THE
WORLD ABOVE

ROBERTO MAGINI

PRESS

VULPINE
PRESS

First published in Italian by Leone Editore in 2014
Published by Vulpine Press in the United Kingdom in 2020

Translated by Julia Gabrielle Barnes and Giuseppe Sofo

Cover by Claire Wood

ISBN: 978-1-83919-315-6

www.vulpine-press.com

For Micio, Micia and Cicciò

Prologue

Mesoamerica 1541

At the foot of the pyramid there were the last representatives of the ancient people of the Mountain of the Sun. The sacrifice had just been completed and the skin of the flayed virgin, wedded to Xipe Totec—Our Lord the Flayed—now covered the head and back of the *tlamacazqui.* After having officiated the rite, the old man was laboriously descending the high steps of the main staircase, supported by two shaven attendants. Under the human mantle one could glimpse his unkempt, hoary mane streaked with blood, and thread-bare, floor-length black robe.

Theoticatl, the young warrior recently appointed as the great orator of the Holy People, awaited him halfway down, on the landing of the central stair. He bore a sumptuous ceremonial vestment: a towering, feathered diadem on his head, an iridescent cloak on his shoulders—this, too, interwoven with splendid feathers—and on his feet were golden shoes fit for none but a god incarnate. He was entitled to those garments: in the course of the latest and victorious battles, he had captured eighteen enemies alive to be offered in sacrifice to the god of war.

Lower down, in the huge square demarcated by the colossal statues of the gods rendered with the most menacing visages and enclosed on three sides by the *mecehuales,* the naked, shoeless standard-bearers supported the highest multicolored pennants on leather trusses. At the center of the esplanade twelve by twelve dozen warriors—all that remained of the old and glorious army—were lined

1

up. In hand were black spears tipped with obsidian, just like the short swords they carried at their waists. Only a few of them showed leather sandals and wore the prestigious and now worn-out parade uniforms; all others were barefoot, free of insignia, and wearing modest clothing or simple loincloths. The wars, the persecutions and the terrible sicknesses had decimated the Holy People and now almost the totality of the army consisted of *macehualtin,* common people of the lower classes, or *mayeque,* peasants with neither land nor rights.

Each warrior had his woman beside him. Some girls wore rich garments of pure cotton and flaunted precious necklaces, indices of their noble lineage, although most of them only wore modest fiber cloaks. They were little more than teenagers, and many couples had been united in marriage that very morning, just before the sacrifice, in one big, collective ceremony. Behind the ranks of youths, on the left, stood a group of girls stripped of all ornamentation and wearing just rough ivory tunics fastened at the waist with a simple cord. Their facial features and skin color betrayed their racial diversity and the warriors who surrounded them left no doubt as to their status as prisoners. On the opposite side of the square more than three hundred men were gathered, kneeling and kissing the ground, half-naked or wearing ragged clothes, these too carefully surveyed by armed guards. They were the *tlatlacotin,* the carrier-slaves that had been captured in the recent battles against the People of the Lake. Next to them, large, overstuffed woven baskets. Standing motionless and silent at the edge of the square was the rest of the population: the elderly, women, children and the few young people who had been chosen to stay. The silence was absolute and the tension palpable. The *tlamacazqui,* high priest of the Holy People, placed his right hand on the head of Theoticatl and began speaking: "The white-skinned man with metal clothing came from the place where Tonatiuh rises, and though welcomed by us as a friend and liberator, he has removed his mask and shows us now his true nature—a rapacious predator. Deceived by his flattery and false promises we joined him, and with him we fought the battles against the oppressor and eternal enemy. Thanks to our help, he was able to accomplish unimaginable feats and, in just a few moons, the entire domain of the People of the Lake, won through the course of many moon cycles and with the blood of countless battles, dissolved into nothingness.

"For us, however, the remedy has proved worse than the disease: the greed of this foreign dog knows no bounds, his appetite is never sated and he now takes any opportunity and invents any excuse to plunder and massacre even those who were his friends. And those who are not murdered at his ruthless hands are exterminated by the loathsome, terrible diseases he has brought with him from his faraway lands.

"More and more of them come from the sea, swarming like locusts, and our lances, our brittle blades and our valor can do nothing as they come down against these monsters with their incredible weaponry. Shameless double-crossers, not only did they not grant us the promised lands, but day after day they are even taking those which belonged to our ancestors. They alight everywhere, destroy our *teocalli* and our altars to erect crosses and impose their laws.

"By now we are reduced to a shadow of that which was the glorious, holy people of the Mountain of the Sun. But you, Theoticatl, you will resurrect it. More plentiful and powerful than before.

"By your strength and courage, as the son of poor *macehualtin,* you came to wear the insignia of the *pipiltin* nobility, and when the last descendant of the sacred *tlatoani* lineage was murdered at the hands of this wicked invader, the wise men did not hesitate in the selection of a successor. And upon you, who have given the highest example of obedience in sacrificing your woman to the gods and demonstrating unparalleled courage in battle as well as wisdom in the command of and respect for the elders, they wished to bestow the prestigious insignia and entrust the route map of the mythical hero of the Holy People, Gonna the Explorer, kept hidden for generations in one of our *teocalli*'s secret places…the route that will show you the way and which will bring you, in the footsteps of those who came before us, to the garden of the Curved Mountain.

"All have heard of this place of delights, awarded by the gods to their children on earth, but no one knows where it is and many doubt that it even exists. But the Garden of the Gods exists and, with the help of the map, you will learn how to find it. There you will plant the last seed of our sacred race, there you will establish our new dwelling and there you will remain. Forever. And no foreigner will ever set foot there.

"As a reward for your dedication, the twelve virgins taken from our former ally, this villainous enemy, have been awarded to you. You will use them as he has used our wives and daughters, you will not allow them to sleep under your roof, and the male children that they will conceive by you—though they be your own flesh—will be offered in sacrifice to the gods to repair wrongs and renew the memory of future generations.

"My two students will accompany you on this journey," the high priest continued, indicating the two shaved-headed youths beside him. "They have just come out of the *tlamacazcalli,* but they already know to perfection each rite and each rule of the Book. Heed their counsel and ensure that they may impart the word and wisdom of our forefathers to the children of the People.

"The *tlatlacotin* will carry all of the riches of our people for you: gold, silver, precious stones, exquisite seeds, rare birds whose splendid feathers will never fall into the hands of our wicked enemy, who will break our altars and damage our *teocalli* no more. Because in the moment in which you will have left the Mountain of the Sun, this place will turn to stone, so that when the insatiable vulture spreads its wings in these lands, we who remain will already be dispersed in the nearby valleys and mountains, and to welcome him he will find nothing but weeds and wild dogs. You now receive the route map and the symbol of power, linger no longer," concluded the high priest, while his aids passed him an ancient roll of rabbit skin and an obsidian spear whose shaft was adorned with precious stones.

Theoticatl rose to his feet and, holding his gaze, grasped the two sacred relics from the bony hands of the high priest. Then, without a word, and after a curt bow, he turned away and resolutely descended the last stretch of the steps. The silence was broken by the officials' barked orders, and a long column of men and things immediately formed behind the young *tlatoani* and began to move slowly towards the main gate.

The goodbyes had already been said, and on the silent, tearless faces one could find all the sadness of one who will never again see the faces of his friends, nor retrace the paths between the comforting surroundings of the dwellings in which he had grown up.

The journey seemed endless, fraught with perils and endless afflictions that put a strain even on the most toughened physiques and resolute tempers. The diplomatic ability of Theoticatl always managed to avoid confrontation with the populations that were encountered from time to time during the long pilgrimage; they came in peace, not for conquest, and paid for everything necessary for their livelihood in gold, precious stones, much sought-after feathers and cocoa seeds. Most of the time they chanced upon small, isolated villages of poor people, perched atop hills or on high ground, where no one would think to attack such a menacing army.

Only on one occasion were Theoticatl's warriors forced to fight. Word of the magnificent treasures that they carried inevitably preceded them, and the possibility of possessing who knows how many riches, vigorous slaves and beautiful young women could only provoke the greed of the most bellicose peoples.

One day, in the middle of a gorge dominated by large, fortified settlements, the long procession was attacked by a crowd of screaming warriors.

The reaction of Theoticatl and his men was immediate, terrible, and ruthless. In the course of a few hours the offending army was annihilated and the few survivors were forced to disburse rich tributes to persuade the victors not to sacrifice or enslave them, and to forgo dominion over their lands. From that day on the renown of the Sacred People's treasures was not the only word to precede them, and none dared hamper their passage.

But where enemy weapons had no authority, the thirst of the deserts and the hunger of the desolate lands, the chill of the mountains and the snares of the forest took their toll. The objective seemed unattainable and endurance was put to the test more than ever, but every time their discomfort was about to gain the upper hand, the emergence of the profile of a mountain on the horizon or the conformation of the curve of a river shown accurately on the map rekindled hope in everyone's hearts and spurred their spirits to press on.

More than seventy moons had elapsed since they had left their homes when the refugees found themselves passing through a narrow valley that climbed among the foothills of snow-capped mountains, which rose ever higher. A limpid river teeming with fish cut through the valley, but increasingly a waterfall or a full tributary forced the travelers to take long detours or go on painful marches in reverse in order to wade through surer waters and be able to proceed. As they climbed in altitude, the valley narrowed into a progressively cramped and rugged gorge, while the landscape was changing rapidly in appearance. The meadows gave way to dense coniferous forests and these, soon after, to ever sparser shrubs, growing lower and thornier to the point where there was nothing but cold, rough rocks, bare of all vegetation, to be trodden underfoot. As if that were not enough, a strong, cold wind from the south channeled through the narrow gorge, whipping relentlessly at the travelers as if to urge them to go back.

Meanwhile, the river had transformed into a raging torrent flooded with impetuous, turbid waters, and it was becoming more and more difficult to draw nourishment from it in order to feed the multitude of derelicts who proceeded now by the sheer force of desperation. Curiously, however, while the air was becoming progressively cold and bitter, the water of this torrent remained continually warm; the temperature seemed even to rise gradually as their altitude increased, and the disturbing phenomenon never ceased to arouse mixed feelings of hope and superstition in the troop's spirits. Consternation was at its peak when, one gray, autumn dawn—after having overcome with great difficulty the drop of the thousandth waterfall—they found the road blocked by a sheer cliff so high that they could not see the top of it. The rock was completely devoid of holds and so smooth as to make climbing inconceivable, nor were there any visible outlets. And turning back would mean new hardships, new sufferings, and new casualties. Where to go, then?

The map ended with the image of Tonatiuh, "The Shining Sun," and gave no other indications. The stores of food were dwindling and several weeks had passed since the refugees had encountered the last human settlement.

While the gathered counselors and the *tlatoani* were discussing the decision to be made and the bitter prospect of turning back, their arguments were suddenly interrupted by the cries of an explorer. At first the men could not locate the source of the noise, and only when the call was repeated several times were they steered in the right direction.

Behind a bizarre camel-shaped rock, just at the point where the stream gushed out of the mountain and almost completely hidden by a thorny hedge, the opening of a tunnel was visible, high enough that a man of average height could barely squeeze into, and then just walking sideways with knees bent.

"Wait here," ordered Theoticatl, among the first to rush over. "You," he continued, pointing to the guide, "go ahead of me and light a torch."

The two men advanced slowly into the narrow corridor. In some places the water overflowed from the river, making the cobblestones slippery and balance precarious, but after about ten meters the tunnel began to widen out until the two could move forward with their heads raised and without their backs pressed to the wall.

Perhaps it was sheer fate or some higher will that ensured that everything happened precisely then. The fact is that the guide, slipping on a stone, suddenly lost his balance and Theoticatl, trying to avoid being hit in the face with the torch, whirled around to find himself with his back to the river.

Something in front of him caught his eye. "Stop!" he cried, snatching the torch from his attendant's hand and bringing it urgently towards the wall.

Right at eye level, at the center of a tiny moon carved into the rock, there was a bas-relief. The edges were worn away by time, but the image was still clearly recognizable, and only a human hand could have carved it. It was the image of Tonatiuh, identical to that charted at the furthest boundary of the scroll. Theoticatl was assured that he was not hallucinating when the guide, who in the meantime had shifted his gaze in the same direction, issued a muffled gasp and bowed to the ground to kiss his feet.

There was no time to linger. Theoticatl, torch in hand and heart in an uproar, started forward ahead of the guide at such long strides that he could barely keep up. A new force drove him and his feet no longer perceived the roughness or hidden dangers of the earth. He was moving almost at a run, heedless of the danger of slipping and falling into the turbulent waters, overcoming obstructions and bypassing boulders that blocked the path with all the agility of a cat.

After a seemingly infinite jog he suddenly stopped; about twenty meters ahead the tunnel bent at a sharp angle to the right and he realized that, despite the distance, he could clearly distinguish the wall's change in direction. There had to be a light source beyond the curve.

At the height of exaltation, he quickened his pace. As he progressed, the faint glimmer became clearer and clearer, just as his hope turned to certainty. After passing through a last, tight curve, the ceiling of the tunnel suddenly ceased and his eyes were dazzled.

The long journey was over. Theoticatl had just entered the heart of the Curved Mountain.

When he returned to his people late in the afternoon, a new light shone in his eyes: "The Garden of the Gods is at the end of that road," he said, indicating with a wave the mouth of the tunnel and thereby responding to the silent question written on every face. A roar of cheers, shouts of exultation, joy and victory filled the narrow gorge and, amplified by the echo of the walls, rose to the highest peaks of the surrounding mountains.

In short, the energy of the men became frenetic. Expert stonemasons, with increased energy and renewed vigor, widened the first section of the tunnel to facilitate the passage of the people and bulky loads. The carriers, laden for the last time with heavy burdens, were evenly spaced along the entire length of the tunnel and, for moons and moons, hauled boulders, stones, and endless amounts of earth and gravel inside, dropping all of it into the warm, fast waters of the river until it lapped at the vault in every direction, thus precluding any possibility of access to that passage.

None of the carrier-slaves, however, were permitted to tread on the sacred soil. On the wall of rock at the point where the river entered into the disappeared tunnel, a stone altar was erected, and for three whole days on the other side of the mountain the water ran red.

PART ONE

Chapter 1

September 2013 – Southern Patagonian Icecap

The moon was almost beyond the horizon and, in the clear air, the first rays were sculpting the landscape of sharp contours. A fantastic dawn was looming on the horizon and nothing could foretell the events of the day it declared.

Marco had always been an early riser, and that day too he had gotten up well before sunrise. He did not mind preparing breakfast for his friends who were still asleep inside their little igloo of waterproof canvas. He loved those moments of infinite peace when nothing interfered with the slow awakening of nature, who was shaking off the last shadows of the night. He wanted these moments all to himself, as though he feared that an unwanted presence could change the course of that primordial event, so majestic and never the same twice. While the aroma of coffee wafted through the base camp, his gaze shifted inevitably towards the glacier overlying the mighty rock wall in front of him, which, as the stars disappeared, changed from black to violet, from dark red to pink, finally reaching the whitest white silhouetted against the azure sky.

He was starting to feel at peace with himself, and much time had passed since the last time he had felt that comforting sensation. He had left Rome just five days ago, and already the events of the last weeks seemed a lifetime ago.

One-hundred and ninety pounds well-distributed over six feet and four inches, an athletic physique and the face of a nice guy despite his thirty-eight years and the early graying of his temples, Marco was a plastic surgeon renowned among Rome's elite, as well as an unrepentant eligible bachelor. According to common sentiment, his could be considered an enviable position. He himself—if he looked around—could not help but admit it; even though in his heart—while trying to convince himself of the contrary—couldn't manage to feel privileged, let alone accomplished with his deepest aspirations. He felt a constant and indefinable sense of dissatisfaction, of incompletion, of unattained goals. Something told him that all of his successes in the workplace and in the social sphere did not amount to what he really wanted. He felt that he'd been pulled into some gearwheel, into a sort of perverse mechanism that—after having lured him with false promises—had maneuvered and driven him step by step towards pre-established and conventional goals, as if it had been someone else who chose on his behalf, preventing him from being the true master of his own destiny. It was not that he despised what his privileged position allowed him, but in the fulfillment of each whim, there was never a feeling of full satisfaction. He often had the impression that that much-needed something was there, one step away from him, ready to be caught, but by an inexplicable and sardonic twist of fate it continued to slip away from him each time he was about to grasp it.

Maybe—he told himself when he felt this dissatisfaction most poignantly—he should have devoted much more of his time to the great eschatological problem, because only by fixed points and very solid faith would that serenity of the soul be brought, hard-sought and never reached, capable of giving a meaning to existence. He even came to envy the iron religiosity of the believers, but the intransigence of their dogmatism was irreconcilable with his desire to run free, without bridles, gags or impositions; and the instinctive respect that he felt towards any idea—even the most outlandish and unconventional idea—brought him to tolerate everything and everyone except the intolerant. Moreover, every time he sought to flesh out the issue with philosophers, priests, theologians or other experts, he had never gained much certainty or reassurance. In fact, most of the time he had come out of those meetings more confounded, confused and doubtful than before, and he had come to the conclusion that—even if he got his act together, and with all the best intentions—he, by his own strength alone, would never succeed in unraveling the tangled skein. Maybe he should have simply blindly trusted someone to light the way, but he was wary of false prophets and had never been able to shake off his visceral discomfort with prepackaged relics, rituals and sermons.

He loved simple things. When he could, he holed himself up gladly in his old country home in the Roman hills to pass entire weekends in perfect solitude. Walking behind the lawnmower while his two cats trailed along in curiosity, he felt much closer to his goal. In those moments his imagination—his best friend, as he called it— roamed freely and without constraints, and could offer adequate responses to many questions. Not that he felt devoted to monastic life or hermitage. In fact, he loved company, especially female company, enough to be considered a veritable womanizer in his circle of friends. He did very little to convince them otherwise—in some ways he was even pleased by this reputation—but in his heart he knew that, in reality, things were not quite as they thought.

He had to admit: he had broken hearts, many of them, throughout the course of his eventful romantic life, but never for carelessness, opportunism or insensitivity. With each new love affair he had always been totally convinced that he had finally found the woman of his dreams, his soulmate, "the one." But every time, just as the goddess of the moment fell into his arms, in a hidden crevice of his brain a switch flipped—as if by a curse or some arcane spell unleashed by hostile and malefic forces—and the much-coveted being, the woman who up until several seconds previously represented fulfillment, culmination, lost all attraction. At that point, he tried vainly to fight back and to pick up the pieces of all that was crumbling, but eventually, inevitably, he had to acknowledge the truth: he had gotten carried away by passion, he had exaggerated, magnified his own feelings, let himself be taken in.

Thus, he was forced to begin the painful matter of gradual and progressive detachment every time; it was designed to extricate him as painlessly as possible from the web in which he had tangled himself. And he'd always felt like a hypocritical and deceitful worm when, after a long campaign of persuasion—in which he had become masterful—he uttered the fateful words: "But we'll stay good friends." Because—he knew before saying them—as soon as he turned the corner he would fade into obscurity, vile and cowardly, and he would falsify papers sooner than stumble across his old flame.

Looking back, he realized that he had probably spent a lot more time burning bridges than building new relationships, and when he was in the mood to beat himself up he even got to the point of self-diagnosing Casanova Syndrome: this is the insecurity of those men who, in order to believe in themselves, need constant reassurance and, rather than loving, have an absolute need to *feel* loved. But he was not slow to absolve himself of blame; certain behaviors could not be labeled, they could not be the result of mere egoism, let alone be dictated by indifference or a lack of respect for others. His quest for true love, even if often misguided, was a legitimate and altogether natural aspiration; somewhere in the world there had to be the woman capable not only of arousing that feeling within him, but also of making it endure and resonate for a lifetime. So the feelings of guilt subsided, his confidence returned and, with this, he resumed his endless search.

There was, however, the time when even the hardened *tombeur de femmes* had to suffer the humiliation of defeat and, though his vanity was still laboring to digest it, he often wondered what outcome the whole ordeal might have had if the foul deed had not arisen: Marta, established and cyclonic editor of a weekly women's magazine. He had met her by chance, obliged by the president of his club, who was also a dear friend, to attend the conference that the woman was to hold at their headquarters. "She's commendable, believe me," he said, referring to the spokeswoman. "Let's not make our usual bad impression by making her talk to brick walls or the usual crowd." So, resigned and disappointed at having to forego another more attractive invitation, Marco had obeyed, and he showed up punctually and prejudiced against the meeting which would be on some aspect of the feminine condition; he was ready to put up with the usual platitudes on equal opportunity, women in power, and the female presence in politics, the rights denied and so forth.

But he immediately and happily changed his mind. The woman had struck his fancy the moment she had climbed up to the podium. Tall, black hair in a short bob with the ends brushed forward to graze her cheekbones, full, dark lips and a simple, tight charcoal suit which extolled her slender, athletic figure and, at her neck, a single strand of gray pearls above an unfairly chastened décolletage, which was not bad at all. She was a monument to Valentina: a real knockout of a woman.

At first Marco was only attracted by her physical appearance, by her intriguing look, the aristocratic nose and inviting lips, but as soon as this object of so much admiration began to speak, all his attention shifted immediately from her body to her words. No, she was not at all the obtuse passionflower, frustrated and rattling off memorized doctrine to the audience in the usual precooked political jargon in the party sacristy. She was deeply convinced of what she was saying, the ideas which she espoused where her own, and as she spoke she became zealous to the point where she had a light in her eyes that caught you and carried you into that world of liberty, equality and justice of which she dreamt and burned with all her strength to achieve.

After the report, Marco maneuvered to get himself assigned a seat at the table next to her and, heedless of the world that surrounded him, he monopolized her for the rest of the evening. They made a date for the next day and, that next day, another for the day after.

It was thus that a full, overwhelming, passionate relationship, such as he had never had before, began.

She was a volcano of ideas. She loved follies, and was known to wake him in the middle of the night to talk to him about a project or a thought, and to pull him out of bed to drive him to a spot tucked away on top of the world to see the dawn. With her, there was no time to stop and think or to look around and strangely enough, rather than disorienting or wearying him, that sea of initiatives filled him with life, restored and invigorated him. On more than one occasion it happened that he found himself whistling in the operating room after an entire sleepless night with her, running after one of her many crazy ideas.

He felt reborn, regenerated; he lived every moment fully, extraordinarily, euphorically. Until that infamous day. They had been together for six months when Marco, one Saturday morning, had gone to his home in the country to finish up some work that he had started some time ago and never seen to completion. The ceaseless events of the last months had brought him to ignore his beloved refuge perhaps a bit too much, and, an honest man, he kept the house in order; he had always mowed the lawn, taken care of the plants and fed the cats. He wanted to see the state of things for himself. Anyway, that weekend Marta would be engaged in an editorial meeting and he would have the opportunity to recharge his batteries and enjoy one of the first weekends of the incipient spring in peace.

He had not even had time to open the front door when he heard his phone ringing, and it was the hospital calling to say that a patient he had operated on the day before was having problems. He could have given some kind of directive by telephone and postponed the visit until Sunday evening, if not Monday morning, but that was not his style, so, disappointed and angry, he closed the door and made his way back.

Before heading off to the hospital, he made a quick trip home to change clothes and there, waiting for him, he found the bitter surprise: Marta, in his room, in bed with his best female friend and in a compromising position.

Marco still wondered how the relationship would have ended if the hospital had never called, if he had turned a blind eye and had not proved deaf and unmovable in the face of her apologies, and then her accusations of "bigoted-moralist-backwards-hypocritical-sonofabitch" that Marta spun into a frightening one-breath crescendo.

But it had happened. The solemn blow had made him think hard about his bachelor status. The "big four-oh" was approaching by leaps and bounds, and not a day went by that his mother, a widow of many years, did not repeat the usual spiel: "You have to get your head on straight, son, you have to find a good woman, a housewife, without too many strange ideas…I don't want to become your children's old granny!"

Perhaps his mother was right, he told himself, and that was probably the motive that had pushed him to turn all his attentions to Claudia, a girl from a good family, the daughter of a notary, cute, intelligent, politically correct in every way and, more importantly, predictable by every token.

The recent, tragic experience had burned him inside. All of a sudden Marco had lost his taste for improvisation; he no longer desired to live for the day, he wanted a fixed point, a quiet harbor, a person he could count on at any time, day or night. And what pushed him even more in his determination was also the fact that in that circumstance, as had never happened before, the conquest was neither easy nor taken for granted.

Claudia, in addition to being beautiful, was also a great catch and she already had a flock of suitors. So Marco had had to work hard to win the fierce competition, and that commitment, too, out of the ordinary and not such a given, must have helped to convince him that he had finally made the right choice and—something previously unthinkable—to induce him to articulate for the first time in his life the fateful word "marriage."

"I couldn't have made a better choice," he told himself again and again, seeing how his fiancée could navigate every situation with grace and elegance. But the more he repeated it, the more he was struck by the feeling that the very predictability which he so coveted and desired was inexorably undermining his certainty and his dogged endeavor to convince himself. So it was with great enthusiasm he had accepted the suggestion from his friend Karl, the mountaineering master in Ortisei, to join the expedition organized by his Chilean colleagues in a remote, secluded region of the southern Andes on the border between Chile and Argentina. It had been Sergio, his inseparable childhood friend and longtime student of the expert rock climber, who introduced them six years earlier.

He looked much older than his thirty-five years and, although no taller than Marco, his enormous size made him look twice as big. From a jungle of perpetually disheveled oakum-colored hair which covered almost all of his head and face, two small, sky-blue eyes peeked out, radiating through premature wrinkles and a gibbous nose flanked by cheeks made ruddy by both the high quantity of sun and the wine of the valley.

Marco had immediately found harmony with that sensibly minded man who was more than a bit jarring with his countenance of an enormous bighorn sheep.

Karl was not a man of many words, but those few times that he intervened in some discussion with his unmistakable Teutonic accent, he was accustomed to getting straight to the point of the argument, and always in a good way. His quietness had the power to transmit certainty, so as to convince Marco himself to overcome his primal fear of heights and take some mountaineering lessons with him.

While Sergio was more devoted to large enterprises and the continuous pursuit of perfectionism and pushing limits, Marco and Karl favored quieter, more contemplative climbs. Rather than exceeding higher degrees of climbing difficulty, their goal was to get to unknown, untouched places, where they could sit silent and immobile to admire the scenery.

In the evening at the local club, while Sergio was—more often than not—engaged in heated discussions with other guides and hikers over how to conquer a drop or pass to a higher grade, Marco and Karl tended to refrain from chiming in and preferred to listen to all that talk in silence with a good glass of grappa. Sergio's exuberance, however, did not bother them at all. In fact, he acted as a liaison, as a facilitator, within the company.

On the fifteenth of September the three friends gathered together at the Fiumicino airport, ready to fly off towards the unknown land. Karl had joined them in Rome the day before on a domestic flight and all of them, to avoid mishaps, had stopped to sleep at Marco's house.

Claudia had offered to accompany them to the airport, and she was also making the effort to return the van they had rented for all their baggage. During the whole journey, the men, with ill-concealed embarrassment, had limited themselves to a few trite, circumstantial phrases; they all felt almost a sense of discomfort or a vague sense of guilt regarding their companion. Claudia was not very talkative either, like when Marco had told her that he would be participating in the expedition. Only after check-in had she thrown her arms around his neck, hugging him with unusual force almost as if to hold him back, but without shedding a tear and remaining in total silence.

In flight, staring through the window at the white bed of clouds that blotted out the land, Marco had mulled over that parting, not knowing if he had been selfish, insensitive or stupid when "Bye, beautiful. I'll call you when I arrive in Santiago," was the most that he could say to her. And almost unconsciously, once he had passed through the exit that would lead him to the terminal, he had uttered the fateful phrase.

"*Finalment ai suma,*" he absentmindedly said aloud. That motto, uttered by the first king of Italy who reached Rome, for some mysterious reason had become inculcated in his brain, transforming into a sort of victory cry of his after a successful venture, the resolution of a problem, or the achievement of a goal. In retrospect, the bridegroom was trying to banish the nagging thought that uttering that phrase—and specifically in that circumstance—had been a real act of liberation.

Chapter 2

Marco was so absorbed in his thoughts and taken with the magnificence of the mountain that he only noticed the presence of Karl when his friend's giant shadow merged with his own.

"Hey Karl," he acknowledged without looking back.

"*Hallo*," said the other, purposely emphasizing the German inflection copied from his friends. Cup steaming in hand as he sipped coffee, even he could not take his blue eyes, reduced to two narrow slits, off the imposing rock face.

"Gorgeous, huh," Karl said at one point, with a wink to the peak.

"Yes, gorgeous and hard…you're going to struggle to get me all the way up there."

"Oh don't worry. The only snag is that it's a bit tall, but it's certainly not more difficult than others you've done without problems."

"Hopefully," Marco mused, unconvinced. He had accepted the challenge, but he feared that he had overestimated his ability. Karl's words, however, had given him a new dose of confidence.

They were still sipping coffee with their eyes turned to the face and its surrounding peaks when their contemplation was interrupted by the shouts of Antonio and Manuel, who had just walked out of their old ridge tent. They were engaged in a vibrant debate for a change, and with a little effort you could catch a few words in their strong dialect. They were the leaders of the expedition, who come Andean summertime would become the ski instructors in Ortisei, and in the Italian summer they would return home to organize excursions in the Chilean-Argentine Andes on behalf of a few travel companies. Karl had worked hard to incorporate them fully into the circle of fellow mountaineers and to put them in contact with important Italian and foreign tour agencies. The two felt that they owed him a large debt of gratitude and, knowing his preferences, wanted to reciprocate by organizing a special excursion, far out of the common tourist routes, at a faraway spot in the vast mountainous region near the southern border between Chile and Argentina.

They were natives of the capital, but passion for the mountains and their work had led them to those latitudes countless times. They had just discovered that spot themselves, though, having discovered it almost by accident only a year before. On the other hand, a lifetime would not suffice to explore even just a tiny part of the infinity of peaks, gorges, ravines and crevices in the vast glacial territory of the Andean cordillera, three hundred miles long and eighty wide, forming a nearly impassable partition between the two nations.

Both were of uncertain age, were short and stocky, boasted a thick growth of smooth black hair that whipped across their olive-skin faces with every movement, and had lively charcoal eyes; at first glance they could be mistaken for brothers, but they were not even distant relatives. If you did not see them in action with your own eyes you would have never believed them capable, with their stocky physiques, of climbing like geckos, using only their hands and feet on walls almost devoid of handholds. They were born climbers; they had mountains in their blood.

They had come to get "the Italians" at the airport in Santiago with an off-road vehicle that must have been a Land Rover in a past life. Its owners treated it like a son. They had totally repainted it—the tires were saved by chance—with such a shocking pink that it would be impossible to camouflage even in the depths of the Amazon rainforest.

"So, *primero,* thieves think twice before robbing it, and, *segundo,* if we get lost in the mountains we can find it much easier," Manuel laid out for his stunned fellow adventures. In truth, so many

23

such modifications had been made to the car that it wouldn't have gone unnoticed even painted black in the dead of night.

Just needing to fix the luggage carrier in the ingenious Duralumin cage—which overflowed by a foot on all four sides of the little roof and was devised in such a way as to enable rapid loading and unloading of luggage without having to resort to so many laces, straps, various rope and rods—and the party was already on its way south.

Their destination was thousands of miles away and the guests' vacation days were numbered. Thus, they had unanimously decided not to stop in the capital and to head straight for the specified destination.

The first night they had spent in the car sleeping fitfully while Manuel and Antonio alternated maneuvering the SUV through the chaotic traffic of the only road that, according to its label on the map, should have been a freeway. As they traveled away from the capital, traffic was sparse, but the trucks had continued to slow their grueling march to a drag.

The second night, after having gorged on steaks three fingers thick and being awarded a long, refreshing bath, they were able to rest their joints on a real bed as guests in one of the rare *hospedajes* along the way.

The next day, having arrived in Puerto Montt, they took the Carretera Austral, which was more than eight hundred miles long and paved only in portions. It was the obligatory route for reaching the extreme southern part of the country by land.

The countryside, which was nearly uninhabited, was of unparalleled beauty. Immense lakes of an abyssal blue succeeded one another in the endless pine forests, and increasingly the road intersected with impressive waterways, spouting from the glaciers of the Cordillera, rushing wildly towards the ocean with spectacular leaps of frosty froth.

On the fourth day, even the solid Carretera remained nothing but a dim memory and the SUV began to climb in low gear up a narrow trail carved by the streams of the first thaw and riddled with deep, dry ditches dug by waters that had abandoned them for easier routes.

It was then that Marco, Sergio and Karl realized the usefulness of the two thick and sturdy steel axles and the marine plywood fixed to the sides of the Land Rover in special brackets. In a moment, they could be extracted from the slots and thrown across natural obstacles, thereby allowing the car to overcome them quickly and unimpeded. Sometimes, however, the banks of the streams were so far apart that these boardwalks did not work, and the drivers could only leave the main track just to find it again after long, winding detours. As if that wasn't enough, as they progressed to higher altitudes while continuing southward, a new traveling companion joined the group: a freezing, incessant wind which blew with ever-increasing insistence through the rocky peaks and gorges of the mountains. The sky, on the other hand, remained consistently clear and bright except for a few brief showers, and the place continued to churn out vistas of unspeakable beauty, true corners of earthly paradise.

On board, despite the limited space available, the unforeseen obstacles and the fatigue of travel, discontent did not dominate; the fatigue was in fact abundantly compensated for not only by the magnificence of the landscape, but also by a mixture of euphoria and exultation of those who know what it feels like to walk on untouched land. Moreover, Manuel and Antonio were proving themselves to be travel companions of a unique harmony in addition to expert guides. Proud to show their friends the beauty of their land, they talked from sunrise to sunset, and often engaged in extremely animated, incomprehensible arguments among themselves, so lively that it seemed that they would come to blows at any moment. Until, suddenly, they burst into loud, resonant laughter, slapping one another on the back so hard that the car swerved dangerously.

That morning their animated discussion alerted Marco and Karl to the two Chileans' awakening.

"*Bien*," Manuel began in his mixture of Italian and Spanish after joining them, encircling a cup of hot coffee with numb fingers.

"Little wind. *Esto es el giorno ideale para subir a la cima…Usted verá que extraordinario espectáculo!*"

Both Chileans, by necessity, had had to learn Italian by forced march, but they were still able to make themselves understood with their mixture of idioms. Especially Manuel, who of the two was definitely more outgoing and loquacious.

The guides immediately sat down around the camp table and, as usual, began to gobble down an impressive amount of long, thin tortillas, warmed on a clever steel plate soldered over the spout of a gas stove.

"Now I understand why they've brought an entire warehouse with them," said Marco, raising his voice so as to be heard by the two gluttons. "I thought we'd be able to feed an army, but with those big mouths it'll be hard to make it through to the end of the trip!"

As always, the last to set foot outside his fiery red igloo was Sergio—also known as Little Serge, when you wanted to send him into a rage. He looked fresh out of an imperial suite. Dapper, clean-shaven, perfumed and every hair in place, wide-frame sunglasses with white frames, high SPF sunscreen on his cheekbones and nose, a designer headband across his forehead, and the latest jumpsuit just pulled off a high fashion mannequin; he was trying to use this outfit to make up for his biggest, unspoken torment: his height.

For the occasion, he had also had the heels of his climbing boots raised to the mythical threshold of three-quarters of an inch, and that was more than evident in his satisfied expression when he could converse with the two Chileans while looking them straight in the eye, without having his nose up like he always did with the other two Watusi.

He had been a classmate of Marco's in elementary, middle and high school, and had remained his inseparable friend even when he had opted for law school in college. Constantly romantically occupied since the first hairs on his chin sprouted, he had married right after graduation, but came back single after just a year of stormy marital strife.

In eternal struggle with weight, he tended to accumulate pounds despite a strict diet which consisted almost exclusively of yogurt, vegetables, and various concoctions that were nauseating just to look at. And that morning too, after having merely sipped at a brew of indefinite color without deigning to look towards the coffee, tortillas or sausages, he was quick to harangue his friends. Eyeing the steel Daytona ergonomically tucked above the cuff of the suit, he began giving his directives—namely, those established by Karl and the two Chileans a long time ago.

"According to Manuel, it should take four hours, more or less, to reach the top of the rock face and about half an hour to get down the other side onto the plateau below. From there to the base of the towers, the land is totally flat...Even at a snail's pace, we should reach our destination, maximum, at three in the afternoon, and then we'll have plenty of time to pitch the tents, eat dinner and go to bed with the chickens...So all the scenery-fanatics," he continued sarcastically to no one in particular, but knowing he had hit the mark, "will be refreshed and rested tomorrow morning when they will see for themselves how much our friends have busted our balls."

Admittedly, neither Marco nor Karl could wait to summit the mountain because, if even half of what the guides reported throughout the trip were true, they would be able to witness a sight utterly unique in the world.

Manuel and Antonio had already climbed up there twice, and the description they gave of the place was too specific and richly detailed to just be the fruit of their imaginations. Beyond the wall, they had recounted, stood two towers in the shape of giant blades on either side of a very wide fork, and in their anterior concavity the two towers were lightly angled inwards. Once at the summit of the rock face, the climbers would have to drop down beyond this and onto a nearly flat, frozen expanse in order to reach the base of the fork. The front of the fork and the blades looked out on a large, elliptical chasm bordered on the opposite side, several miles away as the crow flies, by a high cliff in the shape of a giant, headless bat with its wings spread and slightly inclined forward, seemingly wanting to seize the two pinnacles opposite. Furthermore, according to the guides' tale, all the walls around the pit were of such an immaculate white that you could not distinguish the point where the icy crust ended and the rock began.

The whole ravine was entirely covered by an impenetrable barrier of blinding light. From dawn, the sun's rays were captured by the great wings of the wall opposite the ravine and from these, reflected onto the front faces of the blades and the fork. It was thus that a kaleidoscopic play of reflected light was created among the many facets of the enormous natural mirrors on either side, producing flashes and thunderbolts which struck from different angles and continually changed direction, generating a true natural wonder. With extremely dark sunglasses, you could just make out the edges of the enormous elliptical chasm, but not the bottom. Additionally, the Chileans added, the amazing phenomenon lasted the entire day because even when the sun was on the other side, its rays continued to reflect onto the two towers and the fork below by way of the deep notch between the two wings of the mighty bat-wall.

The first time, Manuel and Antonio had watched the show from the tower to the right. The astonishing phenomenon had struck them to the point that the next time, in lieu of climbing the side tower, they had chosen the path of the central gully and once they reached the top of the fork, had tried to descend into the abyss.

They still remembered with dismay what happened next—and they were certainly not the types to be scared easily. For a hundred meters or so of their descent, they had not encountered any difficulties, but at the end of the icy crust, when Manuel had tried to hammer a nail into the vitrified rock, it had instantly disintegrated for a long stretch like a fragile crystal plate, and if Antonio had not had crampons firmly planted on the iced-over section, which had enabled him to recover his companion by the strength of his arms alone, the two would never have lived to tell the tourists of their venture.

Chapter 3

"Okay," said Karl, "guides lead the way. Then you go, Sergio…so," he added, returning to sarcasm, "you can tell your descendants that you were the first Italian to climb this mountain. Marco will climb up behind, and I'll close the rope and prepare the way for the return…And now, you misfit southern farmers, get going, because we've already wasted too much time talking."

The climb was much more difficult than expected, especially for Marco, the most inexperienced and unsure of the group. "You're the usual thoughtless fool," he repeated to himself as the difficulty and distance from the bottom slowly increased. "The next time they suggest a stunt like this—provided that there is a next time—think twice about it before throwing yourself in like a jerk to show the world how great you are. And don't think about it just once, think about it a thousand times…And now how could you put it? You feel like going up to them and saying: dear-friends-excuse-me-if-I-made-you-travel-halfway-across-the-world-but-I'm-so-scared-that-I'm-shitting-myself-so-if-you-don't-mind-let's-go-back-down-to-the-valley-and-let's-all-go-back-home? You got the guts to do that, asshole?"

But he gritted his teeth, held firm, and forced himself to keep going. And his satisfaction was great when he yelled, "*Ai suma!*" as he managed to get his foot on top of the wall, even if just to remain faithful their plan.

Now the two towers soared in front of the climbers in all of their austere beauty. Slightly angled, almost as if they wanted to be looked at sideways, they seemed like two huge guards placed there to protect the area from any desecration.

To the farthest horizon not a cloud obscured the white of the mountains and the clear blue skies. Although the wind swept exasperatingly across the summit, the friends, who until a few minutes previous had suffered a great deal from the icy lashing, were now sweating. The light reflected by the large rock-wings hit the spot right where they stood, creating such heat that they were forced to hurry away from the cut of that fiery blade. And at that moment, all of them, enchanted by the flurry of flashes and glares emitted beyond the towers, had to agree that the guides had certainly not exaggerated in their description, such was the magnificence of the sight they beheld.

After having some refreshments but not yet fully recovered from the surprise, the five resumed their movement, descending a few hundred meters to the foot of a gentle slope which soon led them to a large, frozen basin with a slightly sunken center, which they would have to cross diagonally to be able to reach the base of the tower that they would climb the next morning.

Antonio and Manuel were ahead of the group by about thirty meters. The type to be impatient with any restraints, as soon as they reached the plateau they had detached from the rope and were now proceeding freely and briskly in the direction of their destination. The other three, however, loyal to the Teutonic directives, continued to walk in single file while securely connected to the climbing rope. And it was this that saved them.

They had just passed the halfway mark and only a few hundred meters separated them from the small creek that the guides had chosen as bivouac for the night when a muffled roar, as powerful as thunder, froze them in place. In the dead silence that followed, the friends looked around, stunned, their minds harried by the strangest conjectures. But the response was swift.

After a few eternal seconds the noise, which seemed to come from everywhere, was repeated even longer and more deafening than before, and the whole mountain began to vibrate and shudder violently. There was a tremendous cracking sound and suddenly a deep fracture opened in the ice, zigzagging across the ground like a lightning bolt, and instantly crossed the entire plateau while it widened as if two invisible hands had grasped the icy crust and were bending the two halves inward.

The ground tilted alarmingly and the two Chileans, who at that time were marching right across the line of the fracture, were instantly swallowed by the ravine. The others, now in an elevated position, began to slide slowly toward the yawning mouth of the pit, which continued to widen a few feet below.

Karl, at the end of the line, reacted promptly and calculatedly by planting an ax into the ice with a clean blow. A second later, Marco did the same and their downward race stopped abruptly with Sergio, screaming and terrified, whose legs had already slid into the void.

Keeping hold on the ice axes with one arm and pulling the rope with the other, Karl and Marco had just managed to bring Sergio onto the ice sheet when it broke apart further uphill, and fell unimpeded into the abyss. Fortunately the slab on which they found themselves was wedged horizontally between the walls of the crevasse and remained in place even when the enormous weight began to plunge it downward.

The three, terrified and deafened by the tremendous noise of the ice grinding against the walls, could do nothing but continue clinging to the rope and ice axes in an attempt to not slip and stay balanced on the trembling platform, while the sky receded rapidly from their view.

After a seemingly endless time the uproar ceased; the ice slab was somehow floating in an ethereal silence inside an immense cavern of ice with a hemispherical dome. They would surely have been dashed to pieces on the bottom if, after a flight of more then a hundred feet, there had not been a deep reservoir of water from the thaw there to welcome them.

The impact, however, was tremendous, and while the pressure of the water returned the sunken rubble to the surface, a block of ice in free fall hit one of Karl's legs. His piercing scream mixed in with the ominous creaking of the ice dome that was closing over their heads.

Chapter 4

An agonizing quiet descended, broken occasionally by Karl's groans. Sergio showed no signs of life and Marco, who had remained lucid the whole time but was forced to watch as a helpless spectator, was now staring numbly at the translucent ceiling of the cave which diffused a cold, hazy light. He let himself be rocked, motionless and indolent, on the frozen raft that floated near the shore. His mind refused to accept the enormity of the circumstances; it seemed to him that he was living in a bad dream from which he would soon awaken, and he did not know whether to scream or close his eyes and go back to sleep.

"This can't be real," he repeated to himself continually, but Karl's moaning did not take long to bring him back to reality: he was buried in an ice dome, which barely allowed for a glimpse of the distant cavern walls and, despite the dim, ghostly light, he was struggling with the feeling that there was no way out of that trap.

Some time passed before he managed to take some initiative. He felt pain everywhere, but all his pieces seemed to be in place. He tried to turn on his side and after a while, with a few pangs and no small effort, he managed to get to his knees.

Karl was lying a few feet away from him; he was alive, but in a state of confusion and, even before Marco got over to him by dragging along on his knees, he quickly noticed the unnatural angle of the leg.

"No," he uttered dejectedly.

He did not see any blood. *At least the artery was spared,* he thought, calming himself minimally. His first impulse was to try to straighten the limb, but he held himself back; he would run the risk of even more serious trouble by acting recklessly. He needed help.

"Sergio!"

Marco took his eyes off the broken leg and, still skating on his knees, he neared his other friend. Sergio was on the edge of the raft curled up in the fetal position, immobile. Marco felt reborn after hearing that his pulse was regular, and sighed deeply in relief when, after a first cursory inspection, he found no major injuries. Or so it seemed. Marco was emerging from his state of inertia and his mind, in processing more and more of the situation, began to swirl into full speed and spur him to action. He slid a hand under Sergio's body in search of the cell phone that his friend always wore at his belt. His own, mistakenly left on all night, had run out of battery overnight.

"Goddamn it! We really needed this!" he cursed for the lack of reception.

Keeping his balance precariously on the smooth, rocking floor, Marco was able to get off the ice slab, which in the meantime had run aground on the downward-sloping shore of the reservoir. Then, he began to slowly drag his friends onto the mainland by pulling on the rope that still held them together.

Karl was recovering at that very moment and every movement tore howls of pain from his mouth.

"Karl, can you hear me?" Marco asked after stretching him out on the shore, once he had verified that his cell phone was completely silent.

"Yes...yes," stammered his friend.

"Try not to move. You have a fractured femur," he instinctively instructed, regretting having spoken even before he was done. "But...but don't worry because one way or another we'll take care of it," he added, perhaps to reassure himself more even than the wounded man.

"I have to leave you now, Karl. But just for a minute. I have to see how Sergio's doing. In the meantime, you lean your head on this," he added, slipping off and rolling up his jacket.

He had not yet finished arranging it properly when the silence of the cave was broken by desperate cries: "Help! I'm falling, I'm falling, I'm falling!"

"Good, good, Sergio. Stay calm. It's all okay," Marco shouted, darting over to him.

"Oh God, God, God…What the fuck happened!"

"Don't work yourself up, Sergio, everything is under control. I'll explain soon. But first let me check and see if anything's broken."

To not remember anything that had happened, he must have hit his head, Marco thought worriedly. On top of that, from knowing him all his life he knew that the confident attitude and swagger vaunted by his friend in all circumstances was nothing more than a smokescreen to hide his inherent insecurity. The last thing he wanted, therefore, was to cause even more agitation, but in that situation there was no room for pleasantries or mincing words. So, once it was ascertained that Sergio was whole and capable of discerning and wanting, Marco did not hesitate to inform him of the happenings.

"There must have been an earthquake," he said, continuing to knead Sergio's neck and limbs. "This is a seismic zone—I read that in the guidebook when we were traveling. A huge hole opened up in the ice and…and we wound up inside. Then, up there, the dome closed and…okay, to cut to the chase, we were trapped below. As if that wasn't enough, neither your cell phone nor Karl's has any reception and mine's battery…"

"What are you saying!" snapped the other, twisting to a seated position. A quick three-sixty around him sent him instantly into despair. "Fuck, fuck, fuck…This isn't possible! We're fucked, we're at the end of the line!"

As gloomy as his own thoughts were, Marco realized that Sergio had gone off on a tangent. He could not be of much help, at least at the moment; if there was any remote possibility of getting out of this mess, he had to find the right way on his own.

"But now calm down and listen to me," he shouted in Sergio's face, shaking him by the shoulders. "We can't lose our heads and we

35

need to examine the situation like we should, not fly into a panic…it's useless now. And then…and then, the last of it hasn't been said yet."

"Yes, and who's going to pull us out of this shithole?"

"One thing at a time, please. Try to stand up and tell me if you feel something wrong somewhere…Unfortunately Karl wasn't as lucky as us, he has a fractured femur and I need your help to immobilize the leg."

The sudden call to duty was able to at least partially mitigate the anxiety of his friend, who after being brought slowly to his feet began to pat down his entire body. "It hurts a bit here," he remarked, rubbing his right shoulder and arm, twisting it in every direction to test its functioning. "I feel like I'm on a boat…and I also have a lot of ringing in my ears. But…but I seem to be all in one piece."

"Good. Then you stay here close to Karl and help him if he needs anything. But don't touch his leg for any reason, please. I'm going to try and see what's become of the other two."

"What happened to them?"

"I don't know what to tell you," Marco replied. "I only know that they were several meters ahead of us when I saw them disappear into the crevasse and…I'm afraid that there isn't any water where they fell," he added after a glance around the perimeter of the reservoir.

His fear was soon and tragically confirmed: the bodies of the two Chileans were lying mangled on the solid rock a hundred feet away, half-buried in ice. Marco rushed to free them, but it was enough to just look at their faces to see that there was nothing more to be done. "At least they will face no more troubles," he found himself thinking, shuddering at the thought of the fate that was reserved for him and the other two survivors.

Anguished, he made a move to go and report to his friends, but after a few meters he stopped abruptly and almost ran back in his steps; this was not the time for tears and renunciation, he had to react, think of something, if he wanted to escape from the absurd situation, and not give up immediately.

Like a man possessed, he began to furiously remove the blocks of ice that still covered the two bodies, and overcoming all reluctance, he began to slip off their backpacks and even their belts without wondering whether it was right or whether he had any idea of what he was doing, but something told him that if he wanted to survive, that was the way to act.

Once he had loaded everything that was transportable onto his shoulders, he started to make his way back. Though sweating under the enormous load, he was beginning to miss his jacket. Beyond this, raising his head he saw that the little light coming from above was waning faster than expected. It would not be long before darkness fell. He had to hurry. Sergio was sitting on the edge of the reservoir with his legs crossed, waiting for him. Upon hearing his approach, he looked up at him and despite seeing him loaded down like a burrow he did not even get up to help him. He stared at him from a distance with a distressed look. And when he saw him shake his head back and forth meaningfully, he became even more distressed. "We're fucked. We'll never get out of here. It's over, it's over, it's over…"

"Stop that!" Marco shushed him. "Turn on the stove and warm up a bit of water instead of standing there crying like a little girl. I'll look for the flashlight in this backpack and take a look at Karl's leg."

Sergio, who was always ready with a rebuttal in any situation, accepted the order wordlessly this time and was visibly relieved that someone was there to take initiative.

Karl had silently witnessed the whole spectacle. He was lucid again and you could read all his pain in the pulled expression on his face.

"Karl," Marco began once he was beside him again, "we must try to reduce the fracture. It will hurt like hell, but there's no other way for you to—"

"Do what you have to do," Karl interrupted in a whisper. "But do it quickly, because I can't even breathe with this pain."

Marco did not even pray. Using the super-sharp hunting knife that Karl always carried at his side, he began to cut the fabric of the suit from the bottom and up the entire length of the leg. He wanted to show great care, but when he stripped the limb, he was white-faced as he directed the beam to the point where the leg had been struck; mid-thigh, from the purplish, jagged edges of a large cross-wise wound, the sharp white tip of a bone stump protruded.

"Mother of God," he gasped. But he recovered quickly: "Pass the case of medicines," he ordered Sergio to conceal his apprehension and at the same time desperately racking his brain for the most elementary notions of orthopedics, now lost in the mists of time. In preparing the first aid kit he had certainly not reckoned on a disaster of this magnitude; in addition, for space reasons, he had had to cut the pharmaceuticals to a minimum, in spite of which he had aimed to stuff in enough for varied emergencies.

Before beginning to work, he made Karl swallow two tablets of analgesic and then he dissolved a packet of Euclorina in the hot water before beginning to gently cleanse the edges of the wound. Then came the difficult part.

"Karl, I can't give you any more painkillers. We only have a few and they may even make you keel over...Here, bite this," he added, passing him a handkerchief. If you absolutely cannot bear the pain then let me know, but try to endure as much as you can...there is no other way to deal with this, unfortunately." Karl, handkerchief between his teeth, assented with a nod of his head. "You now, Sergio, hold down his thigh here at the groin. Like this," Marco showed him. "With both hands...you got it?"

"Yes...yes."

"Okay. So keep it firmly in that position and do not let go while I pull."

"Alright."

Then Marco filled up his lungs to bursting, grabbed Karl's leg just above the knee, and began to pull it towards him with all his strength.

The pain must have been terrible even for someone of Karl's caliber; after a few moans from the handkerchief, he saw fit to lose consciousness again, thereby clearing the way for the makeshift orthopedic to proceed without much regard for the thankless task. In spite of this, Marco had to make several attempts before he had the feeling that the bone stumps had meshed together. A quick look inside the wound confirmed that the were perfectly aligned.

"God willing, we've got it...Now hold it steady like this and do not move it for any reason. Understood?"

"Yes, yes. Don't worry."

Once again Marco cleansed the wound and surrounding skin, which was encrusted with dried blood, using near-boiling water, from which emanated the reassuring smell of bleach. Always on hand in the pouch there was thread for stitches, a pair of scissors and a needle holder with which—this time with much more expertise— he sutured the edges of the lesion with multiple internal and external stitches. Finally, after having disinfected the sutures and bandaging with gauze and plaster, he pulled over and re-sewed the pant leg to the best of his ability.

"Now hand me two hatchets...Mine and Karl's, they're the same length."

Sergio, who in all his life had never even witnessed the extraction of a tooth, was about to faint after seeing all those stitches go through living flesh without even a touch of anesthetic. Just to get away from the sight of the operation as soon as possible and breathe some fresh air that did not smell like antiseptic, he leaped up to follow the order without even a thought of contesting anything that had to do with the length of the axes.

After detaching the handles from the metal part he arranged them alongside the leg and, while Sergio held them still in that position, he immobilized the limb in multiple places using the backpack straps and the belts taken from the guides.

At the end of the operation they were both drenched with sweat, but almost frozen from the cold. It was now the dead of night in the huge cavern. To save battery, they decided to turn off the flashlight and the only source of light now was the violet glow coming from the gas stove, on which they had just concocted a frugal dinner of tea and tortillas. To protect themselves from the bite of the deepening chill, they prepared a single bed using all five sleeping bags as a mattress and covers, and immediately after dinner they slipped into it without even taking their boots off.

Karl was feverish, but he slept deeply because of the sedation. The silence was broken only by the torment of the water dripping from the ice sheet that slapped into the water below at irregular intervals. Sergio's talkativeness had ceased. Before going to sleep he continued to tinker frantically with the phone, moving from one point of the cave to another in desperate search of reception, but he eventually had to give up, and the battery would not last forever.

At that moment, neither had the courage to voice their thoughts aloud. It was Marco who broke the silence.

"Look," he said softly, "there's no reception at all down here...so there's little hope of outside help."

"Mm," Sergio commented laconically.

"Ergo, we have to find the way out on our own."

"But then, they won't hear from us for a while, they'll send someone to look for us!" observed the other, showing that he was only following the logical line of thinking.

"Try to think," Marco continued patiently. "With that mountain of ice up there, I don't think your phones will localize very easily. They could get to the car using mine, but it'll be days before they notice our disappearance. Then, supposing that they are able to find our base camp right away, even more days will go by before the rescue teams arrive. After which, hoping that they manage to find the few nails that we planted in the wall, they'll have to make a wild guess to figure out that we wound up down here; up above there's not even the shadow of a trace of our presence left. But let's assume that they are able to find us fast enough; how much effort, do you think, will they put into transporting the drill up here to break up all that ice?...Believe me, at the end of the day, they would get down here just to recover three bodies long dead from hunger and cold."

"Mmm, but if they find us...as we wait for them to get us out, they could drill a hole in the ice and pass down things we need to survive."

"Come on, Sergio, try to keep your feet on the ground here. You know that I want to agree with you, but if you poke around in your brain for even just a minute you'll soon come to my same conclusion pretty fast; where we're at, there's not a hope in the world for outside help; so live with it, we have to find our own way out of here."

"Now, though, you're the one rambling. Will you tell me where the fuck we're going to find a way out? I'm not sure if you've noticed, but we have been buried alive!"

"Lower your voice please, you'll wake Karl up."

"I'm sorry; it's just…it's just that I can't even begin to imagine how you think we'll be able to find a way out of this trap."

"Well, for that matter, I have an idea."

"What's that?" replied the skeptic, paying close attention.

"I'm not sure if you've noticed one thing: the water that collects down here in the reservoir overflows on the other side…so much so that we had to move onto this shore to sleep where it's dry."

"Yeah, so what?"

"We're in full thaw, Sergio, and that water will have to go somewhere. Don't you think?"

"So?"

"So we should follow it. It's our only means of escape."

Sergio was silent just long enough to digest the concept but then, as if bitten by a tarantula, he threw the blanket off, grabbed the flashlight and jumped to his feet, ready to rush and check it out.

"Stay where you are!" Marco ordered him, holding him by the jacket. "Can't you see that it's pitch black? If we move now we'll only lose time and also risk running out of batteries right away. Let's try to rest instead, because a few hours of sleep can only help us. You'll see; tomorrow morning, with the light, we'll make up for the lost time."

Sergio, taken as he was with the desire to escape, remained still for some time, standing in silence and assessing the situation. Finally resigned, he surrendered to the logic, bent down and slipped back under the covers without a word.

They did not bid each other goodnight. Laying with their backs to one another and the cover pulled up above their ears, each retreated into his own thoughts in the vain attempt to get to sleep. This came only after quite some time, and for as welcome as it was—both being wrung out and exhausted in their very bones—it was only a restless half-sleep marred by continual, distressing nightmares. And as soon as the first light of dawn filtered through the ice dome the two, as if by unspoken command, sprang to their feet in unison.

Chapter 5

"Prepare something to eat," Marco ordered. Karl was still asleep and Sergio, while stamping the ground in anticipation, immediately and wordlessly began to pull all of the breakfast necessities out of the backpack while Marco, short ax and torch in hand, started out for the first exploratory tour.

The water overflowed on the downward-sloping side of the reservoir at one point only. In an effort that spanned millennia, it had carved a deep groove in the rock through which it flowed in slow streams, feeding a sort of brook which, after a few meters, fanned out into many small, divided rivulets. The light barely touched down there and in order to avoid retracing the same route several times, Marco began his search systematically, starting from the first branch on the left.

It was a succession of failures, and each accomplished nothing but to increase his anxiety and despair. Each rivulet inevitably trickled off in a dead-end at the foot of an ice hollow, or wormed into a burrow into which it was impossible to continue even by crawling on the ground.

After a good half hour of fruitless attempts, Marco went back for breakfast. "Nothing to do over on the left," he relayed immediately, answering his companion's unspoken question, who did not dare to ask as he handed over a bowl. "Let's try the other side," he continued, trying to stem his friend's panic before it started. "We'll go together; the rock there is too steep and slippery to go down alone."

"That will mean that we'll use rope and nails if necessary."

"Sure. You hold it and I'll extend or retract it as necessary. That way, it won't take as long to get down and back up."

"Okay."

"How is Karl, though?" asked Marco with his mouth full.

"Well…a little while ago, when I left him, he was going a little crazy. But as far as I can tell, he wasn't doing too badly."

Despite the reassurance, Marco went over to the other side of the reservoir just the same to check on the state of the injured man. Karl was feverish and babbling in his sleep, but Marco still managed to make him swallow a few sips of tea with an antibiotic by holding his head up.

The second exploratory tour was also a series of failures and disappointments. It so happened that upon entering, the tunnel suddenly widened out and thus reopened their hearts to hope, but after a few meters the appearance of an ice wall or in impassible bottleneck plunged them back into turmoil. And climbing back up the slope to the starting point became increasingly difficult and tiring.

The last three streams, located in the most precipitous part of the cave, were yet to be explored. Breaching the original method, Marco set off down the middle one. He was almost resigned and beginning to doubt his bright idea and every move he made—turning the flashlight on and off continually so as not to deplete the batteries too quickly—was mechanical. The first twenty meters were promising enough, then the reflection of light on the wall of ice made him realize that he had once again reached the end. And there were only two last possibilities for hope.

"Fuck, fuck, fuck!" Sergio continued to chant after the announcement of yet another failure. "It's over, it's over, it's over…"

"Shut up!" a curt command interrupted from below.

Marco was tied up in acrobatic contortions in an attempt to turn around in the narrow alley to avoid being forced to go back again when, laying against the floor of the tunnel, it seemed to him that he heard a noise. And as soon as the echo of complaints died down, he neared his head to the floor of the tunnel to press his ear to the wall.

In the absolute silence, the noise reached him more distinctly. It seemed to be the same produced by the bathtub in his home. And a noise like that could not depend solely on the paltry rivulet over which he was crouching.

"It's empty behind here," he shouted more to himself than to his friend, shutting off and setting the flashlight on the ground. He immediately grabbed the ax with both hands and took to raining furious blows on the bottom of the tunnel. The ice, made porous by the thaw, gave out easier than he expected and after just three hits from the ax handle, he found no more obstacles, and it sank into the wall up to its hilt. Extracting the shaft, Marco groped for the flashlight and turned it back on with trembling hands.

A gigantic black eye had appeared on the white wall and it seemed to want to carefully scrutinize his every move while the noise, which a few seconds before had been barely perceptible, had suddenly been amplified as if on the other side of the wall it had started to rain heavily.

Like a man possessed and with strength renewed hundredfold, Marco began to enlarge the hole until it was large enough to be able to insert the flashlight, and then his arm, and then his head. And when he directed the light beam downwards, the spectacle that loomed before him made up for all the hard work.

Beyond this, the trickle that was lost at the foot of the ice wall formed a small waterfall. But there was not only one waterfall back there. There were ten, a hundred, a thousand of them, much, much larger than that supplied by Ariadne's thin thread that had led him up to that point, and all in a wonderful symphony of various crystalline sounds; they flowed in from everywhere into a single large reservoir. The water that overflowed from this coursed into a deep cleft in the rock and there, at least at first glance, the icy roof seemed high enough to be able to push forward in an upright position.

As though regenerated by the discovery—albeit perturbed by a vague sense of unease—Marco began committing himself to breaking down the last barrier that obstructed the way, while Sergio—

who had regained his hope, along with his mania—could no longer stop asking for more news or dispensing his valuable advice.

Half an hour later, the two friends were again on the other side of the little lake. Karl was still delirious. There was the massive problem of how to transport him. Also, as he was obviously unable to carry a load on him, they had to make a selection of the essentials to bring with them including the wounded man, all the backpacks and the tents.

They filled the backpacks to capacity and tied the sleeping bags on top. They decided to abandon the igloos where they were, but with the Duralumin rods and tent fabric they prepared a sort of hammock equipped with straps to be placed behind the neck and shoulders so that they could keep their hands free to support and help themselves along the way.

Before setting off, they went over to their Chilean comrades, tidied up the bodies, took from their pockets the few personal effects to be returned to the families, and covered them with the canvases of the igloos, holding them down on the sides with blocks of ice. They recited a short prayer and then after a final, emotional farewell, took leave of the improvised graves to return, mournful and pensive, to their starting point.

"You go down first," said Marco, breaking the silence after slipping on his backpack. "Then I'll pass Karl and his backpack to you with the rope."

They did it just so, and once they reached the bottom of the tunnel they proceeded across the breach in the same order until they reached the edge of the reservoir. At that point, after securing Karl's backpack over his chest, they lifted his improvised stretcher off the ground, arranged their straps, and bypassed the expanse of water; they walked along the little creek, keeping their legs apart and placing their feet on the rocky embankment just above the surface of the water.

As they proceeded downwards, the flow of the stream became more and more substantial thanks to the contribution of the other

46

tributaries, up to the point where they were forced to wet their feet in the icy water, while the increasingly impetuous current produced such a resounding roar that they were forced to shout to be able to communicate.

Although they were careful to turn it on only when absolutely necessary, the flashlight was emitting a dimmer, reddish light. On the other hand, the icy vault had become higher and higher so that even Marco could proceed with a straightened back and no longer bent double as he had been forced to do in the first section of the road—for Little Serge, this was never a problem.

After more than an hour's slow and labored walk, the cleft between the rocks suddenly opened out into a large hole at the bottom of which the creek—after almost a five-meter drop—was thrown into a veritable underground river. For the two, it was enough to glance at the whirlpools below to see that they had arrived at the point of no return: those freezing waters of seething foam could mean salvation or their tragic end. And they did not even have the possibility of choosing; exhausted by fatigue and almost frozen by the cold, they would not be able to go back even half the long, bumpy way they had just been. And all uphill, too.

Without even stopping to think about it, they slipped the stretcher off, propped it precariously on the right bank of the waterfall and knotted the rope to the carabiners.

"Let's continue in the same order," Marco suggested. "So you can go first this time too."

The joke only barely managed to make his friend's mouth twitch in the semblance of a smile, but it had the power to end the lingering.

While Marco supported him with the rope, Sergio lowered himself slowly into the river. The water was almost up to his neck and, even though he was held up by the rope, he could hardly remain standing against the momentum of the current.

Then it was Karl's turn. Marco, after having tied his knees and ankles together using the straps off the stretcher, slid slowly down, holding it with the rope. Finally, assuring himself that his companions were no longer below him, he placed the ax between the backpack and his back, pocketed the flashlight, made the sign of the cross, heaved a deep breath, and dropped down in a ball.

When he plunged into the water, Sergio and Karl were already far away and he did not even have time to stand up because a sudden jerk of the rope dragged him immediately into the middle of the current.

As much as he was protected by the watertight seal, Marco felt his skin being pricked by a multitude of icy needles. The fury of the water was tossing him about and preventing him from adjusting the speed of the descent, and his groans and curses were endless each time an elbow, knee, or some other sensitive part went crashing into a rocky outcrop. Often the backpack caught on something and halted his course, but one yank on the rope took him right back into the stream. Other times, however, his feet were the ones to hit Karl's head or shoulders and free him from the traps and snags in which he had gotten stranded.

After a few minutes of lunatic racing, the cold had rendered him nearly numb. Marco had ceased reacting and allowed his inert body to be carried almost indifferently by the water in the absolute darkness towards an unknown fate. Meanwhile, the underground river was swelling dramatically, becoming faster and more violent, and at one point Marco had the sensation of rubbing his face on the tunnel ceiling and it no longer had the smooth texture of ice, but the coarse ruggedness of rock.

"This is the end," he said to himself, trying to store away all the air that his lungs could hold, snatching it out of the narrow gap still between the water and the ceiling. He felt strangely lucid and was meditating on what he would experience shortly, in the act of dying; how much time would pass between the time when the water entered his throat and when he would lose consciousness? And how much would he suffer?

Marco was about to give up, he was ready to let go, to stop fighting. He felt his lungs bursting in their selfish and spasmodic demand for oxygen. *Enough, I'll end it now,* he thought, tempted to put an immediate end to the terrible nightmare by opening his throat to the lethal water. But his survival instinct took over.

He had exceeded the limit of his endurance when, through his eyelids, he perceived a weak light. In a last, desperate, superhuman effort he forced himself to resist. One second, then another, and another, to breaking point. And suddenly, as if by magic, he felt himself cast out of the mountain into a blinding light while his lungs, with a hungry snarl, filled with a mixture of air and water spray.

Chapter 6

It was the rope that saved him again. While his limp body fell through the void, Marco felt himself suddenly stopped and then, with a violent jerk, pulled backward towards the mountain wall. Luckily for him, the tremendous impact against the rock was cushioned by his backpack and sleeping bag.

He could not see anything. At first he accepted this as quite a natural occurrence because of the sudden transition from the blackest dark to the bright light of day. But when everything around him continued to appear blurred and hazy despite the passage of several minutes, he began to seriously worry. "Perhaps the lack of oxygen got to my brain?" he said to himself in anguish.

He could not make any sense of it all. Every now and then he was hit by a burst of cold water, a load noise was roaring in his ears and it was necessary before he came to understand that his sight, thank God, was still quite good, and that all that fog was nothing but an impenetrable wall of water. It was then that, looking up, he realized that he was hanging by the rope from a tree trunk that protruded from the terrace of a rock face to his left. Just above him he could see Karl's feet, inert and dangling from the other side of the trunk; but instead of being taut, the rope that hung from the carabiner was writhing like a crazy snake lost between the splashes from the waterfall. No trace of Sergio.

"Mother of God, hopefully nothing happened to him!" Marco moaned to himself. The water at the base of the waterfall should have been pretty deep, but this did not reassure him in the slightest. The carabiner must have come unlatched from him on its own…provided that he did not unlatch it himself, he thought, and—knowing his friend—took the second hypothesis almost for granted.

He stayed in place for a long time, peering down in a vain attempt to see someone or something and calculate the height of the jump, but despite all his efforts the visibility ended just below his feet in a sea of spray and infinite rainbows.

At that moment, however, concern over what could have happened to Sergio and for the health of Karl were selfishly offset by the joy of still being alive. As though pervaded by a strange euphoria, and certainly not indifferent to the difficult situation, he allowed himself to be calm and peaceful in the void while a flurry of abstruse considerations crowded his mind.

"I'm changing my life!" he heard himself screaming, as if to overcome the noise of the waterfall, after some kind of audacious succession of flights of fancy and algorithms produced by the gray matter of the brain. And at that point he could not even begin to imagine how prophetic those words would prove to be.

The sounds of his own voice managed to snatch him from the static state of apathy into which he had fallen and bring him back to reality. Karl was hanging motionless in the void. Perhaps he was still alive, but if he wanted to help him he first had to take care of himself. And quickly, too.

That was easier said than done. The chill, which up to that point had almost anesthetized him, was slowly melting away and gradually the human mechanism resumed functioning and one after the other all the scrapes, bruises and dings came to the surface in a terrible flood; in almost every part of his body, Marco felt a crescendo of excruciating pains, and every movement caused him an unspeakable pang that even made breathing difficult. But he was able to react.

He clung to the rope and with a bit of strength from his arms and a bit of help from his legs, he brought himself slowly up to the level of his friend. Karl was unmoving, his mouth half open, eyes closed. With both hands occupied, Marco was not in any position to check his pulse at either the wrist or throat; from the coloring of his nose and the sliver of his face that was not hidden by his beard and the woolen hat pulled over his brow, he did not look deceased.

Swinging himself through the air, he grabbed the rope from which Karl hung and inserted it with a click into his clasp. Then he harnessed his friend with the rope hanging from his belt and knotted the free end around his waist. Luckily for him, the long exposure to water had completely stripped the tree trunk of its bark, so that when he looped the rope overtop, it was slimy and slippery, and as soon as he pulled a bit on the rope he felt himself projected upwards like a musket ball.

While he shot up like a rocket, he congratulated himself; if he had not taken steps to bind the ropes in a single carabiner, the huge counterweight would certainly have hurled him beyond the trunk and driven him down to the bottom of the waterfall. But the knock that his head got when it slammed against the hard wood made him drastically reduce the self-commendation.

But the difficult part was yet to come. Still half-dazed, he secured the end of the rope, to which he had harnessed Karl, to the trunk with a noose in order to free himself for maneuvering. Then, with a great effort, he pulled himself astride the plant, but with its slippery surface the wood—which had been such a faithful ally moments before—suddenly was the most treacherous enemy, causing him to lose his balance and systematically drag him back into open air every time he managed to climb on.

Marco hardly had the strength to get back up and none left to spend cursing. He was moving in slow motion now. Every slight movement elicited groans of pain from his mouth, but after a series of countless failed attempts he finally managed to find a way to hold firm onto the trunk by crossing his legs underneath it, and soon after he began to push hard on the rope, forcing it sideways towards the terrace with his fingers. The task was facilitated by the slight downward tilt of the trunk. Despite this, he soon found himself with broken nails and fingertips reduced to a bloody pulp, but he gritted his teeth and, inch by inch, managed to move slowly out of the waterfall's spray and then, after an infinite spell, onto solid ground.

He was exhausted, dazed by fatigue and pain, but he still could not stop. With slow strokes he retrieved the rope that was fastened to his waist and after having securely fixed it to the first root of the semi-uprooted plant that he grazed with his hand, he pulled it towards himself with a sharp yank. The noose unfastened instantly and released the enormous weight, which tumbled down towards the terrace all at once and the violent jerk that his hands received simultaneously—had he not had the foresight to secure that rope to the plant—would certainly have catapulted him into space. And so began the slow recovery operation.

Karl's weight was truly incredible. Marco felt that his strength was about to abandon him, but he forced himself to endure and managed to carry his friend, inch by inch, onto dry land. It was only after having dragged him several meters away from the spray of the waterfall that he let himself drop to the ground, at the very height of exhaustion.

The thought of his friends tormented him, but in that moment he was spent. As he laid motionless on his back, unable to take any initiative, the world around him caught his attention for the first time.

He was lying on his back in the middle of a meadow. There was a great light all around, but rather than a blue sky above him there was a one solid, immense, white ceiling; a sort of gigantic dome that seemed brightly lit by powerful spotlights hidden away someplace. The meadow's tall grass precluded his vision to the sides, but did not prevent him from making another disconcerting observation: during the long ride in the heart of the mountain he had to have descended several hundred meters; however, considering his still-saturated clothing and the prevailing climate in those altitudes, he should have felt like an icicle inside a freezer. Instead, he had the sensation of being immersed in the same gentle warmth as when in late springtime he would lay in the front yard of his house in his home country. Even the grass—compared to the miserable thorn bushes, yellowed and withered by the winter cold that pervaded up until the day before—was incredibly high, fat and flourishing and, even more surprisingly, there was not even a breath of that icy, relentless wind that over the last few days had not given respite to the ill-fated party.

A bee buzzed a few inches from his nose and Marco, as if he had nothing more important to think about at that time, observed the movements of the insect who presented itself to the inner corolla of a lemon-yellow flower in order to quietly suck the nectar.

Soon, though, curiosity won out over his fatigue and the delivered man, in an attempt to reorient himself with something among all those oddities, first brought himself to a seated position and then laboriously to his feet, taking great care not to abuse his joints too much.

To his right, just above the trunk of the plant from which he had hung, there was the massive column of the waterfall; on his left, however, the meadow stretched as far as the eye could see up to meet a distant wall with the same whiteness of the ceiling. A multitude of unrecognized flowers broke the deep green of the grass with splashes of color, giving the observer the impression of being inside a giant greenhouse where the owner had, perhaps a bit carelessly, sown grasses and flowers chaotically and with a culmination of incomparable beauty.

In front of him, two or three miles away as the crow flies, loomed another concave white wall. The meadow in which his feet stood did not seem to touch it, but instead seemed to stop—like a roof garden—just a few hundred meters ahead.

Marco lifted his gaze again. The immaculate dome rose skyward until it was lost somewhere, while behind him its downward inclination was increasingly steep and ended behind a thick barrier of tall trees that towered over the meadow like a large amphitheater.

"Where the fuck am I!" he wondered privately, more and more confused and disoriented. The pain forced him to sit again. And he was still massaging his aching knees, elbows and ankles when Karl's cries distracted him from his questioning.

With his heart pounding, he crawled over to Karl on all fours like a limping dog along the length of the rope.

Karl had resumed raving, but thank God he was alive. The doctor, beside himself with joy, thought that a state of semi-hibernation had saved him from drowning. Feeling his forehead, he must have had a high fever, but at his wrist a regular pounding—though rapid—was discernible. The fractured leg, moreover, was still perfectly straight and bound to the other with the restraining straps, and it was only at that time that Marco remembered with relief that the case of medicinal products was safely inside his backpack and not Sergio's, where they had originally put it when divvying up the things to be carried along.

"Sergio…what could've happened to him?" Marco wondered, his anguish mounting, while with broken nails and martyred fingertips he tried to untangle the still-wet, taut backpack straps in a vain attempt to open it. He was torn between two conflicting impulses: on the one hand, he wanted to understand Karl's condition more thoroughly; on the other, weighed down by a distressed foreboding, he definitely wanted to investigate the fate of his childhood friend.

He chose the second option. Karl, after all, was still alive, and Marco could not do much to help him at the moment regardless. So he left his backpack and managed to get to his feet and drag himself towards the waterfall, being very careful not to slip on the muddy ground. Once he reached the edge of the terrace, he clung onto his saving tree trunk for safety and leaned down, but only to confirm what he had already had occasion to observe when he was still hanging in empty space: it was impossible to see anything through all that fog. He decided to walk along the edge of the meadow, gradually accelerating his pace as his joints resumed functioning with some difficulty. He advanced while keeping a safe distance from the ravine, leaning gingerly from time to time to take a look at the bottom, but only after a hundred meters, when the curtain of water mist thinned out, did he manage to get a more precise look at the situation. And what he saw made him tremble.

The jet of water shot out of the mountain with violence, tracing an arc of impressive dimensions, then enlarged as it plummeted down before one's very eyes and ended, after a gap of two or three hundred meters, into a reservoir of seething foam bordered on the other side of the waterfall by a rock face. The noise produced by the enormous milky ribbon was nothing short of stunning, and the height of the jump had nothing to envy of the highest and most famous waterfalls in the word.

There and then, Marco could not help but stop and admire the enchanting grandeur of the sight, but the thought of his missing friend—made even more painful by the size of the drop—was fast to return him to the urgency of the moment. He resumed marching quicker and quicker close to the edge of the sort of natural balcony until he reached the outer corner at a near run and when, having reached his destination, he cast his eyes downwards, and was effectively winded.

Before his eyes there was an immense valley. The water beneath the waterfall which was barely visible was nothing but the furthest stretch of a real lake, in the middle of which was a squat, flat barge of an unusual shape with two oarsmen on board, which at that time were directing the boat towards the shore and rowing in an erect position. Between them, in the center of the boat, lay a body.

"Sergio," Marco breathed with a pang in his heart, immediately recognizing the unmistakable colors of his jumpsuit despite the distance. "Mother of God, he could not have gotten out of a drop like that alive!" he considered disconsolately, shifting his gaze to the shore where a large group of people was gathering, which only served to increase his astonishment. They appeared to be nude or wearing skimpy bathing suits and had their eyes on the boat; despite the noise of the waterfall, their excited voices could be heard all the way up in the meadow.

Perhaps it was his sixth sense, or the bewilderment, the sensation of being in front of an impossible occurrence, that prevented him from crying out and revealing his presence to all of them. The fact was that Marco, instead of calling for help, threw himself down at the edge of the terrace while watching the scene in secret. It was this instinctive gesture that saved his life once again on that absurd day.

Chapter 7

As the boat approached land, the people on the shore swelled in number. Almost all of them came from a single road that ran along an out-flowing river of the lake, and was lost along this, following the rocky outcrop of the waterfall. "Their village must be behind that partition sort of thing that marks the lower bank of the lake," Marco reasoned with himself. "It certainly must not be just a handful of houses, judging by the number of inhabitants."

The observer was struggling with these considerations when the distant voices suddenly ceased and the crowd, which was silent as their heads bowed, split to form a narrow passage which made space for a train of characters straight out of the past. Leading the procession, preceded by two nude heralds bearing high rectangular banners on straps, marched a handful of soldiers in bizarre greenish uniforms with identically colored round shields on their left arms and long spears at their sides. Two men in black robes followed in lordly chairs supported by twelve bearers. On the bench sat a man who looked quite sincerely unique.

Marco was not able to make out his features, but by the reflections emitted from the diadem on his head, the staff borne in his hand and the countless jewels that glinted on him, he deduced that he could not be a simple tribal leader and reflections of that sort were not given off by broken glass or any old junk. No, that staff, that jewelry and that headdress were definitely studded with precious stones, that character was a real king, and the throne on which he was seated—and judging by the number of bearers in the procession—could not be anything but solid gold.

He was growing more and more confused, and to him it felt like he was attending one of the typical historical reenactments of a village with much flag-waving and ridiculous characters in historically accurate costumes playing their roles. But this hypothesis did not have him convinced. He needed to see things more clearly.

He moved a few feet back, turned around, stood up and trotted back to the starting point. After taking a look at Karl—who, fortunately, was no longer delirious and was breathing regularly—he hastily pulled the binoculars from a side pocket of the backpack and flung himself down on the edge of the terrace.

Now Marco could observe every little detail of the spectacular parade. Once he adjusted the focus, he felt like he was in the very midst of the crowd gathered on the shore, like he too was participating and acting in the ceremony. The amazing procession concurrently concluded with the arrival of another array of illustrious characters, also in sumptuous vestments and covered with jewels. They were all arranged in a semicircle behind the royal sedan chair, which had in the meantime been set on the ground near the shore while the twelve servants now kneeled at its sides with their arms crossed over their chests.

"No, it can't be a country festival…and it can't be a tribe of highlanders either," Marco kept repeating, bewildered by so much pageantry. Only the guise of the king clashed a bit with the grandeur of it all. Squat and portly, his feet barely reached far enough to touch the embroidered cushion underneath them. Despite the distance, he could make out quite clearly his ruddy cheeks, piggy eyes and snub nose, but especially the strange oblong shape of his skull which, although exhibited by almost all of the dignitaries assembled behind him, was not racial, given the normal shape of the heads of the commoners. Marco had heard of or read somewhere about an ethnic group that used to obtain such deformation as an indication of high birth, but at that moment he could not remember what it was, as much as he racked his brain.

Sergio seemed to have his eyes open but he showed no signs of life, and it was beyond clear that the cause for the crowd's flocking together was just the discovery of his body in the middle of the lake. Marco, however, could not yet explain why no one had yet taken the trouble to carry this object of so much interest onto dry land, despite the boat being anchored a few meters from the shore for some time already.

Soon the two mariners began to systematically undress Sergio, and Marco was truly amazed when, after a lot of tinkering, they managed to solve the mystery of his parka's zipper and began endlessly opening and closing it, exclaiming at the astonishing discovery with vibrant gesticulations each time. "It's not possible that they've never seen a zipper in their lives!" he pondered perplexedly, recalling that he had seen garments with that type of lacing in even the remotest villages of Black Africa.

In the meantime a human chain had formed between the boat and the shore, which passed along every object found on his friend hand by hand. The first to possess them were the two black-robed men. One of them seemed quite advanced in age; a sparse fluff, as white as his bushy eyebrows, encircled his balding head like a halo; standing, he was supported by resting his hands and chin at the top of a long staff as he seemed to observe each object that was passed under his nose with an indifferent, almost absent, expression.

The aspect and behavior of the other man were, however, diametrically opposed. With a head of long black, thick hair that gave the impression that he had not seen a barber since it had sprung up on his head, he was of a robust frame, medium height and an authoritarian countenance; he was the real leader. While he confabulated with the warrior who stood respectfully beside him (the commander of the guard, judging by the height of the plumes on his garish uniform), he passed along each item and garment that was exhibited to him, and only after having examined it with extreme fussiness did he deliver it to the lord seated on the throne. The astonishment of the onlookers reached its height when the Rolex came into the hands of the latter. The foreign sovereign initially fumbled with all the watch's small buttons and extendable wristband for a while and after having attached it around his wrist did he begin to summon the dignitaries crowded around him to show them the new marvel. And all vied to see, touch, and press the mysterious object to their ears.

When the task of plundering was completed, a new transfer began. This time in the opposite direction. Now it was the men on the shore who passed boulders and stones of every size to those in the water until, in the vicinity of the vessel, a base large enough that a large rectangular slab of white stone could be arranged by the labor of six robust bearers. Only then was Sergio's bare and lifeless body taken from the boat and placed on the stone in supine position. Immediately after the man in black completed a detailed examination, he went down into the water fully dressed and moved slowly behind the makeshift altar.

Marco had followed all the preparations with growing apprehensions and at that point he did not need a wild imagination to guess at what would follow. The images spoke for themselves now: that character was none other than a high priest and on that stone an ancient, terrible rite was about to be consummated. "No, it cannot be, it's not possible!" he continued repeating, trying to convince himself that it was only a game, all a macabre staging. But the events that followed gave tragic confirmation to his darkest predictions.

Silence had fallen on the lakeshore. Even the sound of the waterfall seemed to have softened for this exceptional event, and while a thick column of smoke rose from a bonfire near the lake, all eyes were locked on the officiant, who suddenly held between his hands a long dagger with a black blade. In dramatic sequence, the priest raised it high in the air and brought it down violently into the victim's chest; with a quick and expert gesture, he then dipped his hand into the gash, extracted the heart and raised it in the air, still dripping with blood, to show the excited crowd, from which a roar of cheers arose in unison.

"No!" Marco choked through clenched teeth. "No, you fuckers! No!" The near-certainty that Sergio was already dead at the time of the execution was not enough to soothe his pain. He was paralyzed, pinned to the ground by anxiety and terror. Then he was seized by uncontrollable tremors, and while his choked sobs died in his throat a single, absurd word had been hammered into his mind: Aztecs!

Chapter 8

Petrified by grief and fear, Marco remained motionless, speechless, staring with wide, tear-clouded eyes at the terrible sequence of images that had not yet come to a close. The executioner, still clutching the heart in his hand, sprinkled its blood in the four cardinal directions in an act of blessing. Then, assisted by two shaved-headed aides, he began to dismember the victim and the pieces were passed from hand to hand to the shore where they were in turn deposited on a large, copper-hued grill settled on the coals of the fire that had just burned down to embers.

Soon the entire population starting with the king and high dignitaries began to feed on the summarily cooked human flesh, to the extent that nothing remained of the victim but a few bare bones tossed to calcify on the embers. Only the head was left intact, stuck like a macabre trophy on the point of a long pole held erect by a completely naked herald.

It was a while before Marco, stunned by the turn of events and unable to accept what had happened, could look away from the valley and worry about Karl's condition. He could not, must not, lose him too; only his experience and expertise could get him out of this absurd situation which he still had a hard time believing.

Meanwhile, his suffering rapidly gave way to a sense of powerlessness and the growing fear of coming to the same fate as his friend. Flattening himself to the ground as much as possible, Marco began to crawl slowly backward with bated breath, and only when he was totally sure that he could not be seen from the valley did he dare to get back on his feet and allow himself the right to run back in the direction of his only companion still left alive.

Karl had begun raving again. His moans were abundantly covered by the noise of the waterfall, but it was not enough to reassure his friend, who was haunted by other pressing emergencies. He had to seek shelter for the night, first of all; to remain encamped on the moist and muddy soil was unthinkable, and things would not improve a lot by shifting farther away from the waterfall, either. The temperature was dropping quickly, announcing the sunset, and he was beginning to feel the cold through his wet clothes. Camping on the grass would risk sickness, and if this held true for him, it was out of the question for Karl; in the current conditions even a common cold could prove fatal.

But concern for the cold and the dampness of the night was nothing compared to the fear of being discovered. At that time, his only imperative was hiding. But where? Until then he had not noticed any signs of human presence, but he could not trust appearances. The forest, he thought, was the only place nearby where you could at once hide and find protection from the rigors of the night.

After several unsuccessful attempts, he managed to find the best way to carry Karl by loading him up on his shoulders and pulling him by an arm and his healthy leg. Then he began heading for his preselected goal in small steps, continually shooting inquisitive glances, ready to seize upon any suspicious movement.

The closer he came to the forest, the higher the meadow's grass and shrubs grew, coming to the point where they blocked his vision. All in all though, that natural shelter, though a hindrance to the walk, did not bother him at all in light of the scene to which he had just borne witness.

After a few hundred meters the grass ended suddenly in front of a thick barrier of tall, compact brambles so high as to constitute a kind of wall, and Marco had to make his way along it for some distance before he found an opening large enough to pass through while dragging his friend.

Beyond the hedge the grassy earth ceased in order to make way for plants that became increasingly imposing as they climbed upwards. Eager to find a hiding place, Marco was not in the ideal state of mind to begin studying the local flora (if anything, it was the uncertainty of the fauna that occupied his full attention at the time), but this did not prevent him from noting that there were mostly pine and fir trees around him. Occasionally, however, the conifers gave way to giant deciduous trees with trunks unquestionably at least a thousand years old and with such full, majestic foliage that you could pitch a circus tent under each of them. It was easier to proceed at the foot of these immense umbrellas even if the tangled vegetation of the undergrowth forced him to frequently deviate his path.

Karl's weight seemed to grow by the minute, which necessitated that he make increasingly lengthy stops to catch his breath, and when the slope became too steep for his strength, Marco decided it was time to stop. He laid his friend in a wide clearing and covered him with a thick layer of dry leaves and pine needles then, painfully resisting the invitation of that temptation, he went back down to the meadow to go recover the backpacks.

His track was still clearly traced in the high grass, so it did not take long to find them. Precisely for this reason, on the way back he proceeded facing backwards, lifting and straightening the trampled stalks in an effort to erase all traces of his earlier steps. This operation, however, took a good deal of time and night overtook him suddenly while he was still at the edge of the forest.

He stood dumbfounded. Not even during his repeated trips in the equatorial regions had he ever witnessed such a sudden sunset; the transition from day to night was instant, like lightning, as if the landlord had decided at a certain point to turn off the light by flicking a switch with his finger. But once again, there was no time to waste trying to find a logical explanation for this new, perplexing phenomenon.

Marco had always had a keen sense of direction, but at the time, in total darkness and without a single reference point, finding his way in the woods proved to be a rather difficult task. Partly because he was not going to risk using the flashlight. He was wandering aimlessly for about half an hour and was almost resigned to the idea of not being able to track Karl down before dawn when he was suddenly piloted in the right direction by his friend's loud snoring. But he realized that he had reached his destination only when he stumbled into the pile of needles and leaves where he had buried him.

He still could not concede to a well-earned rest. Still in darkness, he pulled the pouch of medicines from his backpack and unrolled the two sleeping bags. He attached them together with the zipper to form a single blanket and tucked both himself and his friend underneath while supporting his head. But only when he was sure that not even a little light would leak out from the improvised shelter did he venture to light the flashlight. Holding it tight between his teeth, he directed the beam of light to the injured leg and, between curses, managed to untangle the still-saturated straps from the restraints. This, he was able to verify, had held up better than he had expected given the ill-treatment during that interminable day, but the swollen, purple wound did not look so good. Marco disinfected and tried to treat it as best he could; he pulverized one tablet of antibiotic and one of antipyretic in the lid of the water bottle and, after having dissolved the powder with a little bit of water, slowly poured the contents between Karl's lips while he held his head up. The wet blanket weighed on his head like a ton of cold bricks, but at the end of the long operation he found himself bathed in sweat just the same.

He could do nothing else for the moment; he just needed to rest. The night before he really had not slept a wink, and the day that had just passed was nothing short of incredible. He burrowed into the vegetal covering, but in spite of his fatigue sleep was a long ways away. Before his eyes the entire sequence of the gruesome ritual was still flashing, in which he saw the body of his best friend cut up and devoured. He still could not get his head around the thing and every time the images of the sacrifice returned to his mind, the idea of meeting the same fate put a knot in his guts. At the same time, he was besieged and tormented by a rising tide of thoughts and concerns, and each did nothing but increase his anxiety, plunging him deeper into despair.

Chapter 9

It was Karl's voice that roused him from the dreamless sleep to which he sank after hours of restless dozing. Just as his eyes opened, Marco had a moment of disorientation in the gloom of the forest, but the sudden recollection of events hit him like an avalanche. "Shut up, please!" he pleaded with his friend, covering his mouth with one hand. "We're in danger!" Karl, as dazed as he was, quieted instantly. He was perfectly lucid and, to all appearances, seemed to have recovered well enough.

The clearing was a cacophony of the twittering of a thousand bird voices. High up among the treetops, there was a gap large enough to allow the eyes to wander for a large tract overhead, and while Karl looked around quizzically to try to focus on their environment, Marco stood in silence, watching him with bated breath as though he wanted to give him some time to prepare for the bad news. He did not know where to start. Given the precarious state of his friend he did not want to shock him even more, but in his urgent desire to escape he could not wait to bring him up to speed on everything, if only to have two heads together to seek a remedy to the predicament.

Tactfully and carefully choosing the right words, he recounted the previous day's tragic events, from the terrifying descent through the mountain to the slow climb through the woods at night, and as he got into the details—including the absolute uselessness of the cell phones—he felt the mountainous weight slide off his shoulders.

The South Tyrolean listened to him in silence and Marco saw him wince, reading all the dismay, disbelief and incredible pain in his face when he got to talking about their mutual friend's miserable end. Occasionally, Karl lifted his eyes to the immaculate vaulted ceiling that could be glimpsed between the trees and then habitually lower them to his leg imprisoned between two sticks. At the end of the story he remained silent for a long time as if to digest the full extent of what he had just learned. "We'll never get out of here," he said almost to himself, his voice barely audible.

Those words had the same effect on Marco as an unexpected punch in the stomach. "But...but how can you say that! How can you, without having seen, without...without...someone like you, and with your experience, your...Come one, don't be crazy. You just talk like that because you see yourself tied up like that. Think about healing instead, then you'll see that you'll find it, you, the right way to get out of this. Of course you'll find it. I'm sure that you'll find it. Don't tell me that..."

Realizing that he had raised his voice too high, Marco instantly quieted but continued to stare at his friend's face with the imploring expression of one who is waiting for a change of heart, but Karl remained silent, and in his eyes he saw a definitive ruling, the same that he knew in his heart was true, though he refused to accept it. Indeed, although not a born mountaineer, he had come to understand on his own that it would be an impossible task even for someone with Karl's experience to climb that mirror-smooth wall with such a marked degree of curvature. And then even if he were in perfect physical condition. Nor was there any possibility of ever sending phone signals outside; the first to notice them would doubtlessly be the inhabitants of the valley, and being discovered would certainly be the last calamity that the two could bring upon themselves considering the welcome committee at work in those parts. For the moment, they could do nothing but sit in silence in the hope that it had occurred to the rescuers to go and look on the other side of the towers instead of where their tracks ended.

The underground river to which they had entrusted their last hope had transported them through the heart of the mountain into an ancient volcanic crater in the very irregular shape of an hourglass.

The several mile-long, elliptical valley formed the base of the lower cone and was surrounded by concave walls as smooth as a mirror, which, after reaching a maximum point of convergence at about eight hundred meters, diverged upwards to form the inverted cone of the hourglass that corresponded to the abyss in which the two Chileans had attempted to descend. The two cones, however, were out of alignment with each other at the level of the isthmus, so that it was impossible to see the sky from the level of the valley or for the valley to be seen from above.

But the amazing jokes that Mother Nature was generously dispensed to pull did not end there. In remote ages volcanic eruptions gave birth to this crater and had acted on its particular composition, molding it with enormous pressure and temperatures into a glassy layer as smooth and fragile as a mirror, which in a bizarre play of lenses imposingly funneled the sea of light from the mouth of the crater, inundating the valley for the entirety of the day. And this explained the instantaneity of the sunrises and sunsets in that god-forsaken place.

Additionally, the volcano was not completely extinct. From the top of the terracing on the opposite shore of the lake, you could in fact make out the deep inlets in the wall of rock from which enormous geysers of boiling water rose almost continuously, mingling with the icy water from the glaciers and precipitation. The resulting thermal transfer was striking, and generated a huge cushion of warm air which spread in every direction and gave the valley an almost tropical climate and, rising to the top, prevented the glacier above from closing the isthmus of the crater. This last was quite useful for both air intake and acting as a natural watershed, and when it rained or snowed (which was quite frequent, even in those parts), a dense network of streams was created which, running down either by waterfall or pouring down the walls, helped to feed the lake waters and irrigate the soil below.

The bank on which the tragic rite had been consummated, with the exception of some sandy stretches, was almost entirely covered by polished white pebbles which in the evening were collected in some small white canoes and the big vessel that had transported Sergio on his last trip, but proceeding to the left in the direction of the area of enduring volcanic activity; the gravel perceptibly made room for a white cliff of boulders which emerged ever higher and mightier and stood near the geysers like so many stone pyramids.

The lake was surrounded by a long stretch of a large, grassy meadow that was passed through each night by a team of workers armed with scythes who cropped it with care. Beyond the meadow was a whole series of small plots of land perfectly squared and bordered by irrigation furrows, many of which cultivated sweet corn. Entire families, children included, were busy plowing, hoeing, watering and cultivating those lands from the first light of the morning until late evening, when they retired to their homes on the edges of the fields. These were stone huts with rooftops made of glassy slabs and, as a peculiar detail, none had its doors or window facing the lake, so that at night you could not even see a glimmer in them from the terrace.

Further on, beyond the fields and orchards, a lush forest grew all the way to the opposite wall of the crater. The leaves of some plants were such an intensely bright green that at certain times of day, the light seemed to reflect off the surrounding rocks. In that part, the intervention of human hands was also evident; they had been arranged in neat rows according to decreasing height in such a way that prevented them from casting shade over one another. Everything was perfect. It was a true sliver of paradise. But a haven of forbidden fruit.

From the type of vegetation and the clothes the people in that region wore, it was easy to deduce that there must be a hot, humid, tropical sort of climate throughout the entire year. There was also a fairly mild temperature on the terrace where the two survivors had wound up, but despite the few hundred meters that separated it from the valley, the influence of the outside world still made itself heard. The plants, for example, were typical of more temperate climates and, judging by the humus present in the undergrowth, were certainly subject to seasonal variations that took place outside the crater.

During the night, in fact, the temperature dropped several degrees and during the daytime it sufficed to climb around the high parts of the forest to immediately perceive a difference; it was like switching from the spring warmth of the Roman hills to the crisp, clean air of the Dolomites.

Much of the lake remained hidden beneath the terrace and it was impossible to make out its inner bank, as near the waterfall it was not possible to see that part of the valley obscured by the rocky spur delimiting the lake.

After medicating the wound and changing the bandage, Marco went to fill the water bottles in a stream he had come across the night before while he was climbing through the woods. Upon his return he found his friend sitting with his back against the trunk of the tree under which they had slept. He had emptied out the entire contents of the backpacks and was fiddling with the little camping stove. "Luckily, this was spared," Karl announced without taking his eyes off the flame, satisfied, after turning it on.

Neither of them had touched food since the previous day and the fact that Karl was hungry was comforting. By mutual agreement they decided to use the stove. Being careful not to overdo it with the flame would ensure that they would not run a great risk; on the other hand, after the drenching they got the day before and the humidity of that night, they both really needed to swallow something hot.

While the tea steeped, they put two tortillas on the steel plate to heat up. The cellophane had miraculously saved two entire packages of them. They had already discovered that some water had gotten into another and transformed the contents into such a soft and slimy paste that it would make any stomach turn, but the two thought it best to air-dry the contents and stow them away for future famines.

The tortillas, although covered by the upside-down nonstick pan—along with the teapot, the only to survive the disaster—also smelled delightful. "Let's hope that there's no one else around here," Marco said, drooling with hunger. "I read somewhere about some race of aborigines—I don't know which—with such a keen sense of smell that they can detect odors from incredible distances."

"Mm," grunted Karl in response to the good news, which was relayed precisely to hurry him through breakfast.

"But if it's any consolation," the other hastened to improve, "last night I didn't notice any trace of human presence…To be honest, it's not like I've had much time to go around and check. We'll have to stay tuned in and be very, very careful not to pull any shit if we don't want to get ourselves in a mountain of trouble."

"*Natürlich*," agreed Karl, "but I'm convinced that no one but us has ever been up here. Remember what happened to the Chileans when they tried to come down here? These walls, in addition to being smooth as mirrors, are fragile as glass…look," he added, showing Marco a fragment of silvery-white rock recovered earlier among the few stones in the clearing. "It has razor-sharp edges, but if you try to put a nail through it, then look what happens…No, if it's giving me so much trouble," he concluded, convinced, "those people down there have never even tried to come up here."

It took some time to discover, but actually the place where they had wound up was almost entirely excavated within a large recess of the mountain, but only a small slice of the terrace protruded from this. During the primordial volcanic eruptions, the magma must have met a particularly hard rock at that height and, not being able to melt it, had modeled it in that manner. And the same thing must have happened to the rocky outcrop located beyond the waterfall. By contrast, the less resistant rock found above and below the terrace had been warped into gigantic caverns, so that from the valley one only saw one small, jagged peak of the mountain. The remaining part of the meadow, the entire forest and almost all of the upper cavern remained completely hidden from view, and that was probably the reason for which the natives had never had a great desire to risk breaking their necks to go and nose around those parts; otherwise, they would not have been stopped by a simple vitrified wall.

For those who lived there, however, it was another matter entirely. Over the millennia, the flat section of the terrace and the less precipitous part of the cavern had accumulated a thick layer of dust in the air, and on that soft and fertile topsoil a wonderful hanging garden had come into being, perennially watered by numerous streams descending from above. On the edge of the terrace where the earthy layer was lower, the grass rose high enough to just graze their ankles, but proceeding in the direction of the forest it grew higher until it overcame the shoulders of even a giant like Marco.

The thick barrier of shrubs and bushes between meadow and forest was so fraught with brambles that it could be crossed—and not without difficulty—at only a few openings. In the forest however, an infinite variety of trees had dug in their roots, and they were of increasingly imposing dimensions as one climbed nearer the summit of the majestic amphitheater. Many plants, surely thousands of years old, were veritable natural wonders and for many of them it would take four or five people to embrace the trunk at its base.

Near the waterfall the forest rose upwards in a gentle slope, but nearing the southern end of the terrace it became steeper and more precipitous. The meadow below, however, following the elliptical path of the crater gradually narrowed to a sickle until it closed completely at the extreme pole of the volcano's rim in the still-active area below.

"It'll be just like you said," agreed Marco, relieved as he came to his friend's same logical considerations. "Anyway, I prefer to do it Saint Thomas' way. If you don't mind, then, I'll take another look around. But you —and this is the doctor talking—try not to make any unnecessary effort; try to sleep instead, because you really need it. Then when I get back I'll try to find somewhere a bit more sheltered for the night; maybe it's the shade, maybe it's the proximity of the waterfall, but the moisture here soaks into your brain."

Karl simply gave a tacit nod of assent and Marco, after spreading out the sleeping bags—and everything else still in need of a good drying—out of the shaded area, started off to explore their new world.

73

Chapter 10

For the exploratory tour, Marco had put on khaki Bermuda shorts, a denim shirt and an old pair of tennis shoes. And he had to thank an inveterate habit of his that he had them at his disposal then. Several times in the past it had actually happened that he found himself hiking after a tiring climb along lengthy stretches of flat land for which it was well worth the trouble to get rid of the cumbersome climbing outfit, tie it onto the backpack and put on those lighter, more comfortable clothes to walk freely and unimpeded.

His bare legs reminded him of the multitude of thorns that he had encountered in the comings and goings of the previous evening. Thus, to reach the meadow he thought it opportune to skirt the stream from which he had drawn the water for the water bottles just before; a bit longer of a walk and surely more tortuous than the previous, but at least it would make him less of a martyr.

He had just set foot in the meadow when his innate curiosity got the better of his fear. Proceeding first in a standing position, then on all fours for a long stretch and finally crawling on the ground, completely oblivious to the dew that seeped into his clothes, he slowly approached the terrace, this time while heading towards an observation point a bit more distant from the waterfall compared to the one from the night before. Once there, he pulled back one by one the blades of grass that obstructed his view, and only when he was totally certain that no nose down below was pointed upwards did he dare to focus his binoculars on the valley.

Down below there was a glimpse of peaceful, normal life, and were it not for the black spot near the shore from which weak coils of smoke still rose, nothing would have suggested the gruesome spectacle of the day before. No trace remained of the sacrificial stone or its foundation. In the middle of the lake, right in front of his eyes, the two fishermen were pulling in a long net, patiently disentangling the night's catch. Several women sitting on the ground near the shore were weaving baskets and mats of different varieties using flat, green strips pulled from some kind of quiver strapped over the shoulder to their backs while the children, cheerful and chattering, were playing chase and diving repeatedly into the water. On the lawn bordering the shoreline there were groups of young people busy competing with each other in wrestling, archery, and combat with short, gleaming swords little longer than daggers. Further on, other men, women and children were working in the gardens and fields.

Even from his new viewpoint, Marco was not able to see the stretch of valley hidden below the rocky spur. To satisfy his curiosity he would have to push much farther to where the curved terracing increasingly approached the southern pole of the crater, but that part of the meadow also seemed fraught with briars and he had too many important things to be pondering then to waste his time satisfying his curiosity. With a tinge of regret, he put the binoculars in the pocket of his backpack and backed away with due caution—as always—from the edge of the terrace and turned back in his steps.

While crossing the meadow, his gaze lingered on the infinity of wild grasses that grew there with every step. There were also several species of mushrooms, many never before seen, but fortunately for him he knew the fatal amanita well enough and most of the toxic mushrooms, and his now well-founded rural experience enabled him to immediately identify known and definitely edible plants among the many varieties. Additionally, in the thick barrier of brambles that divided the meadow from the forest there were several flowering trees that almost certainly indicated the future possibility of harvesting ample fruit. All in all, he thought to himself, he would not run a great risk if in his hunger he wanted to try a taste. The stores they had managed to bring along would not last forever, given that they had rescued very little apart from the tortillas and a few teabags.

While he climbed into the woods following a new path, his ears caught the sound of a stream. The many novelties of the morning had made him forget even thirst, but the appealing temptation called it immediately back to mind. Partly because, despite the coolness of the forest, his throat was completely parched.

He kneeled at the edge of the brook and rolled up his sleeves, stretched his greedy hands under a small waterfall, but retracted them in a flash; he had expected cold, but it was in fact the diametric opposite. Overcoming his bewilderment, Marco tried to put only the tips of his fingers in. "It's really hot, then," he exclaimed upon verification that he had not had a sensory hallucination. The source must not have been very far away and Marco, so as not to belie his inquisitive nature, decided on the spot to go and take a look by continuing upstream.

At first the cheerful, winding stream meandered among the tall trunks of trees, but as the slope of the land gradually increased, its path became steeper and interspersed with ever higher leaps of water, forcing Marco to use his arms to help continue climbing while keeping close.

After a long and tiring hike, the forest suddenly gave out in front of a lunar-like landscape, an expansive, immaculate scree devoid of vegetation from which white boulders cropped up here and there, their stone smoothed over time into the most bizarre shapes, in a sort of open-air contemporary art museum. Here the stream, which in times past must have had a reach far superior to the current one, had dug a broad, heavy natural staircase that—for as steep and irregular as it was—allowed him to proceed more expeditiously.

The staircase ended in a smooth, flat landing bordered on the left by the rocky spur that, after flanking the waterfall, continued to rise upwards, creating a real partition wall inside the huge cavern. The stream popped out at the foot of an opening in the rock about five feet high and wide and Marco, after using his ax to swipe away a thick network of webs that were blocking the entrance, warily climbed inside, scouting ahead with one hand bearing a lighter. To enter he had to lower his head a good deal, but he was able to immediately raise it when his eyes noticed by the dim light of the flame that the ceiling rose progressively into a sort of dome over a large, ellipsoidal cavern, reaching a height of twelve or thirteen feet in some places.

After crossing the cave floor, the stream crept to the right in a bottleneck beyond which Marco discovered another room, much lower and smaller than the main one.

It was an old accessory mouth of the volcano, modeled in that manner by lava emission. Before springing from the subsoil, the water that flowed across the floor must have passed in close proximity to a zone that was still active, heating up like so, but not much altered in its organoleptic characteristics. In fact, although not drinkable because of the high temperature, or its decidedly savory taste, the mephitic fumes of so many thermal waters were not felt in the cave. Additionally, the presence of the stream gave the place a discreet warmth without creating excess moisture. Marco did not stay to think about it for another moment. His decision was immediate: the cave would become their refuge.

Excited by the discovery, he immediately started down the return path and so as not to have to go back down to the meadow and then climb up to the creek again as usual, he decided to cut through the woods diagonally. As for paths to follow—as in interpersonal relationships—he had always been a staunch supported of the "direct route," but after half an hour of useless wandering he was beginning to doubt himself. If he were in a slightly bigger forest he would surely have gotten lost. In fact in some places, the daylight could barely filter through the trees' foliage, preventing him from establishing reference points with which to navigate. As if that was not enough, the thorns had resumed their interest in his legs like angry cats, but between one curse and another he managed to grasp the positive angle to it: the tangle of brambles and vines was a further, indirect confirmation that neither human foot nor animal paw of a certain size had ever trod over the virgin soil to leave traces of their passage. And with this comforting consideration he felt a strange sensation which was not merely relief, but he was still far from grasping the true essence of it right then.

The sound of the waterfall yanked him out of his thoughts to lead him in the right direction, and after making a few more loops he finally arrived at his destination. Karl was sitting with his back against the usual tree and, for a change, he had interpreted the physician's recommendations in his own way. Surely he must have moved down to the clearing several times to recover the now totally dry sleeping bags and backpacks, and he had arranged everything that had been spared neatly around himself. He was warming up the usual tortillas on the plate. Some steaming tea was ready in the pot.

Guzzling greedily, Marco relayed that morning's important discoveries between mouthfuls. "It's probably just like you thought, there must not be a soul around here...And let's hope that no one decides to come poke around now that we've wound up here."

"Yes, but we will have to be very careful not to make mistakes, just the same; those down below will still be wondering where Sergio's body shot out from and we'll get ourselves into real trouble if they discover us, as a vitrified wall will certainly not deter them."

"Oh, for sure. But for as much as I could see, I don't think that they suspect anything, all the time that I was observing I didn't see anyone raise their eyes up here."

Marco continued reporting to his friend every little detail of his first hike. He was visibly pleased to be able to finally relay some good news, and when he got to the part about the cave he even seemed euphoric, like a child making his first discoveries. Karl kept listening in silence, interrupting only occasionally, but a faint smile was hidden under his bushy beard.

The journey from the clearing to the cave was slow and painful. Especially for Karl, although to avoid excessive jolting Marco preferred to follow the well-trodden path back down to the meadow and then enter the forest at the point where the thermal stream ran and would lead them to their goal.

Karl tried not to show it, but the leg must have been causing him immense pain; he could hardly contain his groans when his friend, who was holding him, accidentally slipped or tripped over some obstacle along the slope. The final steps, then, were an ordeal for both. Marco had to stop on every step to catch his breath and let Karl rest, but in the end he managed to step up onto the landing in front of the cave and drag his companion up by sheer force.

"What do you think?" he asked proudly after showing him the suite.

"Good," Karl commented abruptly and Marco, who was well acquainted with his stinginess in terms of appreciation, knew that this was the highest compliment that could be expected from him and was more than satisfied with the response, so he arranged his friend on the balcony next to the entrance with his back against the wall. Then he went back down towards the woods to retrieve the backpacks and upon his return he began emptying them, arranging the contents inside the cave in the spots where the most light reached.

Apart from a bit of food and the gas cooker (with one reserve tank) they had saved very little, and the most precious thing to have survived the disaster was unquestionably the more than one hundred meters of climbing rope that had saved the two friends from certain death. Moreover, in addition to the hunting knife that Karl usually carried at his side on each excursion, the hammer with the bag of nails for climbing fortunately were also spared.

Karl immediately got down to the practical elements: "The gas cans have very little left in them, so they're best left for emergencies."

"Ah, you're right, but what will we do without a cooker?"

"We'll light a fire."

"But…what about the smoke?"

"Oh, I don't think we have to worry about that very much anymore. While we were out in the woods I saw a ton of sticks and broken branches on the ground. Gather the driest, and they won't make a wisp of smoke when they burn. We'll put the moister ones outside here or in front of the fire before burning them...Don't worry, nothing will happen, you'll see; we'll just have to be careful not to make too big a flame before sunset and not burn leaves, pine needles or green wood; we're in a very withdrawn part of the mountain and the little bit of smoke coming out of the cave will already have dispersed along the wall before they'll be able to notice it from below."

Marco just needed reassurance and was more than relieved by his friend's convictions, so he gladly embarked on the commute between the cave and the forest to begin the task, carrying massive bundles of dry, resinous branches on his shoulders up the path again and again.

Chapter 11

Just like the previous night, darkness fell suddenly upon them. The crater sank into night instantly, which raised Karl's eyebrows despite already being aware of the singular phenomenon. Now, however, the situation was much less dark for the two survivors; they were protected from the night's dampness, were wearing dry clothes, had a fire for cooking and illumination—and, luxury of luxuries—they even had hot, running water.

Outside was silent, and this was only broken by the occasional barking dog or the cry of some other unknown animal. In the cave, which was dimly lit by the light of the improvised bivouac, Marco had just finished dressing the leg: "Tomorrow we'll apply a more suitable brace," he said as he adjusted the dressing material in the first aid kit.

For dinner, in addition to the usual tortillas they split a can of tuna and also allowed themselves each a generous swig of brandy, which had been miraculously saved, but both sharply felt the lack of a good coffee, which had been lost with what was left in poor Sergio's backpack.

After medication, they both slipped right into the sleeping bags which were laying by the fire. Their backs felt every little protrusion in the floor, but those pesky bumps did not prevent them from falling asleep. What *did* keep them awake was the overwhelming sensation of helplessness in the face of their present circumstances. Up to that moment, their every move had been dictated by emergency, the immanence of danger and immediate necessity, but now, in the silence of the cave, their awareness of the enormity of the event and the uncertainty about tomorrow began to gain shape and texture.

During the excursion that morning, Marco thought he had heard the sound of an airplane flying far above the mouth of the crater. He had held his breath in the hope of identifying its route and his heart opened at the thought that it could be a reconnaissance aircraft, but little by little the noise vanished completely, leaving him with the impression of having imagined it.

"At this point, they'll have begun looking for us," Marco said softly, speaking more to himself than to his friend, who was perhaps already falling asleep. "It's been three days since they've heard from us."

"Well," said Karl, obviously as awake as he was, "I don't want you to lose more sleep or get more distressed than you already are, but one thing is for sure: no one has ever come in here besides us. And even if they had…"

Marco did not need clarification—the tragedy at the lake was still vivid in his mind—but he insisted: "But even the people down there had to get in here somehow!"

"For sure, but definitely not the way we got in. It may be that once they entered, they were trapped inside. You know, an earthquake, a landslide…something like what happened to us. That said, if there's a way out down there, would you feel like going to look for it after what happened to Sergio?"

"I still can't believe it," Marco said, evading the issue, slipping away from it on the logical considerations of Karl. "I think that they're Aztecs. Or Mayans. Or their close relatives. Of course I'm no expert, but those outfits, that ritual…It's just…I dunno, it's all crazy, just crazy, totally crazy."

"No doubt about it. But I think that figuring out who these people are or where they come from is the least of our problems right now. If that's the case, I'm afraid that we'll be in here for a long time. We'll have to organize ourselves the best we can, then, if we hope to get out of here. I realize that in my condition…"

"Don't be stupid!" Marco hushed him. "If you weren't here, I…I would be absolutely in over my head. Like I said, you should only think about healing now. Then, you'll see, we'll find a way to get home. Let's do this: tomorrow I'll go out on another exploratory tour to study this place a bit better. You, on the other hand, you'll sit your butt right here in the sun and rest…You just need to rest, Karl. You'll see, if you believe me then in just a few weeks you'll be even more agile and sprightly than before."

They stayed up talking late into the night, but even after having wished one another a good night they both continued ruminating at length on the prospects of the future. Marco thought of his mother, alone on the other side of the world. When would she get the news? How would she react? And Sergio…every time he thought about the incident he was overcome with grief and disbelief. Claudia…The last time they had spoken on the phone was three days ago, the reception was bad and they were only able to exchange a few trivial remarks about the weather and landscape, as if they both wanted to avoid more challenging topics. His job…who would postpone his appointments? Postpone? Cancel! Aztecs, Mayans…He passed from wakefulness to sleep without realizing it and finally, in spite of the little spikes on the floor, managed to sleep for nine hours straight.

Chapter 12

The inevitable smell of tortilla woke him late in the morning. Karl must have been awake for quite some time and had dragged himself soundlessly to the entrance of the cave. He had already prepared breakfast and seemed to be in decent condition.

"Let's take a look at that leg," Marco said as soon as he got up, feeling almost apologetic for having remained idle for so long.

The unwrapped thigh did not make for a pleasant sight. The skin around the sutures was red and swollen. There must have been the beginnings of an infection and the resources in his first aid kit could certainly not replace those of a hospital; the antibiotics would be exhausted within a few days and the gauze, even if recycled, could not last much longer. He had to be a bit more effective if he wanted it to last for a reasonable amount of time. He carefully washed the used gauze bandages in the hot water of the stream and hung it outside to dry. When he needed them, he would sterilize them in the pot of tea. Then he began to concentrate on the wound.

With scissors and tweezers he removed the central stitches, and without paying much attention to his friend's pain level he put pressure on the edges of the tumefaction, pressing into it to squeeze out serum and pus until only bright red blood came out. Before replacing the stitches he cleaned the wound with gauze soaked in disinfectant and finally bandaged it with the last remaining gauze bandages.

"Torture's over," he announced at the end of the operation. "Now lend me that knife because I need to make a quick trip into the woods. And while I'm gone, you're to sit here and not move that leg for any reason. Got it?"

A grunt of assent authorized him to leave the scene for a good half hour. On the way back he carried two branches as straight as golf clubs, strapped them to the sides of the injured leg and, eyeing his handiwork, adjusted them to the right length by attaching them to a sort of metal bracket at the bottom so that the sole of the foot remained slightly elevated off the ground. To make the brace, he had had to sacrifice a piece of the precious climbing rope, but on the other hand, at the end of the operation they were both more than happy with the new arrangement.

"How does it feel?" Marco asked after rearranging the restraining straps.

"Um, okay...My leg actually feels lighter," responded the concerned party, moving his limb back and forth a bit.

"Great. And now, since we stink like two goats, let's take advantage of that hot water. Come on, pass me your clothes, I'll wash them in the stream. And while they dry I'll try to fix up a softer bed for the night. Then, if you don't mind, I'll take another look around to see if I can find something different to chew on...I know that I'll miss them soon, but all of those tortillas are starting to come out my eyeballs."

Marco spent the rest of the morning shuttling between the forest and the shelter with backpacks full of pine needles and dry leaves, which he dumped each time in a corner of the cave to create a bed two feet high and as big as a parade ground; then, after grabbing a bite to eat, he took to the road to the meadow.

As he had already had occasion to notice during his previous journeys, there was a wide variety of mushrooms in the forest, but he only collected the ones he knew well; he did the same with the many wild grasses that he ran into throughout the meadow. From time to time he came upon birds similar to seagulls, who glided low and slowly over the grass in search of food. Other birds, however, only took flight at the last second, right under his feet, and the sudden flutter of wings nearly caused him a heart attack every time. But none of the birds seemed to be very bothered by his presence. In fact, despite his repeated—and vain—attempts to nab at least one on the fly using the ice ax like a club, they continued to fly calmly and peacefully around him as if nothing had happened.

Gathering food could mitigate at least a little bit of his anxiety and distract him from his darkest thoughts, but an unconscious command guided his zigzags around the meadow, as well as his attentive hunt for fruits and vegetables, pushing him step by step in the direction of the edge of the terrace. And the second that the backpack was filled to the brim, he dropped it to the ground, pulled out the binoculars from a side pocket and walked, prudent and circumspect, towards the edge of the meadow, to a spot even more distant from the waterfall than the previous one.

Judging by the crowd that had gathered on the shore the evening of the sacrifice, Marco surmised that behind the rocky promontory there had to be something much more sizeable than a simple village of mountain-folk hidden away, but never in his wildest dreams did he imagine discovering what was actually there. When he finally managed to point the binoculars in the desired direction after a lengthy and tortuous tour through the meadow, his breath was taken away; behind that rock there was another half of the valley, and towards the back there was an entire city. A fantastic city.

The city was structured in a quadrangle against the opposite wall of the crater; it was encircled on the other three sides by a massive, perfectly chiseled wall of such a bright white that it seemed like they were built of enormous blocks of sugar. The main gate was directly opposite the observer, at the southern edge attenuated by the circle of walls, and it was there that the road to the lake began. All of the buildings inside the walls were also constructed of white brick, but the reflection given off by their walls was nothing compared to the light reflected from the roofs of the palaces, temples and many other public buildings. A warm, intense light, like that of the sun at its zenith. There was no doubt about it: those roofs were entirely covered in gold. At the extreme edge near the mountain rose a great pyramid erected on four levels and surmounted by two temples, whose magnificence could be guessed at. A long central staircase led to the top of the pyramid and each level gave off the same, identical gleams which emanated from the palace roofs. And this spectacle was not consummated in gold.

Being a city built in a progressive ascent on the slopes against the opposite wall of the crater, from his high position Marco also had an overview of the whole road network, which would have aroused the envy of any city planner. From the main gate one would enter into a semicircular plaza from which five avenues fanned out, and they in turn were intersected by other semicircular roads. The central avenue, which was the largest, ran straight towards the plaza where the pyramid stood, cutting the whole conurbation diagonally. The other four, however, after branching out radially for about three-quarters of their path, also converged at the corners of the square so as to create the striking image of a giant octopus stretching out its tentacles to seize the entire pyramid. The square had at its center a kind of miniature pyramid, and was surrounded on all sides by tall obelisks interspersed with fountains and giant, squat statues.

And it was certainly not a ghost town. The square and every street were swarming with people—especially the main avenue, where a real open-air market was active. Almost all the buildings near the square were topped by gilded gables; high, multicolored banners adorned the entrance of every temple and palace, and there was no street corner that was not embellished with fountains and flowering gardens.

But the splendor of the enchanted city reached its apogee in two giant, stone jaguars planted on either side of the main gate. With their immense eyes glowing green, it seemed as though they wanted to peer into the valley in every direction and that the sculptor had frozen them in the act of leaping from the walls towards potential aggressors.

It was unique, indescribable. Marco had never in his life seen such magnificence concentrated in one place, despite having traveled the world far and wide.

Eldorado, Eldorado, a voice in a remote corner of his brain repeated, almost as if to convince him of an impossible, absurd truth, beyond all reach of logic, just like the idea of being confronted with a Mesoamerican civilization transplanted into the bottom of the world. And yet…

With difficulty he managed to look away from its beauty and direct it outside the walls, where he discovered several plots of cultivated land and many small, modest huts which were quite similar to those near the lake. The water for irrigation had to be taken from the river, but this could only be viewed from a small handle protruding like an elbow from the rocky spur.

Marco would have remained there in awe infinitely, but looking at his watch he realized that several hours had passed since he had left the shelter and he had no intention of being caught again by nighttime before going back. Also because he trembled with the desire to report his new and amazing discoveries to Karl. Furthermore, he was beginning to feel a little peckish, and this turned into real hunger at the thought of the backpack abandoned in the middle of the meadow.

That evening they dined on wild herbs first boiled and then sautéed along with a few mushrooms, seasoned with the oil from the last can of tuna. Not so long ago Marco would have had a lot to say about those daring combinations, but after all the tortillas gulped down over the last few days, it seemed that he was eating the food of the gods. Both of them, while they gorged themselves with flavor, could not help but consider that the little bit of salt that escaped the wreck, although used sparingly, would sooner or later be used up, and this—even Karl, who was no dietician, knew it—was indispensable to man for survival, and not all foods contain a sufficient quantity. The prospect made them grow solemn. To quiet the sad thoughts which threatened to spoil their enjoyment of the beautiful feast they took to the bottle and, so as not to skimp, allowed themselves both a generous ration of brandy.

Throughout the entire evening and late into the night, Marco held court, reporting his exciting discovery and focusing on the minute details, as if he were afraid that he was not believed: "If those aren't the Aztecs or their close relatives," he concluded at the end of the long report, "I'll eat a dog, and its tail."

"Well, I don't know what to tell you," Karl commented. "What you've said is indeed a lot to think about. But you have to agree that your hypothesis isn't so easy to digest; it's not like you can take a ride around the hinterland of Central America and arrive down here at the end of the world. And to what end, then?"

"Ah, I wouldn't know how to explain that."

The next morning Karl was already much better; after the usual dressing of the wound and a quick breakfast of tea and leftovers from the night before, Marco took the opportunity to start exploring another slice of the new world a little earlier than usual, this time focusing upwards, in the direction of the mountain.

The refuge was at an extreme edge of the big natural amphitheater just steps from the rocky partition that, after bordering the lake, rose higher yet for several hundred meters until it completely closed the huge cavern obliquely. Above the forest on the right, there was the huge, white scree which became steeper and steeper as it proceeded upwards.

It was an extremely arduous undertaking to proceed in the midst of this rubble, both for the marked slope of the land and because the gravel slid almost continuously under his feet, often causing him to take one step forward and two steps back, or freeze in place with bated breath when a stone, in spite of all his precautions, began rolling down and dragging more gravel with it. The forest and the distant roar of the waterfall offered a decent cover for the sound of these small avalanches, but the cavern's echo seemed to amplify it hundredfold. Nevertheless, he did not give up, and continued to climb the insidious slope in his firm determination to conquer the summit, which called to him temptingly.

In ancient times, lava had dug an infinite number of ledges and niches into the foothills of the rocky wall, which in that moment were entirely occupied by one or more nests. The chirping was deafening. Among the various unknown species that Marco saw once he had reached his goal, the most numerous seemed to be the large gulls, whose feathers were such a pure white that if it were not for their round, black eyes and orange beaks, they would surely blend into the surrounding rock. Several birds looked like cormorants, others like giant pigeons, but they all seemed to live in harmony despite the tight spaces.

In all likelihood, the man considered, they had to be non-migratory birds, born and raised inside the crater for countless generations and, as Darwin had taught, the unusual characteristics resulted from natural selection due to isolation. Additionally, they must not have dropped down into the valley very often; otherwise, they would not have proved so indifferent to human presence. At most, some specimens flew in a small arc out of the nest, only to return after a short glide.

It was mating season; each female was depositing her eggs or brooding and Marco was unable to resist the impulse to make a move that would have made him ashamed a few days ago. Right before his eyes, at his fingertips, there were five eggs little larger than those of a quail. Disturbed by the stranger's proximity to the nest, the mother had just moved away, but she would return soon.

Just three days had passed since Marco was trapped in that godforsaken place, and without even realizing it he had already fallen into the role of a hunter-gatherer who walked the savannas at the dawn of humanity. The search for food had become a primary need for him, and even when he had just finished filling his stomach, it began working his mind to find a way to satisfy it again soon.

Marco reached out to the nest and furtively snatched an egg, cracked it softly on the rock, then divided the shell into two small cups and, being careful not to spill even a drop on the ground, took them to his lips one after the other, sipping the contents greedily. Right after that he grabbed another which quickly followed the same fate, but the return of the nest's rightful owner deterred the man from taking a third egg. The female realized the raid and immediately went berserk; then the predator, fearing that her outburst could alarm the whole avian community to the risk and thereby see himself deprived of this God-given gift, made a lightning decision. All at once he snatched the bird from its nest, wrung its neck and tucked the body in his backpack.

The surrounding birds, however, remained relatively unperturbed and continued to chirp calmly and quietly, completely indifferent to the crime he had just committed; so then rather than repenting, the wrongdoer only sighed in relief, satisfied and reassured, then withdrew the last three eggs from the nest. He was tempted to take a more substantial stash, but he chose not to test his limits and elatedly began the slow descend back "home."

Chapter 13

Two months had passed since the day of the tragedy. Thanks to Karl's manual skill and with Marco's help the two survivors were able to make their refuge almost comfortable, creating utensils and dishes from wood and stone, with even a sort of fireplace carved into the wall for burning wood and cooking. Even the entrance of the cave, which had been suitably expanded, was barred during the night by a customized door. They had used a kind of liana that grew in every corner of the forest to assemble the pieces, and though it was almost impossible to cut it had several extraordinary properties: its tightness, plasticity and maneuverability could compete with that of the climbing rope. Moreover, the thin fibers of which it consisted were as resistant and elastic as nylon, and could also be used as excellent thread for sewing. Using the same creeper they wove the nets of two comfortable hammocks so that they could finally lie down on two real beds and sweep away all the dead leaves and pine needles that infested every corner.

Early in the morning, after a hearty breakfast, Marco left the shelter to go find as much food and wood as was commissioned by his friend for a project. It looked like Karl was improving and, although he needed two crutches, he was now able to move in and out of the shelter easily and without assistance. Soon he would be able to get down the higher steps and venture into the new world, and Marco could not wait to be his guide and finally show him in person the amazing discoveries that up to that point he had only been able to describe. As Karl became self-sufficient, he felt entitled to move farther away from the shelter for longer periods of time, often for the whole day, gradually expanding his patrol tour to new territories and simultaneously moving forward with a project of his own.

He had found his ideal place to implement it near the waterfall, and after having cleared away all invading grass and shrubbery, he had cleared out even the smallest stones. With rudimentary tools he had then tilled, hoed it smooth and divided it into many sectors, which he passed by day after day to enrich with neat new rows of edible seedlings and bulbs that had been taken together with their roots in the course of the daily expeditions. His little garden did not even require much work; the mist from the nearby waterfall provided for it and each seedling, thanks to the excrement collected from the nesting area, invariably took root and grew with prodigious rapidity. Some were already blooming, and soon they would give their seeds for days to come.

It was now the beginning of summer and even the trees had begun to make their contribution to the table. They were wild plants and their fruits were miniscule, but no less succulent. From the dense bush at the edge of the forest hung branches of gigantic, immature blackberries, while the thorny bushes in the undergrowth began to produce an endless variety of delicious-tasting berries.

Meat was never lacking at the table in the refuge. Every two or three days Marco climbed up to the nesting area to stock up. To access it more easily he had traced a small path in the gravel using clods of earth and soft clumps of grass that he had carried up, which not only made the trek up the scree easier but also much quieter. Usually he went up in the evening, when all of the birds had already returned to their nests. The place was swarming with new chicks and the eggs continued to hatch at an exponential rate. Shrewdly and carefully choosing a different department of his supermarket, he withdrew only the bare essentials from the nests and, before leaving, also gathered a nice block of droppings.

In the meantime, his friend had pulled another trick out of his sleeve. The cooking salt, however rationed, was now reduced to a pinch; since the thermal water was slightly savory, Karl had filled a pot to the brim and boiled it till the entire contents evaporated. On the bottom of the pan a thin accretion of small, transparent crystals was left behind; when scraped off with a wooden spoon, this had proved an excellent substitution for the precious condiment. However, it was unthinkable to continue procuring it that way and risk harming their only metal container—in addition to the teapot—which was used for cooking, but the genius of the cave had already thought up a way to produce a more substantial quantity and with much less effort by concentrating the water in a small tub carved on the outer wall of the shelter where evaporation, combined with sunlight and the heat from the constantly burning fire on the other side of the wall, would contribute as well.

Every day after the daily gathering of food, Marco never missed his daily appointment with the valley, but as he had already inspected the furthest recesses high and low with his binoculars, he had never once seen even the slightest hint of the presence of animals of a certain size. Looking around he saw chickens, turkeys, rabbits and numerous small dogs that howled day and night like giant coyotes. The plows were pulled by arm power alone and what was particularly curious was that nothing moved on wheels. Every load was either carried on shoulders or on a hand sledge dragged on wooden runners, and it never ceased to amaze the observer that these people were able to build a city of such extraordinary range and not yet know how to use a wheel.

And then there was the fish. Marco also felt the lack of this; every time he saw the fishermen unload baskets of the delicacy on shore, it seemed to him that he caught the scent of barbecue in the air. He did not resist the craving, and scoured top to bottom every free stream that ran down through the woods and every ditch that streaked the meadow, but he had not found even the slightest trace of aquatic life: not a prawn, not a fish, not even the shadow of a tadpole.

Chapter 14

It was a hot day, the day that Marco reached the threshold of sending his soul to God by putting a tragic end to his earthly journey. That morning it was too hot to go work in the garden, the stocks of poultry and eggs had already been procured the day before and he had no intention of going for a stroll in the meadow or through the woods to acquire more food. He decided that it was time to take a look at the southernmost stretch of meadow, from which he would be able to visually perceive the entire valley.

The endeavor was not as simple as it first seemed. He had tried other times in the past, but for one reason or another he had had to give it up. In the area of the scree, for example, the way was blocked halfway through by a high, rocky promontory as smooth as glass; in the woods however, he had stumbled into such thick brambles that he gave up after just a few meters. The way by the meadow was better, he then thought, but even then he had to give up after a few unsuccessful attempts. In fact, contrary to the vicinity of the waterfall, where the terracing was almost completely covered by a sort of grassy savanna through which it was possible to proceed without too many problems, in that other part of the meadow it was a real pain to move even a few feet without getting flayed alive, as it seemed that all species of brambles, stinging plants and thorny bushes on earth had mutually agreed to take root in that one spot. Marco had already tried to find a passage several times, but the wall of thorns seemed endless, and the further they ventured the thicker they grew. For this reason, and especially because of the many pressing tasks of daily living, he had decided to postpone and postpone the expedition to a day when he had fewer worries on his mind. And the day had finally arrived.

Armed with gloves and a long staff with a sharp stone hatchet affixed to the top, Marco began to open a passage in the middle section of the meadow where the undergrowth seemed a bit less dense. From time to time grassy lots opened in the barrier, in which he could advance somewhat more expeditiously. And it was in one of those open spaces that he risked tragedy.

Marco was proceeding through the tall grass with long strides, when the handle of his tool accidentally bumped against a rock. A prolonged thumping rose from the ground and the man instantly jumped back in fright. He was already whirling around to flee any danger when the corner of his eye caught sight of a reptile, like a huge lizard, retreating rapidly. His hunter's instinct overcame his fear and Marco, throwing caution to the wind, launched into swift pursuit of the prey, but suddenly, after just three steps, he felt the earth fall out from under his feet.

As he was falling, right when it seemed that nothing would be there to stop him, he managed to grab at a shrub that was sufficiently rooted in the ground. Despite the protection of his gloves, Marco felt countless thorns bite into his flesh, but he did not dream of letting go. Kicking repeatedly into the void and pulling with all the strength of both arms, he tried to reach other roots and pull himself up as best he could, but only after several frantic attempts did he finally manage to get back up onto the edge of the meadow.

Facedown in the grass and panting with fatigue and terror, he absently threw his gaze towards the point from which he had just climbed, and he thought he perceived a hole or a ditch a little deeper than the others, but when he craned his neck he shivered. A few inches from his nose a wide chasm opened, cutting the meadow in two. And below, far below, he could see the blue waters of the lake. The chasm into which he had sunk was not even very narrow—almost twenty meters stretched between one bank and the other—it was just that the tall grasses and hedges prevented him from seeing it in time.

With his stomach still in knots and any ambition to hunt instantly shelved, the miracle slowly rose to his feet and inclined his head into space to try to understand something of that strangeness. The cleft spread to the outer edge of the terrace without shrinking, so he decided to walk along it in the opposite direction. This time, however, he proceeded much more prudently, pushing aside each blade of grass and testing the ground with the rod of the hatchet at every step before planting his foot. The gap showed no signs of narrowing even a millimeter on that side, as though a giant had taken the trouble to cut cleanly through the entire terrace with a huge ax, but Marco, ever more intrigued and determined to get to the bottom of the matter; he was not daunted by the obstacles and after a bloody confrontation with an army of vines and brambles he managed to reach the top of the forest. Here, though, he did not find the usual scree to welcome him, but rather the rocky promontory that he had come across during previous excursions in the upper area, which was also divided perfectly in two. And that was when, looking up, he thought he finally found the right explanation for that freak of nature that had almost cost him his life.

On the wall of the mountain, several meters above the chasm, he noticed a large opening through which a small stream flowed; it barely had the strength—and then, only for brief stretches—to break away from the rock as it fell, but by the size of the mouth from which it poured, it was easy to deduce that in times past there must have been a waterfall of exceptional size in that spot, much, much larger and more imposing than the one that had carried him into the crater.

Evidently, the patient attrition of the water had succeeded where even the violence of volcanic magma could not, and the hard stone, millimeter by millimeter, millennium after millennium, had been cut cleanly from the edge of the terrace to the side of the mountain, thus precluding any possibility of accessing the other side. With some climbing rope and nails in the wall it would have been quite easy to do by climbing the promontory, but that was also the best way to be discovered and it was not the best place—what with that treacherously smooth rock—to attempt crossing in the middle of the night.

No, at that point he did not see any chance of overcoming the obstacle without incurring danger and Marco, disappointed and upset, was forced to give up the expedition and just observe the forbidden land from afar. On the other side the meadow progressively narrowed as it approached the south wall of the crater while the forest, on the contrary, although it grew close to the mountain, grew much more expansively and left a lot less room for the scree above. Marco knew that he would not settle for just a glance, but at least for now he would have to be patient.

Chapter 15

One evening, while returning from the usual afternoon trip to get food and observe the valley, Marco immediately sensed that something was not right. Karl was not engaged in one of his usual projects, which was strange for him. Instead he sat motionless and silent, fixated on the weak flame in the fireplace. Despite the glow of the hearth his face was a ghostly white and his forehead was beaded with sweat.

"What's wrong, Karl?"

"I don't know. I feel exhausted. I've been shivering. I think I even have a low fever. I'm afraid that it's my leg. I feel it pulling…and it hurts a bit when I put weight on it."

Marco, assailed by a terrible premonition, rushed to inspect his thigh. He felt a pang at just a glance. Just above the scar there was a bulge. It was not that pronounced but it was purple and tense. The wound had healed perfectly and several days ago Karl had been freed of his crutches to move in an out of the shelter with the aid of just a stick. Having taken for granted that the wound was completely healed, Marco could not comprehend what had happened and he continued to observe the bulge, trying to understand why a complication was arising so late.

"An…an abscess must have formed down here," he said at a certain point, resolving himself to speak. "A foreign body, perhaps. I'm afraid we'll have to make another incision, Karl," he added flatly, avoiding looking his friend in the face so as not to betray his apprehension. "It will be painful, but…"

"Do what you have to do," Karl said curtly.

Marco washed and carefully shaved the thigh around the scar, sterilized the razor on the embers of the fireplace—it was an antique collector's object that had belonged to his father, and which he had providentially decided to bring in the tragic attempt to save themselves—and gave Karl the usual handkerchief to bite. Then he took action.

Beneath the bulge there was none of the buildup expected with an abscess, but bloody, putrid tissue. Marco felt his blood run cold then and there, and lingered as though stupefied, observing the rotting flesh, incapable of making any decisions. Recovering himself from his paralysis, he slipped his fingers into the wound in feverish search of small bone fragments, pieces of cloth, unabsorbed stitches or some other foreign body, but he found none. On the other hand, even if there had been, it would have been an impossible task to recover them from the sea of decaying tissues. Gripped with anxiety, he tried to pull as much necrotic material as possible from the sore, oblivious to the pain that could be caused to his friend, who continued to endure the torture with real stoicism.

At the end of the atrocious suffering, there was a deep aperture in place of the bulge. Marco cleansed it several times with near-boiling water, and after having inserted a gauze soaked in disinfectant for drainage, he bound it up with the old, dry, sterilized bandage. He could not do anything else.

The next day, he did not leave the shelter at all: "Today I want to tidy up the stairs," he announced, anticipating Karl's complaints, who would surely push him to go out for the usual rounds. Staying close by he could not only keep him company, but also more closely monitor the situation and look after him if needed. To distract him, he chatted with him at length about this and that, about any topic, but without ever touching upon that which most oppressed him.

Karl, sitting on the ledge next to the entrance of the shelter with his back against the rock, only contributed to the conversation in monosyllables, continuously looking ahead with narrowed eyes. But he did not give the impression of being asleep, or fixated on something in particular. It seemed, rather, that he was absorbed in deep though, like he was trying to mentally solve a difficult and complicated problem. He did not eat lunch, and at dinner he just swallowed a few spoonfuls of vegetable soup and only then at the echoed insistence of his friend.

During the night, convulsive tremors accompanied by bouts of delirium preceded fever, which reached extremes; Marco had his work cut out for him trying to contain it with cold wraps on his forehead, hands and feet. And the next morning when Marco undid the bandage to begin medicating, the room was instantly filled with a sweet, sickly stench that took them by the throat.

Marco's face blanched. He knew that odor; he had only smelled it on rare occasions, but it was a smell that was impossible to forget. Paralyzed, he stared at the rotting wound for an infinite time, while a jumble of disheartening thoughts accumulated in his mind. *There's no other solution, we have to amputate,* he thought, *but how, and with what?*

It was probably his lengthy dwelling on the wound that betrayed the anguish that gripped him. He winced when Karl's voice broke the silence: "It's gangrene, right?" It was more of a statement than a question. Deceiving him would be a lost battle, but Marco tried just the same.

"Actually...yes, there is festering," he admitted, seeking to assume a professional tone, "the infection must have extended upwards a bit...through the lymphatics, probably, but..."

"It's gangrene, right?" Karl interrupted quietly, but with a firmness that allowed no minced words or misleading speeches.

Marco felt cornered: "Yes, Karl, this is gangrene," he admitted with a whisper. "We'll have to amputate the leg," he added after a silence. "It will hurt very much without anesthesia, without...I could stun you, though, and then try to do it as quickly as possible. The bleeding, then, we can stop with a tourniquet, and the cut...yes, then we'll cauterize the cut with a hot knife," he continued, freewheeling in spite of himself by clearly expressing all the difficulties and alleged risks. "It will be very hard for you to bear, but one way or another, you'll see, it'll come to head and——"

"No!" Karl interrupted peremptorily.

"But——"

"No, Marco, we're not going to talk about this."

"Try to understand, this is the only remaining possibility to prevent the disease from——"

"Marco," Karl interrupted again in a quiet voice, "you know better than me that what you're proposing is only a palliative, a desperate attempt to postpone what is already decided."

Faced with so much determination, Marco did not have the strength to argue. He looked his friend in the face, raised his eyebrows with a resigned sigh, then bowed his head and was silent.

"You shouldn't blame yourself for anything," Karl began after a long pause. "You did much more than what you could've with the limited means at your disposal. Now, though, if you really want to help me through this, listen to what I have to tell you."

Marco assented with a nod, and it seemed that Karl was focused fully on his thoughts as if to summon up his ideas before speaking again: "You know, Marco, few are granted the right to know 'the hour.' Most would prefer never to know when they're going to die. It's probably just ignorance, this unknowingness, this desire not to know which will keep them alive and ensure that they take care of their bodies and their interests, pursue new goals and achievements as if they were going to live forever. Oh, don't worry," he said, giving the slight hint of a smile, "I'm not going to lecture on life lessons. But I do feel like I can say one thing about it."

He paused briefly to collect his thoughts, then continued: "I am convinced that if there is a God, he cannot be an abstract entity who can only be reached by a select few with abstruse theories or scholarly exegesis of 'sacred texts.' I am of the belief that the way to get to Him is much simpler, more straightforward: God is in the beauty that surrounds us, and each moment is beautiful. That's why, despite fearing it like all the others, I consider it a great privilege to know and face death with a calm, clear mind. And in the presence of a great friend, too." Marco listened in silence, speechless with emotion.

"Do you remember our trips to the mountains?" Karl added with unusual fervor. "What do you think we were looking for in those lonely, untouched places, if not the presence of God? In the face of such beauty we felt satisfied, even if only for a moment. But as soon as we went back down to the valley, there we were, taken again by the craving to search for other enchanted places in the unconfessed hope of discovering another one capable of satisfying this urge of ours longer, if not permanently. Look around you, Marco, and tell me: is this not the place that we've always searched for? And also ask yourself: in the past, how many have been given the chance, the good fortune to make a discovery of such unimaginable magnitude?"

He paused to catch his breath: "I knew you would object," he continued. "This was not your choice, you're stuck in this place, you're stripped of the liberty to decide here, you're obliged to silence, fear. But—and answer me truthfully here—do you think that maybe all these impediments, all these influences are much harder and more difficult to bear than those imposed upon you in the so-called civilized world? How would you have spent your days outside of here? Do you think that you'd be able to find that something that you always search for, which would be able to make you feel at peace with yourself and fill the void that oppresses you? Believe me, Marco, surely others of these will exist all around the world, but this is a great place to find oneself. It's also a nice place to die. That is why I ask you, I beg you to grant my last, great wish: help me to face this last ascent with a calm spirit and I, I promise you, will always remain by your side."

Marco had never heard so many words come out of his friend's mouth, much less such intimate and personal topics. Nor was he ashamed of the river of tears that flowed uninterrupted from his eyes while he listened.

Karl passed away after just three days. Up until the end, his skilled hands had continued to carve a long, gnarled stick on which, in a marvelous sequence, grotesque zoomorphic figures with serpentine bodies came to life and enveloped the staff from top to bottom, creating a harmonious ensemble of incomparable beauty that was at once tragic and fascinating. A true masterpiece. It was the legacy that Karl left to his last friend. He entrusted it to him a few hours before lapsing into a coma.

Marco, overwhelmed with grief, dug a deep grave in the meadow at the edge of the forest. He dug it with a stone hoe, with a knife, and even with his nails. Then, as Karl had asked him to do, instead of cutting flowers for the grave, he covered it with sod. And to mark it, in lieu of a cross, he planted a sapling.

For days and days he lived like an automaton, feeding himself only what turned up close by and drinking directly from the streams. Dazed by the pain, the only inhabitant of that new, solitary world, he wandered through the meadow and through the woods like a lost soul living hand to mouth, without objective. But his steps led almost continuously back to the grave in search of answers. By now, perhaps to overcome the loneliness or to break the oppressive silence that surrounded him, he got into the habit of talking aloud. "You shouldn't have left, Karl. You didn't have to leave me here alone. In this prison with no hope of escaping, of fleeing, of seeing my mother again...without being able to scream from the despair. There is some truth in what you said, but for all my effort I can't fully share that belief with you. I don't deny it: we were granted a sensational discovery, incredible, superior to any more pretentious claim, but how can we feel gratified if we can't communicate it to anyone? No, Karl, I'd love to agree with you, but for how hard I try I just can't. It's like...it's like we hadn't found anything at all. Get it? And now I'm alone, terribly alone. Alone..."

Chapter 16

Several weeks had to pass before Marco regained a semblance of normal life. Thin, beard unkempt, long, shaggy hair graying so it seemed that he was reduced to a St. Simeon Stylites; but in spite of his apathy, indolence and lack of interest, the pangs of hunger had continued to push him in search of food. And it was probably just this primordial instinct that kept him alive. Since he had first found himself in the crater he had not had any issues of sustenance, but autumn was approaching and he already felt the first stirrings of it. Contrary to the valley, in fact, where people continued to go about in loincloths, at the height of the meadow the temperature was becoming chillier every day, especially in the nesting area. In short, the earth would not offer a lot to feed him for much longer, and the cold would become more dangerous. He had to provide for future needs if he wanted to survive the winter.

The developments in the weather fully confirmed his predictions. Within a few days and with surprising speed, the leaves changed from green to crimson, from ocher to yellow, until they assumed all the shades of leather and, while the trees despoiled of all their foliage, the temperature dropped precipitously until he was forced to dress up in a jumpsuit, gloves, hat and heavy climbing boots that were almost forgotten in a corner of the shelter with the belief that they would no longer be necessary.

Slowly, almost by inertia, the man returned to his ordinary activities and day after day the labor was able to dissuade him from considering extreme solutions. Many of the fruits that were stored in the shelter when Karl was still alive were rotting at a discouraging rate and he could not come up with a way to slow down the rapid deterioration, but the supply of meat in the area of the nests remained abundant, although for quite some time there were no more eggs. On the other hand, he made an exciting discovery in the middle of the woods: majestic, centennial trees bearing branches laden with a sort of black, oblong walnut with a very hard shell, but with a big, meaty, nutritious seed inside, and they tasted delicious. The plants were too high, though, to consider procuring the fruits up above, and it would be sheer folly to try to procure them through a clamorous shaking. But mother nature provided for him.

When the leaves began to fall, an infinite number of the nuts began to fall with them at an exponential rate. Marco stocked up on them every night before going home, but within a few days the rain turned into a veritable hailstorm, so he was forced to anticipate his evening procession under those plants far in advance in order to be able to pick up as many as possible; although there were no mice or squirrels in the woods, the competition was fierce. The ground was swarming with little, near-microscopic worms, capable of infesting the inside of a walnut in just a moment, while an army of red ants of Herculean strength dragged an impressive quantity of God's bounty away as though they were on tiny conveyor belts.

When the falling ceased, the days were reduced drastically and the night became long; it had grown hellishly cold, but every available corner of the refuge was filled with nuts, berries and late fruit, while next to the mantelpiece a reassuring amount of wreaths of dried mushrooms and roots hung. The shells of nuts were also burning, which was a wonder, and the indispensable provision was that they did not create even a wisp of smoke.

Marco meanwhile had begun to cure the few winter vegetables and wrest new tracts of earth from the wasteland for future sowing. Towards the end of the summer he had, in fact, put up to dry whole bundles of edible herbs and every night after dinner he withdrew a bunch, peeled the dry inflorescence from the stems and after crumpling them in his hands, he let them fall onto the table from above while simultaneously blowing on them in order to remove the impalpable bran pellicles from the tiny seeds. A long, tedious and not very profitable task given that some seeds had to breathe for a whole night, but if there was one thing that he could dispose of limitlessly it was time. After several weeks of patient work, he thought that he had accumulated more than enough seeds for spring planting. And then he wanted to do something on a whim.

He ground a few handfuls of seeds in order to obtain a coarse, ocher-yellow flour, then mixed together a bit of warm water, a pinch of salt and his substitute and, after having kneaded it for a while and flattened it to form a bun half a finger high, he placed in on a stone slab lying on the embers in the fireplace. He turned it over and over several times, being careful not to let it burn, and while the color of the cake turned slowly to hazelnut, the shelter was slowly saturated with a heady scent. Marco got tears in his eye when it was finished baking and he brought the dough, still warm and fragrant, to his mouth and savored every last crumb in religious contemplation.

Chapter 17

With the passing of the days, Marco began to appreciate the little things in the new land again and, more importantly, establish a definitive routine. If suicide was not the right solution to his problems, as he had come to believe after the deepest and most dangerous moments of despair, if he had to go on living he might as well do it with dignity and give a meaning to his existence, and not dwindle away like a stray animal. At least as a sign of respect to Karl's last wishes and as revenge against those who forced him into silence and segregation.

He had begun washing at the end of each day again, shaving with his old razor to sweep away that beard that during his dark days had obscured his face completely. But not his hair; that, he had left to grow. "After all, they're good protection against the cold," he said to himself, not wanting to admit that long hair was one of the many satisfactions that the so-called civilized world had always denied him.

Every day he went to the edge of the meadow in the valley to observe and monitor the events from nearby. That place, which was almost within reach and yet so far away and surreal, had become his only recreation. There was no one waiting for him at the shelter anymore and it was sad, if not downright agonizing, eating alone in that cavern in broad daylight. He had thus gotten into the habit of fully exploiting the few hours of daylight available and staying out for the whole day.

In the morning, after a hearty breakfast of leftovers from the previous night, he took a good amount of nuts and roots from the pantry for lunch, chose the appropriate tools for the task before him and after he closed the door behind him, he did not return to the shelter until late evening. Day after day he was creating a dense network of paths and walkways that allowed him to reach every corner of the meadow, the forest and the nest area quickly and silently. He knew these paths to perfection, and the idea of being caught outside the cave by the sudden night no longer frightened him. Nevertheless, when it was about to get dark, he took the road back just the same; in those days the temperature was not at all pleasant at night and, as he had already had occasion to check many other times, there was little to see below after sunset.

Towards evening, in fact, all activity around the lake ceased; the two fishermen pulled their boat to shore, the farmers returned to their blinded homes and the women, children and artisans walked towards the town from the shoreline. Shortly thereafter the main gate of the city walls was blocked as if the inhabitants had to defend themselves against some kind of external threat, a custom that was completely inexplicable to the observer. And just as night fell, all forms of life disappeared even from the city streets. For a little while torches or some other source of light were seen moving about, but then even those went out, and only a few lanterns placed at the corners of the main streets and the braziers lit atop the pyramid were left to validate the existence of the mysterious city.

One day, Marco went to the meadow early with the intention of obtaining new land for planting. In preparation for the trek ahead he preferred to travel light, wearing only what little was left of his shirt and shorts, as he thought that the physical exertion would protect him from the cold. The crisp air was his stimulus and so as not to stop halfway through and then be forced to set out again on a full stomach, he had chosen to skip lunch and wait until late afternoon, stopping only after completing a good quarter-acre.

"Perfect," he said to himself, looking pleased with the result of his hard labor. The land was freshly worked; it was littered with potholes and craters and looked like a minefield after the detonation of all buried explosives. "Cleared and plowed in one fell swoop.

Tomorrow I'll remove all the stones...after some hoeing, and fertilization...it'll be ready for planting."

Though he was exhausted by the labor and his back felt broken, after the task was completed he did not want to abandon his habitual pastime so he went back to his observation point just the same. His hunger was great, but he staved it off with all the nuts and roots that he had brought with him; he gulped them down almost to bursting and shortly after, either from exhaustion or from the lethargy that accompanies digestion, he passed from wakefulness to deep sleep without even realizing it.

He was awakened by his own shivers in the middle of the night; it was pitch black and he had goose bumps. He rose slowly to his feet, groggily rubbing his arms and stretching his numb legs. He was already about to start back toward the shelter when, turning his eyes towards the valley, he instantly froze and rubbed his eyes; right then, in the area near the lakeshore, a small procession was coming.

A second later Marco was flat on the grass with his binoculars focused on the valley. Dark as it was, he certainly did not run the risk of being seen, but blending in and not making a sound had become a conditioned reflex. The cold stung horribly, but this encore was so appetizing that it pushed any discomfort to the back of his mind and it did not even occur to Marco to run back to the shelter for something to cover himself; he remained flat in his spot, frantically maneuvering the binocular dials with frozen fingers until the focus was quite good.

The procession mainly consisted of women and children. The first few, of which were little older than girls, wore long white robes cinched at the waist by a simple cord; the children, both male and female, were instead completely naked, the youngest in their mothers' arms and the others led by the hand.

The group was flanked by six soldiers in parade uniform, each bearing a long torch. A man in black robes with long, shaggy hair led the procession, and Marco felt a pang in his heart as he immediately recognized him as the executioner of his friend. He had not seen him again since the day of the sacrifice, but the appearance of that lugubrious character had remained indelibly burned into his mind, and that was enough to sweep away the last remnants of sleep and give his skin more goose bumps than the cold possibly could.

The procession halted near the shore. The warriors planted their torches in the ground so as to illuminate a large semicircle of beach, then turned their backs to the group and positioned themselves at ease. And only then, with a sign from the high priest, did the women break the line and begin to undress: "Ah, that's why…" Marco said to himself, convinced that he had finally unveiled the mystery of the absolute absence of doors and windows facing the lake, and he felt a sort of excitement in being the only spectator and violator of a ceremony prohibited to all others.

Many girls took turns bathing in the lake waters, others chatted among themselves, combing or oiling each other's bodies. The lively, cheerful children threw themselves repeatedly into the water and played tag on the shore, but oddly enough none of them dared to exceed the perimeter marked by the torches, as if it were an impassable boundary.

Marco watched the scene motionlessly until the procession started on the road back and slowly disappeared from view. The singularity of the scene together with the beauty of the women and the joy of the children engendered in him a mixture of curiosity and a need for human contact, which created the urge to attract their attention.

Chapter 18

In the days that followed, Marco never missed this evening engagement. His life now revolved around the nightly meeting. Winter had arrived, and the contrast between the weather in the valley and on the terrace had become striking. Down there, despite the few hours of daylight, the vegetation was lush and luxuriant, and the people continued to move about in loincloths and bathe in the waters of the lake like they did in summertime. Up above, however, the situation had changed considerably in recent times. The trees, with the exception of pines and evergreens, were stripped of their foliage and there was little left to scrape together at the table besides several varieties of mushrooms and a few edible roots. But he did not worry himself; his garden continued to produce, albeit with difficulty, and with diligence in regards to wastefulness and the supplies accumulated over the last few months he would be able to make it to spring. But as for livelihood, he had nothing to worry about; he still had his work cut out for him dealing with the numerous other daily necessities.

He wound up adapting his rhythms to the days, which had been shortened to nothing. He continued to use Karl's sleeping bag as a pillow even though his own could barely keep out the cold during the night. On the other hand, the thermal water on one side and the embers in the fireplace on the other helped to maintain an acceptable temperature in the shelter. In the morning he lounged in bed a little longer than usual, but as soon as the daylight seeped in through the small cracks in the door he ceased the procrastination; he threw himself out of bed, pulled on the jumpsuit and did not stop moving for even an instant until late evening.

The first and most burdensome task of the day was the hunt for firewood. For some time now he had run out of dry branches, and the weeds below the shelter and the shells of the nuts which he consumed daily were just barely adequate to rekindle the fire. To get new wood, he was now compelled to penetrate even deeper into the forest by creating new paths every now and then along which, at strategic points, he would pile the branches that he found on the ground; every evening as he returned from his usual rounds, he brought a bundle back with him on his shoulders. With the cold, even the dried wood was not quite as dry as in the summer months. To not make smoke he was forced to lay it out dry for a few days near the fireplace before burning it, and then use it very sparingly. But in spite of all his precautions, the fuel was running low on all sides, and Marco was beginning to wonder with growing concern when the day would come that he ran out of everything. He had to find a remedy to the nagging issue if he did not want to suffer the cold or eat raw food, but he could not think about solving it with the strike of an ax or by making smoke signals using wet leaves or pine needles. Even at night, especially when the light of the full moon lit the entire crater.

In the course of his regular trips in search of stones suitable to be made into tools, he often happened to stumble upon peculiar rocks that stood out because of their black color. A bit larger than tennis balls, they weighed much less than the surrounding rocks, but not so much as to give the illusion of being coal, as it might have seemed at first glance. Marco, however, was filled with impatience to get new fuel and wanted to figure it out on his own; one morning he picked one up and hit it against the wall with the sharp part of the hammer. The stone split in two much more easily than expected, revealing a multitude of little black, bright crystals on the inside, each not much bigger than a grain of rice. He tried to open others, but the contents were always the same: nothing particularly promising.

But hope is the last thing to die and, despite all evidence to the contrary, he had picked up a dozen and deposited three or four on the embers of the fireplace in the hopes of watching them transform quickly into the same number of balls of fire. But while the wood was consumed, the stones, deaf to the mental encouragement of the stoker, remained black and inactive, totally indifferent to their surrounding environment.

He realized that he was as hungry as a wolf when the embers began languishing under the ashes. In the pursuit of his delusions he had forgotten to put something on the fire to eat, and that was a task that he was allowed to carry out only in the dead of night.

In a hurry and more than a little annoyed at the waste of time and the precious wood that had gone up in smoke, he emptied his backpack of the last geodes and used them to fix the andirons which normally supported the steel plate long since removed from the gas cooker and now used as the usual cooking plate. He threw some wood on the embers, arranged the plate on top and, rod in hand, began blowing repeatedly on it.

The sticks were just beginning to burn atop the flowing coals, , and Marco was about to lay down the rod when a sudden bang like a gunshot almost made him tip over backwards. He had not yet recovered from the shock when his attention was caught by a purple light that appeared suddenly under the plate. The glow, accompanied by a growing crackling, gradually increased in intensity until it became the brightest of blowtorch flames.

As though hypnotized by the dazzling light, Marco continued staring open-mouthed at the phenomenon for a long time, completely oblivious to the smoke that was saturating the room, but he instantly roused himself when a corner of the plate, which had suddenly started glowing, began bending downwards. He kicked the sheet and sent it flying away from the hearth, at which point the uncovered, glowing pile rose in a spray inside the fireplace, emitting a great shower of sparks all around him that lit up the whole shelter. Hands raised to shield his eyes from blindness, Marco could see through just a narrow slit in his fingers that the jet sprang from the cavity of one of the broken geodes.

The show ended abruptly after a few minutes and the smoke-clouded room was silent. Still dazed, Marco cautiously approached the fireplace and used a stick to pull what remained of the portentous stone from the embers. It seemed like the shell of a coconut emptied of pulp and was still hot. Of the many crystals that were inside just earlier, not a trace. The other black stones, those still whole, instead continued to bask, totally dormant, on the hot coals.

With renewed hope, Marco immediately devoted himself to new experiments to study his exciting discovery in more depth and try to find out if he had finally found the much needed alternative fuel source, but after a whole night spent breaking stones, making himself hoarse by blowing on them and filling the room with smoke, he came to two thrilling conclusions: first, the black stones burned only when opened and exposed to a particularly lively flame; second, that while giving off a considerable amount of heat they emitted such thick, acrid smoke that it would be impossible to use them either to heat the room or, more importantly, to cook.

"Coal...sure, why not...damned rocks!" he found himself yelling dejectedly from the doorway of the shelter, his throat parched and his eyes bloodshot from the smoke and fatigue; he angrily flung the empty shells of the thankless stones into the woods.

After the ill-digested disappointment, Marco decided to fall back on more traditional energy sources. In the woods there were several large branches and even whole fallen trees lying on the ground. Pure madness, in every way, to think of cutting them where they lay. So Marco, having eyed up the best suited to the task, slid them slowly down from the woods to the meadow below. With the help of the rope and some wooden rollers, he dragged them without too much effort near the waterfall and there, with a sledgehammer, ax, stone wedges and a much scrutiny, he reduced them to small logs that would swell the wood pile that he had been accumulating day after day by the shelter door.

The few moments of light that remained after the time passed gathering firewood were spent caring for the garden, tilling new stretches of land or searching for the few varieties of wild berries. But during every chore, in every moment of the day his thoughts were always and constantly turned to the nightly procession, especially wondering who the women could be: "Priestesses, perhaps," he posited, thinking of the men who accompanied them. But this was a deduction that did not have him completely convinced. Their presence at such an unusual hour and so far from prying eyes could uphold this hypothesis as well as justify the absence of doors and windows overlooking the lake, but were the guards there to protect or supervise them, since they seemed to feel holy terror at the thought of straying beyond the illuminated area? Marco kept beating his brain in an attempt to resolve the question and every evening, as soon as night fell, he yielded to the call of the sirens of the enchanted valley. One, in particular, intrigued and attracted him more than any other.

She looked scarcely eighteen years old. Not very tall, but with a harmonious and graceful figure and long, smooth, raven hair well past her shoulders, her behavior was totally unique. As soon as the group arrived at their destination, she exchanged a few words with her friends and immediately withdrew to the left corner of the strip of beach encircled by torches. There, she undressed, laid her tunic on a rock and plunged quickly into the water. But unlike her friends, who took just the time for a quick bath before going right back to the shore to talk to each other or amuse the children, she used all the available time to swim. With slow, regular strokes she safely moved away from the shore until she disappeared under the terrace right at the point were the observer was stationed. Perhaps, Marco supposed, mentally calculating how long it took until he saw her reappear beneath him, she went all the way to the opposite shore of the lake before going back. She was a skilled swimmer with an impeccable technique, and from above you could barely see the trail left in the water by her quick passage.

When she returned to shore the man in black robes was almost invariably waiting for her; he watched her closely the whole time she dressed. There must not have been much good blood between the two. The girl, in fact, seemed not to listen to him when she was addressed, giving the impression that she was annoyed and almost resignedly suffering the attention, and as soon as she finished pulling her tunic over her still-wet body she ran to her friends, as though eager to be rid of an unwelcome presence as quickly as possible. And this behavior earned her the fixed attention of the interested observer on the terrace a number of times.

One evening, right at the moment when the swimmer was coming out of the water, something completely unexpected happened. Around the area demarcated by the torches a troop of warriors suddenly materialized, and a crescendo of screams and anguished cries instantly rose from the group. A stampede followed during which the hysterical mothers ran from one point to another on the shore in search of their children, then threw themselves in the lake like they wanted to escape impending danger. But the soldiers must have prepared for this strike well in advance. Following a precise plan, they moved compactly in one direction and surrounded a woman who was running with her two sons, pinned them down and tore the elder of the two from her hands.

Then something even more surprising happened. While the mother whose son had been taken desperately screamed and writhed in a vain attempt to break free from the soldiers' iron grip, the girl who had so aroused Marco's attention, leaped towards the kidnapper with a stride worthy of a sprinter and with a masterful trip she rolled him to the ground. She had just recovered the child and was racing towards the shore when she was surrounded by other soldiers who flocked suddenly from that direction as well. But she did not give up. She kept fighting with animalistic fury, and when at last he was immobilized and rendered helpless by the overwhelming number of opponents, many of them took to massaging their bruises and meditating on the surprising resources of the fairer sex. "No, they can't be priestesses," the astonished witness concluded. And the answer was not long in coming.

Chapter 19

At dawn the next day, Marco was woken by a repeated, prolonged sound like that of a foghorn. He had already heard that sound at other times, but never at such an unusual hour, much less from so close by and in an almost obsessive manner.

"Something big is about to happen down there," he said to himself, jumping out of bed and rushing to his observation spot with binoculars in hand without even having swallowed a mouthful. In the valley, in fact, the scene was quite different from usual. There was not a living soul in the fields or the lake, the streets were deserted and the few people that were still traveling along them were all hurrying in the same direction.

Their common goal was the main square which was already crowded in spite of the hour, and the preparations there were chaotic. Some workers were just finishing up with fencing off the route between the pyramid and the small structure situated in the center of the square. On top of the latter a canopy supported by four coiling columns had been erected, and under there other workers were arranging two massive golden thrones with some difficulty. Hundreds of bright-colored banners adorned the entire structure, the sides of the square and each step of the great pyramid. An army of warriors in parade uniform was advancing up the main avenue and upon entering the square divided into two neat rows that proceeded to position themselves at the foot of each banner. Were it not for the gloomy presentiment that oppressed him, Marco would have delighted in the magnificent choreography.

By midmorning all the inhabitants of the valley were huddled around the demarcated area. The long sound of the horns was repeated three times in a row and the whole city fell silent. Right after, a procession of figures who were already notorious to the observer, came out from a side street of the square: the golden throne, carried on the shoulders of twelve bearers, and behind this the crowd of illustrious rulers splendidly dressed. Even with the binoculars it was impossible to make out their faces at that distance, but Marco had no trouble in immediately recognizing the two figures in black tunics at the head of a second procession that was simultaneously moving towards the door of the temple located on the right side of the square.

Behind the priests was a golden throne supported by four bearers with shaven heads, on which sat a figure wrapped in a short purple robe. A young man, judging by his size, and probably tied to that chair, given his wriggling. Marco did not have to engage much of his perspicacity to guess who he was and what awaited him.

A row of twelve women in modest dresses followed, disheveled and of indeterminate age, each flanked by two warriors and bound together at the neck. While the royal procession halted at the center of the square, the other arrived at the foot of the pyramid and began to slowly climb up it along the steep central stairway over which the most recalcitrant women seemed to be dragged by force.

The procession was accompanied by the continuous, obsessive metallic clanging of castanets and cymbals, and a growing rumble of drums and other percussion instruments in the hands of a group of acrobatic characters who strode forward dancing, shouting, gesticulating, jumping and twirling left and right as though possessed. With towering plumes of iridescent feathers on their heads, their faces hidden behind ridiculous, grotesque masks and their bodies weighed down by ungainly, multicolored costumes, they looked like a troupe of minstrels. But the spectacle that unfolded was not very amusing. When the procession came to a halt at the top of the pyramid, the king and his officials had already resumed their place under the canopy and on the steps of the structure at the center of the square. And so began the ceremony.

The young boy was taken from his chair, undressed and stretched out across the stone altar in front of the temple to the left. On the other side, the twelve women were also stripped and the various segments of the rope that held them by the neck were fixed to big hooks protruding from the edge of the balcony. Meanwhile, the old priest was made to sit in an alcove in the front façade of the temple on the right-hand side. It seemed that he was put there more to be venerated like the statue of a saint than to officiate a ritual. Its real director, for a change, was his young confrere, who in the meantime had assumed position behind the sacrificial altar.

Marco had no doubts as to what was about to happen, but how much actually occurred exceeded all imaginings. This time he could hear the chilling roar of the crowd when the priest dealt the mortal blow. But this time the victim was little more than a child and was still writhing on the stone when the murders hand, stained by innocent blood, pulled the heart from his chest.

And the ritual was just beginning.

While two novices helped the executioner to dismember the body of the small victim and lay out the pieces on the continuously lit brazier in front of the altar, across the way the twelve women one after the other were pushed into the void, so that they hung by their necks, and each execution was accompanied by new shouts of encouragement from the crowd.

The hanged women had just ceased kicking in the last throes of their agony when they were withdrawn from the terrace, dragged to the altar, then beheaded by another zealous character. While their heads were driven again and again in full view onto the balcony's hooks, the bodies were lifted at the hands and feet by valiant warriors and sent rolling down the sides of the pyramid, at the bottom of which there were other butchers waiting by prepared grills.

Upon completion of the sacrifice, the priests slowly came back down the pyramid steps and headed towards the royal canopy. Behind them, two young servants carried a huge gold tray on their shoulders on which laid the still-smoking limbs of the boy. After the king triumphantly raised what had to be the little victim's liver into the air, he brought it to his mouth and bit in with a dramatic flourish; the loud roar that went up from the crowd was discernible to even the distant observer's ears. Soon after, between sounds and dancing, the macabre feast began. Lined up like a tribal community, the dignitaries and warriors took turns feasting on the flesh dispensed by the skillful hand of the priest while the remaining population competed for pieces of the other victims.

At that point Marco was overwhelmed by a mixture of horror and nausea from his dismay and disbelief at the events of the grisly ceremony, which culminated in bitter retching.

Chapter 20

He returned to the hut in the afternoon at a slow, trailing pace. He was stunned, shocked, he could still see the images of the severed heads, horribly mutilated bodies and humans who fed on their fellows. As empty as his stomach was from the previous evening, the very idea of eating made him sick. As he entered the cave he threw himself onto the bed, falling instantly into a restless slumber full of ghosts and terrifying nightmares.

He woke suddenly, bathed in cold sweat. It was already dark and the embers of the fire which, against custom, had gone unfed upon his return, had gone out altogether. The cold and his hunger forced him to get out of bed to stoke the fire. He still had an upset stomach and the acrid taste of vomit in his throat, which he tried to wash out by gulping down a stream of icy water. This partly worked, but when he tried to swallow something solid he was again assailed by nausea.

He had just bent down over the ashes when, thinking back to the horrors of the morning, he gasped. "The girl," he said in anguish, springing to his feet. A moment later he was outside of the refuge with binoculars in hand, and as he ran at breakneck speed through the forest and across the meadow he found himself praying to the Almighty not to break the slender thread that still bound him to life.

All were present on the shore of the lake, but the scene was not the usual one. The king was there in person this evening to witness the spectacle. He was seated, as usual, on his golden throne surrounded by the twelve porters; at his back, however, there was not the typical crowd of dignitaries, just a small group of warriors.

Grouped on the sidelines, the women and children watched in fearful silence what was unfolding in the center of the illuminated area where *she* stood, the lone swimmer, tied to two poles with her arms and legs spread, the woman who with ever-increasing tyranny was monopolizing his every thought. Behind her loomed the grim figure of the priest. It seemed that he was whispering something in her ear, but suddenly his murmurings were cut short by the girl's swift reaction; spinning rapidly, she spat directly in his face. In spite of the night and the distance, Marco was able to discern the sudden change in the priest's countenance; wiping his face with the sleeve of his robe and with bulging eyes he grabbed the woman's tunic from behind and tore it off with a furious gesture.

As overwhelmed as he was by this turn of events, Marco could not help but be enchanted by the beauty of the naked body that in the past he could only catch glimpses of from the gloom of the cliff. It was not possible to make out the girl's face in the backlight, but everything suggested that it could not betray the harmony of the whole. The man's ecstatic contemplation was soon broken by the brutality of the priest, who snatched a whip from the hand of the warrior beside him and without waiting for orders from anyone, dealt the first, terrible blow.

The long whip of braided rope wrapped around the woman's body several times like the coils of a serpent, imprinting the mark of its ruthless embrace with every lash, but not a groan nor invocation escaped the victim's lips; she stared at the king with her head high and unconcealed disregard as he sat grinning before her.

Marco witnessed the torture with tears in his eyes as if the blows were inflicted upon his body, and cursed his own helplessness more than ever. Trembling with rage, he felt his blood boiling. *Enough with that filthy butcher,* he thought, biting his tongue until it bled and holding back the urge to stand up and scream his wrath to the torturer.

The warrior to whom the task of imposing the sentence must have been assigned was the one to seize the priest's hand as he continued to rage on his victim like a man possessed even when she lost consciousness and hung motionless between the two poles, supported only by the ropes that encircled her wrists. Silence fell, and when a soldier decided to use his sword to sever the ties that held the girl she poured forward; the show was over. The porters hoisted the throne on their shoulders and resumed the way home preceded by the priest, leaving a few men behind to guard. And only then did the women, withheld no longer, dare to run to the aid of their friend.

The girl showed no signs of life and Marco, out of self-hatred and a heart overwhelmed with worry, continued staring at her with bated breath until he saw one arm move slightly. But that weak motion was certainly not enough to beat away the anxiety and anguish that was tearing through him. And to think that he had begun to feel almost a mixture of admiration and sympathy towards this simple, hardworking people, forcing himself to see them from a perspective different from his own, coming to justify them and even to convince himself that certain rites could not be condemned without taking into account the culture and traditions of a people among whom—as he happened to have read about certain pre-Columbian civilizations—being sent as a sacrifice to a god could even be considered an honor. But that morning's barbaric executions, that race for the consumption of human flesh, and above all the fury and absolute lack of compassion in regards to a helpless girl whose only crime had been to attempt to spare the life of an innocent, did reanimate in him all the subsided hatred for those vile, bloodthirsty creatures. At the same time, he felt pervaded by a new feeling and yearning for the victim, which was neither simply admiration nor lust. That woman had conquered him, day after day she had taken possession of his whole being and he felt that he would even be willing to give his life in that moment just to be able to hold her to him, comfort her…tell her that he loved her.

Chapter 21

Several months had passed since he had set foot on that land. The watch, which he continued to wear on his wrist purely as an ornament, by fate or coincidence had stopped on the very day that he buried Karl. Since then Marco had almost lost all concept of time and when he managed with some difficulty to overcome the depression and apathy to which he had sunk after the death of his friend, he had given up keeping track of the days.

Actually, in earlier days he had tried to make a sort of calendar, tracking each day with a tally on the wall next to his bed using a climbing nail, but not long after he realized that waking up to see that crooked-stroked register indicating the inevitable protraction of his imprisonment, it did nothing but exacerbate his frustration. So it was that one morning, as soon as he awoke, rather than drawing the usual tally on the way he found himself drawing the imagined face of the woman he loved, transforming the many tallies of days passed into as many stems in a flowering meadow.

Spring was just around the corner. The days were lengthening again and the temperature was rising. The sun's rays, no matter how indirect, had given a bronze color to his skin, while the hard work and spare diet had swept away any trace of excess body fat. Marco continued to shave daily, sharpening his trusty razor on a block of stone, but he still had not touched his hair and a long, flowing ponytail fastened with a shoestring now reached down his back.

Once again he tucked away his parka, which he wore only during the most frigid hours of the morning and evening when the cold made itself known. For the rest of the day he wore just a ragged loincloth made from the last shreds of his Bermuda shorts. It was not modesty that compelled him to cover his nakedness, nor was it the need to protect his sensitive parts from the thorns that grew everywhere. He had simply imposed a rule upon himself: "I am a man, not a beast!" he instructed himself again and again, although there were so many moments of despair when he felt his iron resolve falter.

He now knew every corner of his land by heart, each vein of spring water, every stream, every tree, every bush, every blade of grass that grew in the forest and in the meadow; everything in that little world to which he was confined was well known. He had only too much work to do, but it was monotonous, repetitive, so much so that he harbored a growing sense of dissatisfaction and his footsteps were increasingly leading him subconsciously to the edge of the fissure. Sometimes it happened that he would sit with his binoculars for hours, scanning the other half of the terrace and the more he dwelled on the details the more he desired to reach that promised land, so close and yet so far. Partly because there was at least one thing on the other side that was particularly attractive.

From the first day that he set foot on that land, Marco had always noticed a multitude of bees in the meadow, but he had never been able to find even the shadow of a honeycomb. After relieving the flowers of their doses of nectar, the bees rose into the air and invariably aimed towards the other side, only to immediately disappear from the view of the powerful lenses of the binoculars. Their nests all had to be over there and he often found himself drooling while fantasizing about that sweet temptation. But it was neither the desire to be able to reach other significant resources for food and firewood nor the possibility of pushing to the southernmost pole of the crater, from which he could finally claim the satisfaction of beholding the last stretch of valley thus far precluded, which so heightened his desire to reach the other side. Above all it was a challenge to feel alive again, to overcome at any cost.

For a long time already he had been racking his brain over how to bridge the twenty meters of void that separated him from the other side without being noticed, but each new solution that came to mind had some flaw and was systematically discarded either because it was too risky or because it was impossible to realize with the limited means at his disposal. The proper idea came to him quite accidentally.

One morning while he was working in the garden, the silence of the meadow was suddenly broken by a frightening crash, followed closely by a prolonged, increasing racket. The noise was coming from the upper area of the forest and was rendered even more deafening by the cavern's echo; it seemed endless and Marco, whipping around in that direction, saw that all of the commotion was nothing more than a gigantic plant, long dead, that was falling down flat on its side like a huge elephant and breaking all the branches and smaller trees that it met, bringing them down with it as it fell.

Marco was so panicked that he found himself running towards the shelter at breakneck speed: "But where the hell am I going!" he said to himself, stopping in his tracks after covering nearly half the meadow. Back to himself, he then walked to the edge of the terrace, multiplying his usual precautions to a maximum once he came crawling in proximity to his goal. His heart opened when he arrived and realized that he had been scared for nothing.

In fact, all was quiet in the valley; the fishermen were gathering their nets, the peasants worked in the fields and the women wove their mats with impunity, as though nothing had happened. But the noise must have been perceived well enough, because children and teenagers on the shore all had their noses pointed upwards and were shouting excitedly to each other while motioning towards the terrace several time. Logical deduction: what had just happened was neither a novelty nor an extraordinary event for the locals. After all, one had to consider, there were heaps of fallen trees in the forest.

His heartbeat had not yet resumed its normal pace and his courage was coming out of hiding when a bold, ingenious plan began taking shape in the survivor's mind.

Chapter 22

It was a warm spring morning when Marco, after rising early, proceeded towards the chasm with a determined step to realize his idea.
Within the stretch of meadow near the forest there were some old
pine trees that, by growing a ways apart from the others and on fertile, flat soil, had reached exceptional dimensions. One in particular
seemed to have been planted there specifically to meet his needs. It
was about fifty meters from the fissure, but it was as tall as a redwood.
If you cut it the right way, not only would it bridge the emptiness
of the crevasse, but it would also fall in the meadow instead of atop
other trees, as would surely have happened in the woods. It was
certainly not an insignificant undertaking that he set before himself
because the diameter at the base of the plant exceeded two meters,
but his workshop had churned out an infinite number of tools during
the winter and he would do it in such a way as to find all the time
necessary for the task. He just had to begin.

With strength, and being careful not to make the slightest noise,
he began shredding the bark with a sharp chisel made of stone. In
the beginning he worked on the low branches, but left all those that
would be visible from the valley when the tree fell attached to the
trunk. Each branch was first bound, then clipped to the base and
gently lowered to the ground. Marco took twenty days to complete
the preliminary work, then he started on the trunk. He attacked it
first from the side of the chasm, and by working hard for another
month he created a bore notch of almost half a meter. This done, he
moved to the other side and squatted down and commenced the
tougher, riskier final phase of the enterprise.

At first he only dedicated his free time to the job, being as occupied as he was with the many day-to-day tasks, but when he began to notice the first encouraging effects he flung himself into it headlong and neglected all other activities. He attacked it in the morning, then allowed himself a short lunch break and soon after got back to hacking away at the trunk without stopping until later at night, often after sunset, when his arms begged him to stop.

At the end of the day, by dint of being leaned and bent forwards, it was a struggle to stand up straight again; despite this, he never dreamed of missing his usual appointment with the nighttime nymphs. Step by step he went to the meeting on time and then, without caving in to his pangs of hunger, he sat and watched them until they left.

He returned to the shelter in deep night, stoked the embers and after cleaning himself up, he began preparing something to eat. That was a moment of future plans, but also of nostalgia and remembrance. His most poignant thought was always that of his mother, left alone to mourn his disappearance; he knew that she would never be resigned to the idea that he was dead, nor would she give up hope until the end of her days. How much longer would her fragile heart endure? Marco would have sold his soul to see her again, or at least to let her know that he was still alive, that he was well, that he loved her. And Claudia? With the passage of time, the features of his bride had gradually grown blurred and faded in his memory to make space for an increasingly imposing, idealized image of the Goddess of the Lake, as he had already christened his impossible love.

Chapter 23

She had not appeared since the flogging. "She didn't make it, she didn't make it!" he repeated disconsolately, whenever the hope of seeing her reappear among the others was dashed. The ceremonies at the pyramid never ceased to haunt him and his despair was transformed into anguish at the thought of what could be in store for her if she were still alive. He already despaired of seeing her again when one evening, after days and days of endless waiting, he saw her reappear in the middle of the procession. At first he did not believe his eyes, but there could be no doubt: it was impossible to confuse her with another. And then he wept for joy and exulted as he never had in his life.

The others no longer existed to him. They were all nymphs of an enchanted world, but among them was Venus herself, and Marco had eyes only for her. He followed her every move, noted every motion and he accompanied her stroke after stroke along her entire path when, having recovered her strength, she resumed her usual swims. The Goddess of the Lake had become the pivot around which his life revolved, his only consolation. But he was prevented from meeting her, hearing her voice, and this fostered a growing desire in him to find at least one point of contact with her. So it was that one evening, the urge prevailed over reason, and the admirer indulged in an action that in moments of lucidity would be called foolish, to say the least.

It was a full-moon night and the waters of the lake reflected the light like luminescent mirrors. From his position, Marco followed the swimmer, holding his binoculars with one hand. Almost unbeknownst to him, the fingers of the other sank into the damp ground, clutched a handful of hearth and, as though with a mind of their own, they began to shape it into a sphere slightly larger than a ping-pong ball. His mind calculated the time, and when the girl came to be almost at the edge of the terrace under which she would soon be eclipsed by his hand, without hesitation, dropped the dirt.

Reason returned an instant later. "Are you out of your mind? This time you're in shit over your head. And you're here alone, hunted…" The reprimand was interrupted by the impact of the ball on the water just a few feet away from the girl. In the silence of the night it seemed to Marco that he distinctly heard the splash, but perhaps he just confused that with the sound of his heart.

The swimmer stopped instantly and looked around in astonishment; the noise she had just perceived was unmistakable, but it was impossible to throw stones that distance from the shore. So she tilted her face to look up as though sure of discovering someone there. So much so, she can't see me from so far away, thought Marco, trying to reassure himself while still cursing his own stupidity. He pressed his chin to the ground trying to shrink, but did not look away, while his heart kept pounding in his throat with slow, deaf thuds that echoed in his head. The girl did not continue to the other side, but stayed peering upwards for a time that seemed infinite to Marco. Then she roused herself and with long, smooth strokes she returned slowly back to shore where, despite the inevitable stares of the priest, she took longer than usual in putting her clothes back on. Before catching up with the other women she threw one last, long look in Marco's direction.

"I acted like a complete idiot, only a brain-dead idiot could have gone so far," Marco chastened himself, contrite, heading back to the shelter while his legs still trembled. And the next night, like clockwork, he found himself in the same place, at the usual time, ready to do the same, insane thing he had done the previous evening. This time she stopped short, immediately directing her gaze upwards, and once again she did not proceed towards the opposite bank, but stayed in place as if waiting for a new signal. Then, slower than usual, she returned to shore, swimming on her back with her eyes glued to the terrace.

And again she was silent with her friends. "She got it. Yes, I think she got it. She didn't rat me out!" Marco exclaimed, euphoric. The next day, the Goddess of the Lake did not tarry even for a moment to talk with the others. She headed right for the outcropping rocks, hastily undressed, dived into the water and in quick strokes reached her now habitual destination. Where she stayed put, waiting with her face upturned. So Marco gathered all his courage and dropped a ball, then another and another in rapid succession: "I am mad. And I don't give a damn."

"Maybe she didn't understand," he reflected the next morning while he worked on the trunk. "She could think that it's a natural phenomenon, a crumbling of the ground…No, I need to do something more if I want to make her understand. It's a risk, I know, but it's a risk I have to run. Absolutely…So, what do I have to lose now?"

On the eighth day, a beautiful orchid fell along with the usual ball of mud. With his binoculars, Marco followed the woman all the way to the shore. Here he saw her turn her back to the priest, dress herself and bend forward between the rocks to collect something that she slipped deftly down her neckline. Finally, at the height of exaltation, he saw her look back in his direction and lift the palm of her hand in a furtive manner before reaching the group.

Fantastic moments followed. Every night the two unfamiliar lovers met promptly at the secret rendezvous point, and each time the girl's suitor sent her his message of love: a flower, a delicious-tasting berry, a splendid feather and anything else he could think of to pay homage. He would have liked to surprise her by sending and object unknown to her, even just a piece of foil, but the attentions reserved for her by the priest were a clear demonstration of how much she was subjugated and unfortunately if she were to be found in possession of a foreign object in the world in which she lived, there would be serious trouble for her. So Marco had shelved the idea, while he racked his brain for something truly unique and valuable to send without putting her in danger.

In the area of the scree it was not uncommon to find geodes of volcanic origin. The first few times, Marco was fascinated by their glittering contents. However, it was almost always a matter of calcite crystals or small quartz rocks that were not very transparent. Despite this they had proved very useful for their hardiness in shaping stones into awls, chisels, wedges, and many other practical tools. At the beginning he had stocked up on it, but with time he accumulated so many that he no longer knew what to do with them and had ceased picking them up. But one day he came across a strange-looking geode. Judging by its weight, oblong shape and its light straw color it might have been a petrified ostrich egg, and Marco could not help but put it in his backpack. When the dry hammer-hit that split it in two shook it near the waterfall, his breath was taken away: in the little treasure chest, sealed for millions of years, a host of fantastic blue crystals had come to light, as bright and transparent as spring water. A real treasure.

For several weeks, Marco neglected every other task and devoted himself body and soul to his new job. First off, with the tools left to him by Karl, he separated the main crystal, from the others, for it was the prettiest and purest. Later, with the tip of one of the climbing nails and with maddening slowness (errors were forbidden) he bored a hole into the stone holder in which the gem was set, and at the end of the operation he slid a string spun from intertwined fiber and wool through it.

The task was complete. The jewel was so beautiful in its natural state that working it in a different way would just have ruined it; despite this, the jewel would not elicit much of a stir in the valley because the sculptor had already noticed many others of the same sort shining at the ears and neck of dignitaries, warriors and these very night-owls. He could risk it. After emptying an egg of its contents, he slipped the jewel inside and sealed the shell.

The masterpiece fell from above that evening and appeared promptly on the girl's neck the next. She was showing it to her friends as though she wanted to communicate her discovery to him; as he had imagined and hoped, while the women admired it and passed it around they did not give the impression of being very dazzled by it. And at the sight of this, Marco was at once comforted and his heart filled with joy.

Chapter 24

The "contact" had regenerated him, had given him a new lease on life. After the wonderful addition of the jewel Marco once again plunged heart and soul into his work, more determined than ever to finish it in the shortest possible time. He had pushed almost to the marrow of the tree and to prevent it from disobeying the bore cut and crush him, he had begun to insert thicker wedges into the notch.

In every moment of the day, while he continued to chop at the wood fiber by fiber, his thoughts were always turned to the Goddess of the Lake. He was resigned to the idea of never being able to meet, never be able to hold her to him. He was happy just the same, and the absence of physical contact was compensated for by the friend that was his imagination, who, after having kidnapped his beloved from the valley, transported her to the meadow to follow his laboring and listen to his discourses. And he talked to her about everything, responded to her silent questions in great detail, and sought to dazzle her with descriptions of the many wonders of the world he came from and to which he would one day take her with him after having freed her.

One afternoon, his internal monologue was interrupted by an almost imperceptible tick coming from the heart of the plant. As though bitten by a tarantula, Marco sprang to his feet and began to push against the truck with all his might: "Damn it! By talking to yourself you even started getting auditory hallucinations, here," he told himself. But there was still three handbreadths of wood to be cut, so he resignedly sat down again in his usual spot, convinced of the need to devote a lot more of his time to the grueling job. But soon he heard an identical tick. "I didn't make that one up!" he exclaimed, jumping to his feet again and positioning himself to push on the trunk with both arms. "Shit!" he snorted, not hearing any more warning signs for a while.

He was about to resume sitting when he heard a different sound beneath him, a "*thunk*" this time. And another "*thunk*" after a little bit, and then another, and another, at first almost imperceptible and at intervals of a few seconds apart; then more distinctly, dry and tight, as if at the base of the trunk all the strings of an enormous guitar were snapping one by one. And at that point Marco, now certain of reaching his goal, planted his feet on the ground and began to apply force like a man possessed, tensing his muscles to breaking point while rivulets of sweat ran down his forehead and face and clouded his vision.

It seemed that that mule of a plant was completely deaf to his solicitations and would hear absolutely nothing of tearing itself away from its lofty position. But it suddenly came to life and, as if by magic, began to slowly bend forward, gradually accelerating its fall while at once the ticking at the base of the trunk turned into a deafening roar that was increasingly magnified by the cavern's echo and the cracking of the branches that broke off and fell to the ground.

He cast an eye upon the felled giant, then his feet were carrying him towards the edge of the terrace at a sprint, but to a remote spot far from the place that would draw curious eyes. In fact, just as he had feared, this time not only teenagers and children were there on their shore with their noses pointed upwards, but all were present, including the fishermen. At this sight, Marco really feared that he had trusted too much in lady luck and had done the irreparable. Soon, however, the curious gazes began to fall one after the other and each, having taken stock of the novelty, returned to their usual occupations. But a good bit of time still had to pass before the lungs of this improvised lumberjack would resume sucking in aid and his legs, which had turned to rubber, would again be able to hold him upright.

Happy as a clam about the narrow escape and doling out thanks to all number of saint, Marco returned boldly to the scene of the crime. It did not yet seem real that that devil, who for so long—he did not even remember how long—had held him fixed to its trunk, wringing every last drop of sweat from his pores, now lay at his feet, defeated, bridging the two distant worlds in a firm embrace. The cut had been made in a workmanlike manner, and the tree had fallen perpendicularly to the two edges of the chasm, extending over each by several meters. It weighed so much that it would not have budged even in the face of cannon fire, partly because the plant's high branches, which had been driven deep into the ground during the fall, helped to keep it firmly in position. Additionally, the branches within view of the valley which he had purposely left attached to the trunk created a perfect camouflage, while those stumps cut on the upper side acted as comfortable holds for hands and feet while crossing.

There was no reason to stay transfixed and observe the promised land from a distance. Marco hoisted himself onto the trunk and, after having tested its stability by rocking his body to the right, left and center, he stretched himself out face down and began to crawl across with the slowness of the sloth, careful not to dislodge even a twig. He thought that he was probably exaggerating with the precautions; the trunk allowed him to advance easily without having to do any stunts and its diameter was such that it would have been able to conceal two of him side by side, so he did not run any risk of being seen from below.

Despite this, it took him almost half an hour to span the few meters that separated him from the coveted shore. In a paranoid excess of precautions, despite having no reason to doubt the hold of the land, he overshot the opposite edge of the fissure by a good distance and finally, after bringing himself back up to a seated position, he made the leap: "*Ai suma! Ai suma! Ai suma!*" he repeated to himself just as he touched the ground, restraining himself from shouting for joy and at once performing a tribal dance of his own invention. He was euphoric, radiant, more than convinced of having just outclassed the Columbian expedition, though, at least at first glance, the world in which he had landed did not seem all that different from the one he had just left behind. At that time he could not even begin to imagine what incredible upheaval the conquest of that wretched strip of land would bring him.

Chapter 25

Marco was jumping out of his skin with joy; he trembled with the desire to explore the new land and he did not even know where to start. He had come to the edge of the woods, which on that side was also separated from the meadow by a barrier of brambles. He decided to head for the southern pole of the crater that bordered the latter. Along the way he encountered many streams that were wide and deep in relation to the short distance they traversed. The overflow from the thaw had broken the banks of several streams, creating great swampy expanses in the middle of the meadow—real quicksand in some places—so that Marco was forced, despite the near absence of brambles on that side, to advance at the same slow pace and he wound up taking much longer than he expected to reach his coveted goal; once achieved, however, he was finally able to gaze out over the entire valley.

The river, after being eclipsed by the sheet of basalt that bordered the lake, reappeared four or five hundred meters downstream and after tracing a wide bend to the left it was directed straight towards the opposite side of the crater rim and then disappeared forever into the mountain. There were also many small plots of cultivated land on that side, interspersed with farmers' huts which were very similar to those found near the lake, but close to the left bank of the river one could glimpse the golden roofs and white stone walls of numerous, magnificent palaces surrounded by green trees and flower-filled parks.

But the landscape on this other side was completely different. Not a blade of grass grew in that place and the arid, gravelly soil was littered with huge piles of crushed white stones, interspersed here and there with smaller stones that gave off amber reflections: "There it is...the quarry and the auriferous quartz, too," the observer determined, not very amazedly. While not a geologist, he knew a bit about minerals and therefore did not believe that he had gone too far in having just identified the parent rock of gold.

But besides the peculiarities of the soil, it was the activity going on below that kept his attention. Beyond that branch of the Acheron and guarded by armed warriors there was a multitude of the damned—men, women and children—covered in white powder from top to bottom and intent on squaring stones or crushing rock material with big masses of stone, and many, many other ghosts coming and going from black sockets in the mountain carrying baskets of gravel on their backs or dragging large sleds bearing huge boulders of rough stone.

Marco stood scrutinizing the crowd of derelicts until he saw them get back in line to continue their journey towards the city, but when he decided to leave his post it was too late. The night overtook him suddenly in the middle of the meadow when he had not even covered a quarter of the way back. Then and there he was disoriented, unable to make a decision. It was unthinkable, however, to venture into the night on that unknown, marshy terrain with the risk of winding up in a ditch or collapsing into one of the muddy sections. He had to stay on that side overnight. As if that were not enough, that was the first morning he had not even swallowed a mouthful and, as he wore only a loincloth, he was beginning to feel the first of the nighttime frost. He decided to seek shelter in the woods and once he crossed the barrier of thorns, he was finally able to lie down under a thick layer of dry leaves and pine needles like the first day of his arrival. But this time he was half-naked and the improvised cover could barely protect him from the cold and the damp of the night, and it stung like hell.

But it was neither the cold, nor the itching, nor the discomfort of the bed that made him think. What distressed him more and would not give him peace was the missed meeting with the Goddess of the Lake, the first after the fateful contact: "That's it, now, that's what she'll think! That something happened to me. Or, worse yet, that I have gone away…I'm not sure I can afford these errors, I can't miss this meeting, for any reason, not even once. Never, never, never."

Chapter 26

He slept little and badly, and got up even before the day began, numb and with his stomach in knots. From the bleak grayness of the light coming from above he deduced that, fittingly for his mood, there must have been very bad weather above the crater. Maybe it was snowing outside, but inside it never snowed, nor was there a breath of wind. He had a full day ahead of him before the longed-for meeting, so he decided to maximize on it and take the opportunity to take another look around. He was very hungry at that time, and he could only hope to find something to eat in the nest area. So, he decided to continue climbing through the forest.

To be able to push him to this decision, his hunger pains must have taken away his faculty for understanding, making him completely forget what he had already had occasion to observe countless times from the other side: the ascent, in fact, immediately proved much more challenging and difficult than expected. The trees grew along narrow, flat ledges separated by high, rocky steps or precipices so steep that they forced him to cling constantly to the shrubs in the undergrowth and pull himself up by his own strength in order to proceed in fits and starts. Not to mention the tangle of brambles and vines that were seriously intent upon running a cutthroat competition with those that grew on the other side.

Here and there along the way he ran into bushes of known, edible berries, but they were still not ripe and tasted unbearably bitter. He was tired, cold, and the call of his food supply and the bed that awaited him in his warm, comfortable refuge grew increasingly domineering. After about half an hour's hike he was on the verge of giving up on the pursuit and heading back when, after hoisting himself forcefully onto the umpteenth ledge, he found the road blocked by an obstacle.

Behind a thick barrier of creepers he glimpsed a strange rock whose dark color clashed sharply with the whiteness of the rocks that he usually came across. Intrigued, rather than to divert his path and avoid the obstacle, he wanted to see things more clearly and unsheathed his knife to begin cutting the bushes that separated him from the "thing" that made a particular sound when the dry branch of a plant eventually fell onto it.

Marco's heart skipped a beat. Hunger, fatigue, lethargy and despondency were instantly swept away to make way for a state of excited disbelief. He had known that sound for a lifetime, he could not have been mistaken, and it was a delightful sound, a divine music of immense promise that he never, ever dreamed of being able to hear again for the rest of his existence. Because the mysterious object that had just made that sound could only be solid metal.

"My God, let it be true," he found himself praying, afraid of being contradicted by the facts. With both hands and strength increased tenfold, he then began to uproot and eradicate all the shrubs and vines that still separated him from his certainties. In the excitement of the moment he did not even feel the bite of the thorns in his flesh anymore, and only when he had pulled away the last curtain of vines did he unravel the mystery: in front of him, atop a huge carcass of sheet metal only slightly rusted by time, towered the unmistakable rotor of a helicopter with one blade broken in half. Judging by the patches of dark green and brown paint on the parts of the sheet metal that were not yet eroded by rust, he deduced that it must have been an old military helicopter. Fortune had it that the aircraft had not blown up despite the major impact with the ground.

"It must've run out of fuel…or maybe the trees cushioned the blow," Marco hypothesized. "But how did it get all the way down here?" he wondered, considering the distance that spanned between the place where the helicopter was and the mouth of the crater. The pilot probably sank down here because he was attracted by the mountain's light show, he continued to conjecture. Then, either because he was dazzled by the glare or because of engine failure, or whatever other reason, he must have lost control of the chopper and crashed. At that point the upper cone of the "hourglass," acting both as a slide and a springboard, must have made the aircraft run a long course gliding for it to have landed in exactly that spot. It could be a plausible explanation, but in that instant the incident was at the bottom of the list of his concerns; the infinite possibilities of the huge mass of sheet metal in front of him were running through his mind in rapid sequence. All the gold that shone on the roofs of the valley was nothing in comparison.

Working with the knife and his bare hands, Marco continued to make his way through the brambles. In the collision, the nose of the helicopter had been wedged into the ground and scrunched into itself, but the entire fuselage was intact with the raised tail trained on the valley; by consequence, given the steep slope of the cliff, the tail rotor had to be about eight feet above the ground. The cabin's entrance door was reduced to a heap of twisted metal, but the side doors were still intact, with the left one slightly ajar.

When approaching the aircraft, Marco almost fell to the ground by tripping over the missing piece of the bade. He picked it up off the ground, weighed it in his hands with repeated nods of approval and then cradled it in his arms like a precious child before deciding to stand it upright and in plain sight against the trunk of a plant. Taken by the desire to examine, he leaped and grabbed onto the edge of the hatch that was situated over three meters above. Then, placing his feet on the left skid and pulling himself up with his arm strength, he managed to stick his head into the narrow opening.

At once he cried out, let go and fell away like a dead body. A second before he had found himself face to face with the smile of a skull that stared at him with a sardonic expression, and even before he hit the ground he was already cursing himself. And he cursed even more so when, at the end of his spill, he felt himself sinking into the middle of the bush that, on the one hand, stopped him from falling down the steep slope, but on the other came close to flaying him alive.

"Freaking imbecile! And to think that this isn't the first body you've had to see!" he swore as he worked to extricate himself with difficulty from the infinity of brambles that imprisoned him. Shortly after he was as determined, resolute, and bloody as a Christ on the cross when he leaped for a second attempt. This time he managed to keep control over his primeval revulsion, but before slipping inside the cockpit he reached out his arm to move the bulky sentinel a bit off to the side. Maybe a bit too much to the side, because the skull, which his fingers had barely toughed, broke away cleanly from the neck and began to roll downwards with a hollow-box clacking that gave him the chills. But it was not the time to begin philosophizing over antithetical human behavior when faced with the living and the dead and Marco, mustering his strength, pulled himself up with his arms and then, using his elbows, managed to pass his torso through the narrow opening to enter fully into the interior.

It took a little while for him to get used to the diaphanous light transmitted through the Plexiglas windows obscured by vegetation and dust accumulated over the course of decades. Then, slowly, the contents of the fuselage began to take shape. Upon impact with the ground any objects that were not fastened down were thrown towards the cockpit. Near the entrance, the cervical vertebrae of the beheaded corpse were lost inside a camouflage suit steeped in putrefaction while from the sleeves of the same suit protruded long, skeletal fingers—which as of yet were still intact—outstretched to claw at the steel floor. The poor man must have dragged himself to the door in rather bad shape, and he had probably managed to open it halfway, but death had caught him on his way out.

In spite of the ominous presence, Marco was itching with excitement. Wherever his eyes landed he saw fantastic objects from "his" world, and each of these was immediately associated with its thousands of possible uses and each discovery fueled his desire to rummage everywhere. Turning his gaze upward towards the tail of the aircraft, he saw in the dim light many reinforced metal crates hovering eerily in a grid of straps. He longed to go snoop around, but refrained from doing so; moving in that direction would run the risk of breaking the delicate balance which for many years had held the helicopter in its unstable, tilted position and the hassle that could come of it would not go unheeded by the ears in the valley.

"You'd better not go looking for trouble," he told himself judiciously, and slipped slowly in the opposite direction, towards the cockpit, supporting himself on each foothold that he encountered along the descent. At the bottom, hidden under a chaotic mess of heterogeneous material, another grisly discovery awaited him: the skeleton of the pilot lying forward, still held in the pilot seat by its seat belt, with its head twisted under its arm in an impossible position as though to peer sideways at what was happening behind him.

The new encounter with death succeeded in mitigating much of the euphoria of the explorer and bring him back to reality; he could not continue to rummage haphazardly in the dark, he had to calm himself down, act sensibly and less incoherently if he did not want to get himself in an ocean of trouble. He decided not to touch anything, climbed cautiously up to the exit and after having fallen back to earth started to run towards the shelter. He was dead tired and hungry, but the discovery had caused him to forget every discomfort, even the thorns that he had not yet managed to pull away, and he had no intention of postponing what he had set out to do.

In less than two hours, he had returned to the shelter and was back to the starting point bringing the hammer, the bag of nails, climbing rope, and a long stick fitted with a hatchet. Before leaving the cave he had snatched something from the pantry that he devoured along the way without even realizing it, and crossing the bridge each way he did not even deign to look at the valley, but continued to mull over his next moves, which were already clear and well defined when he reached his destination. Without wasting any time, he took up the hatchet and began to clear all branches, brambles and vines from the aircraft that over the years had encompassed it in a kind of vegetal cocoon. Just this preliminary task took up the whole rest of the morning, but in the end there was not so much as a blade of grass around the helicopter and the surrounding trees. He could move on to the second phase.

After several failed attempts, he managed to throw the rope over the tail boom, catch the end of it and tie it around itself with a slip knot, bringing it slowly higher as he fully tightened it. With another throw—he got it right the first time around, this time—he slipped the rope between the main branches of a sturdy tree located behind the aircraft. The plant bifurcated more than ten meters from the ground, but the steep slope of the terrain meant that the fork was at exactly the height of the tail of the helicopter.

End of the preliminaries. It was time to develop the keystone of the whole strategy he had concocted, planning and revising in his mind all morning. The "nail strategy."

Having recovered the top of the other part of the tree, Marco wrapped it around the base of another plant but did not bring it full-circle around, but doubled it through the ring of a climbing nail to three-quarters of the circumference. Then he pulled it towards him, but blocked the ring from coming out with another nail driven in sideways, and brought it back under tension. He repeated the same operation on other trees nearby, sometimes twice on the same trunk, until he was more than certain of his calculations and at the end of the operation tied the rope securely to a last plant. With this simple trick, he calculated, pulling out the nail that was used as a retainer, the rope would slip away from the ring, stretching for more than half the circumference of the trunk.

After checking that the rope was good and tense, Marco returned to the helicopter and used the handle of the hatchet to begin disengaging it from the stone and earth that held it fast in its inclined position.

He had just taken away a few stones when the aircraft, like a giant awakened after a long dormancy, came to life and began to slowly bend backwards with the growing creaking of twisted metal that was amplified hundredfold by his fearful ears. "Let it hold!" Marco found himself praying, more tense than the rope. "If the rope breaks, there's going to be a real mess here." His prayer was answered. The tail boom, after dropping an arc of about one meter, just when it was gaining speed, stopped mid-air without unbalancing the helicopter. And the rope, although tense as a violin string, held the weight.

There was silence, and only then did Marco, emitting a puff of all the air that was trapped in his lungs like a humpback whale, realize that he had sweated more in those last few moments that he had during the whole morning trek. Even considering his soft legs, the aircraft had not made a lot of noise. Nevertheless, to avoid any unpleasant surprises he embarked just the same to make the effort to descend the entire slope, go racing to the edge of the meadow and come back up the steep climb to the helicopter. Only after ensuring that everything was calm and quiet as always in the valley, could he complete his work.

He tied a strap to the ring of the nail that served as a retainer on the first loop, then planted a foot against the tree and pulled it to him with a jerk. The nail slipped away without any resistance and the noose, which was no longer restrained, snapped out of the ring like a whip, thereby lowering the helicopter's tail by another half meter. The rope was stretched to its maximum but still held and the helicopter, with the front ends of its skids now firmly on the ground, gave off only a slight creaking. Then it was the same for the successive loops. To prevent the aircraft from slipping despite the rope's hold, Marco had erected a barrier of rocks and brambles behind it, but when it came down to it this turned out to be an unnecessary precaution; at the seventh loop the helicopter's skids rested fully on the narrow, rocky ledge.

"*Ai suma!*" he exulted again. Everything had gone the best way. Finally, after much toiling, he allowed himself to peacefully and calmly open this great treasure chest from the sky, still far from imagining how luxurious and precious its contents would prove to be.

Chapter 27

Before initiating his systematic examination of the helicopter, Marco pulled the stripped remains of the two crewmen and buried them beneath a mound of stones, partly for the sake of human compassion and party so as not to have to constantly see that spectacle of the tragedy that occurred who knows how many years prior. The corpse lying next to the door of the fuselage wore a giant revolver that hung from his belt: "Um, unusual for a soldier!" Marco considered, turning it over in his hands and removing it from its holster. Although he was no novice in the realm of firearms, he had never held a Springald of this kind in his hands before; it was so big, long and heavy that it really looked like the caricature of a gun.

Just above the handle, Colt Magnum was engraved in the steel. It had several rusted patches on the barrel, the trigger, and also the hammer, which pulled backwards with some difficulty although it did not seem too badly limited. Thanks to the protection of the holster, the drum was not in the least affected by rust and still revolved pretty well on the central pivot, and the bullets that were housed there, like the ones stuck in the weird belt that hung from the holster, shone like they were freshly forged. Under the light the inside of the barrel appeared to be perfectly smooth. All in all, putting it back in order would not be an impossible task.

"It just needs a good cleaning and oiling," said Marco at the end of his close scrutiny. Of course, with sandpaper and lubricant a bit better suited than the crude bird fat that was the best he could manage in the situation, he would have been able to have a lot more success in a lot less time, but he concluded magnanimously that you could not have everything in life. While inspecting the weapon, however, he could not help but consider that the cannon would certainly not put him in a position to compete on a level playing field with the people of the valley. "At most, I could shoot myself in the head if they were to discover me!" he said optimistically. That thought darkened his mind somewhat, but only a bit: a small, passing cloud come to somber the splendor of that great day just for a moment. Marco decided to put away the gun and belt in a corner and move on.

Next to the right side door, which was still barred, a sturdy steel arm was welded—the support for a machine gun, probably—with its joints locked by rust. On the floor of either side of the fuselage ran two long leather seats and, in the space below the seating surface, there was an unbroken row of rusted drawers. Marco did not even pause to think about it. He bent down, grasped the handles of the top drawer in his hands and—considering the state it was in—pulled it towards him with a vigorous tug. He cursed when he bumped his head against the edge of the seat behind him after he flipped backwards; the drawer, contrary to all appearances, had slid out of its compartment in a fraction of a second, freezing at the end of its track. But the rust there was real, only the drawer was fitted with ball bearings that were still perfectly oiled and it traveled on two tracks that were still mirror-smooth and even the pull of a little finger would have been sufficient to remove it.

Massaging the lump that was forming on the back of his head as rapidly as a fungus, Marco got back up to his knees. And he just avoided the roof of the passenger compartment when, casting his eyes inside the drawer, he could not keep himself from jumping for joy. Inside there was an endless array of fabulous work tools lined up in perfect order and contained in their respective compartments by elastic straps that were still intact: screwdrivers, wrenches, files, awls, chisels, a hammer, pliers, pincers and many small transparent containers full of screws, bolts and nails of all kinds. And it seemed to him that he breathed the air of home again when in the corner he unearthed two large tin cans the color of petroleum still sealed, with LUBRICATION FOR BEARINGS printed in Italian.

Without even finishing his inventory of the top drawer, Marco rushed to open all the others in a frenzy of excitement. And every discovery multiplied the riot and exaltation in him. In the one next to the first he found a handsaw with two spare blades, a short-bladed wood saw as sharp as a razor and, under a dividing partition, some discs of sandpaper and a drill with many tips made of wood, iron and cement. The bay below the handle displayed its battery power, but the chuck did not even try to move when Marco hopefully pulled the trigger. Wishfully thinking that this might just stem from a bit of simple oxidization, he withdrew a screwdriver from the other drawer and used it as a lever on the lid of the container, but after sending it flying he found the battery embedded in a greenish con-cretion, much to his disappointment. Despite this, something told him that the thing would lend him some degree of satisfaction just the same, with or without batteries.

From a longer drawer that was almost in the tail of the fuselage a shovel, an ax, three long, steel pegs, and surprisingly a crowbar, popped out. In another container there were two rolls of wire and a long rope made of synthetic material one inch thick and never used. Above, attached to the wall, he found the first aid cabinet with drugs, tourniquets, syringes and even some surgical instruments. The med-icines were long outdated—from the mid-seventies—but Marco knew very well that properly preserved they had a far longer life than indicated. Even the few surgical instruments, although obsolete, were still in fair condition and the man, upon finding a scalpel with some spare blades, two hemostasis clamps, needles and suture thread, could not help but to revisit Karl's tragedy in his mind: "And to think that this was all here on our doorstep, at our fingertips." But the regret for what could have been was soon ousted by other ex-traordinary discoveries. Out of a cabinet came aluminum tins, plates and plastic cups, various steel cutlery, several packets of biscuits and cans of meat whose contents were certainly inedible, but whose containers were a real treasure. And the most important discoveries were yet to come.

During his first hasty inspection of the morning, Marco had already noticed the presence of numerous stacked crates at the end of the fuselage. After swiping his hand over the windows of the tail in a tricky attempt to get a bit more light to filter inside, he walked over to the crates and undid the leather straps that still held them firm in their place, but when he tried to disconnect one from the pile he was met with unexpected resistance. It was extremely heavy and he had to make a huge effort to remove it from the stack, put it down and then drag it behind him as he walked backwards holding the handle with both hands.

He cursed when he got to the exit and realized that the crate could not pass through the opening even when turned lengthwise, while the door would not budge an inch on the rusty track even when he pushed it with the crowbar. Marco was champing at the bit, he had just about had it with all the mishaps; he was madly tempted to solve the problem to the tune of hammering but restrained himself. To push the process along he softened a bit, went to pick up a screwdriver and sandpaper from the drawer, and squatting on the floor he began to resignedly wear away the numerous encrustations.

It took a good hour to get the door to slide just enough to pull the crate through and in the light of day he finally realized why it weighed so much: it was not made of wood, as it had seemed to him in the dim light of the fuselage, but rather of solid metal well-protected by a thick layer of dark green enamel. The lid made no resistance when he tried to lift it.

Inside the case, still wrapped in wax paper and well lubricated with paraffin oil, there were pieces of a submachine gun. At the bottom, a plastic bag containing an instruction booklet. In all languages, perhaps even Aramaic, but not even a line of Italian. Frantically, Marco continued on to drag one crate after the other out of the fuselage and throwing them open as soon as they were on the ground, pausing only to give a quick look at their contents. At the

153

end of the transfer there was a real arsenal in the helicopter. In a great crescendo, the crates revealed another submachine gun identical to the first, hundreds of magazines, cartridges and eighty burnished steel hand grenades.

Marco was still struggling to believe his luck. In the morning when he had discovered the aircraft he had immediately realized that it would bring about many useful things, but that which had arisen far surpassed all of his expectations. At that point, perhaps by association of ideas, his thoughts ran to the valley people—the black priest in particular—and a satisfied smile suddenly appeared on his lips.

"I wonder who they were!" Marco kept musing, thinking about the two men in the helicopter. At first he had taken it for granted that they were soldiers, but the more he thought about it the less convinced he was. Why, for example, did neither of them have dog tags? What was a cowboy gun belt doing on a soldier? But it could not be a matter of drug traffickers because despite having ransacked it from top to bottom, there was not even an ounce of drugs in the helicopter. Guerrillas? Arms dealers? Mystery.

But determining the exact profession of his two saintly benefactors was the least of his worries then. He was definitely in high spirits but his fatigue, sleepiness and hunger had reached an alarming level. Moreover, even if the days had lengthened substantially, it was getting late and this suitor was not going to miss a meeting two nights in a row. It was time to give it a rest and pack up, taking only the belt and the gun which was already strapped at his hip; he had all the time in the world to complete the inventory.

He was about to descend from the helicopter when his gaze fell casually onto the crate on which he had just placed his hand for support while jumping to the ground and which he had bumped into each time he had dragged a crate behind him throughout the entire afternoon. It was fixed to the floor near the exit. On the side facing outwards it was completely hidden behind the big door that was not completely open, but peering through the narrow gap between the two walls he could glimpse the edge of a trunk.

The man's heart began to beat wildly and once again hunger, fatigue and sleep disappeared instantly. Marco began to scrape feverishly at the last section of the sliding door's track until it opened completely, fighting against time. Then he devoted himself to the chest, but it took a heart attack caused by a metallic thud before he sprang away from the opening. Inside the box there was a shapeless heap of gears. At first glace it seemed completely rusted, but when Marco went to scrape it clean it with a screwdriver tip, a small piece of solidified sludge broke off the block.

Maybe it was chance or maybe it was a higher will, but the fact is that at that very moment the crater was flooded by the rays of the setting sun. A sudden flash came from inside the container and the man, as though irradiated by divine light, knelt in front of the tin altar, hugged it and sobbed like a child; he had just found his ticket to the valley.

That evening, Marco looked at the woman through different eyes. The little spark that had set the fire that now raged inside him, the ray of light that in an instant had transported him to the high heavens had been nothing more than the reflection coming off the steel cable of a winch. He did not have a clear idea in his mind of how or when, but of one thing he was already firmly convinced: in one way or another, that cable would end his isolation, with that cable he would reach the valley, with that cable he would hold his Goddess in his arms.

Chapter 28

Days of hectic work and dreaming followed. Often the darkness surprised him as he was still trying to dismantle pieces of the helicopter, but it did not bother him anymore; he had commuted from one side of the chasm to the other so many times and he knew each hold and spur of the felled trunk so well that he could make the whole journey even in darkest night.

He had already brought the smaller treasures to the shelter moving, of course, only in the dead of night and always after his habitual meeting with the girl, when there was not a living soul left in the lake. But he had preferred to leave several working tools protected inside their compartments in the helicopter, in which he had set up his second laboratory.

First and foremost he devoted himself to the winch. The trunk in which it was housed and the grease that covered the gears, no matter how rusty the first and how solidified the second, had preserved the contents in very good condition. The container, by contrast, had been infiltrated by rust, especially on the outside where the bolts and anchoring screws were almost one with the floor and Marco, despite the many new tools at his disposal, was forced to an exhausting chore. Several screws were placed in blind spots so inaccessible that it was an impossible task to unscrew them without skinning his fingers, and he had to spit out the blood before managing to unscrew them without breaking them or giving in to the insane temptation to summon the valley's entire population with the sound of his hammering.

Champing at the bit, he forced himself to calm down and in the end, except for a few completely rust-eaten pieces, he managed to recover almost all the bolts and screws with much of their thread. Then it was the gears' turn. With a wipe and a screwdriver he freed them one by one from the thick encrustation, replacing it from time to time with a good amount of bearing grease. This job also took a lot of time, but at the end of the operation each component was good as new and a light pull on the clip was enough to make the steel cable, now docile and obedient as a dog, roll off the spool seamlessly and in absolute silence to its full extent, which was seventy meters exact.

At that point Marco moved on to carefully study the scheme of connecting rods, wheels, and couplings through which the driving force of the helicopter was sent to the winch and multiplied by the gears many times over. But before daring to remove a piece he carefully noted every detail with a notebook and a pencil that he had found in a driver's seat pocket. On a separate page, his idea took shape simultaneously.

In its initial state this was science fiction to say the least; furthermore, Marco had not at all taken into account the material he had at his disposal, so when it was time to move from theory to practice he was forced into a constant commute between the work table and the helicopter to search for the right pieces to fit the design. And if the operation ran aground for lack of a spring, a pin or a simple bolt, he erased, corrected, replaced, redesigned from top to bottom until he could overcome the obstacle. Little by little the project was completed, the futuristic machine had been turned into a heap of parts fixed up a bit everywhere and often held together with unseemly wire. But, at least on paper, it should work.

The primary goal was to find a way to replace the driving force of the helicopter with manual power. Marco knew how to work with his hands a little bit and even though his knowledge of mechanics was lost in the mists of time, the principle of the lever—that of the pulley in particular—was still engraved in his mind, and he had based the whole gimmick on just that principle. To his great fortune, the gears and bearings of the tail boom of the helicopter were preserved as good as new in their caps, which were still sealed and well-oiled, and despite looking like it was broken down into a devastated pile of junk, the engine was still able to provide a nice contribution of belts and sprockets.

But beyond a shadow of a doubt, the real trump card proved to be the drill. On it Marco had mounted a toothed wheel fitted to the side of the crank, connected by a chain to another much smaller wheel, which in turn coupled to the spindle perforation. This yielded a prototype that was not very hi-tech to look at, but with a singular purpose: turning the crank with force the big wheel multiplied the revolutions of the small one, and this imparted enough rotation speed to the spindle to be more than sufficient for drilling all kinds of materials. It had taken forever to figure out, but in the end he got himself a helper able to meet demands that not so long ago he would only have been able to dream about meeting.

The nose of the helicopter was an inexhaustible source of raw material, whose sheet metal was crumpled and torn in places at the moment of the disaster. It was easy enough to grasp at part of the ragged edges with pliers and pull them apart from the rest, so when the aircraft was not able to provide the ready pieces Marco withdrew a piece of sheet metal, brought it near the waterfall and there, with a bit of the drill, the hammer and the file, he molded it in the desired manner.

The first, fundamental achievements churned out of his shop were the pulleys. With the hacksaw, now permanently bound to his hip like the inseparable knife, he worked five large wheels half a foot tall and three fingers thick from the tip of the felled pine tree. Working then with a chisel and mallet, he carved a deep groove on the edges and at the center he made a hole large enough to hold a ball bearing tight, complete with an axle. He mounted one wheel inside a bracket plate fitted atop a steel ring and below, hanging from the prongs, a sturdy hook; the other four however he paired side by side, two at a time, inside two other brackets. Once he prepared the pulleys, Marco went in search of the appropriate supports from which to hang them and it did not take him long to locate them at the foot of the forest in the form of two large beech trees that grew almost opposite one another on either side of the chasm, only a few meters away and readily accessible from the meadow after clearing the bramble barrier.

The system was designed to easily transfer even the heaviest loads from one side of the chasm to another. During the night, he climbed the beech trees and secured the rope to them at two different heights. The single pulley would be kept in balance by the weight of the load on the sliding cable and the operator would not have to do anything but regulate the descent with another rope secured to the ring of the bracket. The two double pulleys allowed for lifting the load from the ground to the height of the hook; they were hung from a branch of the same plant by way of a movable pulley, which would reduce by three-quarters the force required to lift.

It was late fall when Marco began silently transporting the heavier material by night. Everything went as planned and within a few hours, even with the huge hassle of having to shuffle from one side of the chasm to the other every time to tie and untie the load, he managed to send across all the crates and casings already stacked up and slung below in the days prior underneath the departure station with the intent to complete the job in one night alone. He left the winch for last.

This was the most valuable piece by far, repository of all his dreams, but it was also over four hundred pounds and just the thought of seeing it end up in the bottom of the lake made him crazy. It had taken several days to lower it without making too much noise along the cliffs and steep slopes of the forest. It had proved much smoother for him to carry it across the meadow towards the chasm on wooden rollers, then up to the departure station with the help of the movable pulley.

At the moment of transfer, given that the steel cable was welded to the hub, he would unwind it all from the reel and fix it to the arrival trunk with a carabiner. So not only would that relieve a lot of the winch's weight, but he would also have a way to recover it by means of the cable if the box were to be dropped from the hook, even though he ran the risk of having to go down and dump it in case he could not get it back before dawn. As a precaution, he had also wrapped the restraining rope around a branch of the plant at the origin, which would allow him to both restrain the load more easily thanks to the friction offered by the bark, as well as operate on the edge of the chasm from which point he would be able to oversee the proceedings of the entire operation.

As soon as he undid the noose that held the bracket, Marco immediately felt the enormity of the weight and had to lean forward to avoid winding up upside down. At first everything went smoothly and he continued to guide the cable hand after hand in a slow and uniform motion, but when the load passed the halfway mark, all of a sudden he felt a vibration in the air, as though in spite of all his precautions the cable stretched between the two plants was lowered enough for his hair to brush against it.

Marco went cold. If the load dropped even lower, then it could be stranded on the edge of the chasm and then it would be a super-human feat to recover it by the strength of arms alone. Panicking, he then began to work the rope in long strokes until it nearly flew between his fingers and he did not stop until he heard the distant clang of a metal box against the arrival trunk. Drunk with joy and not caring at all about the noise pollution, the man crossed the bridge in a flash and ran to embrace the pile of junk that had not betrayed him, then performed for it his usual shamanic dance as a way of showing thanks.

Chapter 29

As overworked and overwhelmed by his labors as he was, Marco had never missed his nightly meeting and never on one occasion did he neglect to pay homage to his distant companion with some little gift. But she was not to be outdone and, ever punctual with their meeting time, she had continued to search for the presence of her unknown lover without ever betraying herself to her companions. The suitor was well aware of the risks they were both running, but these meetings had become his only reason for living and, for some time now, an integral part of his crazy plan.

He committed himself to this for the entire winter. The spray of the waterfall, though greatly reduced, still produced more than enough noise to allow him to work in its vicinity without overdoing it with the mallet and the ax like he did in the days of the thaw. With his new tools and proven nail method, he managed to take down another small pine in a reasonable amount of time, and once he stripped it of branches he carried in on the usual rollers to the waterfall beside the tree that had saved him and Karl almost three years ago. This was apparently still in good condition, but the long exposure to water could have made it rot inside and he, not at all willing to run risks, had shouldered the considerable amount of work in that thankless, additional task. And only after having attached the two trunks under the arch of the waterfall did he feel comfortable hanging the pulley.

Then he started on the winch. After having planted it a few meters from the waterfall, he fastened it securely to four poles planted deep in the ground and, exaggerating his precautions, nailed it to the earth with four long, iron pegs. Some time ago he had condemned himself to assemble the many pieces of a heavy wooden wheel with a crank-fitted hub that was situated on the pins of two planks planted behind the winch, linking it to the first gear of this same by way of a driving belt and, the instant in which the trunk could no longer contain all of the cable necessary for the operation, he pierced the side and added a coaxial capstan fixed to the roller. End result: a system of advantageous, rotating levers that were capable of allowing their operator to lift impossible weights with minimal effort. He had to work a little to give the heavy wheel—which also functioned as a flywheel—some momentum, but when it picked up speed, the power of inertia kept it going almost on its own. The cold season, which had not slowed the activity of the indefatigable worker, who during the long winter nights had brought a bit of homework and, with the help of the omnipotent creepers, had made a good basket that was lightweight and durable which would be attached to the cable. There was nothing left to add.

It was the beginning of spring, his third spring in the crater, when Marco weighted the basket with some stones and began to lower it down. The waterfall was showing the first signs of the thaw and day after day it traced a wider, more impressive arc, allowing the basket to descend behind it without danger of being hit by the jet of water or noticed from the outside.

The only downside of the whole system of rotating levers was that they unrolled the cable with maddening slowness: six turns of the crank to move down one meter, sixty for ten, four hundred and twenty for the lone steel cable. Every hundred turns of the crank, Marco stopped the wheel and ran to look out over the precipice to make sure that the cable was not whipping right and left, and continued to inspect its movements even when the basket was already long vanished between the sprays of the waterfall.

Everything was going as planned, but not all the difficulties had been dealt with yet. At that point, Marco needed to do his calculations well. Combining the steel cable with the climbing rope and

162

then the rope he had found in the helicopter, he obtained three hundred meters of cable. At a guess, more than enough to cover the distance that separated the meadow from the lake. But he could not settle for approximate calculations; he had to know precisely the distance between the pulley and the surface of the water, but he certainly could not do so by arming the basket with buoys because the rope, which was heavy enough with that already, would always be stretched with tension. Marco already had, however, a solution in store for this last problem.

The helicopter's alternator contained a coil of copper wire as thin as a human hair, but durable and endlessly long. After passing it through the pulley, he tied a weighted buoy underneath, made from leather and foam padding taken from a seat of the helicopter, and lowered it slowly down. His destination seemed unattainable, and while the coil unwound rapidly between his hands he had a growing fear that this was not the greatest idea. He was beginning to despair when suddenly the thread lost tension: "*Ai suma!*" he said excitedly, and immediately brought the cable back to tension and dropped it back in the water several times to be sure of the result. At that point, after making a sign of recognition, he began to recover the copper cable without rewinding the coil, but walking backwards through the grass: two-hundred meters was the final verdict. One thousand, four hundred and fifty-eight turns of the crank and a good quarter of an hour of elbow grease separated him from the lake.

Chapter 30

Marco had ceased sending the girl his daily tributes. A few days ago he sent the drawings, made on scraps of writing pads, depicting the waterfall, the lake and the terrace as they should appear to the eyes of someone who was looking from the opposite shore. The final touch: at the bottom on the left, a small still life depicting an ear of corn, a pumpkin, a tomato and their respective seeds. Marco was well aware that the paper on which these messages was drawn, which was unknown to the valley, added danger to the danger, but it was time to risk it all.

After slipping the little "landscape" into an eggshell sealed and weighted properly, he sent it down to his beloved who, punctual as usual, was waiting in the usual place. For several nights in a row he sent the same message. She, he thought, would certainly be racking her brain to understand why the images were so endlessly repetitive, but this itself was the provocation, because at a certain point, when the preparations were coming to an end, he modified the drawing by adding ten well-defined, long, black lines in the top right corner. Which became nine the next evening, then eight, then seven, six, and so on until the last message with just a single mark.

On this he had drawn the girl in the act of swimming along the route of an arrow that led under the arc of the waterfall, where the basket and the cable leading to the terrace appeared with the stylized figure of a man intent on retrieving it. He could not have done a better job; the message would be more than clear to her.

That night Marco did not manage to sleep a wink. "Let her understand!" he kept praying, tossing and turning in his bed without finding respite.

There was still light the next evening when Marco began to slowly lower the basket. In the days prior he had repeated the operation so many times that he had already memorized the exact number of turns of the crank that separated it from the lake. At the end of the rope, he halted the winch and walked towards his usual observation point.

He was quite ahead of time. The fishermen had just moved the boat to shore and were unloading baskets of fish, and in the fields and vegetable gardens beyond the clearing, the farmers had not yet retired their tools in their little huts.

The minutes seemed like hours, never passing. After an agonizing wait, the night fell suddenly, but Marco still had to wait for the arrival of the much-anticipated procession. On the other hand, from that moment on, everything happened with astonishing speed. Having exchanged just a few words with her friends the girl walked swiftly across the shore, and after having stripped, rather than putting her tunic on the rocks she made a bundle, tied it with the cord that she wore at her waist and squatted on the ground to tinker with her ankle.

Marco continued to spy on her every move with trepidation. The shadow of the rocks did not allow him to see what she was doing, but he knew, wanted, needed to believe that this unusual behavior could only mean one thing, but he could not take it for granted. The whole operation only took a few seconds, then the girl plunged into the water and moved away from the shore with slow, regular strokes.

Come on, keep it up, don't stop, Marco urged her, swimming with her all the way, and when he saw her freeze at the point where she used to stop in expectation of the usual message, his heart stopped with her. It began to beat wildly when she, after a moment's hesitation, began to swim with greater vigor and determination than

165

before, heading straight in the right direction. And when she was hidden from view, disappearing below the terrace, he almost flew as he raced to the waterfall to halt a step from the precipice. There, after harpooning the cable with a grapnel and stretching it to him with all his strength, he sat down to wait.

Marco almost took it for granted that with the full thaw, there would certainly not have been dead calm down there. To help the young girl reach her goal more easily and mitigate at least part of the fibrillations, he had added three floats with a meter of vine holding each. Despite this, the worm of doubt never ceased dogging him. "Let's hope she finds it in the middle of all that mess...in the dark...in the cold..." he continued to agonize while the rod sent him irregular, repeated vibrations from the cable that weighed a ton and he had to work like the devil to be able to keep it in tension. But it was not the fatigue that wore him down.

After an exhausting wait, he thought he felt a jerk. His heart jumped into his throat. Another wrench, harder this time, then the cable was stretched taut. "She's there, she's there, she's there!" he cried, letting go of everything and jumping to his feet. Marco reached the winch in a heartbeat, leaned forwards, unfastened the snare from the wheel and gripped the handle with both hands. As eager as he was to re-cover his dear, he forced himself to be calm. The basket should have been far enough away from the cascade and the swimmer should have been able to come across quite easily with the help of the buoys, but the whirlpools and eddies of the currents could hinder her attempts to climb aboard and it would be an unforgivable mistake to ruin everything in haste after so much toil.

Soon, however, he decided. His heart skipped a beat when, at the first turn of the handle, he felt no resistance. But he quickly re-covered when, after three more seemingly unladen revolutions, he felt the sensation of something heavier than usual: "She's there, she's there. Yes, she's there. She's there, she's there!" he repeated endlessly in a mixture of hope and excitement as he reeled in the cable. He was crushed by two conflicting desires: on the one hand, the thought of the girl being naked and exposed to the cold lash of the waterfall urged him to turn the handle as quickly as possible; on the other hand, the fear that a reckless maneuver could unbalance the basket and make it fall into the void made his skin crawl. So he tried to pretend that in the basket there was the usual ballast from his trial runs, but it was impossible to think that way.

It was the lock of the hand wheel that warned him, while he was still lost in these reasonings, that the basket had arrived at its destination. After fixing the crank firmly two turns in the opposite direction so that the cable would not be too tight, he immediately locked it and, in an excess of zeal, picked up an iron bar from the ground and slipped it sideways into the winch's gears to further block it. Then, finally reassured, he ran towards the waterfall.

Along the journey that separated him from his goal, he pulled the small flashlight from the bag at his hip, the one that had made a narrow escape at the time of the disaster. The batteries, though jealously guarded and sealed always in a piece of cellophane, were almost depleted and the flashlight emitted a light so dim that it barely lit his toes. Nevertheless, as soon as he reached the edge of the precipice, Marco directed the equally weak beam of light towards the spot, just below the level of the meadow, where he would find the basket.

She was there, curled up on herself and protected solely by the mantle of her long hair, which almost entirely swathed her shoulders and back. She was visibly shivering from the cold, but as soon as she noticed the light she lifted her head and the palm of her hand in greeting, perhaps, but more likely to better focus in the backlight on the person who was illuminating her. Strands of wet hair hid her forehead and face, but it was not the time to stand there and stare.

Clamping the flashlight between his teeth, Marco picked up a ladder fitted with hooks off the ground, slid it downwards, hooked it to the basket and anchored it to the edge of the terrace: "Come quickly!" he yelled, motioning with a hand to come up. He certainly did not think that he was addressing a multilingual, but the gesture had to have a universal value. The girl, in fact, did not make him repeat it and slipped the bundle, which was still tied to her ankle, under her arm and gripped the ladder, quickly reached the summit and, after a moment's hesitation, grabbed the outstretched hand.

Chapter 31

The first, magical contact with that little hand which was so cold but full of trust would remain indelibly imprinted in his mind. Marco, terrified by the idea of losing her at the last moment, pulled her with all his might; the girl was lighter than expected and almost fell on top of him and made him lose his balance. They fell onto the grass entwined, and to anyone who would have seen them then, embracing and illuminated by the faint light of the flashlight on the ground, would have taken them for a pair of lovers who had known each other forever.

They stayed like that, in silence, pressed against one another, while time seemed to stand still. Marco had closed his eyes, thinking he was dreaming, he did not want to be roused for any reason and he came to himself only when he felt the uncontrolled tremors of the little body in his arms. Cursing his chronic absentmindedness, he broke the embrace, jumped to his feet, pulled off his jacket and immediately helped the girl put it on, fastening the zipper on the front, while she obediently and wordlessly helped him do so. Then he took her by the hand and, still unable to believe the miracle, led her down the path to the shelter.

Occasionally he turned to illuminate the narrow pathway for her with the flashlight. And he never ceased talking: "Watch that bramble…There's a rock here…Here there's a step…" He intended to reassure her with his voice, but at the same time he was letting off all the accumulated tension from that endless, incredible day. It did not take long for them to reach their destination: "Here, sit down here," Marco told her as he accompanied her to the dark bench in front of the fireplace after he closed the door behind him. Wasting no time, he kneeled down on the ground, pushed aside the ashes with one hand, leaned a bunch of thin strands of straw against the few remaining embers and began to gently blow on it several times. He felt the girl's watchful eyes upon him, and he was dying to turn around and look at her face, but he knew that she was shaking from the cold in spite of his jacket; he had to warm the room before anything else.

When the flame sprang up, he added a handful of straw and increasingly thicker twigs until he had arranged two logs that immediately took to glowing and crackling with a beautiful flame, hot and fragrant. The fire became more intense almost right away, slowly illuminating every corner of the room, and Marco turned to his spectator with a triumphant expression: "*Ai suma!*" he was about to proclaim, but the fateful words died in his throat, and as though thunderstruck he was unable to get up. Long, raven-black hair framed an enchanting face. Mirroring the lapping tongues of flame, two big black eyes were fixated on him with an ecstatic expression, and in those long, vaguely Egyptian eyes Marco read an ocean of antithetical feelings: fear, admiration, shyness, gratitude, awe, trepidation. The line of her thin, black eyebrows was intense faded upwards, giving her eyes an exotic and terribly fascinating quality. Her high, pronounced cheekbones accentuated a tiny, perfect nose. Her warm and sensual rosebud lips opened to a set of small teeth whose whiteness created a wonderful contrast with the slightly sallow skin of her face.

His mouth wide open, Marco was unable to tear his gaze from the heavenly vision: "But…but you're really a goddess!" He said, reaching out a hand to brush her cheek as though to reassure himself that he was not dreaming.

In all probability, she was running through the same considerations because with the caress her lips parted in a dazzling, childish smile: "Ctzatzichi," Marco thought he understood, hearing the crystal clear sound of her voice for the first time. "Catizachii"—or something similar—the girl repeated, pressing her index finger to her chest to indicate herself. But the man was not listening, he was in another dimension that no longer had contact with the earthly world, because the melodious sound of that voice coming from the empyrean creature had abducted his soul. "Chatiztacqui," she insisted.

It was the slight change in the girl's expression, as she was evidently fearful of not being understood, that brought him back to planet earth. Shaking from the state of ecstatic contemplation into which he had suck, Marco reciprocated with a warm smile. "Marco," he said quickly, imitating her gesture as he pointed to himself. "I'm Marco."

"Maaco?" she asked.

"No, Marco."

"Maaco!"

"No, listen" Ma-ar-co" he said, articulating each syllable of his name.

"Ma-aa-co," the girl said conclusively.

"Yes, no problem, Maaco is fine," he conceded euphorically. "And you, Chatì," he added in return, compromising with the business of names. The pronunciation problems were the least of his concerns at the time, and what he wanted above all else was to reassure the girl. He was terrified that the cave in which he lived, the food he would offer her, the isolation to which he confined her would disappoint her, disgust her. He wanted to amaze her, astound her with objects unknown to her, but he feared that these objects could scare her and by consequence raise a barrier of distrust and fear between them.

She was beautiful. More than once in the past as he watched from afar, he thought he saw a bit of peculiarity in the skin and facial features of her and her companions, different from those of other women in the valley, as though they belonged to a different race. He told himself that his impression was probably owed to the fact that he saw the former only in the dead of night by the dim torchlight, and the latter always in broad daylight. The fact is that Marco, having been struck by her extraordinary and unexpected beauty, was blown away and for the first time in his life he was insecure of his own physical appearance. Who knows how she sees me, he found himself thinking.

The idea that she might not be pleased froze him. In the long months of waiting, as he prefigured the moment of their meeting, he had prepared countless speeches and explanatory gestures with the goal of breaking the ice, of making a good first impression…But instead he stayed put and stock-still, looking at her with a stupid smile on his face, unable to articulate the slightest words, shifting his body weight from one foot to the other from time to time in an awkward manner.

It was she who took the initiative.

Embracing her while she slept under a sleeping bag which was widened so as to form a single cover, Marco could not get to sleep even though it was already the middle of the night. Chatì had to be around eighteen years old but she was already a woman in every way and the man could not help but wonder why she had no children, as almost all of her companions did—even those who appeared to be younger than her. He stroked her hair softly so as not to wake her as he admired her magnificent facial features, just barely illuminated by the soft glow of the dying fire, and he could not help but think back to Karl's words.

When, in the solitude and despair of days gone by, would he have been able to imagine that the valley that he feared and hated would give him a gift that he had vainly sought at the very ends of the earth? He had just barely learned her name, but he felt that he had never loved a woman with such transport and consuming passion. Contrary to what had always happened, not only had he felt no ebb in his desire once he had reached his coveted objective, but he felt something irrepressible within himself, something he had never felt before in his existence. "You were right, Karl, this is a great place to die, but also to live. And I am finally alive. And I want to live this life to the fullest."

Moreover, everything made him believe that she, after having sought him out without even knowing him and giving her whole self without asking anything in return, reciprocated his feelings in full measure and it could not have been youthful recklessness that would push her to embark on an adventure from which she would not return. No; given her actions throughout the entire ordeal, her choice was a reasoned one, the choice of a mature woman who was master of her own actions.

Chapter 32

The new presence revolutionized his daily living in a radical way. Finally he had a reason for living, a purpose to fight for. The woman that he felt he loved more than himself had given him a tremendous gift, perhaps undeserved, and he now wished to reciprocate by fulfilling her every desire. But it was Chatì who heaped him with many other prodigious gifts before he could do anything in return.

It happened on the morning following "the abduction." She was still sleeping deeply when Marco, before the sun rose, had slipped out of bed and tired to noiselessly rekindle the fire. He wanted her to wake up to a warm room and a welcome breakfast, but in his stealthy bustle of preparations he tripped on her tunic, which was forgotten under the bench. The man cursed as he realized, collecting it from the ground, that despite the proximity of the fire it was still a sopping mess. If he had hung it out to dry the night before it would have been ready to wear by now, because his wardrobe had little to offer the newcomer.

Contrite and determined to quickly remedy his inattentiveness, he untied the cord that bound the tunic and unrolled it, but in the act of draping it over a chair next to the fireplace he felt several strange lumps. His heart skipped a beat. Summoning all the patron saints, he began groping the protrusions with an expert hand, seeking tactile confirmation of his diagnosis, but when he got nothing from it he decided to turn the garment inside out. He was not mistaken: hanging here and there inside the tunic, there were a number of canvas pouches with a white wax-like film that was waterproof. Each as large as a pants pocket and almost full to bursting, Marco knew that they contained exactly what he wanted. Manners told him to wait for the owner's awakening before opening them, but the temptation was too great and he impulsively opened one and spilled the contents into the palm of his hand.

A handful of perfectly dry pumpkin seeds came out and he, unrepentant of his transgression, ecstatically contemplated the invaluable asset for a long time before putting it back in the bag, being careful not to drop any on the ground. Then, as if seized by maniacal rapture, he rushed to open the other pouches. Out came kernels of corn, small potatoes from which sprung tender roots, pepper seeds and many, many other varieties of seed both known and foreign.

"Ah, les femmes!" he said at one point, sniffing the aroma given off by a small earthenware container that he had just unwrapped, found inside a bag. But in a not too distant future he would be putting his foot in his mouth for this chauvinistic review: "Well done, well done, well done, Chatì!" he repeated, choking down exclamations of joy with every new discovery. He longed to run and wake her up so he could hug her, kiss her and thank her for having outclassed all his expectations.

He approached the bed. She was sleeping the sleep of the just, curled up in the fetal position. The sleeping bag had fallen slightly from her shoulders and despite the shadows Marco noticed the reddish scars left on her back by the whip, and that mutilation caused all of his anger against the perpetrator to well up inside him again: "But how could you…fucker! How could you do harm to…to…May you burn in hell with all those around you!" he proclaimed. He did not want to interrupt that innocent sleep, but he could not resist: "Chatì," he called, sitting down on the bed next to her. After some feeble protesting, the sleeping beauty squinted her still-sleepy eyes which suddenly widened in an expression of alarm, but they soon focused on the well-known face and the bewilderment faded instantly, giving way to a sweet, serene look while the smile of a happy little girl appeared on her angelic lips.

She whispered the man's name softly, drawing him to her.

They woke in the early afternoon as hungry as wolves. Marco began to prepare lunch, as she carefully followed his every move and let out repeated exclamations of wonder at the sight of objects which to her eyes must have looked like so many devilish contraptions. Chati's wonder amused him, and he began speaking to her, describing the various objects that were unknown to her. Then he had an idea: he went to pick up one of the bags found inside the tunic, slid a few kernels of maize into the palm of his hand, and showed them to the girl questioningly. "Mahis," she said. "Mahis, mahis," she repeated insistently, showing that she had understood the intent of the question.

It was thus that Marco began learning an ancient, unknown language whose sounds had died in the night of time and, thanks to the patience and intelligence of his new companion, slowly came to unravel the mysteries of the terrible and fascinating people of the valley whose remote origins were lost between reality and legend.

The gods had bestowed upon their earthly children the Garden of the Curved Mountain, where the Holy People lived in peace without knowing the sufferings of hunger, disease, death. Only one thing was forbidden: no child of the gods could ever leave the Sacred Soil. A man hungry for knowledge, however, had dared to defy the law of the gods and had secretly crossed the sacred boundaries. He return to the Mountain years later, by which time no one thought they would see him again. He brought the seed of evil with him. The council of elders sentenced him to life imprisonment, but it was too late. The man's stories of the magnificence of the places he had visited and of the many people he had encountered during his long absence had enchanted many of the inhabitants, who came to rebel against the will of the sages. The people then began a fratricidal war and death, torment, and desolation broke out in the Curved Mountain.

The gods, outraged at the ignorance of their ungrateful children who would not settle for that which they were given, enacted their terrible vengeance on the valley. And a mysterious disease claimed men, women, the elderly, youths and children, who began to die one after the other. The few survivors then decided to leave the Garden of the Gods, promising that they would return once they had atoned for the transgression and the wrath of the gods had subsided. Gonna the Explorer guided them, and their journey was long and arduous. Wherever they trod, enemies were ready to chase them away or capture and enslave them. And many others perished by the wiles of the journey, by hunger and disease. But one day the miserable group of survivors came to the Mountain of the Sun, a land of delights teeming with vegetation and food and, most crucially, uninhabited. They decided to stop there and for centuries the Holy People lived in peace and prospered in total freedom.

However, the gods had not yet fully savored their vengeance, and just when the People had become convinced of having found their final dwelling place, they sent a new and even harsher punishment. Not far from the Mountain of the Sun there lived a warrior people whose appetite for conquest was never satiated, and who constantly fought with the neighboring nations. They lived in an immense city located in the middle of a lake, rendered impregnable by the surrounding waters. A fantastic city with roofs of gold, whose canteens were continuously filled with fish, birds and rare fruits that were given in offering by the subjugated populations.

Enchanted by such magnificence, the inhabitants of the Mountain of the Sun adopted the language and customs of the People of the Lake and many also took to worshipping their gods, who proved so benevolent towards those powerful people. But the People of the Lake did not accept their friendship. On the contrary, they fought and subdued them like all the others, and demanded from them increasingly weighty tributes of gold, feathers, precious stones and, above all, lives to be sacrificed to their terrible gods.

And for the Holy People, the greatest punishment was yet to come. One day the white-skinned men came from the sea. They possessed terrible weapons, capable of killing from incredible distances and blow through even the most resistant shields as though they were dry leaves. They fought on fearful monsters and wore clothes of hard metal that neither sword nor arrow nor spear could scratch. The People of the Lake welcomed them as children of the god who had abandoned their land, and headed towards the point where the sun god Tonatiuh appeared, but with the promise to one day return. But this was mistaken, and the mistake was paid for in blood.

Even the people of the Mountain of the Sun were deceived by the men who came from the sea. With promises of freedom, slaves, wealth and new lands they joined forces to fight the oppressor, but in doing so sealed their own fate. When the lake city was conquered and all its people subjugated and enslaved, the white-skinned man not only reneged upon his promises, he began fighting against, looting and exterminating their former allies. The People then asked their gods forgiveness for having repudiated them and, convinced that they had at last atoned for all their sins, they retrieved the scroll bearing the path of Gonna the Explorer and went in search of the Curved Mountain. The return journey was no less harsh than that which had brought them to the Mountain of the Sun, but guiding them was Theoticatl, a young, brave and wise *tlatoani* who knew how to instill confidence in his people in the most difficult moments of deepest despair, and who led them after endless sufferings and hardships all the way to their long-awaited destination.

And when the people took ownership of that ancient, sacred ground, Theoticatl gave the order to forever seal the only entrance to the valley so that the children could not commit the error of their fathers, and then he ordered them to thank the gods for having guided his steps and thereby forgiving the ancient misdeeds; at the point where the river entered the mountain he built a stone altar on which all the *tlatlacotin* who had accompanied the exiles on their journey were sacrificed.

None of the people could get out of the Curved Mountain, and every stranger who dared to cross its sacred boundaries would be given in sacrifice to the gods. Only the slaves taken from the white-skinned man were allowed to live in the Garden. They became the exclusive property of the *tlatoani*, who could dispose of their lives as they pleased, and over the centuries all of their male children were sacrificed to the gods so that all the powers of their old infamous enemy were transferred to the warriors of the Holy People. Chatì was thus the great granddaughter of those slaves.

Chapter 33

Marco had devoted several months and met with no small number of difficulties in order to understand and piece together the various fragments of the long and fantastic story which he was still struggling to believe, despite the irrefutable evidence that bridged the many gaps and gave a logical explanation to several of his questions. In the early days, when he had not yet mastered the girl's language, he interrupted her all the time, sometimes to repeat an unpronounceable word a few times, sometimes to work to comprehend the meaning of a phrase, but with his mastery of the new language his requests for explanations had become even more pressing, so urgent was his desire to penetrate yet deeper into the mysteries of the unknown, timeless people.

Chatì had immediately proved herself to be an unparalleled, infinitely patient teacher, but although she was also animated by a great thirst for knowledge, she did not have her student's predilection for learning languages. With time the two had reached a sort of compromise by adopting a particular dialect: that of the valley enriched with numerous expressions borrowed here and there from Italian, English, French, or even totally made up. And day after day the two strangers came to understand one another and communicate, managing to convey their respective states of mind.

Chatì explained how the first *tlatoque*, the sovereigns, were righteous and honest men, and even though they had the power of life and death over slaves, they developed a great respect for them. They were also loving, caring fathers to their daughters, and to make the terrible detachment of the male children from their mothers less painful, they had them taken to the temple, which was called *teo-calli,* immediately after birth.

At the beginning even a *macehualtin,* simply a citizen, could aspire to the insignia of the *pipiltin* nobility if not, indeed, to that of the great orator. At the head of various orders only capable men of great value were named, and only the most deserving *pipiltin,* who were honest and had years of experience, could become part of the council of wise men. But with the passage of time, the most powerful *pipiltin* reached an agreement among themselves and resorted more and more to deception and violence, making it so that the high insignia became hereditary. The power was thus passed into the hands of a few families, which would become ever richer and more powerful.

And evil was heaped upon evil. The two high priests, the *tlamacazqui,* were always appointed by the council while the *tlatoani* was elected either by the council or by the *tlamacazqui.* According to the law of the Book, the priests had to devote themselves exclusively to the care of the temple, to officiating the sacred rites and to teaching the *tlamacazcalli.* While the insignia were being limited to the hands of a few, the *tlamacazqui*—who always came from the richest and most powerful families and were certainly not accustomed to living on donations alone—wound up abandoning the old rule and used their power to begin demanding ever richer tributes to the *teocalli* and asking greater privileges for themselves every day.

The offerings to the temple turned into obligations, and with the accumulated fortunes the *tlamacazqui* began to buy the support of many more powerful councilors and *pipiltin* and thereby to control the council's decisions, amending many rules in the ancient Book.

The stature of the god Xipe Totec was thus removed from the temple to make way for the old gods of the old enemy of the lake. And from that day on the Holy People was forced to worship Tlaloc, god of the earth and rain, Huitzilopochtli, god of the *tlatoani* and war, and above all, Quetzalcoatl, the serpent god, in whose name the Order of the Serpent was founded; in theory this was the guard of the great orator, in practice it was an army in the service of the priests.

When several *pipiltin* realized the accumulated power of the *tlamacazqui* they tried to restore the old order, but it was too late. Some of them were stripped of the insignia and forced to live as simple *macehualtin,* but many, many others were secretly eliminated. It was then that the *pipiltin* who had been deprived of their insignia rebelled and led the revolt of the *tecuhtli,* the dignitaries of the countryside, but this was quickly suppressed and curbed with violence; the few survivors of the massacre were enslaved and used to construct the city walls, called Aplaia, to protect it from new revolts. And when the last wise *tlatoani,* now deprived of all power, tried to rebel against the sacerdotal order, one morning he was found dead, poisoned, in the bed of one of the slaves. Blamed for his death, she was forced under torture to confess to the crime she had not committed and then dragged to the top of the pyramid to be stripped of her life and her skin.

With the support of the councils at their service, for nearly forty years now the *tlamacazqui* only allowed stupid, corrupt *tlatoque* who were obedient to their will to be elected. The slaves of the great orator had become their slaves and those who did not submit to their wishes wound up on the sacrificial stone; their male children were no longer delivered to the temple at the time of birth, but raised to adolescence and sent to be sacrificed only after being forced to fulfill the hidden desires of some *pipiltin,* many aspiring priests and the *tlatoani,* thereby breaking their mothers' hearts twice.

Chitoontecl—this was the name of the *tlamacazqui* who had whipped Chatì—had had his eyes on her from the moment she reached puberty, but he had never managed to make her capitulate. The young woman's refusal must have deeply wounded his immeasurable pride and, though it was difficult to believe, break even his stony heart. Because the horrible man had proceeded to pester her even more than before rather than send her to be sacrificed, he went so far as to forbid any man from touching her, even with just one look. One day, after yet another rejection the proposals turned to threats, up to the point where he promised her that if she had not ceded to him within twelve lunar months he would take her by force and then drag her to the top of the pyramid so he could skin her alive with his own two hands.

But it was not just the slaves who were persecuted by the priest. The entire population except for the few families who still retained some power lived in fear of winding up in his clutches, or in those of his worthy servant Mohotzuma. Additionally, with the return to the rite of the People of the Lake, all the youths who had reached puberty—except, of course, the children of the powerful *pipiltin*—became part of the warrior orders of the eagle and jaguar, and every five years, after long, hard training, they faced each other in the Flower War: a bloody battle in which each of them had to capture alive those who until recently had been brothers and friends to offer in sacrifice to the gods in order to obtain the coveted insignia of the serpent, whose benefits were enjoyed by him and his family. The wives of the warriors who were killed or sacrificed were also sacrificed, or sent to work in the stone quarry along with the *tlatlacotin* or—and this was only for the most beautiful and desirable—given as gifts to the more faithful *pipiltin.*

In the course of her long stories, Chatì was often overwhelmed with sadness and could not hold back her tears when she thought of the fate of her friends whom she had abandoned in the valley. In particular that of her sister Xeetha: her son was the boy whose sacrifice Marco had witnessed. The father of the two women was the former commander of the Order of the Serpent, a hard man, but fair and brave. To ingratiate himself to him, the *tlamacazqui* had given him a slave of the *tlatoani,* who was loved and respected as a true wife, and his daughters had cause to fear nothing while he was alive. But one night an unknown hand had struck him in the back while he was heading home, and before his body was finished burning on the pyre his banners had already passed into the hands of Puqutec, a stupid, dishonorable man who was a faithful servant of Mohotzuma, who sacrificed their mother and sent her and her sister to become slaves.

"We have to do something for those poor girls," Chatì repeated continually. "We cannot abandon them to their miserable fate," and Marco, on hearing the report of so many misdeeds, had adopted the woman's sentiments. He was distraught when he saw her sad and anguished when the talk turned to her friends, and he would do anything to alleviate her suffering. But his selfish instincts prevented him from acting; he could not, did not want to jeopardize the greatest gift he had ever received in his life. Nevertheless, a daring and extremely dangerous plan was already taking shape in his mind.

Chapter 34

He already had everything needed to achieve this feat at his disposal. Nevertheless, it took some time to put in place. With a few poles and the flexible, durable branches of a plant that were similar to rattan, he replaced the basket pulley with a cage that was two square meters in which ten people could fit, if uncomfortably. Meanwhile, Chatì's small, delicate hands had become calloused from braiding fibers of portentous vines to amass a rope as thick as a wrist which, combined with the climbing rope, reached a length equal to that of the cable winch. At regular intervals, they had added rings for hands and feet which could both assist in climbing on and off and to stop and catch one's breath.

The plan was to lower the booth with the winch while the new rope, attached to the same logs from which the cage hung, would be dropped. The cables together would not reach the water, and the remaining twenty meters would be spanned by a rope ladder attached to a trap door in the middle of the floor. Marco, after having lowered both Chatì and the cage, would join her a moment later by coming down the later, and then they would descend to the lake by way of the ladder.

The idea of not making the cage descend all the way to the surface of the water offered a double advantage: it reduced the weight of the rope and they could pick up the ladder in just a few seconds, thereby preventing the possibility of any unwanted access to the cage. As for the weapons they would carry, Marco had first thought to use the submachine guns, but immediately shelved the idea; to give the entire group of women and children enough time

185

to escape, the whole operation would have to be carried out in complete silence. He had to find a more discreet solution, which came to him from the bars in the cockpit seats, which were similar to the bows of crossbows.

Marco had to make several attempts before he was able to develop a prototype of a powerful weapon that was accurate and easily reloaded. That done, it was effortless for him to build an identical one in much less time, and then use a small file to refine some small pieces of sheet metal to create many slender arrowheads. But even Chatì had done her part to prove herself invaluable by crafting highly resistant strings to fit the bows, then by finding the most suitable sticks of wood on which to apply the arrowheads and directional feathers.

While the two finalized preparations and tested the whole system with almost obsessive pedantry, for some time now in the clearing beside the lake there was a whole succession of dignitaries and workers laboring to fence the area in, to raise golden canopies covered with feathered tapestries and everywhere raise multicolored banners, flags and pennants. For their part, the youth had intensified their daily exercises in the middle of the lawn, often drawing them out late into the evening; they were preparing for the terrible Flower War.

On the day, just as with other fateful events, the two were awakened early by the prolonged sound of the horns from the valley. Despite the hour, there were already a lot of people massed around the fenced perimeter and many other villagers were coming from the city and the entire suburb, and when the well-known royal procession arrived at its destination shortly thereafter, there was not a living soul in the lake, the fields, the gardens or any road of Aplaia. Marco and Chatì followed the development of the event with a mixture of curiosity and trepidation, passing the binoculars repeatedly between them while she briefed him on the details: "The short man seated on the throne at the center of the stage is *tlatoani* Cuzupuma, the great orator…even though the only great thing about him is his belly and his bottom. The old man who is being carried on shoulder is Taoquazatl, the elderly *tlamacazqui*. And the one behind him is that dog Chitoontecl…but you already know him."

In truth, Marco did not need an introduction for any of the three; their faces had been indelibly imprinted in his mind. Instead, it was a completely new face that drew his attention, that of a character who at that time was assuming his place behind the two highest priests: "Mohotzuma!" Chatì exclaimed, anticipating his query and betraying with her voice a rage and contempt comparable only to that which she expressed in pronouncing the name of the hated *tlamacazqui*.

The man, who was wearing a gray tunic bigger than himself, clashed more than a little with his simple vestment in the middle of the crowd of dignitaries wrapped in gorgeous cloaks; he would even have been mistaken for one of the many lackeys in their service if everyone present were not moving away obsequiously in his wake. Chatì had described him countless times, but Marco had never gotten to see him in the flesh before. More bones than flesh, when the lenses brought a gaunt, sunken face into focus, whose ashen pallor— very much comparable to the color of his tunic—was interrupted only by two gloomy, dark circles topped by equally dark and bushy eyebrows and a completely bald head. This image fully confirmed his partner's description: the drawn, ageless face elicited a shiver just by watching it.

Mohotzuma, she explained to him, was Chitoontecl's murderous hand; Chitoontecl was the one who was entrusted with the *tlamacazqui*'s dirty work. He lived and acted in the shadows, unscrupulously eliminating all obstacles interposed between them and their conquest for power on behalf of the priest. Everyone in the valley knew of his misdeeds all too well, but nobody—save few, who were still powerful *pipiltin* belonging to some of the most ancient, noble families—dared go against him. Because the extensive network of spies and informers in his service, as well as the fate reserved for the reckless few who dared to criticize the infamous couple, was equally known to all. The lack of official offices in fact allowed him to act without having to hold himself accountable to anyone for his actions, to the point where he was feared and revered to the same extent as a *tlamacazqui.*

"Emerald Eyes," Chatì suddenly exclaimed, indicating a woman who was coming then. In a beautiful, iridescent robe with a huge, feathered tiara supported by two pages, this last person to arrive was by no means the least important, given the bowing of all present while she climbed the regal staircase with a slow gait to take her place on the second golden throne under the central canopy, in position only slightly lower and further back than the sovereign. Marco had never seen her before, but thanks to his partner's detailed accounts he knew her life and miracles, including the gimmick by which the high priest, in contravention of the written rule, had awarded her to the king as rightful consort.

Chatì went on for a long time briefing him on the dignitaries as they took their seats in the stands on either side of the royal canopy, not only on their respective titles, positions and privileges, but also, in a surprisingly informed manner, on the relevant vices, crimes and power games in which they were relatively embroiled. And at the end of the long explanation—which had generated quite a bit of confusion in the mind of the listener—he could consider each of the notables a tried and true whitefly for having remained completely unscathed by the bloodthirsty arrows of their hostess.

In the meantime, the army was arriving in its entirety. Leading the line were the men of the guard in their distinctive parade uniforms: a long cloak, green on the back and yellowish on the breast, headdresses in the forms of serpents' heads with open mouths through which the faces of the warriors could barely be glimpsed, round shields colored with yellow and green meanders with a stylized image of the serpent god at the center, swords at their sides, leather sandals on their feet.

"The guard of the great orator..." Chatì informed him. "The guard of Chitoontecl, that is to say. They are the most feared warriors of the valley. Today they enjoy many privileges and when they retire from the service they get the best lands with the most robust servants to work them. But things were so different for them when they still wore the insignia of those back there," she continued, pointing to the next two columns of soldiers who were just entering the clearing.

The newcomers exhibited parade uniforms the likes of which Marco had never seen before, and if he had not already been informed by his partner, he would have hardly recognized in them the kids that he had watched compete on that same field for months upon months.

"These here," Chatì continued in reference to the column that had halted at the right-side border of the field, "are the jaguar warriors. Those others, though, are the eagle warriors," she said, pointing to the second column of warriors bearing bizarre headdresses in the shape of bird beaks, directed towards their position at the opposite end of the field. "Those poor guys," she pressed on in a cordial tone, "have been bred from birth for the sole purpose of confronting each other this evil day and fall in that field like so many fresh-cut flowers. They know that most of them will not see the light of day tomorrow, as they know that today they will have to fight each other mercilessly, without looking their friends and brothers in the face. Because only a few will be given the honor of joining the Order of the Serpent and have the fortune not to wind up killed in battle or sacrificed at the top of the pyramid. All the others, even if they are winners, can only hope the next Flower War..."

While Chatì drew out her explanations, the men of the guard were placed around the entire perimeter of the cordoned off area, with the task of at once overseeing the battle's progress and thwarting any head-shots on the spectator's part, as many of them had children, husbands, friends or grandchildren among the contenders. From the eagle and jaguar camps, each consisting of a few dozen men, rose animalistic screams and every warrior sought to intimidate their opponents by waving their long spears in the air, or beating their shields, or feigning daring forays in their ranks, but this was all done especially to self-administer a dose of courage in the face of the impending confrontation.

The deafening noise coming from below seemed to have no end, but at the sound of the horns everyone instantly quieted. In the general silence, the *tlatoani* stood up from his golden seat and walked to the balcony of the central stand where the high priest awaited him, and there he undressed: "Now the Chitoontecl is handing him the agave thorns with which he will pierce the tongue, calves, ear lobes and sacred point. It is a way to thank the gods," Chatì went on to explain. "At the origin of time, the gods shed their blood and that of those vanquished in the battle." Meanwhile, the high priest collected the precious royal blood in a golden cup, and at the end of the gory ritual, dipped a bunch of feathers in it and began to scatter it to the four cardinal points in a kind of auspicious blessing.

The cleansing ceremony had ended. With a new, prolonged sound of horns, the silence of the crowd broke and a ferocious cry arose from the valley. Immediately after, a dozen or so warriors armed with shields and short swords came forward from the ranks of each opposing side, and after staging a sort of ritual dance they hurled themselves against each other with chilling screams, everyone choosing their direct opponent.

Instead of aiming to stab their opponents' weak point and thus earn a quick victory, the duelists sought to prolong the fight as long as possible. Their skill consisted mainly of dodging their opponents' blows while trying to inflict as many wounds as possible, but taking care both not to hit vital points and not to shatter their swords. The crowd went into raptures when a warrior mocked his opponent by hitting him in the back with the flat of his blade, and applauded till their hands chafed when one of the two contenders, dripping with blood from his many wounds and no longer able to stand and grasp his weapon, was overpowered, disarmed and reduced to helplessness by the victor, who handed him alive to the *tlatoani,* who ran over at once. Actually many of those who yielded, in a last, often vain attempt to mock their opponents in extremis, sought death by stabbing themselves with their own weapons or whatever was left of them, and if by chance they succeeded in the attempt, the winner was not praised but booed and jeered at by an angry mob that hurled rotten eggs, tomatoes and even excrement.

The tournament went on like this for the whole morning. Without any delay, the duelists with swords were replaced with ones armed with spears, knives, hooks, or just with their hands wrapped in bandages studded with vitreous slivers. At the end of the battlefield lay fifty corpses strewn with black spots of dried blood, while the largest group of those defeated crouched at the edge of the field with their hands and feet tied behind their backs and surveyed by the men of the guard. Some of them would not survive until the evening with their injuries, but among the ranks of winners there were very few left completely unharmed by the skirmish.

In short, the bodies were piled unceremoniously on a huge pyre hastily prepared at the center of the clearing, and while the scent of burning flesh wafted over the entire crater, the usual procession was directed towards the city and led by the regal party, accompanied by singing and dancing. The defeated army brought up the rear, surrounded by guards of the *tlatoani,* who dragged the dead weight of the injured and the most recalcitrant or moved them by sheer force.

When the long procession reached the main square, the king and the dignitaries made their way to their places in the structure at the center of the square while the priests worked their way up the central staircase of the Great Pyramid; once they reached the top, they brought back the sacrificial altar from the temple on the right. "Soon the *macehualyotl* will begin," Chati went on to explain to Marco, who was increasingly stuck on the fact that it was very hard to focus on the sights, given the distance. After that moment every hero was helped by the guards of the *tlatoani* to begin climbing the central staircase of the great pyramid to the unrelenting rhythm of the drums, bringing his prisoners with him. The first in the long line brought even six or seven with them, and after kneeling to kiss the ground once they reached the altar, they very publicly turned them over to the high priest, receiving in return the coveted insignia of the serpent to the cheers of the crowd. Then, the first prisoner was stripped naked, laid on the sacrificial stone and held in place by four priests' aides, while the *tlamacazqui*'s sharp blade struck his chest like lightning.

The victims succeeded one another without interruption while the blood flowed like lava down the red-tinged steps. As soon as they were removed from the altar the corpses were immediately beheaded, and while their heads were added to the bare skulls of old killings lined up in perfect order in a special shrine, the bodies were sent rolling down the sides of the pyramid and at the bottom were dismembered and the pieces laid out on the hot grilles by other priests' aides.

So the macabre feast was revived, and the crowd satiated itself with the meat of their own children, which even supplied enough to carry home. And it was not over yet: in the evening, twelve women were dragged atop the pyramid in front of another temple, and the scene of hanging and successive quartering was repeated. "They're just a number of the slain warriors' women," Chatì informed him. "The others will be allocated to the mines and the stone quarry or to the service of the winners and the *pipiltin*. And many of them will raise children for the next Flower War."

It was towards the culmination of that endless and tragic ritual that Marco became aware of the metamorphosis that had taken place within him since his arrival. For some time he had been feeling something strange, a kind of inner torment, but he could not identify the reason. He had been horrified and appalled at the sight of his friend's mangled body, and had vomited bile after witnessing the collective sacrifice consummated atop the temple some time later, but new, incredible events had occurred since those early days, scoring and changing his person, cracking his principles, undermining his deepest, most established beliefs at their roots and turning him, day after day, almost unbeknownst to him, into a new being that was quite different from what he was before, but still a stranger to him.

At first, his survival instinct and the constant terror of being discovered and killed like an animal for slaughter dictated his new, compulsory rules for living. Over time, though he almost justified and admired the lost civilization, the never-accepted and unbearable awareness of being deprived forever of his freedom had instilled in him a growing impatience towards his captors. Impatience had turned into deep hatred following the violence inflicted on his wife, whose tales of misdeeds and abuses perpetrated by a few villains among an entire population had created in him a progressive desire for revenge and retribution.

Marco had already perceived this slow change, but no logical explanation ever came to him for the disorienting feeling that tormented him which he, unconsciously, tried to silence and repress every time it reappeared. Suddenly, however, the darkness dissipated before his eyes, and the light of truth struck him with the force of a hammer: he realized that the destruction, massacres and sacrifices through the course of that tragic day had caused him neither nausea nor dismay. Not even pity. He still struggled to admit it, but in that instant he was realizing that the terrible acts of violence and death that he had just witnessed had enraptured, exalted and, at the same time, excited.

So he ceased opposition to the old reasoning and permitted the new being that existed in him to take over, to take possession of his person and pervade him to his deepest roots, transforming him into a new man who he wanted to be: the warrior who was ready to fight and kill. He noticed that this feeling did not bother or frighten him at all, and he realized that neither fear nor the desire for revenge were pushing him down that road, but rather the longing to grapple with and confront the warriors of the valley because he, almost without realizing it and certainly without intending it, had become one of them. Now he had to act.

Chapter 35

Shortly before sunset, Chatì slipped the crossbow's strap over her shoulder and, by way of the ladder which was now permanently fixed to the edge of the terrace, quickly descended into the cage. Once the cage was lowered to the determined point, Marco stopped the winch, walked to the edge of the meadow and went down to grab the rope, using the same ladder. In the days prior he had traveled all the way countless times without any problem, but the thought of Chatì alone in the dark, exposed to icy waters, had blanketed him with an agitation that was such that more than once he stumbled while slipping his foot into the rigs and risked falling. When he reached the cage, night had just fallen.

Before descending, both had coated themselves with a thick layer of grease and soot so as to both blend in and protect themselves from the cold; nevertheless Chatì, who was curled up on herself, was shivering. "Let's go down now," Marco said, holding her to him and rubbing her body vigorously while shouting over the noise of the water. "And stay near me the entire time, please," he continued, sliding first into the hatch. "It's a new moon tonight and you won't see anything down there."

Once in the water, they initially swam backwards until they touched the wall to avoid being sucked in by the currents, and they remained close against it in order to circumvent the waterfall on the left, and after a few meters they began to feel the first warmth of the water coming from the volcanic area, which soon thawed their limbs. At the halfway point they stopped to take a first look. The slaves were already in place, but the scene was not the same as always.

Chatì had not chosen the date at random. From having experienced it before, he knew the custom of singing, dancing and no end of libations to celebrate the entry of new members into the Order of the Serpent, just as he knew there would be a relaxation in surveillance. In fact, as he had foreseen, there were only two warriors following the group. On the other hand—and this, he had not expected—Chitoontecl had brought along two bold youths.

"Damn it!" Marco cursed through his teeth at the sight.

"Oh, don't worry about those," Chatì assured him after a moment of uncertainty. "You see? Their heads are shaved, they're just two students of the *tlamacazcalli* that Chitoontecl usually brings behind him for the evening prize granted to the children of his *pipiltin* friends; they have never seen a naked woman in their lives and they'll be so caught up in choosing their favorite that they won't even have time to notice our presence."

"Let's hope…" said Marco, not so convinced.

As planned, they crossed the lake in a sweeping semicircle to the left, heading upstream first in the direction of the volcanic area to the point of nearly scalding themselves, and then descending back to the valley along the bank in the shelter of the rocks, until they reached the point where Chatì used to dive into the water when she was still a slave among the slaves. Swimming breaststroke so as not to disturb the waters and covered in soot, they were rendered virtually invisible. To be sure Marco had even applied the poultice to his hair, which had recently taken on a salt-and-pepper tone that would have attracted a bit too much attention.

Once ashore, they crept along the waterline until they were just before the cliffs. In total silence they slipped off their crossbows, tensed the bows, fit the arrow nocks to the bowstrings and after having laid them gently on the ground they raised their eyes above the barrier of the boulders just enough to unravel the situation. The embers of the giant pyre had not yet gone out and their feeble glow helped to shed light on the clearing, which was just barely illuminated by the few torches present. As always, the guards were standing in position with their backs turned to the group and at the shore, while the high priest was busy doing the honors of demonstrating the elegance of a completely naked girl to the two students, whose coarse and excited laughter could be heard far behind the rocks.

"God damn it! But soon I'll make you atone for all of them!" Marco hissed between his teeth. "You aim for the sentry on the left, and I'll get the other. Than it'll be better to free ourselves of the two assistants immediately...they'll be harmless as can be, but their legs are too long for my taste. We'll think about Chitoontecl together, afterwards...On my signal, then."

The moment of truth had arrived and Marco, in raising his weapon, suddenly realized with dismay that he had lost all his boldness. His arms had become as heavy as lead and a nauseating cramp was utterly turning his stomach. No, it was not easy to kill a man in cold blood. It was not like shooting at the usual inanimate silhouette. Overwhelmed by the anguishing feeling, he turned to Chatì in the hopes of seeing her caught up in his same hesitation and tell him to let it go, to give everything up and go back home in good order without a shot being fired. Instead he saw that she did not feel the slightest hesitation and was in firing position with her finger resting on the trigger. And that was enough to evaporate any obstacle. Marco took a deep breath, leaned his head on the crossbow and took careful aim: "Fire!"

Each shot fired by the bows were covered by the voices of the women and the shouts of the children; they were just barely audible, and the arrows hissed though the night like two thunderbolts, striking their targets in the determined spots. The guards were pierced from the hollows of their throats to the napes of their necks and fell limply to the ground like two puppets without a groan. They had not yet touched the ground when the rearmed crossbows were already aiming at the napes of the necks of the two would-be priests.

"Fire!" Marco ordered again after a few seconds. But while his arrow flew straight to its target, an unexpected movement by the other meant that Chatì's arrow, after only grazing his neck, deviated in trajectory and pierced Chitoontecl's cheek just below his left ear.

The scream of pain and terror that rose in unison from the throats of the wounded made everyone turn their way. "Shit!" Marco cursed, but before he could stop her Chatì unsheathed her knife, cleared the cliff with one jump and fell headlong in the direction of the student who was groping his wound dazedly, and before he could figure it out she had cut his throat.

Chitoontecl's reflexes were much readier: he instantly spun on himself and with the arrow still stuck in his check he sped nimbly into the shadowed area, disappearing fast in the dark. "No, stop, don't do it!" Marco shouted with all the air left in his lungs as he saw Chatì run off in pursuit of the fugitive.

His companion's unforeseen initiative had caught him off guard, making him linger for a few seconds too long in the shelter of the rocks; but his shouts obtained the desired effect, and while the pursuer stopped in her tracks he was already recovering from his disadvantage, racing across the clearing with the speed of a cheetah to meet and protect her from any danger.

If the appearance of Chatì had created quite a stir in the group of slaves, the sudden appearance of that giant who was three heads taller than any other being that they had ever seen in their lives brought about a veritable wave of panic among them. Terrified screams arose from all sides and everyone, without exception, fled away from the black demon. Only then did Chatì realize her mistake: covered as she was with soot from head to toe, her old friends could not have recognized her and their reaction was more than justified. If they dispersed into the darkness it would be impossible to gather them and bring them all away in the little time available. They needed to be addressed in a hurry if she did not want to sent the whole plan to hell: "Tlachinalli, Peeptel, Zaaptami," she cried, turning to the women closest to her, "I am your sister Chatiztacqui!"

Hearing themselves addressed by name, the girls froze on the spot and focused their eyes on the intruder while remaining a wary distance from her. Chati's words worked a miracle though, because not only did those three who were called stop, but all the others had halted as well. One of them, actually, was returning slowly to retrace her steps: "Xeetha, I'm Chatiztacqui, do you recognize me?" Chatì said to her, careful not to approach for fear of scaring her.

The respondent stopped a few feet away from her and stared at her for a long time with inquiring eyes: "No, you cannot be Chatiztacqui," she pronounced in a trembling voice after a moment of uncertainty. "Chatiztacqui disappeared into the lake more than twenty moons ago. You are jut her dark spirit come from Mictlan to take revenge."

"No, Xeetha, you're wrong, it's me, Chatiztacqui, flesh and blood. I do not come from the place of death, I am alive; I have been alive this whole time. You just don't recognize me because my skin is covered in black...look," she added, scratching her chest with her nails to reveal the underlying skin.

Xeetha moved warily. Her fear was great, but the love for her lost sister invariably exceeded that by far. When she drew close, she reached a trembling finger out to touch her arm, and the long strip that appeared when her nail grazed it from top to bottom swept away any lingering doubts.

"Chatiztacqui! My sister!" Xeetha cried, throwing her arms around her neck. "But...but what happened to you, where have you been all this time?" The words came out of her mouth mixed with tears and joy, and their embrace dispelled everyone else's fear; they all rushed en masse to their recovered friend, swamping her with hugs and overwhelming her with questions.

"There's no time for lengthy explanations now," said Chatì. "Suffice it to say that the night I disappeared I swam to the other side. I had been informed that I would find a basket hanging from a rope behind the waterfall. I got on it and I was brought up there...I was transported to the place where the rare birds go to sleep. It just seems like a small mountain ledge from here, but it is much, much bigger than it seems. Remember how many times we fantasized about the many beautiful feathers that we would have been able to get if we were able to climb up there? Well, he has lived up there since the day the body of the white-skinned foreigner was found in the lake," she went on to explain, indicating Marco: "Those two were close friends, but only he was saved. And he saved me."

"Up there," she added as soon as the others let her, "we live happily. Because there are not only beautiful feathers, but also plenty of food, fruit to no end, and plenty of water for watering the fields. And there's room for all of you…We came down just to convince you to come away with us, and you won't regret it if you decide to follow. Because up there you will live as free women and no longer as miserable slaves." Until a moment ago all eyes had been glued on the resurrected girl as though charmed by her incredible story, but at that point turned in the stranger's direction who, fearful of making everyone scatter again, had remained motionless in his place, resisting the impulse to start shouting at them in order to press them to escape. Silence descended on the meadow again, broken occasionally by the inconsolable crying of a terrified child who sought solace in his mother's arms. Marco was quivering with impatience, but he perceived that the eyes of the onlookers were still suspicious and inquisitive as they regarded him. The plan was taking a turn for the worse; Chitoontecl would not take long to reach the city and give the alarm, and their time for flight was diminishing. He had to resolve the impasse that had arisen as quickly as possible.

"Greetings!" he said, voicing the first word that came into his head, then raising his hands to shoulder height with palms facing forward. "I am Chatiztacqui's liberator…and I have come to liberate you, too."

Hearing him speak their language, albeit with a bit of a strange accent, the women began to scrutinize him with less suspicion while maintaining a safe distance from him so as to be ready to flee in case of danger. One of them, however, broke away from the group: boasting an athletic build, taller than the others and—alone among all of them—her hair was cut into a very short bob. Additionally, in stark contrast with her companions who were almost all wrapped in long, cream-colored tunics, she was the only one to wear a sort of blue tunic that left her legs and left breast completely uncovered and

Marco, despite the tension of the moment, could not help but admire the features of that statuesque body.

The woman went to meet him determinedly and without any apparent fear: "Greetings to you, liberator," she said when she was close, imitating his gesture. "I am Atzcha of the slaves of the *tlatoani*," she continued, putting her hands on his shoulders. "My sisters and I will come with you. Command us and we will follow."

It was just what he wanted to hear. He wanted to plant a kiss on her forehead, but for fear of starting trouble he refrained from doing so and simply smiled, nodding his head repeatedly in approval. The ice had been broken. At this sight all fears instantly vanished and everyone, as though by a clear signal, streamed towards the man with the same manifestations of joy that had previously been reserved for their newfound friend. Marco trembled because of the precious minutes they were losing but at the same time, the sudden change of attitude caught him off guard and the great show of affection overwhelmed him, and he did not want to curb his new friends' enthusiasm by seeming gruff and unfriendly.

He searched for Chatì with pleading eyes and once again it was she who pulled him out of trouble, while her own heart was rejoicing for the reception that her companion was given: "Don't waste any more time," she shouted, her voice overpowering the general uproar. "We must hurry. By this time Chitoontecl will have reached Aplaia and given the alarm. His men will be here soon." Hearing this dreaded name pronounced, they all quieted at once, and Chatì took the opportunity to impart her guidance: "You two," she began, addressing Atzcha and the girl who stood next to her, "get up on a *tinchca* and take my man with you...he will show you the way. You, on the other hand," she continued, turning to Xeetha, "get a few sisters to help you sink all the *tinchaque* here on the shore...except, of course, those that we'll need to escape. Everyone else run and push the big boat into the water and climb onto it in a hurry. I'll join you in a moment."

"But..." Marco interjected, "the arrangements were that the two of us should go..."

"No, try to understand," Chatì interrupted him, "Chitoontecl's escape has upset all our plans, unfortunately, and there is no more time to do what we planned; the big boat will take a long time to get to our destination and if there's no one to guide it in the right direction then there's a good chance that it won't get there at all...And this is a task for just me, because only you have the strength to lift the cage alone with all that weight. The *tinchaque* should be much faster, but only a few of us know how to drive them...explain everything to my companions along the way and leave them under the waterfall as you go up, so that they can give instructions to the others as they arrive...Come on, please, do as I told you, my love, don't waste any more time!"

Marco wanted to be obstinate, but he realized that given how things had become complicated, Chatì's suggestion was the only way forward. Knowing her, he knew it would be an impossible task to convince her to chance her mind: "Don't do anything rash," he finally ceded, squeezing her tight.

"I'll see you up there," she assured him with a smile, freeing herself and rising on tiptoes for a quick kiss. "And...take care," she added mischievously, "to behave well with my friends." That said, she turned her back and began to run towards the shore to go and help her companions push the boat into the water.

Marco stood there watching her as she ran away. He was ravaged by the desire to run after her, to stop her, to drag her away by force, but eventually surrendered and walked with slow, rueful steps in the opposite direction. Atzcha and her friend were waiting for him; they had already descended into the water and were holding a cone steady as it pitched near the shore.

"She is Peepty," Atzcha said, pointing to her companion. "Peepty the red," she specified. And Marco, as absorbed as he was by his concerns, was very impressed when he raised his eyes to the girl who was just presented to him and he noticed for the fist time that even in the shadows her hair seemed to emit fiery reflections, in contrast to the raven-colored ones of the other girls, a genetic memory of some conquistador.

"Hurry!" he yelled resolutely, averting his eyes from the girl and trying to unsheathe a minimum of masculine authority. His recommendation was entirely superfluous: the two companions, after giving him a signal to climb up, pushed the canoe into deeper waters and then jumped on board themselves and without a word immediately began to paddle and set off in the set direction in perfect synchronization, arousing the admiration of the surprised passenger.

Chapter 36

"Did you all hear? What are you waiting for, hurry up here…mothers and children first." If Atzcha stood out for her athleticism and speed of action, Xeetha was no less remarkable in her practical sense and initiative, and while not the doyenne of the group she had great influence over the community of slaves, who were not slow to mobilize or promptly execute orders. In addition to Xeetha, there were another five girls still on the ground, who were in place with her in two tapered canoes carved from the bark of a cork-like plant, but not before lending a hand to use boulders to render useless all other boats pulled onto the shore.

They had just completed the sabotage and slid their canoes into the water when the first warriors appeared on the opposite side of the clearing. Marco was the first to notice their arrival, whose eyes had remained glued to the shore during the journey to monitor the evolution of events closely. He felt a pang at the sight of the soldiers the boat was still just a few dozen meters from shore; as loaded as it was, and driven by inexperienced hands, it moved slowly. Too slowly for his anxiety.

In that moment Chatì was leaning over the stern rail to give her sister instructions, who in the meantime had reached the boat aboard her canoe: "When you get to the other side, stick close to the wall to slip under the waterfall. The float is a few arm lengths further out. In any case, Atzcha and Peepty are waiting down there. There is space for ten sisters, but it's better that you don't let more than six or seven on…with three or four children at most. No more, though, otherwise the load will become too heavy for my man. It will take at least eight trips to go up…Gods of the sky!" she swore, breaking off in mid-speech. "Those fuckers are already here…go, go, Xeetha! And try to get back as fast as possible to take other sisters, so the boat can travel lighter and faster…And you, get moving with those oars," she shouted, pointing to the rowers.

But no matter the strength they put into it, the vessel continued to proceed very slowly and was still clearly visible from the shore, where denser and denser throngs of screaming warriors were arriving. The took no time in spotting it and as soon as they made sense of it they rushed en masse to the canoes; they were sure that they would catch up with a few paddle stokes, but their certainties turned into an extraordinary series of expletives as soon as soon as they realized that these were inundated with water on every side.

It was chaos on the shore. The bravest—or the drunkest, perhaps—plunged into the water with the intention of swimming to the boat but completely unaware, however, of the potential of Chati's crossbow, who in the meantime had started hitting them with quick and accurate shots. Many were shot before they realized that maybe it was better to leave the water much more quickly than they had entered it, allowing the boat to be eclipsed in the dark. But the commanders were not slow to take hold of the situation and after sending a contingent of men to the valley in search of vessels that could float, they deployed all the others on the shore.

The sky was suddenly lit by a swarm of flaming arrows, which at the peak of their arcs remained suspended in the air as though uncertain, then decided to aim downwards in search of prey. The first swarms were lost in the water with an extended sizzle a dozen meters from the boat, but this worked to help the archers to better calculate the distance and adjust the angle of the shot. And a few moments later the first messengers of death began to rain down on the boat.

An infant was shot in its mother's arms, two women were shot in the back while trying to escape the rain, and a fiery arrow pierced through the neck of a girl who was trying to extinguish a flaming arrow on the stern rail. The poor girl was probably already dead when she fell backwards into the water but Chatì, who was right next to her, leaned forward to try to hold her back. And the attempt proved fatal.

She had already grabbed her friend by the hair when an arrow in its blind dive stuck in her back just above her left hip. The stab of pain tore just a groan from her, but it caused her hand to let go and fly to her back. And when her fingers met the cursed shaft, a single, forlorn word issued from her mouth: "Marco." Her companions realized what had happened when the boat was brought out of range and they turned to ask her for instructions.

Chatì was trying to pull the arrow out, but it was stuck too deep and every attempt produced tears of anger and pain from her, hampered by the boat's rocking, and she wound up further complicating the predicament. When after several unsuccessful attempts she managed to pull it out from the puncture wound, from which only a bit of fluid came out, she let loose copious, unstoppable streams of blood.

The companions realized the gravity of the situation and in the general confusion they stopped rowing, leaving the boat adrift. It fell to Xeetha, who was beckoned by the screams, to be brave and take the situation in hand: "Quickly, lower her onto the *tinchca*...Help me hold her, Thalzaa," she ordered the girl seated in front of her. "You, now," she continued, turning to the third passenger: "Get on the scow quickly, there isn't room for four here and we have to reach the waterfall as quickly as possible...And you all keep rowing over there!"

In the meantime Marco, who was completely unaware of the tragedy that was unfolding in the middle of the lake, had circumvented the waterfall and once he reached the buoy he climbed rapidly up to the cage. Atzcha had followed suit, and Peepty remained at the bottom to wait for the arrival of the others so she could give them instructions.

"So are you sure you want to come up with me?" Marco shouted to Atzcha over the noise of the waterfall. In the moment in which he had taken a seat in the canoe he would not have even dreamed of proposing to one of his companions to participate in an undertaking for which he and Chatì had worked for months and months before feeling that they were in a position to face it with certainty, but after seeing them work with the paddle, Atzcha in particular, he was not slow in changing his mind; if they were climbing up together, as envisioned in the original plan before Chitoontecl's escape messed it up, the time that the operation took would have been reduced greatly, and at this point even seconds were precious.

"Along the rope you'll find rings to put your hands and feet in when you want to stop and rest. Never look down. And if you think you can't make it then don't stop to—"

"Do not worry about me," she shouted back. "You go up. I will come right behind you." That woman was coming into his good graces; she kept telling him what he wanted to hear. "Okay," he said curtly, not intending in the slightest to change her mind, and grabbed the rope to begin the arduous ascent. The thought of Chatì in the middle of the lake, still within the clutches of danger, had put wings to his feet. He was thus incredulous when, having stopped at the top of the rope to catch his breath, he felt the woman's head under his feet. But there was no time for compliments. "Follow me," he ordered, grabbing the ladder and helping her up as soon as he reached the meadow. He took her by the hand and then led her to the winch.

Meanwhile Xeetha had arrived at the destination. Throughout the whole trip Chatì ignored the protests of her sister, who wanted to silence her to keep her from fatigue, and continued to give instructions on the manner and timing of the lift. While circumventing the waterfall they had gotten tossed here and there a bit in the boat, but the two rowers had no major difficulties to overcome and could move into calmer waters. It was pitch dark down there, the noise was so great that no one responded to their calls, and the new arrivals happened upon Peepty only when they bumped into her boat.

Peepty was waiting for them standing precariously on the canoe, holding herself up by clinging to the ladder with one hand and to the buoy with the other to avoid being swept away by the current. Xeetha immediately informed her about the incident and the change in plans. She wanted to go with her sister, but she knew that her authority would be needed in order to make things run properly: "You go up," she said to Peepty, "Thalzaa and I will bring Chatiztacqui. You will give us a hand to get her through the opening. But take good care not to slide off the bandage around her waist, or she will begin to bleed again. Chatiztacqui," she said to her sister, "I am going to cause you a bit of pain now, but there's no other way to get you up there. Try to bear it…you'll see that your man knows how to cure you."

They managed to hoist Chatì up with difficulty, but there was no time to catch their breath; they were joined by three other companions on board the third canoe. "You and you go up," Xeetha ordered, touching the shoulders of two of them, "and be quick because there's no time to lose. We, however," she continued, turning to Thalzaa and the other, "let's take the three *tinchaque* and go recover another sister…Hurry, you go, I'll join you soon." The other two canoes had just started out and she was about to let go of the ladder when it slipped out of her hand and began to rise slowly upwards.

"They should be arriving by now," Marco considered aloud, "but let's give them a little more time before retrieving them."

Atzcha was almost not paying attention, she was so taken with the infernal mechanism that the cable wound into, made even more disturbing by the darkness of the meadow that blurred the edges. And when Marco took the crank in hand and made the first revolution, putting the gears in motion, she could not help but leap backwards and let out a scream of fright. But she recovered quickly and, furious with herself for the demonstration of weakness, she regained her composure, boldly approached him and joined him decisively by the crank.

Marco was tormented by the desire to drop everything and run to the edge of the meadow to closely follow the progress of the ascent, but he feared that Atzcha, however strong, would not be able to bring the cage up alone. Thus, he remained yoked to the wheel with her and during the slow operation he tried to explain briefly how the winch worked.

"I can do it alone now," he told her at a certain point, considering that the platform, now lighter from the shortening of the cable, was in the home stretch. "You go help the others get onto the meadow. And be careful not to fall, it's very slippery over there."

When the cage arrived at its destination, Marco immediately had the perception that something was not right. The newcomers were lingering too long in place and despite the noise of the waterfall there seemed to be a crescendo of excited voices. With his heart in his throat, he stopped the winch, and as an icy chill ran down his back he rushed towards the waterfall.

The gloomy foreboding that had inhabited his dreams since the day when Chatì had asked him to act had suddenly taken shape and was manifesting in all its tragic, inevitable fatality. He was shouting, beside himself with grief, snatching the woman from the hands of her companions.

When he had her in his arms he tried to grope around for the flashlight in the pocket of his backpack, which was sitting near the winch. The battery emitted a dim light, but more than enough to instantly make him understand the gravity of the situation. Chatì's face was ghastly pale, and her pulse was barely detectable. Marco immediately noticed the strip of cloth that was tethering her to life. With trembling hands he undid the knot that cinched at the front and, seeing no injuries, gently rolled the woman on her side: a stream of dark blood began pumping from the wound. "Chatì, I have to go to the shelter to get the knife," he said, trying hard to conceal the anguish that gripped him. "You try hard not to move while I'm away. It'll just take a moment to—"

"Marco," she interrupted. It was little more than a whisper, but more than enough to freeze the man in his tracks. "Don't go, please. Stay here with me. Stay close to me. I feel that my life is slipping away...I do not want to die separated from you."

In tears, the man could no longer contain his desperation: "Don't leave me, Chatì, hold on! We are one, the two of us…if you go away, I…I will go with you!" He had lost all control, and was refusing to accept reality.

Chatì's lips spread into a faint smile: "Maaco, you can't do anything more for me…I'm about to go to Mictlan, my love…but I am happy, because the gods have been generous with me."

"No, Chatì, don't talk like that, please!"

"You must not be sad, Marco. You will have my people, my sisters, their children, with you…who will love you as I have loved you, because they have suffered as I have suffered. Do not let them down, help them…it is the last gift that I ask of you." Her voice was barely audible and Marco, petrified with grief, no longer had the strength to respond. "I will wait for you among those stars that you miss so much."

These were Chatì's last words. Desperate, Marco tried to revive her in vain. He clutched the woman he loved to his chest and tenderly cradled her in a long, harrowing embrace. After a seemingly endless time, he lifted his eyes and looked around bewilderedly, and only then noticed the silent group of people who surrounded him, gradually growing in number as the women and children arrived at their destination.

Given the ugly turn of events Atzcha had soon realized that she could no longer count on the man's help. She had accordingly mobilized her companions, instructing them as needed, and had gotten them to help her continue the recovery operation. But given the operators' inexperience every trip required a long time and there were still too many women and children waiting for their turn to climb.

"The warriors have put a big boat in the water and are heading down below," a young girl said, still panting from the trip, pointing to the edge of the terrace which she had just approached. Marco then rose to his feet, picked up his backpack with one hand and walked to the spot from which, in a time long gone, he used to follow his beloved along her lengthy swim. And what he saw once he reached his goal provoked all his wrath.

Lit by dozens of torches, a raft packed with screaming warriors armed to the teeth traveled across the water. It had already passed the middle of the lake and was pointing unmistakably towards the waterfall. The raft was nothing other than the walkway used by the people in the valley to cross the river near the quarry. After having torn it from its place, the soldiers had transported it upstream by forced march, and had then lowered it into the water to use as a boat. A few more meters and the improvised watercraft would be eclipsed under the terrace, and at that point there would be no escape for those left waiting at the bottom.

"Damn it!" Marco shouted at his enemies, completely heedless of being discovered. Like a wounded beast blinded by hatred, he plunged his hand into his backpack, snatched out a hand grenade, pulled the pin with his teeth and flung it angrily down. "Damn it, damn it, damn it!" he cried continually with all the air he had left in his lungs as he pulled an endless series of grenades out of the backpack, one after the other. And he had already sent three into the valley when the first bomb struck its target with pinpoint accuracy.

The raft was suddenly enveloped in a blinding flash that lit everything up like daylight. Then the roar of the explosion came, amplified hundredfold by the crater's echo. A few grenades wound up in the water, but others still hit the target with a chain of light bursts and explosions. The few warriors who were not mangled by shrapnel or swept away by the shockwaves from the explosions sought a means of escape by diving into the water, but many of them disappeared in it forever.

By now only dead, mangled limbs remained on board the partially destroyed raft but Marco, like a vengeful god motivated by blind hatred and implacable fury, kept hurling the deadly parcels until his hand unearthed no more bombs at the bottom of the backpack. The terrified women had witnessed the massacre and were petrified on the spot by his demonstration of superhuman power. But much, much more terrified at that time were the few warriors

210

from the raft who escaped the massacre and those who had watched the stages of the deadly carnage incredulously from the shore. And from that moment on, none of them dared to impede the last rescue operations. And no woman had the audacity to approach Marco when they walked back, and he lifted Chatì from the ground and began to climb towards the shelter at a slow pace.

It was dawn when the newcomers, who were remaining on the sidelines, saw him return to the meadow, their sister in his arms. Marco, after having cleansed the body of the black layer of soot, had then combed her long hair and had finally dressed her in the white tunic that she wore on the day of her arrival.

When he reached the spot he laid her on the grass near Karl's grave and then, with the shovel that he had carried over his shoulder, he began to dig. But when it came time to cover that beloved face, which even in the pallor of death was more beautiful than ever, with black dirt, his legs buckled. He fell to his knees at the edge of the grave, unable to move, and stood looking at her until he realized that she was smiling, just as she used to smile when asking him a favor. And he obeyed.

In continuing to maintain a fearful and respectful distance, the women then saw him fill the pit with huge piles of earth in an almost furious manner. Then they saw him back away and run like a man possessed to the edge of the woods and come back to the grave shortly thereafter with his arms full of flowers that still clung to their clods of earth. Thus they saw him tinkering long with the soil and followed him with their eyes from far off when he turned his back to his beloved and began to ascend slowly towards the shelter without even retrieving the shovel. Then they heard the thud of the door closing behind him and a superhuman cry, almost a roar. Finally, silence. When they dared approach they grave they found it covered with small orchids, Chatì's favorite flowers.

Chapter 37

Everything around him reminded him of his beloved Chatì and renewed his despair. He no longer knew how long he had been lying on the bed, from which he had risen but rarely to drink, dazed by poignant memories that intensified his pain a hundred times over. Marco was about to give himself over to one of the rare moments of numbness that welcomed him when his heart could no longer bear the pain, when he heard a knock. Taken aback, he lifted his head to stare at the door with vacant eyes as though frightened by the unexpected sign of life. The stranger knocked again and then, hearing no response, she opened the door and stopped at the threshold.

The hermit's eyes were so used to the shadows that they were now dazzled, and he could just make out the outline of the figure silhouetted against the light in the middle of the doorway. Only partially recovered from the astonishment, Marco got up from the bed unsteadily in his determination to scare off the intruder who had dared to violate his pain, but the figure cut him off as she headed towards him resolutely: "You are not respecting Chatiztacqui's wishes," she said. "We need you, we were entrusted to you by her and you are killing her a second time acting this way." It was Xeetha.

This was the last straw for Marco, who was already tired from the hardship, little sleep and torment of the last days. His legs buckled, he collapsed back down on the mattress and let the hot tears stream down his cheeks. "You're right," he found the strength to say after so much time, facing the woman in front of him who was silently observing his pain. "I must apologize to you…and to your sisters, too," he added as he got up and started towards the door. But two energetic hands forced him to stay seated.

"Where do you think you're going, looking like that? Do you not think that you already scared those poor girls enough?" Marco remembered the layer of sludge that still clung to his skin, and his hair that was matted and caked with fat, and his long, shaggy beard that hid almost his entire face. He lifted his bewildered face to the woman as if to implore her for advice. Without making him beg, Xeetha looked around silently and went to shut the door, looking around with an inquisitive eye; she found everything she needed and quickly clean him up from head to toe.

"Good!" she commented, smugly contemplating the result of her efforts. "Now you're presentable. Now I can take you to meet your new family...by the way, in case you forgot, I am Xeetha, Chatiztacqui's older sister."

Raising his eyes to look at the woman's face a bit more closely, Marco discovered only then why there had been something familiar about her from the first moment. A few years older than Chatì, she was taller than her younger sister by a few inches but the facial features were the same and her long tunic, which was patched in several places, allowed for a glimpse of an equally harmonious body, although a little fuller-figured.

"I know who you are. I saw your desperation when they snatched away your son, and I cried with you when he was killed. Chatì...Chatiztacqui spoke to me of you very often, as well as your family and your sad story...You were not only her sister, but also her greatest friend. She could not stand the idea of being free while you were still a slave, and she could not find peace with the thought of what might happen to you...We went down principally to save you."

Xeetha was about to cry at the memory of her loved ones, but managed to fight back the tears and flung open the door: "It's time to go. They are waiting for us," she invited him in an unsteady voice.

Marco moved to follow her, but at the doorway he had an afterthought: "Wait a minute," he said before disappearing inside the shelter again. Hanging on the wall of the small cave that connected to the main cavern there was a magnificent cloak of colored feathers that Chatì had assembled. Marco slid it carefully over his left shoulder as she had taught him and grabbed the staff that Karl had given him and quickly trotted back. "I'm ready," he said, preceding his companion through the entrance, who gasped as she admired the object of such a rapid and dramatic transformation.

"Of course…my *tlatoani*," Xeetha mumbled confusedly before deciding to follow him.

When rumor of Xeetha's bold initiative spread, the refugees gathered in twos and threes in fearful silence at the foot of the stairs leading to the shelter. They were waiting for a long time, but although Marco was accustomed to detecting nearly inaudible noises, there was not even a revealing rustle to warn him of their presence. Seen from below with the ominous, carved staff in his hand and wrapped in the long mantle, he seemed even taller and more imposing than when he appeared to them on the night of their escape.

A low murmur of admiration mixed with fear ran through the entire group. Children clung even tighter to their mothers; some women even felt that they stood before a supernatural entity and fell to their knees as a sign of submission; others clutched each other as though for mutual protection. All of them still had before their eyes the wrath and power of the giant who towered over them from above and they feared that he could be turned against them, as they were unintentionally responsible for the death of his partner. Maybe I exaggerated in dressing this way, Marco thought, reading on all the frightened faces the excitement aroused by his masquerade. But Xeetha was ready to pull him out of trouble: "I present to you the Son of the Mountain, the white *tlatoani*, the man who has freed us from our ancient bondage and led us into his world. Many of you were present when Chatiztacqui, before descending into Mictlan, prayed that he would protect us from any danger. Know that our deliverer not only accepted this request, but he even considers it to be a sacred commitment that he has taken on, and intends to keep his promise to the end."

Xeetha's words immediately hit their mark and tore a choral sigh of relief from the group. "You have seen with your own eyes," the woman continued, "how great was his love for our disappeared sister and how implacable his vengeance may be when he is angry. Now he welcomes us into his land with great kindness, and without demanding anything of us. But we, who know the price he had to pay to make us free, will show him our gratitude in all ways." The pause that followed was animated by a strong murmur of approval. "You can be certain that our enemies, even if they cannot see him, they know where we fled, and they will do anything to retrieve us. To punish us, to humiliate us, to make us slaves again. But this does not scare us, because we know that he is with us and that under his protection we will continue to live free and safe in this World Above." Then the dread, the fear and the distrust subsided in one fell swoop, and a cry of exaltation came forth from every mouth.

Marco was visibly relieved by so much proficiency with public relations, but another consideration occurred to him as he continued slowly down the high bounds of the stairs. During her brief pane-gyric, Xeetha had not only attributed to him a rather unlikely parent, but she had referred to the place several times as "his land." Marco had never felt that he was its master, but come to think of it, since it had never been inhabited by anyone before him, it would legally be his according to an ancient border law. The allocation of property had so impressed him and made him proud, but at the same time it had led him to recognize another truth: that "World Above"—he had really liked that last label—no matter how small and limited was now his only world and, save for very improbable developments, it was destined to remain so for all the days to come; there, like it or not, he would spend the rest of his life, there, one day, his bones would rest for good. And not only that.

Chatì's parting should have rekindled in him the old desire to escape. Instead, on the contrary, he felt that even if he found a way to escape he would not have even dreamed of leaving. Because there he had found love, in that land he had found happiness in this world…Chatì still existed. And Chatì was not in her grave, she was

215

in every flower, in every feather, every drop of dew. Everything spoke to her, and she was all these things. And Chatì was also in her people. To forget this world, to abandon those people would mean for him to give up the greatest gift he had ever received in his entire existence. He would never, never leave, never, never abandon that place so full of true life, never, never betray those people. His people.

Such were the thoughts that were streaming through his mind while at the foot of the stairs he was surrounded and pulled at from all sides by women and children at the height of enthusiasm. Xeetha's words had melted any residual fear like snow in the sun and, just like the valley on the night of the escape, everyone was crowding around to see him up close, to touch him, to talk to him. The voices overlapped with each other in a confusion and Marco, struggling to keep up with the tumult of phrases and hear their words, was dazed, but at once moved by such a warm display of affection on the part of people whom he barely knew.

Xeetha stayed on the sidelines for a while either to enjoy the fruits of her speech or to give free rein to the general enthusiasm, but as soon as she had been satisfied that mistrust and fear had completely abated, she stepped back into her role. With a few precise orders that were carried out at once, she silenced her friends, and after having made them line up in single file she presented them one by one.

Marco had already learned of the life and miracles of each of them from Chatì's stories, and often preempted the presenter by calling the woman or the child of the moment by name, and it gave him a world of pleasure to observe the shocked, proud expression of those who found that they were not unknown in the eyes of their new lord. Xeetha also briefed him on the situation: "All in all we rescued four dozen plus five—three dozen plus two women and a dozen plus three children. Ten boys," she pointed out proudly. "Another five sisters were hit by the arrows. One of them left us this morning, one is in very dire condition, but the others will recover soon."

"Good!" Marco said at the end of the introductions. "I think the time has come to introduce you to your new home," and, lifting a child from the ground, he led his subjects to discover the World Above.

Chapter 38

Tenaciously opposed to her reckless companion's repeated attempts at bread making, Chatì had managed to preserve almost all of the seeds from the first harvest and now Marco, while showing proudly the many corn plants that thrived, could not help but thank her for her foresight and think back with a lump in his throat to the many days of hard but happy work that went by with her.

Lost in thought and taken as he was with doing the honors of the house, he had not even noticed having arrived near the little cemetery. The sapling that he had planted at the head of Karl's grave had grown almost six feet. Its shadow brushed Chatì's grave, affording it a bit of coolness, and though all eyes were on him Marco could not hold back his tears as he saw that both graves were covered with flowers.

They were tired but radiant when they gathered for dinner before nightfall. Through the course of the long day Marco had shown his new guests every nook and cranny of his land, describing the characteristics from time to time, the tasks already performed, those to be completed and those planned for the future. The helicopter had done the lion's share, he imagined, but the many objects found inside were also useful for inspiring awe and wonder in the newcomers.

But there was a surprise in store for him. During his long days of hermitage the women had mobilized, and Marco was stunned when at dinner time he was made to sit in the middle of a large semicircle hollowed out of the grass at the edge of the forest. In design it had exploited the natural indentation of a bump in the ground, and even with the limited means at their disposal they had almost completed it. The outer edge on which he was directed to sit had been upholstered with a comfortable straw cushion while on the inside, slightly elevated and enriched by a splendid tablecloth of leaves and flowers, was laden a beautiful feast.

There was everything on that table: roasted birds, eggs, raw seasonal vegetables, sweet potatoes baked in the embers, and all varieties of berries. And many other unknown dishes, but all tasty and flavored with an endless variety of sweet and spicy chilies. How those women discovered and obtained so many gifts from God in such a short time remained a real mystery. Marco, though, enchanted by the magnificence of the spread and bewildered by the many scents that rose from every course, did not stop to ask.

The seat reserved for him at the center of the semicircle was a good head and shoulders taller than the others and he, both flattered and embarrassed by the spot assigned to him from which he could dominate the entire table, could not help but wonder if his seat was conceived in that way simply for reasons of height or because of the *white tlatoani* rank that Xeetha had landed him with that morning.

The girls competed to offer him many dishes, waiting for his judgment with trepidation, and when the visitor tasted and expressed his complete satisfaction with vigorous nods, they melted into squeals of joy and threw their arms around one another's necks, complimenting themselves on the successful enterprise.

For his part, Marco did not even pretend just to make them happy; the hunger that had built up in the days of semi-fasting— piqued by the succession of the uninterrupted succession of aromas and scents—and the need to repress, to stun in some way the despair that would surface in sequential waves, finally freed him from all self-control and inhibitions.

He woke late in the morning the next day. As the memory of the endless flow of the gargantuan feast came back to him he was overwhelmed by a new, distressing concern: "There are so many.

Too many. How will I feed them? How will we get through the next winter? How can I keep my promise?"

Almost unbeknownst to him, he had now fallen into the role of patriarch of his people and was beginning to feel the weight of the responsibility of the assigned role, but in the days that followed he realized with relief that his anxieties had no reason to exist. The women, in fact, were all healthy, young and vigorous, and the liberty had infused in them not only the joy of living but also a great desire to create. Additionally, as Chatì had already thoroughly informed him, they had always been exempted from the humiliating, laborious jobs which were reserved for the other women of the valley instead, so they had developed and honed their natural propensities in a masterly manner. Those who most intrigued him were the Amazons; almost all of them were able to hit impossible targets with bow and javelin, and when Marco accepted the invitation to grapple with them he had to pull away the smugness from his face in a hurry as he learned at his own expense that he had to spit blood to match their marksmanship and that, despite his height and athleticism, he had to sweat his guts out to be able to stay standing in close combat or use his sword to overcome an infinite variety of feints, parries, moves and countermoves of which those incredible warriors were capable, and whose teacher was, unquestionably, Atzcha. In fact the students showed her a blind, unconditional obedience and complied with every request without even dreaming of contravening her orders.

Xeetha, who by tacit consensus had assumed the intermediary role between him and the young community, was meanwhile displaying unparalleled organizational skills; under her watchful eye, within a few weeks the entire meadow on either side of the chasm had been stripped of every shrub and all invading grasses, tilled, fertilized and sown with every kind of seed. All edible tubers, roots and wild herbs that had been found here and there were collected and transplanted in neat rows in gardens of the same species, and next to the streams that ran though the meadow many small pools for water collection had been dug for irrigation.

Day by day the forest and the impenetrable hedge that separated it from the meadow were freed from unnecessary brambles and excessive plants. But nothing was wasted, and whatever could not go to the fire was destined for the construction of mud, straw, leaves and stone huts built on the edge of the woods on the south side of the terrace. In addition to the gardens, next to each hut there were also several aviaries, future homes for different species of birds to be bred in captivity.

Everyone missed the rabbits and turkeys so much that they salivated every evening when they saw the fishermen unload baskets upon baskets of fish on the shore. On the other hand, as Marco had expected, with the coming of spring, a colony of huge lizards had jumped out of an accumulation of stones near the fissure, and despite their monstrousness they were completely innocuous and not in the least threatening; catching them with snares was a breeze, and their flesh proved to be a real treat.

But the real surprise, the most comforting of all, was that the children had immediately proved themselves to be indispensable to the entire community. With their agility they managed to climb onto the smooth wall of the mountain by taking advantage of every little foothold and reaching heights unthinkable for an adult and searching for new nests and much sought-after honeycombs from which to periodically draw the precious sweetener. Some of them had learned to weave baskets, mats and clothes, while others proved tireless in the transportation of blocks of guano from the nesting area to the fields and orchards of the meadow. And the best part was that each of them welcomed such tasks for pure fun, without any obligation.

In witnessing all these rapid changes, Marco saw his fears diminishing day by day and at the same time he felt more empowered to pursue his favorite task. Aided by two skilled workers he had already gutted the entire helicopter, stripping it of every remaining wire, screw, bolt and gear, which were all transported to the workshop near the waterfall, leaving behind only the huge hulk of metal and the skids, which were impossible to carry beyond the chasm. His heart sank at having to leave such a huge mass of metal unused, but he could not consider continuing to dismember it piece by piece in the usual manner and risk destroying the few precious tools that he had at his disposal. To tell the truth, an absurd idea about how to use it had darted into his mind some time ago, but he had not even considered it both because of the enormous amount of work that it would require and because, in order to achieve it, he would be forced to reveal his presence to the world.

Things had changed a great deal recently: being discovered was no longer an issue, and he had more than enough laborers; he would have nothing to lose in the enterprise. But an unexpected obstacle was interposed between his intentions and their realization, forcing him to another compulsory postponement.

Chapter 39

With the return to business as usual, Marco had also resumed his daily inspections of the valley and was recently noticing an unusual and equally disturbing bustle. It was indeed unthinkable that down there they did not know where the fugitives had holed up, despite his orders not to light fires at the edge of the meadow and not to lean over the edge of the terrace for any reason.

Regulations similar to his must have been established in the valley. The locals were careful not to catch themselves looking up very publicly, but with his binoculars Marco had already caught several less-than-stealthy villagers looking up, as they certainly did not expect their every move scrutinized, and did not scrimp on the inquiring glances.

Then there was the unusual bustle of people on the lake shore. Characters often completely foreign to the man's eye, but better known to his new friends, who did not hesitate to inform them that they were mostly timbermen, masons and carpenters. Not to mention the group of musicians who settled permanently on the edge of the plateau, which for some time had begun raging from dawn to dusk in a deafening cacophony and rambling concerts.

The officers of the various military branches made appearances on the spot quite frequently as well, and they were not infrequently accompanied by the abhorrent enemy, Chitoontecl in the flesh. With a sort of turban on his head inclined three-quarters to wrap his left ear, he had the air of a frantic fakir. Followed closely by a retinue of obsequious potentates, he was gesticulating and giving orders left and right, making a concerted effort to keep himself from looking upwards.

All of that did not fail to arouse the apprehension and strong suspicions of the observers, especially when one morning they watched successive waves of massive sledges dragged by hand through the clearing, weighed down with planks, poles, ropes and other materials, which were in turn stacked near the shore, where crews had begun to assemble three large wooden barges at a record-breaking speed, complete with rudders, rails and rowlocks for the oars. Then one night, a strange thing happened.

In the course of his numerous nighttime stakeouts, Marco had never noticed an absolute absence of light in the valley. Here and there, especially within the city, you could still see lamps fixed to the street corners, a stray torch or an illuminated door; and then not to mention the permanently lit braziers on the walls to the sides of the main door of the pyramid. That night, however, and not only near the lake but also throughout the entire city not even the tiniest flame shone out and the phase of the new moon helped to maintain absolute darkness in the crater.

Marco and Atzcha, who had been elected aide-de-camp, stayed at the edge of the terrace observing for the entire night in an attempt to explain the mystery or to preclude any hostile maneuvers, but as soon as the crater was flooded by the morning light, their expectation was not fulfilled; apparently at least, nothing had changed down there. The unusual phenomenon was repeated for four nights in a row. Then the lights came on again and everything returned to normal, leaving the observers bewildered and lost in their growing suspicion and distressing questions.

Exactly one month later the very same event was repeated and the morning after, Marco and Atzcha stayed to watch over the valley for the entire night, as they were still agonizing over what could have been concocted at their own expense in the hours of absolute darkness that had just passed. Once again, everything seemed unchanged down there: the fishermen were pushing their boat into the water, the farmers were on their way to the fields, baskets were being woven on the shore, the musicians had resumed their playing…but something was inevitably going on.

It was Atzcha who noticed a change: "The baskets!" she exclaimed in a near whisper as if to convince herself first.

"What?"

"The baskets. The ones on the right."

After nearly ripping the binoculars our of her hands, Marco pointed them in the direction indicated, but try as he might to better focus on the indicated containers, he could not figure out what his fellow lookout was referring to: "Maybe I'm going blind, but those baskets seem the same as yesterday."

"Look closer…the ones behind the stack of poles."

"Yes, I get it, those are the ones I am referring to. But what strikes you as strange?"

"Last night there were six rows of five layers each. This morning one layer per row is missing. And the pile of poles is lower."

"Are you sure?"

"Very."

"Now it's totally clear," said Marco, "they're taking advantage of the darkness to transport the material to the other shore…"

"What do you think they're doing?" Atzcha asked.

"I wouldn't know what to say, precisely…but I can imagine."

"For that matter, me too. And what do you think we should do?"

"I don't have the slightest idea. I just know that we need to move quickly at this point if we don't want all of this to come to a very nasty end…Come on, let's go tell the others," he said, starting to move away from the edge of the terrace.

The atmosphere was fraught with tension, as the sudden summons was an unmistakable sign that something very serious had happened or was about to happen, and on every face you could read all the anxiety and apprehension about what was going to be announced.

"Listen," the white *tlatoani* began, his eyes ranging over the entire semicircle. "What has been going on down there for some time is now the very clear evidence that the rulers in the valley have no intention of letting us live in peace. Since this morning we have absolute certainty that for two whole moons already they have been working to prepare a very unpleasant surprise for us right under our feet." An alarmed murmur ran through the assembly, but Marco imposed silence by raising his staff in the air: "But don't worry," he added hastily to calm them, "we will know how to send them off." In truth, Marco did not have the faintest idea of how to act, but he know that the only way to avoid the resigned inertia of his people was to inject a dose of confidence, and the expression that appeared on a lot of faces told him that he was, at least in part, successful. It spurred him to invent something else.

"We know that they are many, well-armed, and with the exception of Atzcha and her companions, much better prepared than us in the art of combat. But they have to come looking for us up here, in a land unknown to them, a land we know every inch of. You know well that one of these," he continued, showing his audience a crossbow, "is worth twelve of their bows. Plus, there's a heap of precious metal waiting for us to make many more, and with that same metal we will manufacture blades strong enough to break their swords and arrowheads, the ones that are able to pierce the most resistant shields."

As the various cards that he could play came to mind, Marco almost began to believe his fantasies: "Also, all of you," he continued, more and more impassioned, "were able to witness the power of the stones of fire…but you have not yet heard one of these sing!" he shouted, waving a machine gun in the air that he had purposely placed there before the meeting. "And then I can guarantee that if they dare to disturb our sleep, we will use these to fill their nights with nightmares!" At these words the whole assembly leaped to its feet clapping and screaming, letting loose their newfound confidence, and it was some time before Marco was able to restore silence.

"But," he continued, lowering his voice, "if we want to go that far, we need to prepare to fight. Everyone, including children. We must stop our enemy before he can set foot on our land. A land that shelters and protects us, but that, unfortunately, does not allow us to see what is going on beneath our feet…which we should find a way to see as soon as possible if we want to fend off unpleasant surprises. And unbeknownst to them, possibly…but it will not be easy," he added in spite of himself.

"There could be a way," Atzcha interrupted.

Xeetha, who had resolutely banned unauthorized interruptions during the *tlatoani*'s speeches, sprang to her feet with angry eyes, ready to rebuke the undisciplined woman, but Marco prevented her: "I'm listening," he said, turning to Atzcha and raising his hand to calm Xeetha.

"Thank you, my *tlatoani*," said Atzcha, gracing him with a beautiful smile before continuing: "I have been carefully studying our land for a long time, and I am wondering how I would act if I were in our enemy's place. And the conclusion I have reached is that there are only two weaknesses. The first is under our feet, and everything that has been happening for a long time tells us that this is where their attack will come from; the second, which in my opinion is much, much more dangerous than the other, is the rock that lies beyond the waterfall. Behind that rock they could act undisturbed and unseen, which is not a small thing, working on solid ground and not on the water as they're forced to do now. If I were them, I wouldn't have any doubts in favoring this way…but you can tell that they are either in too much of a hurry to come up here and find us or they are too confident in their strength to get mixed up in so many precautions or, more probably, both these things at once."

"And what would be your proposal?" Marco asked her.

"I think we should move the big wheel to the fissure and replace the cage with a closed cabin. This would allow us to go down to where we want and see what they are doing while at the same time staying protected. It is likely that at that point, as they realize they've been discovered, they'll abandon that way and decide to attack from elsewhere, and it is there that we must concentrate all our defenses."

"Wonderful suggestion!" Marco blurted, whose enthusiasm froze instantly when, in turning his head to the semicircle, sure of meeting the assembly's unanimous consent, he met the flashing eyes of Xeetha, who was incinerating him with her stare for not having properly rebuked the undisciplined speaker. "But…" he added hastily, seeking to appease the wrath of the woman and at the same time dampen the slightly too-complacent smile that had appeared on Atzcha's lips, "I am of the opinion that several changes should be made to your plan. To discover their intentions we will by necessity be acting in the light of day, and this will not allow us to go unnoticed, losing the advantage of surprise…So when we go down it will not be just to look around. The decision has been made," Marco concluded, beating his staff on the ground and calming spirits. "It's time to take action."

Chapter 40

Two weeks later the cabin was ready: constructed of poles and two meters high, each side was equipped with two windows located at different heights that could be opened or closed with sliding doors as needed. Inside, two people could fit comfortably with a good possibility of maneuvering without being hindered. After oiling the machine guns well, Marco got two girls to help him carry two boxes of hand grenades and just as many filled with additional magazines from the shelter to the cabin. He spent a long time with Atzcha fine-tuning everything that was needed, and with the complicity of the night they had cleaned the trunk of the pine tree which over-arched the slit of all branches and debris and after mounting the pulley they hung the cabin and ladder to access it.

On the morning of the operation the whole community was waiting next to the winch. Atzcha was there for over an hour and was giving the final instructions to her friends; she would go down with him and had already loaded the cabin with all their armaments. There were neither encouragements nor speeches, only Xeetha blurted out a phrase before they shut the door behind them: "See you soon, *tlatoani*. And if you have any second thought, remember what they did to Chatiztacqui."

The cabin had just passed the high walls of the crevasse, suspended in space under the vault of the terrace when the two occupants felt their hearts sink in the instant that they realized the extent of the danger they would have faced had they delayed their mission even slightly: on the concave wall defining the inner shore of the lake, the men of the valley had lavished all their engineering skill.

There was no beach, but at the point where the rock emerged from the deep lake waters a pier was anchored, on which impressive amounts of boards, poles, ropes and other materials rested. From the jetty rose a ladder of rope and wooden pegs fixed to the wall. To mount it, the workers had first torn down the fragile glass coating and then planted the support pegs in the more compact rock layer underneath.

The ladder ended at the point where the upper portion of the wall bent almost horizontally over itself to hang out over the lake. There a long walkway of wooden planks supported on numerous harnesses hanging on the rocky face, and to prevent the installation of hazardously inclined planes, the designers had divided the path into flat sections situated at different heights and connected by wooden ladders at the place where the walkway had a progressively more pronounced arc of curvature. On the pier and on every gangway ladder there was an anthill of workers with their heads down, making small holes in the rock, hanging ropes, tying crosspieces and carrying the boards to be laid across the harnesses.

The walkway running parallel to the fissure, which was a short distance away but in proximity of the outer edge of the terrace, where the thickness of the rock was just fifty feet, bent at a right angle towards the crevasse. Once the fissure was reached, it would have been a breeze to climb up to the meadow at night using grappling hooks or flying ladders and create a bridgehead. There were only seven or eight meters left before the task was completed. Just a few more days and at that rate the walkway would have reached its goal.

Marco and Atzcha looked into one another's eyes for a moment almost as if to communicate their reciprocal wonder: on the highly polished glass wall, untouched for whole geological eras, the workers of the valley had accomplished a miraculous feat with incredible rapidity, despite the rudimentary means at their disposal. And without betraying their presence in the least.

"We should have seen this coming, with all those damned drums and fifes," Marco snapped, still cursing his obliviousness. Even

Atzcha could not help a twinge of anger, and immediately grasped the crossbow. "Don't be hasty," Marco restrained her, hopping from one window to the other with the binoculars to study the situation more closely. "As you can see, the best of their warriors are on the catwalks, but not even the shadow of a warrior...I promised you that we wouldn't come down here just to look, but also to do some damage. So, since we're here, let's do as much as possible...let's wait for the bulk of the army before we start the ball rolling."

The cabin had been lowered to a point visible from the opposite bank of the terracing and it was a little boy who was playing at the edge of the lake who noticed it first. His screams first attracted the attention of his playmates and soon after, that of their parents, who immediately began to alert the workers on the other side in loud voices. Grim, prolonged sounds reverberated across the valley and after less than half an hour the first troops of warriors appeared in the clearing, and they rushed en masse to slide three barges into the water.

"But what are we waiting for?" Atzcha said, unnerved by waiting. "If we give them time to reach the catwalk we will be within reach of their bows."

"Stay calm, Atzcha, be patient a little longer, let's make them think that we're not on the offensive...the more people come to the party, the more fun it will be. You'll see...oh, finally, now you show you're alive!" he exclaimed suddenly, cutting off his speech. All the while as he tried to rein in the bellicose impulses of his frenetic partner, Marco had kept his eyes glued to the shore in the hopes of seeing a certain person appear and Atzcha, moving over to peer curiously from the same window, immediately understood the lengthy, dangerous delay: the high priest was coming across the clearing at a gallop, followed closely by the highest echelons of the military, who could barely keep up with him.

Once ashore, Chitoontecl began to gesticulate and shout orders left and right, first focusing his gaze on the cabin, then on the catwalk, then on the rafts. As overloaded as they were with warriors, they were heading fast towards the opposite shore in a sweeping semicircle upstream of the fissure. Their commanders, apparently mindful of the tragic experience the night of the escape, must have given some orders to keep the boats at some distance from the cabin. But they had calculated according to the reach of their bows and not that of the crossbows, which was almost double, and whose arrows they had attached grenades.

"So?" Atzcha asked, becoming increasingly impatient.

"Open the lower door behind me and get ready to fire," Marco finally consented. "I'll take care of the catwalk in a little bit. Now, you aim at the ladder on the wall and try to hit it in places close together in order to interrupt it for a good stretch. Then you can play around as much as you like with the boats and the pier...but wait for my first shot before you start. He put the barrel of the rifle in the slot after ensuring that the weapon was set to a single shot. "Now it's just you and me, you bastard," he whispered through his teeth, "you just couldn't wait to take back your slave-girl, huh? Don't you know that you can't hurt her anymore..." he continued taking aim while his index finger began to press imperceptibly on the trigger.

When he fired, the deafening thunder produced inside the cabin startled both the occupants, especially Atzcha who, as much as she had been warned, had certainly not expected such a bang. A moment later Chitoontecl was kicking at the air, lying on the shoreline with his hands pressed to his groin and Marco, thanking the national ser-vice for his perfect aim, felt an unspeakable pleasure in watching him suffer.

But it was certainly not the time to stand there and enjoy the show. Atzcha, whose moment of fright had passed, had immediately taken action and while Marco turned her way to take a position at the top slot, two grenades had already hit the ladder with pinpoint accuracy, breaking it off the wall for a good stretch about forty me-ters above the pier. The third grenade hit just that, killing men and spilling much of the material from above into the water. The fourth was lost in the lake, provoking a series of flowery expletives from the shooter, whose good mood was immediately restored when the next arrow hit the center of the middle raft. The explosion that followed wiped out almost all its occupants, and when the next grenades hit the other boats, they had already turned into ghost ships; seeing what happened to their companions, the warriors had taken the opportunity to rapidly rid themselves of their bulkier weapons, jump into the water and continue their trip swimming, heading towards the shore or the nearby jetty. But Atzcha didn't allow them to reach their goal, as she churned out arrow after arrow with cold determination and deadly precision, accompanying each shot with insults and expletives against the victims and their relatives.

The workers on the catwalk, who at first had paused in their work to observe in amazement the strange wooden hut that had appeared out of nowhere in front of them, then stood petrified by the sensational onset of the hostilities, but a few moments later, overwhelmed by fearful panic, they rushed en masse in the direction of the latter. Too late, though: Marco let out a long blast on the walkway and on the upper rungs of the ladder. Once he had exhausted the magazine he took the other in hand and repeated the same operation in the opposite direction, then moved to the slit next over to "clean up" the stump at the end of the walkway. The hail of bullets right into the middle of the group of fleeing workers cut dozens down. Some were swept aside by those who were trying to climb over and flew off the catwalk; others lost their minds and threw themselves into the void in terror.

In the meantime, however, some warriors had reached the jetty by swimming and those who had managed to bring a bow and quiver along with them crammed onto the ladder and quickly reached the point where it had been destroyed, then began to shoot arrows in the direction of the cabin. Most of the arrows fell into the water without even touching their target, but occasionally there was one that hit a bull's eye and hit the cabin with a dull thud, and was felt with some apprehension. The risk that an arrow could slip through a slot and hit the occupants grew more and more likely every moment: "Forget the men in the middle of the lake," Marco ordered. "Concentrate on those down on the ladder and the pier;

they're the most dangerous now. I, in the meantime, am trying to complete a certain task."

That said, after pushing a new magazine into the rifle and returning the lever to single shot, he pointed the gun towards the catwalk again. It was now deserted, and of the few survivors, some were lying face down on the walkway hoping to conceal themselves from view or be taken for dead by the occupants of the cabin situated at a slightly lower level; all the others, terrified by the decimation, had rushed in the direction of the ladder and railing and kicking at their fellow sufferers who, having found their path interrupted, were now trying to go back up. The first two shots just grazed a supporting hook, but the third hit it in full, disintegrating it. Other shots went out into space, but more often than not another hook flew out, until a long section of the walkway suddenly gave out a few feet all at the same time, leaning to one side and the boards that laid atop it, no longer restrained, began to slip one after the other into the void, dragging the living and the dead with them. Atzcha's infallible shots, meanwhile, progressed their clean-sweep on the ladder and on the pier until even the last daredevils, realizing their impotence and decimation, chose to throw their bows and quivers away, jump into the water and hurriedly take refuge under what remained of the pier with the serious intent to await nightfall before daring to stick their noses out again.

It had been a real catastrophe. The surface of the lake was dotted with patches of crimson and dozens of corpses drifting and floating on the water. The moans and appeals for relief coming from the wounded were heard muffled all the way up in the cabin but Atzcha, not yet satiated with blood, continued to rage with fierce coldness on them, too. "Enough," Marco said, pulling the gun from the slit and stopping the massacre. Wiping sweat from his forehead with the back of his hand, he grabbed the binoculars and moved to the window that overlooked the beach.

Chitoontecl had disappeared. On the shoreline, in his place there was a big pool of blood, and Marco could not help but wonder what happened. "They've had enough for today," he decreed, averting his eyes from the shore. "And I think some time will pass before they decide to come back here and mess with us…we can go back to the base," he said, puling the rope to send the signal to those above that they were ready to go back up. Everyone crowded joyfully around the two victors in a blaze of joy and exclamations, and from that moment on the cabin started up and down in a continuous cycle, delivering women and children by their turn to enjoy the spectacle of the battlefield.

That night, for the first time in the history of the World Above, a huge bonfire was lit in the meadow and its flames, clearly visible from the valley, were the sign of victory, a true act of defiance against the persecutors. Since they got back to the meadow Atzcha had accompanied Marco for the rest of the day, and that night she had taken her place to the left of the *tlatoani* of her own initiative, drawing Xeetha's critical gaze, who as of yet had not dared to question that kind of entitlement.

Once all the festivities were finished, Marco went to the shelter, determined to get a good night's sleep. He must have dozed off not too long ago when he was awakened by Atzcha and one of her Amazons, both nude, who went to lie down at his hips. The spectacle they gave him of their athletic bodies' perfect figures and the scent of their skin kept him from any attempt at protesting. His head leaned back on the bed, he closed his eyes and gave himself up completely.

When Marco awoke at dawn, he found himself tangled in the embrace of the two sleeping women. He was suddenly seized with guilt: this was the bridal bed on which he had made love many nights and shared only with his beloved. How could he have allowed that such a sacrilegious act be perpetrated? Surely, he thought, he must have been drugged to let go of himself so much…At first he was about to jump out of bed and cruelly drive away the two witches, but this reaction was precluded by the resurgence of a memory.

On more than one occasion Chatì had tried to broach the thorny topic of coexistence with future roommates, at times seriously and other times jokingly but never jealously, and laying out

235

for him his duties of hospitality towards them, duties that were not fulfilled by offering them shelter or simple sustenance. Be he had always glossed over the topic, or limited it to joking without giving it any weight, until that morning.

Perhaps, he justified, thinking back to the night's events, what had happened was just what she would have wanted. Reconciled with this knowledge, he looked at the two sleeping beauties through different eyes, and with a resigned, more than satisfied sigh, he huddled in the warmth of their bodies, letting himself drift remorselessly to sleep.

Chapter 41

The lesson imparted to their enemies proved very healthy. For days no one dared to set foot in the clearing and the corpses dragged downstream by the current were left to rot on the shore of the lake and the pier, which had been reduced to a pile of charred beams from the Amazons' flaming arrows, who in the days following the massacre took care to complete the work begun by their leader, systematically and permanently dismantling the way of access. And in order to deter any headlong rush by those who had not yet entirely grasped the concept, the cabin remained lowered day and night with two people on board with the task of supervising in shifts, surveying everything that had happened in the southern part of the crater.

The first to make their appearances were the wives and children of the fallen, and after hurriedly recovering the now decomposed bodies of their relatives, they cremated them unceremoniously at the edge of the clearing. Shortly after, the workers came back a few at a time with bunches of fiber to weave, and then their children, who happily and cheerfully resumed wallowing in the lake water. But several more weeks passed before the first men dared to set foot on the scene, who to prove their good intentions began to take away what little material escaped the rout and pile it near the shore.

In the end even the fisherman and his solitary aide reappeared. The boat had been one of the first targets of the hail of flaming arrows and the warriors' destructive fury and sustained rather serious damage, but the two got some help from a few young people to drag it well away from the shore, then worked hard on it and within a few weeks they had almost completed the repairs. Considering, however, that the boat was not very well regarded by those above, they did not seem willing to launch it anytime soon. But the lack of fish must have weighed heavily on the valley and the little that was remediable in the much shallower waters of the outflowing stream was not sufficient to meet the demands of the entire population in part because the peasants, in their unwillingness to tempt fate, harvested merely what was absolutely indispensable from the lake area.

It was these obvious necessities that provided the pretext for the startup of the first contact between the two enemy peoples. One morning, while the fisherman and his helper were finishing up work on the side of the boat facing the lake, a lone arrow suddenly stuck in the plating of the bow one step from them. The thud startled them both and as soon as they discovered the cause they were certain of having escaped by some miracle and were more than convinced that the subsequent shots would be much more accurate than the first, so they rushed to seek shelter behind the boat. The older of the two, however, whose running was slowed by his lame leg, had time to notice before he was around the hull that there was a small roll of bark wrapped around the shaft of the arrow. It did not take long to realize that perhaps he and his friend had not been chosen as the first sacrificial victims in a new show off strength. His spirit was calmed, but he was still not entirely convinced of his reasoning, so he stopped running and approached the arrow with his eyes fixed on the terrace.

Two weeks passed before a delegation formed in the clearing, made up of the fisherman, a herald complete with a green banner, then color of truce (as Atzcha explained, visibly pleased), a *pipiltin,* who must have been related to a rooster for how bedecked he was in feathers, and twelve serpent warriors in parade uniform, visibly unarmed, carrying on their shoulders three stretchers overloaded with crates and baskets of different sizes. Everything was loaded quickly onto the boat which was then rapidly pushed into the water by the zealous warriors, but only the fisherman went aboard; the herald, the *pipiltin,* and all the others instead remained stationary on the shore with the single task of ensuring that everything should take place in accordance with the agreements. While the ship took to the water heading towards the prearranged destination, the cabin began to descend from above. It did not stop at the usual point, but continued its course until it paused about twenty feet above the water and soon after, from the trap door of the platform, a cable with a richly laden net began to descend, filled with ointments, potions, medicines, rare feathers, geodes of fantastic crystals and many, many other goods which were sought-after and almost impossible to find in the valley.

Nothing, however, compared to the "treasure" that was sent to the World Above. Inside the cages brought from the boat were rabbits, turkeys, and even two puppies, and the baskets were filled with seedlings and seeds, tanned rabbit skins, cocoa beans, and following the unchallengeable request of the white *tlatoani*, two baskets of fish caught in the creek just before dawn.

It took several days of lively discussions and heated debates before the proposal contained in the pictogram sent downstream was accepted by the council of wise men. The most obstinate resistance was coming from the high priest who had survived even the latest wound; he was blinded by hatred and smoldering with a relentless desire for revenge against the mysterious "Son of the Mountain" (this was the most plausible interpretation depicting the signature scrawled at the bottom of the picture), who had not only stolen the object of his desires but had also physically crippled him twice in a devastation fashion. Chitoontecl at first did not want to hear reason, but the lake was of vital importance to the economy of the valley and the discontent of the people, which was now at such an alarming level that it would surely culminate in open revolt, so in the end— upon the recommendation of even the more far-sighted Mohotzuma—he had to bend to their wishes.

There was another big party that night when roasted fish made its first appearance on the table in the World Above. At the end of the dinner as he took small sips of a delicious hot drink made of honey and dissolved cocoa powder, Marco looked around himself, pausing on several faces. Some women were talking among themselves around the table still, but the majority were in the center of the semicircle, singing and dancing. Even the smallest children took part in the festivities with the most hilarious dance steps while the older ones, divided into "good guys" and "bad guy," roamed far and wide across the meadow to reenact the epic exploits of the recent battle.

Those faces were all smiling and happy, and in that moment Marco realized he could not trade a single one of their smiles for all the gold that shone on the roof of Aplaia. On his frantic quest for answers he had traveled the world, accumulating experience and knowledge of different peoples and cultures, fleeing from a life that was not his. And now, looking around, he was wondering if he had finally reached his long-awaited goal, if the answer to his eternal questions was not right in front of him, in that little strip of land trapped between the narrow walls, in those faces, in those smiles, or maybe in one of them…

"What are you thinking about?" Xeetha asked, pulling him from his thoughts.

"I was thinking…I was thinking that you're a wonderful woman," he replied suddenly, following the logical thread of his thoughts.

Uttered with a wide, innocent smile, those words provoked a completely unexpected reaction. Xeetha's face blanched white as a sheet and then became red as fire; the woman looked around as though bewildered, as though she wanted to make sure that no one else had heard; then she lowered her eyes to the ground and quickly lifted them to meet the man's eyes briefly in a sort of mute invocation; finally, she turned her face the other way to gaze at a distant, imprecise point on the other side of the crater.

"Please…you fool!" she defended herself in a whisper and with an unsteady voice, fidgeting with the cord that cinched at her waist with nervous fingers.

"And…and what do you think they'll do down there now?" said Marco, angered with himself for having once more filled his lungs with air without thinking about the consequences of his words, seeking to bring entirely different topics to the conversation.

"Well," she answered, grateful for the escape that he had offered her, "we can't be deceived by appearances; the exchanges this morning do not mean real peace, they were dictated by necessity, by self-interest. They were just a wall of smoke lifted before our eyes to obscure our view and make us believe the opposite of what they think and what they plan to do. They were defeated by one man and a group of poor women, slaves moreover, and a warrior who respects himself will never bear such grave disgrace…So you can be sure that they will never settle for our perfumes and our necklaces, that they will not sleep from our potions and they will not rest until they see us again, at their feet or at the top of the pyramid."

"Yes, I am convinced of the same," Marco condescended thoughtfully.

From that day on, the instances of contact between the two worlds became more and more significant and numerous. The villagers were happy to swap seeds and animals for artifacts that only the *tlatoani*'s older slaves were able to produce with real mastery, but only a few were rich enough to afford them. The first to come into possession of them, despite his stubborn opposition to the agreement, was the same Chitoontecl. He was closely followed in this by Mohotzuma, the powerful *pipiltin,* a few courtesans and a handful of other magnates. They also occasionally fell into the hands of those in the working class. In fact, although the fisherman was compelled to deliver all the exchanged goods to the authorities, he often managed—with a few extra baskets of fish to be sent up with the rest on the sly—to scrape away a bit of everything for himself, which he then resold under the table at affordable prices to less wealthy people. He had thereby come to establish a relationship of mutual convenience as friendly as it was profitable between him and the inhabitants of the terrace, much to the great satisfaction of both parties.

But, as Xeetha had rightly pointed out, the truce in place was not destined to last, due to both the wounded warriors' and their commanders' pride, and above all the implacable hatred that Chitoontecl harbored for all the inhabitants of the World Above and the Son of the Mountain particularly. The high priest had dared to set foot again in the clearing long after all the other inhabitants of the valley showed their faces. He was visibly limping and always kept a safe distance from the shore, and was always well protected by the shields of a handful of warriors by whom he was constantly surrounded. Marco almost regretted not having aimed for his head in that moment; if he had, there would probably not be so many difficulties in smoothing everything over. This could always be remedied by a well-aimed rifle shot, but such an action could negatively backfire on the World Above, whether successful or not, by giving the enemy a pretext for breaking the truce that had been formed so painstakingly. On the contrary, leaving things as they were, it was not to be excluded that the inhabitants of the valley would realize on their own sooner or later their own mutual benefit derived from the agreement.

Marco, however, had no illusions: the World Above could not let its guard down and run the risk of being caught by surprise a second time, but it would have to stay alert, ready to thwart any offensive attempt from below. And this condition might be achieved and consolidated, giving rise to the project that had been dreamed of for so long, but which until that moment had always been delayed.

Chapter 42

The carcass of the helicopter, now emptied of everything that could be removed, lay abandoned in the woods beyond the top of the crevasse. Marco had never resigned himself to the idea of leaving all that God-given material unused. On the other hand, he had always had to surrender to the evidence: with the scarce tools at his disposal, he would never had been able to take advantage of the infinite potential of that enormous mass of solid steel as he would like, and in all those years the rust had managed to set in only in a few spots. The three hacksaws would be destroyed if he used them to cut and work the whole body, and even the few precious drill bits were already largely worn from his previous work. He needed something that could melt the metal.

But at this point there were a few problems. First: what temperature did he need to reach? He had not even the faintest idea, nor could he consider burning the entire forest to experiment. The only way to get to the bottom of it without being forced to cut downloads of trees would have been to concentrate the heat in a small space, one free from thermal losses. This very much in contrast with the size of the aircraft. So the second problem was that the helicopter needed to be broken down into lots of small pieces, and the tools required needed to be much sturdier than those on hand. The third and last problem was that he also needed to find the proper fuel for the task.

It was in the shelter that he found the solution. He was grabbing his notepad to devote himself to a few scribbles of the project when his eyes fell on the bent corner of an old, warped steel plate, evidence of its dramatic arrival in the World Above. A memory flashed through the man's mind, of the fateful night when the plate started glowing: "The black stones!" In one fell swoop he had solved the first and the third problem, and the only thing that remained was to use his ingenuity to create the tools ad hoc.

Scattered here and there in the meadow were several boulders that were not possible to move both because of their size and because they were too deep in the ground, but for some time Marco had been eyeing one that was suited to his idea. Cuboidal in shape, it was more than half a meter high and the women most skilled in manual labor did not have to work hard to dig a shallow basin with a drainage channel. It was a bit more challenging to create a dome with a truncated cone shape to go on top, whose vault culminated in a large hole sealable by a stone stopper. At the base of the chamber four small vents were left open into which just as many rabbit-skin bellows were inserted. Under the precise instruction of the project manager, the stonecutters had unsheathed all their mastery in gouging the negatives of two hammers in a couple of stones, the two arms of a long pincer and the molds of several other tools. Some final touch-ups, and everything was ready for the fateful test.

Upon impact with the ground, the helicopter nose had crumpled in on itself, collapsing in several places. The moisture content of the soil in which it had been embedded for many years and the lack of protective paint that had been scraped off by the impact had taken care of the rest: the rust had invaded it inside and out and when it was pulled from the ground it was reduced to a jumble of corroded, contorted metal spikes that were quite easily removed even with the few basic tools they had available. Then they ransacked the entire scree in search of black stones, and Marco pronounced himself satisfied only after having made them make a pile next to the furnace that was more than sufficient to fill it to the brim at least three times. The next morning, while the workers were busy splitting the small geodes in two, he himself arranged them neatly in the furnace, laying the half spheres against the wall with the cup containing the crystals turned inward, and bridging together the combustion chamber by alternating layers of wood mixed with other black stones crushed to layers of metal.

When the fire was lit at dawn the next day at the level of the lower opening, the bellows began to operate at full capacity, and not five minutes after lighting they heard a crash followed closely by a growing crackle. The noise soon became so loud that everyone, thinking of Marco, began to fear that the walls could explode at any moment, but no one dared to leave their assigned station. After reaching its crescendo the hail of gunfire gradually began to die down and make way for a more intense, more deafening noise similar in every way to that of a jet plane at takeoff. After a quarter of an hour, the women working the bellows were exhausted by fatigue and almost roasted by the heat. The fire continued to rage inside the furnace, but from the lower opening, through which an inferno of blinding flashes could be glimpsed, not a single thing came out.

Despite the heat, Marco's heart was caught in an icy vice. His confidence was waning in correlation with the fuel and his head was swirling in a sea of thoughts that were hardly comforting. He was distressed and almost on the point of issuing the order to lift the lid to add new fuel to the furnace, while recognizing that this would have led to a sharp fall in internal temperature, further expectations and, most likely, crushing defeat. But what alternative could there be at that point?

"Yes!" he cried suddenly, falling to his knees and shaking his fists in the air repeatedly. "Yes! *Ai suma, ai suma!*" he continued to scream, jumping around the furnace like a maniac regardless of the confusion caused in the onlookers by his very undignified behavior. To dissuade him from gloomy thoughts a trickle of incandescent magma popped out from the mouth of the furnace a few moments before and now, like a snake with variegated red and black coils, it was slipping sinuously, faster and faster along the gutter.

Soon after, his cry was joined by the excited exclamation of the workers. Those closest to the furnace remained motionless, as if mesmerized by the fiery band that continued to leak from the mouth of the furnace, and they were roused from the enchantment only when

Atzcha yelled for them to return to their duties. In pairs, according to precise instructions, they then rushed to pick up off the ground the stone panels secured to wooden handles and gather the precious liquid inside, while the other spectators in their enduring incredulity thronged around them for a closer look at the scorching hot cast that slipped ever more abundantly into the molds.

When the fruits of their labors were brought to light, though rough and spurious compared to the models of the technologized world, there was a succession of hugs and euphoric cheers while the *tlatoani,* whose mood had just reached historic lows, was rapidly regaining ground and far surpassing its former norms.

Chapter 43

From that moment on nothing hampered the major project. Within a few months, by dint of hammer blows and the strength of pincers, the helicopter in its entirety had been dismembered and reduced to parts that could be easily inserted into the furnace. Each time, the latter necessitated a considerable contribution of valuable timber, but the white *tlatoani* with his eyes on the future gave orders to procure this mainly through heavy pruning; in this way they would not only avoid deforestation but the plants would benefit from it in strength and productivity. And though for the last few castings they could not help but to fell some of them, each was immediately replaced by a sapling of the same species collected from a nursery that had been installed at the edge of the forest.

Marco had already delegated these tasks to teams of experienced workers who were able to carry out the job alone. For his part, supported by the Amazons, he had worked round the clock setting up a real blacksmith shop whose stone anvils, reinforced with steel plates, resounded from dawn to dusk with a sledgehammer crashing down on hot rods, and two rudimentary stone wheels spun by pedals entered into operation with the purpose of sharpening blades. Day after day, the helicopter was thus transformed into an arsenal of swords, arrowheads and spears, and an infinite quantity of nails and tools. He had also paid special attention to the forging of two scimitars designed just for him. The steep was moved from the forge to the anvil, from the anvil to quenching and then again to the forge an infinite number of times, and the grindstone turned for days and days before the craftsman was satisfied by the sharpening and the oriental look of the blades. On the hilts, in the hardest, flame-tempered wood, he had molded the imprint of his hand and when they swung his swords the metal gave off flashes of light that was reflected like lightning on the infinite mirrors of the mountain.

"We did a great job," Marco said at the height of satisfaction to the nearby diners during dinner. In the afternoon the last batch of steel had been liquefied and the arrowheads that came out of the molds had been attached to the shafts.

"We could not have done any better," Xeetha agreed. "But surely they haven't been sleeping down there this whole time," she added, indicating the valley with her chin and vocally externalizing the concern that brooded constantly in every heart.

In fact, the frenetic activity which in recent months had keep the inhabitants of the World Above quite busy, had served to mitigate some of their anxieties, but now that the most challenging part of the undertaking was brought to completion, these reemerged in full force. Even so, despite the hard work, guard duty at the cabin had never ceased and for some time the watchmen were noting new and disconcerting levels of unrest in the valley.

The fisherman continued to cast his nets into the lake and appear on time for appointments to exchange goods, the children never ceased cackling, running, and diving into the water, and the washerwomen, artisans and the usual frequenters of the lake area continued to carry out their usual activities undeterred. Everything apparently proceeded normally, but a less naïve observer would easily notice that on the contrary much had changed down below. The gardens and fields, for example, were no longer as populated as they once were; one had the impression that the few farmers who came and went kept their business to a minimum. And if one could see that in the countryside, it was even more notable within the city. Aplaia seemed unusually quiet, deserted, as though asleep. In the streets, in the squares, in the gardens, there was no longer the usual bustle of people who were busy and engaged, the markets were nearly deserted and the constructions sites were almost all strangely still. Especially concerning—rather than comforting—was the fact that the youths had not resumed practicing on the clearing.

"This time too, they're not putting much effort into hiding their intentions," Xeetha continued, again the interpreter of the communal thought process, "only a totally brainless person would be beguiled by all that normalcy. That beating, rather than deter them, only served to make them more cautious. For sure, they've been planning some new attack for a while. And from right over there," she added, nodding in the direction of the waterfall and agreeing reluctantly with Atzcha's hypothesis. "And the worst part of it is," she concluded thoughtfully, "that this time there is no way of knowing what they're up to down there."

"But there might be," interjected Atzcha.

"Yes, and how might that be?" Xeetha rebuked skeptically.

"If you let me finish maybe I can explain it," the other retorted angrily.

Since she had established herself in the seat to Marco's left, Atzcha had transformed even more in his shadow. During the day she was always right behind him and her nightly visits to the shelter in the company of her students were no longer a mystery to anyone. And she did not do much to keep them a secret. Hardly. The things was stirring up a huge amount of resentment in the community and Xeetha was a willing spokesman every time the occasion arose. "During the night," the warrior continued, softening her tone of voice as she turned to the *tlatoani* as though she wanted to be understood only by him, "we could lower someone from my group down and send her to inspect the other side of the valley so as to—"

"Yes, that's a great idea!" Xeetha interrupted again. "Just imagine that those down there didn't put sentries everywhere on the lookout: your faithful friend would not even have time to dip her paw in the water before finding herself belly-up at the top of the pyramid good and ready to be skinned...Not before, however," she continued in a clipped tone, "delighting our friends' ears with all she knows about us...No, you can forget it, we're not even going to talk about it," the woman said, thinking that she had closed the topic.

Atzcha was about to retort when Marco, sensing an oncoming storm, interjected loudly amidst the bickering: "I think both of you are right." The heads of the two combatants turned to him in unison looking almost offended at the intrusion and not quieted by any accounts. "That they are preparing another nasty surprise for us is beyond a shadow of a doubt," continued Marco, staring straight ahead so as to address everyone and no one. "And we can also be sure that they can't wait to get their hands on one of us to wring out everything she knows about us. On the other hand, we cannot be caught by surprise a second time. When they come back, besides being numerous, they will also be much, much more cautious and dangerous than before, and in spite of all our weapons it won't be easy to fend them off if we don't know their intentions in advance. We will have to run some risk, but that doesn't mean we have to act mindlessly; as few as we are, we cannot afford to lose even a fingernail off one of our own."

"So?" the two asked in unison.

"So…so…" Marco snapped, beginning to lose his temper because he did not have even one intelligent proposal to offer: "before rushing into it let's think it over a couple of times, and we'll find the right solution!"

Atzcha and Xeetha were only partially satisfied, but judging by his tone of voice it was not the time to press the issue, so they nodded in silence and Marco was able to breathe a sigh of relief, although he was aware of having facilitated a merely fragile truce in the course of which the two rivals would certainly work over the rules. For some time now, in fact, he had noticed that the skirmishes between the two leading ladies were growing more and more frequent and toxic, with the risk of leading to open conflict at any moment. He tried to mediate in every possible way, to quiet tempers and contain repeated attacks, but he realized that the task was becoming increasingly difficult. A little voice was whispering in his ear with increasing insistence that he could be pulled into the fray but, like an ostrich with his head in the sand, he preferred not to broach the subject. Not even with himself.

Chapter 44

The defensive system that was developed to cope with the new attack relied entirely upon the assumption, which was almost taken for granted, that the attack would come from the waterfall area. The rock wall that flanked it protruded from the mountain like a huge wedge, which after bordering the lower bank of the lake rose up and gradually narrowed to close into the mountain far above the terracing, reaching over the outer edge by thirty years and thus creating a sort of natural curtain between this and the northern part of the valley. About as thick as the meadow was high, the opinions of the former slaves were very discordant. There were those who spoke of a hundred or so meters, but others—the most reliable, perhaps—at least double that. There was so much discrepancy of opinion that Marco was infuriated each time he tried to get something more precise out of his informants. On the other hand, how could they have imagined, when they still lived in the valley, that it would one day become vital for them to know the exact shape of this insignificant rock ledge that divided them from their enemy? Enemy who, at that point, could consider circumventing it, or climbing over it, or, why not? Puncture it, even.

Unfortunately, the noise that the waterfall made, which had so long been their ally, was now playing a diametrically opposite role by covering up any noise nearby. For some time Marco, on the advice of his collaborators, had arranged ambushes and guard duty near the waterfall and the southern end of the crater to try to glean some useful evidence, but until that day, aside from the usual ranks of poor wretches directed daily to the quarry and the mines, the sentries had never noticed anything suspicious. Evidently, they thought, the bulk of the laborers had to move before dawn or, yet more likely, stay there right behind that rock.

In any case, the residents of the terrace had not remained lifeless after the painstaking metal casting. They now possessed more than enough weapons, but they also had to prepare the terrain to be suitable for those weapons. Atzcha had provided valuable suggestions in this regard and Marco, who was not to be outdone, had added his own. Together they dictated the plan.

From a hundred meters away from the waterfall, the workers began to dig several holes in the meadow about a meter and a half in diameter and almost twice as deep, and after having planted sharpened pegs point-up at the bottom, they covered them with a fragile lattice of rods which were then camouflaged by a thin mossy carpet that was perpetually watered so as to keep the grass from yellowing and betraying their presence. The earth that was dug from the holes in the meantime was gathered into a high defensive wall of stakes and stones, starting from the waterfall, flanking the forest for the whole length of the booby-trap area and then traversed the meadow to the outer edge. And as the work progressed, the top of the fence was fortified at regular intervals by long, sharp stakes with the dual purpose of hindering the assaults on the anterior side and then to support the battlements on the opposite side.

The invaders had to be stopped at all costs in the determined stretch of land, which ended at the edge of the forest, and then at its forefront at the wall, and at the other two sides, the edges of the meadow, one of which looked out over the waterfall and the other over the lake. If their enemies were able to overcome the defensive wall, they could easily gain the woods and spread in every direction in the dense vegetation and the defenders at that point would have a retreat beyond the chasm as their only means of escape, where it was not easy to resist a long siege or a well-planned attack.

Atzcha had delegated to her faithful pupils the task of instructing the others in combat, but every day she personally tested each recruit's level of preparedness, assigning roles and strategic positions based on specific skills. She was tireless and very exacting, but the example she set was infectious and in just a few weeks from the group of former slaves remarkable marksmen had come forward, some even able to compete with the Amazons. But certainly not with her.

The days were visibly getting shorter, but every minute of light was devoted to exercises and work, often enduring until after dark by the light of makeshift campfires. After a frugal supper, while two girls took turns at the cabin for the night shift, the others retreated hastily to their huts. And shortly thereafter, all was quiet in the World Above.

With increasing frequency and now complete indifference to keeping up appearances, Atzcha left her lodging at night to go to the shelter. She was almost always accompanied by one of her students— even more than one, not infrequently—and Marco, as exhausted as he was by the day's fatigues, had not even dreamt of protesting to these visits which only seemed carelessly furtive; the thermal water, the skilled hands and fabulous bodies had a portentous, regenerative effect on him; and if then the next morning he was struggling to get out of bed, the memory of the events the night before abundantly compensated in mood and spirit.

One evening, he was undressing when he heard the door of the shelter thrown open behind him: "By now I thought that you hadn't made it out alive tonight," he said without turning around, looking forward to the rest of the night.

"Actually she is not coming tonight. It's her turn for the watch, and there's no reason that she shouldn't do it like all the others. Including me."

Recognizing the voice was like a cold shower for Marco. "Xe…Xeetha! And you…what are you doing here?" he stammered when, suddenly turning around, he saw her towering behind him, one step from the bed.

"I'm sorry, my *tlatoani*…" Xeetha continued, sounding a bit less harsh, "but I needed to talk to you."

"And what is so important that it cannot be postponed until tomorrow morning?" he scolded her angrily, disappointed in his hope.

"Look," the woman flared, raising her voice and putting her hands on her hips. "Either you live in a world that is only yours, or you are so blind that you cannot even see an inch past your own nose to realize what is going on around you.

"What are you talking about?" he asked innocently.

"What am I talking about!? I'm talking about the situation that you brought about…as if there were not already enough fear and anxiety about what they're planning for us down there."

"I still don't understand," he tried to defend himself.

"I don't know if you noticed, but that wall-rider and her worthy companions now consider you to be theirs, their property, a plaything to amuse themselves when and how they please. They have created a vacuum around you…They pretty themselves up for being the chosen ones and go around telling everyone about their exploits. In full detail. And you think that the others are made of stone? They are women, dear *tlatoani,* and all young, healthy and strong, and you know—or perhaps pretend not to know—that they were not raised to be farmers before they came up here, but for completely different purposes, principally to satisfy men in their every desire. And in the World Above, in case you've forgotten, there is only one: you. Chatiztacqui would never have approved of your behavior."

"Mm," Marco grunted, brooding after a long pause. He had assumed that his nightly encounters were now more than widely known, but had not thought that they would arouse any resentment. On top of that, he was very disappointed to learn that his exploits were regaled to everyone at night. He had had a presentiment that sooner or later the chickens would come home to roost and that it would not be at all easy for him to go on pretending like nothing was happening but now, under the pressure of the prosecution, he was beginning to feel a vague sense of guilt. Bluntly and with her trademark frankness, Xeetha had made it clear that by insisting upon this selfishness he would run the risk of creating incurable rifts in the community with unpredictable consequences in an already precarious situation. "But…but it will be a problem trying to tell all this to…" he muttered in a low voice, speaking more to himself than to his interlocutor while his mind analyzed in quick succession the relevant pros and cons—for himself, of course—of the possible cessation of the now-reinforced ménage à trois night.

The woman made him lie down on the bed and, sprinkling her hands with ointment, began to massage his back and loins with care: "As for Atzcha's reaction, if I were you, I wouldn't worry too much," she reassured him, pretending to have understood his concerns in a completely different way. "After all, you did not order her to take her shift on the watch. If anything, she should be angry with me. Don't you think?"

"Bah," Marco commented, not at all following the convoluted reasoning of his lover.

"I understand your concerns, and I realize," Xeetha continued, assuming a tone that was at once complicit and ironic, "that we cannot hurt her feelings too much and hurt her self-respect by treating her like the last of the chicken coop; her work is too essential to us and no one could do it as well as her. And this unfortunately she probably also realizes is her strong point, and we know that she can be dangerous and vindictive when things don't go her way."

"That is just what I wanted to tell you," the tall man lied, not at all willing to clarify the real reasons for his hesitation.

"So, getting back to us," Xeetha proceeded, glossing over the blatant lie, "I really think we should invent a good excuse to sweeten the bitter pill she'll have to swallow."

"Mh," Marco grunted again, who in spite of himself was beginning to resign to the idea of subjecting to his duties. "I'm afraid so. And what do you propose?"

Oh," responded his satisfied partner, feeling the approach of the surrender, "knowing her nature, we could organize a beautiful ceremony during which you could give her an important emblem in front of everyone. You could…I don't know…name her the supreme commander of the army of the World Above. What do you say? It might work; she's one who cares about these things."

The proposal was too immediate and articulate to have been formulated on the spot, Marco considered, realizing only then that he was being manipulated by a wily puppeteer. He pretended not to notice though he was rather annoyed by the scam, assumed a thoughtful expression, and held the deceiver on tenterhooks for a while before speaking, both to make her realize that she had not succeeded in duping him like a fool and, above all, because he was not yet convinced of the soundness of the proposal. "I'm sure," he finally decided to say, "knowing full well how nice our mutual friend is to you, that the plan you're cooking up has been on your mind for some time now."

"Mh," the woman let slip, communicating an admission of guilt without saying too much.

"On the other hand, in these circumstances, I can't blame you. Even if, contrary to what you believe, I'm not at all convinced that she will be angry only with you...In any case, accepting your proposal as a good one, I would be willing to name her supreme commander of the warriors of the World Above. It may seem like a minor quibble, but knowing her type..."

"Well said!" Xeetha finished contentedly, flying over the not-so-veiled accusations. "Then we are agreed to the following: in five days. The time required to organize a ceremony as it ought to be done."

Xeetha had already started towards the door when she was stopped in the threshold by the man's voice: "Where are you going?"

"Who knows where I'm going at this time of..."

She paused when she grasped the meaning of the inquiry. "I...I cannot," she stammered in a choked voice. "I...I am Chatiztacqui's sister...I am old, and..."

"What are you talking about," he replied, moving towards her with a wide smile. "In the world I come from it is rare for a woman less than your age to marry."

Marco sensed the internal upheaval that his words and attitude could cause in her; he remembered well the reaction elicited by his impulsive joke. She, he had thought repeatedly when considering the incident, would never have had such a disproportionate reaction if she had not felt something particular for him, something very different from simply friendship, and this forced her to deal with her past. Life seemed too horrible to her; she had seen and suffered too much violence, and now she was in love with this handsome, kind stranger; her surprise at this new, unexpected feeling and the fear of not knowing how to deal with it made her fragile, vulnerable.

Marco took her gently by the hand and swung the door back into its frame. Then he looked her in the eyes, put his hands on her shoulders and pulled her into a tight embrace. When their bodies touched, a groan escaped from the woman's lips and Marco distinctly felt the tremor that ran through her while she remained still, fighting between anxiety and desire. When he untied her robe and softly kissed her lips, the tension finally broke, and Xeetha threw her arms around him and pulled him to her passionately, as though afraid that someone or something could take him from her, while hot tears of joy ran down her face. She was receiving something that she had never experienced in all her life, and she wanted to reciprocate that gift with all of herself.

"You have saved me twice," she said later, when they were lying side by side. "When you came down to the valley you liberated me from slavery. This evening you have delivered my soul…Now I know what love is, now I can die without regrets, because—" Her voice trembled, announcing new, different tears.

"You already want to put me back in Atzcha's hands?" Marco interrupted, turning to her with a roguish smile.

Xeetha's sad, pensive expression broke into a smile of gratitude, and like lightning she pushed him onto his back and straddled his abdomen: "You're one son of a wall-rider, *tlatoani*. We'll see when I'm done if you still have the breath to say stupid things."

Those movements, those gestures, those words…This time he was to be assailed by memories and suddenly transported far, far back in time.

Chapter 45

From that day on a new order reigned in the World Above. Xeetha finally resumed her role as the white *tlatoani's* alter ego, acting as an intermediary between him and the whole community, while continuing to act as director of projects and all other activities except of course the military, which remained absolutely under Atzcha's authority. She had not received the new directives with much sportsmanship. Marco, in fact, had awaited her vainly in the shelter in the days and weeks following. Evidently, he pondered, she must have been very resentful of the fact that he, the *tlatoani,* in spite of everything that had happened between them, had not lifted a finger to spare her the thankless task of acting as a sentinel. He had a not disinterested sense of guilt towards his former benefactress and so, while continuously refining his defense so as to ingratiate himself in her regard, on the day when she finally decided to visit him again he had thought of a remedy that was even more satisfying than a bunch of speeches to quell the wrath of his intransigent, irrational friend.

Marco implored Xeetha to postpone the scheduled ceremony and he retired to his workshop for days, hammering away at a shield and an appropriately sized leather helmet reinforced with steel plates. Then, separating himself a bit reluctantly from one of the two scimitars, he made it a little shorter and changed the handle to fit the hand of its beautiful wielder. With that gift, he told himself as he melted away in sweat, she would certainly forgive his cowardice and call it quits with her now too-protracted nighttime defections. And when the ceremony was held before the entire gathered community and he awarded her with the high title and then presented her with the helmet, the shield and the beautiful scimitar, he congratulated himself when he noticed the warrior's radiant expression, who seemed to have moved with her weapons and bags to the top of Olympus.

"You were quite right," he whispered in Xeetha's ear contentedly at the end of the ceremony, feeling in his heart and mind that he had leveled accounts with the Junoesque Amazon and entered again into her good graces. But in the days that followed, things did not exactly go according to his predictions.

Proud of her given title, Atzcha never missed an opportunity to make a good show of her insignia to her companions. On her own initiative she had embellished her helmet with a plume of beautiful feathers and spent hours and hours training with the scimitar that had become her inseparable companion. Marco, on the contrary, had thinned out a lot of his training sessions with her and her students; because no one deigned him with her presence at night any longer, there was no reason for her to go look for them during the day.

The direct result was that shortly thereafter, the white *tlatoani* was no longer able to compete with many of them with weapons. But the fact that he was being beaten by women in the martial arts did not bother him too much. What was really hurting him was the fact that in spite of the wonderful gifts and the high-sounding title, Atzcha had not only not delighted him with her presence at night, but she had continued to avoid him during the day. While waiting on the increasingly unlikely possibility that she would rethink, he continued to console himself in Xeetha's arms and every now and then, and according to the wishes of his new partner, he received a new visitor.

But it was no longer the same. He could not deny it: the new entertainers were all brave, intelligent, helpful and also very well disposed towards him, and they would go to the ends of the earth to satisfy his every desire, but he, not being particularly familiar with any of them, felt a sort of ill-concealed embarrassment during these encounters, something that despite all his goodwill inhibited him and prevented him from satisfying them as he would have wished to. His wounded ego was struggling to admit it, but the more days went by the more the nostalgia for the past heightened, major, formidable battles full of emotions that only Atzcha and her uninhibited companions were able to elicit.

To be honest, he had long had another desire, but he had not confessed it to anyone, not even to Atzcha in their best moments: Peepty the redhead. Small, slender but well-proportioned, she could be called a miniature woman. Her long, coppery curls stood out from far away in the midst of so many heads of raven-black hair around the meadow. Her minute nose was surrounded by a myriad of freckles and protruded just above her thin lips which were almost always spread into a sad, but gentle and appealing smile. She was the antithesis of Atzcha. She, cyclonic, quick-tempered, always drawn by competition, dedicated solely to physical fitness and very little inclined to conversations that did not address the martial arts, was always capable of instantly switching from the most amicable laughter to the most furious rages. Peepty, on the contrary, was sober and reflective, but not at all shy. Cultured, refined, of an eclectic mind and many interests, she had great influence in her circle of friends, to the point that she, like Atzcha, had cultivated for herself a group of faithful companions with whom she loved to spend time and discuss many different topics, dispensing advice and tips that were always useful and appropriate, and many hung onto her every word.

Each time after dinner that there would be a knock at his door, Marco was always hoping to see the tawny-haired head appear in his room, but he was always promptly disappointed. That girl had something special that was different from all the others, and it was not just her enigmatic smile or her intelligence that made her so interesting. There was something in her that was mysterious, impalpable, that charmed, intrigued and attracted him in the most compelling way, and more than once he had found himself daydreaming about how it would be if ever she came to visit him.

Infrequently in the past, he happened to pass unnoticed to the other half of the sky. He just could not adjust to the idea that he was not worthy to even be looked at by one of his delegates, it amazed him, it floored him, it mortified him, but at the same time it heightened his desire for his coveted prey, and as the days gradually went by he was able to realize how vain his expectation was, and there were several signs of the erosion of his steely determination not to be the first to make a move, and to give serious consideration to the idea of doing away entirely with his rather uprooted principles in order to start something up with this enigmatic sphinx.

But Peepty's behavior was not his primary concern. What most haunted and tormented him was the thought of what the enemy was concocting on the other side of the rock. It was vital to figure out their intentions well in advance in order to plan the appropriate countermeasures in time, but none of the proposals that had been suggested to him at that point had him convinced, either because they were inconclusive, or too risky, or impossible to achieve.

Almost all the women had volunteered to be sent down, although they all knew it would mean suicide. In fact, despite the complicity of the nighttime, it would have been extraordinarily difficult for them to circumvent the dense network of surveillance that had to have been established in every corner of the valley, especially in the vicinity of the lake, nor was it possible to consider attempting any action during the day. Marco had also thought about the possibility of surprising the enemy with a counterattack by attempting a night raid beyond the outcrop after having circumvented it with the help of the climbing equipment, but he soon abandoned this idea; this kind of an undertaking was already dangerous for him, as he pondered the possibility of mountaineering, let alone for his friends who had never even seen a climbing nail. But the danger was approaching by leaps and bounds and from day to day the need to have some direction grew more pressing. Risky or not, the solution had to be found at all costs, and as soon as possible.

Finally one day at a meeting, a proposal was suggested to him that, risky as it was, would have more chance of success than those which had so far been put forward. "My son Itzac," began Tlachinalli with a note of awkwardness (she was a small woman, thin and very shy, but beloved by all for her great kindness and her willingness to help others in all circumstances), "has always been a very good swimmer, only Chatiztacqui was able to compete with him when we still lived in the valley. He could stay underwater without breathing for an infinite time and catch fish as long as an arm in their burrows with just his hands. He is just over three cycles old, but is much bigger for his age, and he has always solved problems alone."

"Continue," Marco encouraged her, a bit stupefied, as he knew her shyness and was hearing her participate in a meeting for the first time.

"Thank you, my *tlatoani*," she said with a gracious smile, emitting the little air that was left in her lungs in a single breath and then continuing excitedly. "We could lower him down on a moonless night, and he, swimming underwater, could reach the area of the stone that burns. On that stone there will be no guardsmen; my son Itzac however, with reinforced fiber boots that will protect his feet from the heat and make no noise, could then leave the water and by staying on the ground that burns head towards the tall trees. There too, so far away from the lake, there should not be many guards, but even if there were it is much easier to hide in the woods and Itzac, beyond being as fast and silent as a jaguar, is also capable of disappearing behind even a reed…Then it will be terribly easy for him to walk along the outer edge of the valley just below the walls of Aplaia and from there reach the river. In those parts there are dozens and dozens of huts where farmers keep their tools and seeds. My son could wait for morning in one of those stores and the next morning when work resumes he could take advantage of the confusion to slip in with the others…There are boys engaged in quarrying and mining, down there, as many as the stalks in a field of Mahis, and their faces change from day to day. Who will recognize my Itzac in the midst of so many?"

As Tlachinalli unveiled the plan, everyone felt that they were listening to what was by far the most sensible and least dangerous of all the proposals made during the meeting up until that day.

And Marco also felt the same conviction growing in him: "Yours is a very good proposal, Tlachinalli," he said to the woman at the end of her summary proposition, "but it also includes great risks…" he felt compelled to add. "Itzac is still a boy and he is also your only son. Have you thought about this?"

"How can you ask such a thing, my *tlatoani*? Do you not think that a mother is the first to see dangers that may threaten her child? If we were still in the valley he would have been taken from me many moons ago. You know what fate awaited the sons of us slaves, and Itzac knows it too…The son of a slave knows that there is no hope for him, and he grows up very quickly and soon learns things that other, more fortunate boys, come to understand only after cycles and cycles. Despite his age," Tlachinalli continued fervently, "Itzac is already a grown man and he knows well the dangers that he will face. I shudder to think what may happen, but I am consoled by the fact that, however it goes, even if he were to die I would know that he did so for a just cause…and not just to give his blood to appease their wretched gods."

The assembly had fallen silent and all eyes were now fixed on the white *tlatoani,* waiting for a decision. They then turned their gaze to the boy, who until that moment had remained standing in respectful silence next to his mother. Despite his age, he was already taller than her by several inches and his broad, muscular shoulders, which made him look like a giant compared to the tiny, thin woman, betrayed the heavy work to which they were accustomed. His eyes, which were black as his hair, were the mirror of his serious and thoughtful mind, but they looked sad not infrequently. Itzac was neither solitary nor taciturn, but rarely had Marco seen him laughing with his peers in his free time, and one day Xeetha had explained the reason why he acted so timid and reserved.

"What do you think?" Marco asked, turning directly to him.

Itzac lifted his face to the man and held his gaze determinedly: "I was the one who suggested the plan to my mother," he replied laconically.

The entire assembly then turned to the sovereign in a pleading supplication for his approval, but the two males continued to remain silent, keeping everyone in suspense. Marco was impressed both by the apparent simplicity of the plan and the young boy's courage, and as he continued to stare at him with a mixture of concern and admiration, his mind was frantically elaborating on all the implications and risks inherent in the plan in search of a possible weakness, but found none. "So be it," he finally said, repeatedly bowing his head in approval as if to convince himself thoroughly of having made the right decision, which was accepted by all as a liberation.

Chapter 46

Itzac's plan proved to be successful by all accounts and even surpassed their expectations. On the first day of the new moon the cabin was lowered in the evening for its usual guard duty, but as soon as night fell it began to descend to the full extent of the cable. From the trapdoor in the floorboards fell a rope that reached the surface of the lake, and immediately after the agile figure slipped rapidly down and was immersed silently in the obscure, but familiar, welcoming waters. The rope was then pulled back up and the cabin rose slowly until it stopped at the usual observation point.

Everything went as planned, and at midnight the following day Itzac had already reached his companion who awaited him inside the cabin. To avoid suspicion, this had remained lowered for the rest of the night as usual, and was brought back up the next morning at the usual hour.

When the hatch opened and the figure of the boy appeared, everyone thanked the gods and turned to him to storm him with questions. Itzac was able to give everyone a precise, detailed response, but the more detailed it got, the more the exaltation over the successful operation transformed into anxiety and worry; the danger was much more pressing than they had predicted.

The valley's engineers had developed a plan as simple as it was bold, and the hundreds of workers who were doing their utmost day and night behind the partition wall in grueling shifts had proceeded at record-breaking speed. Using the same method they had used the previous time from the lake area, they had fixed a ladder of rope and rungs to a height slightly greater than that of the waterfall and from there, rather than going around the rock, they had taken to boring a tunnel through it that was three meters wide and two high.

The work that was going on back there, the boy reported, was truly incredible. From dawn to dusk and from dusk to dawn, a multitude of workers of all ages and sexes alternated breaking down the hard basalt rock and dragging it away in baskets and baskets of stones and debris, which were then lowered down and piled close to the mountain were they could not be seen in any way by the inhabitants of the terrace. The activity was incessant, and there was no need for bands of musicians to cover the noise that the copper-plated chisels and mallets made, as it was already heavily masked by the waterfall.

Taking a serious risk and going beyond the task that was required of him, Itzac had covered his hair and body with fine white dust, whitewashing every part of himself, and loaded an empty basket on his shoulder to go up to the tunnel and mix in with the workers on the afternoon shift. Without attracting any attention or seeming particularly interested, he tried to listen in on the different conversations here and there and came to learn several things. The tunnel would end just above the waterfall and a long wooden walkway that would allow the military to easily reach the meadow had already been prepared. And it would be just two moons before the excavation was completed.

"It's easy to be scared. And extremely dangerous, too," was Marco's worried comment at the end of the report. "As many as they are, if they manage to come up to the meadow together, it will not be easy to drive them back. We need to invent a remedy worthy of their intention."

"And you already have something in mind?" Xeetha asked hopefully.

"I might have half a plan in mind, to tell the truth," he replied cryptically while peeking furtively at Atzcha, who in hearing talk of plans for war had pricked up her antennae and immediately made a superhuman effort to disguise her interest in the topic. "Follow my reasoning," Marco continued, trying to involve them both in the discussion. "At this point they don't know that we know, and will surely be convinced that they have the advantage of surprise…"

"So what do you think we should do?" Atzcha intervened, no longer resisting the temptation to meddle in the discussion.

"Absolutely nothing," replied Marco, gratifying her with a wide, satisfied smile.

This time it was the *tlatoani* himself who suggested the battle plan: "Once they finish the tunnel," he began at the meeting, "they will try to find a position that is higher and more dominating than our own. With the enemy territory under control, they might settle for spying closely on our movements, set fire to the forest, prevent us from cultivating the fields…They could even force us to surrender without a fight. But we know them well, we know that they could never be satisfied with such an easy and inglorious victory after the humiliation they suffered the last time, and they'll be dying to win the rematch with weapons…and to claim the coveted insignia, too. So all we have to do is play on their great desire for glory and vengeance, and push them to immediately seek their coveted revenge."

Based on the detailed information provided by Itzac, the entire community resumed their work and it did not take long for them to prepare a pathway which, surpassing the waterfall, reached the rocky outcrop at a slightly higher level than where the tunnel would let out. It was sufficient to carve a myriad of small holes into the rock into which feet and hands could be inserted, and then to lodge the climbing nails a bit higher so that the rope railing could be secured. And all of this in broad daylight and with total peace of mind because as the rock wall recessed in relation to the meadow and was always hidden by the spray of the waterfall below, the workers could not be noticed from the valley in any way.

It was a bit more difficult to bore through the rock at the end , but once they excavated a niche in which one could operate squatting in the most comfortable position, the work proceeded much more expeditiously thanks to the steel hammers and chisels, and after three weeks the small indentation was transformed into a tunnel almost five feet deep and nine feet wide, which could hold six warriors armed to the teeth. The entire operation was completed earlier than planned and from that moment on, the grueling wait began.

Marco had just fallen into a deep and dreamless sleep when he was woken in the night by Xeetha's voice: "We're on," said the woman, shaking him with her hand. "Tiachua heard something."

The woman was waiting for him on the landing: "Listen," she said, pressing her ear to the floor and inviting him to do the same. The sound of the waterfall was deafening and at first Marco did not hear anything, but by pressing his ear to the floor too and plugging the other one, he was finally able to hear the busy ticking of chisels that were biting into the mountain. It seemed very close, just a breath away from his ear.

"They're very close to breaking through. They have four or five days to go," she explained once they were back in the meadow, where the whole community had gathered. "From now on, high alert. We can be sure that before they break through they will try to carefully study the ground that awaits them. They will see the fence, and when they see it they'll immediately understand that we were expecting their attack and we are waiting for them right there. They'll be very suspicious then, and we'll have to exert ourselves to make them believe that we did in fact prepare for the invasion, but that we did not expect it so far in advance.

"We know that the law of the Book obliges them not to fight at night, but it will definitely be nighttime when they come out to explore the grounds. So, there can't be anything that will arouse their suspicions here: not a movement, not a fire, not a guard…neither in the meadow nor along the fence. Nothing, absolutely nothing. And when day comes, each of us must go to work like any other day, at the usual time and with the usual tools. And without the shadow of a weapon on us…

"You and your companions, Atzcha, will be up in the niche from tonight onward. There is a lot of moisture up there and it is also really cold at night, so take enough to cover yourselves, and enough food for four or five days should be enough, according to my calculations. You, Puehatl," he continued, turning to the Amazon's best student, "you will lie in wait with the gun on the left corner of the stockade, while I'm on the opposite corner. All others will be hidden behind the fence. And…if any one of you gets the idea to stick even one hair outside the fence before the agreed upon signal, I'll eat her alive."

That evening, Marco went personally to the waterfall to meet the warrior before she climbed up to the landing. Atzcha had just doled out the latest instructions and was adjusting her faithful scimitar along her side. A lifetime had passed since she and Marco had met face to face; he was clearly embarrassed, but he felt compelled to go and speak to her in that particular circumstance.

"You have been entrusted with the riskiest, most difficult task of the entire operation," he said, looking into her eyes and placing his hands on her shoulders, "and I do not think I am exaggerating when I say that it all depends upon you and your companions. I do not know if we will see one another alive again, but I wanted to thank you for the efforts you've made on behalf of all the others. And…I wanted to add…I wanted to tell you…yes, well…I wanted to also tell you that…I've missed you a lot through all of this." That said, oblivious to the gaze of curious onlookers, he hugged her and kissed her on both cheeks.

"Fear not," she told him, breaking away from the embrace with a half smile, "we'll meet again." Then, fitting her long-plumed helmet on her head and securing her shield and crossbow on her back, she strode determinedly towards the via ferrata and her faithful pupils trailed behind her.

Chapter 47

The inhabitants of the World Above did not have to wait long. Thanks to Itzac's undertaking, they had just enough time to take the necessary measures. The white *tlatoani* was had been wrong in his calculations, as the enemy began scoping out the territory well ahead of his predictions, the very night after Atzcha and her companions climbed up to the ledge.

There was a full moon and it was cold that night. Perhaps this was merely coincidence, but it was not unthinkable that the enemy had deliberately chosen a mix of favorable weather conditions before tunneling through, both to take advantage of the moonlight and acting in the hope that the terrace's inhabitants preferred to stay holed up in their shelters rather than stand guard and suffer the frost. The wind was howling away over the top of the crater, sweeping away every wisp of cloud, and the moonlight reflected off the mountain's mirrors lit up every nook and cranny of the unknown land like daylight for the invaders.

On the right corner of the stockade, women and children silently bickered relentlessly over the binoculars, which were perpetually directed at the wall. They had willingly accepted the task despite the cold, not least because Marco had promised a steel dagger with a delicately engraved handle as a reward for the first one to notice something. Antuatl was the lucky one, despite her significant walleye: "They're breaking through!" she had communicated excitedly to her partner on guard. "Run to warn the *tlatoani.*"

A black hole as large as the palm of a hand had just appeared in the milky white rock. Rather than tearing down the wall, the workers immediately made a simple cut along the entire perimeter of the tunnel, leaving only a small portion at the bottom edge intact. If it were not for the powerful binocular lenses and the moonlight, it would have been impossible to distinguish the thin black line of the cut through the mist from the waterfall.

Dawn came. Women and children went punctually to the fields with their usual working tools, all clearly unarmed. Their skin tingled as they felt the eyes of their enemy, but they knew that their every move was spied on and that the enemy was ready to seize upon any suspicious gesture but everyone, including the children, were able to play their part as consummate actors continuing with their daily tasks, playing and conversing with each other indifferently and being sure to not turn their eyes toward the wall. That glimpse of quiet, industrious country life could only reassure the observers of their plan's success. And all of them, surely, were already riding down the nearby paths of glory in their minds.

The light of day had just entered the valley when the stone door tipped forward and fell flat. From the entrance of the tunnel the end of a long walkway appeared, equipped with hooks to stick firmly into the meadow. Then a war cry resounded, overcoming even the noise of the waterfall, and a troop of armed warriors poured from the opening.

The tide of invaders was impressive, and the workers did not have to pretend overly much to feign surprise and fright. Screaming, terrorized and rallying their children, they abandoned their tools on the spot and began running towards the fence, but being careful not to stumble into the well-known booby traps. Once they reached the barrier, they stormed up the stairs that leaned against it and as they reached the top, rather than withdrawing and seeking refuge behind the ramparts, they went down the other side and continued to run wildly towards the only bridge that connected the two sides of the slit, warning all those they encountered of the danger along the way.

And the trap, studied in every minute detail, tried and tested, worked perfectly. If the fugitives managed to cross the bridge, they would have a chance to recover from the shock, regroup and force the invaders to a compromising delay, perhaps indefinitely, in all their hopes of joining the Order of the Serpent. In fact as Itzac had come to learn, the valley's strategists were mindful of the previous carnage and somewhat fearful of the unknown variables inherent to their next venture, and had decided to send the Orders of the Eagle and the Jaguar ahead in reconnaissance, promising as a reward the insignia of the Serpent to anyone who captured the Man of the Mountain or one of his slaves alive; but in the event of the foiling of the final assault, as they finally had a good grasp of the situation, they would be careful not to leave for others the glory that they assumed would follow the campaign. Much more likely, they would situate themselves at the head of their troops to lead without risking their final victory, and so dispelling the warriors of the lower orders' hopes of promotion. They, however, taking this afterthought for granted, were not at all willing to pass up this kind of opportunity as it would be highly unlikely to reoccur during their lifetimes. So they trembled with the desire to attack and immediately engage in battle, in part because the number of slaves was limited and only a few would have the good fortune to capture one alive.

These considerations were mirrored in the minds of their com-manders, who followed the evolution of events from a distance. They too were eager for glory and at the same time were aware of the volatility of their charges (who were certainly not as immovable as those in the Order). They did not wait for the supplications of their subordinates and threw aside any and all precaution, rejecting more cautious strategies and instead opting not to hold them back by giving the order to attack and stop the group of fugitives on the other side of the fissure, since those who had just crossed already had axes in hand and clearly intended to demolish the bridge as soon as they had all crossed.

The warriors that had already run down did not wait for any-thing else, and with shields on their arms and lances in hand they immediately charged with their heads down. They had to hurry and pass their companions if they wanted a chance at the coveted prize, and when some of them began to vanish into the traps only a few began to realize the danger; in the commotion many fell into them, often more than one into the same hole.

The attackers had covered almost half of the distance that separated them from the fence when Marco stood up and let loose the first hail of bullets, followed closely by that of Puehatl. The crossfire of the two machine guns mowed down the enemy vanguards. At the same time, the archers who had remained hidden until the last second sprang out from behind the ramparts and soon after even those pretending to flee joined in, about-facing as planned when they heard the first rounds of the rifles.

The warriors who were closest to their goal were now sure of ultimate success and continued to run towards the fence, but some of them were dumbfounded as they turned their heads back to calculate the advantage they had gained over their competitors; a void was opening behind them, dozens of warriors were crumpling to the ground like bowling pins and many others disappeared into thin air as if swallowed up by Mother Earth. At this sight many froze on the spot struck aghast, only to wind up being overwhelmed by the mass of screaming warriors behind the front line who continued tirelessly to advance, cursing their cumbersome presence. Little by little, however, more began to realize the danger and at a certain point the entire vanguard seemed to sway back and forth several times as though driven by contrary winds before stopping completely a few steps from the fence. The warriors looked around with bulging eyes, unable to make a decision; bewilderment was replaced by fear, fear by panic, then something in their minds clicked and without hesitation they began a chaotic flight, clashing with those who were still unaware of the peril and continued pressing forward with their crazy advance. The attackers' war cry came to be confused with the fugitives' cries of terror, and a total bedlam erupted on the battlefield playing right into the defenders' plans, who took advantage of the confusion and continued firing into the crowd.

The troop leaders, seized by the ugly turn of events and predicting a fate for themselves that was less than glorious, rushed onto the meadow in an attempt to block their men's retreat and push them to attack again. But when they realized that not even the gravest of threats would be able to retain the terrified human avalanche and, when they themselves began to feel the whistling of deadly bullets that were streaking closer and closer to their ears, they changed their minds and joined in the humiliating flight. On the catwalk, among those who continued to emerge from the tunnel and those who were looking to flee there ensued a succession of shoving, yelling, cursing, and counter-orders overwhelmed by the noise of the waterfall. And at that sight Atzcha judged the time ripe for action and six grenades fell simultaneously from above onto the center of the walkway. There was a tremendous roar and the gangplank, partially destroyed under the weight of so many occupants, tilted dangerously downwards until it split into two halves, which were lost in the waterfall with their load of screaming victims.

On the battlefield, the slaughter was still in full swing. The fugitives, hunted and cut down by the firing of guns and crossbows, reached the edge of the meadow and saw that their only way of escape was gone, so they reacted in the most desperate ways. Some lost all reason, rushing into the void in a suicidal leap; others, in the vain hope of escaping the snipers' fire, threw themselves onto the ground and flattened their bodies under their shields; the remaining, seeing no other solution, returned to the initial plan and rushed to attack again, firmly intentioned to sell their lives dearly.

At that point, the shooting of machine guns moved from the meadow to the mouth of the tunnel, forcing warriors who were frozen in their steps to witness the tragedy unfolding before their eyes, terrified and helpless as they were, and after hitting those in the first lines, the bullets began to rebound wildly and shoot inside the tunnel, claiming more victims and prompting mass flight there, too. At a nod from Marco, a girl standing next to him raised a red flag into the air, waving it several times, and the gunfire in the meadow rapidly died down.

It was the agreed-upon signal, and Atzcha and her companions sprang back into action. All in one motion they rappelled down the wall using the ropes to the upper edge of the tunnel's mouth, ripped the fuses of hand grenades out with their teeth, launched them into the tunnel and raced back onto the ledge. After an endless fraction of a second there was a flash, then a roar, and the mouth of the mountain erupted in a cloud of dust, smoke, rubble and bits of mangled bodies. The echo of the explosion had not yet died down and already the women warriors, rappelling back down, reached the entrance of the tunnel. Protected by the thick blanket of dust and chaos that reigned within, they advanced a few meters, grabbed more grenades that they threw forcefully further into the tunnel, then immediately threw themselves down onto their bellies under the protection of their shields. One of them, however, was not deft enough in the maneuver and found herself still standing at the entrance of the tunnel when the second explosion happened, and was hit full-force by the shockwave and thrown backwards into the void. After a brief rush the third bombardment ensued, and this time it was the opposite end of the tunnel mouth that spewed its tragic contents, creating terror and dismay among those who were climbing up the ladders into the tunnel.

The five surviving warriors, still unaware of their friend's fate, had gotten back up and loaded their crossbows to begin advancing shoulder to shoulder inside the tunnel, firing one arrow blindly after another. Along the way they met no resistance and they reached the end of the tunnel before the cloud of dust had lifted.

Atzcha was the first to arrive at their destination and cleanly sliced off, with three dry blows of the scimitar, the head of the first warrior who appeared in the frame of the tunnel entrance as wall as the two stakes that supported the last stretch of the ladder, which was immediately dragged downwards by the weight of its occupants. Those caught off guard did not have time to hold on and pitched down, crashing onto the banks of the stream below; others hung from the broken ladder by a hand or an arm, and they began screaming and kicking blindly into the void looking for a foothold, but many were not so lucky and a little later, as their strength gave out, they were forced to let go and follow the fate of their unfortunate companions.

Atzcha peeked out from the mouth of the tunnel to enjoy the scene and felt no pity at hearing the terrified screams coming from below, and detached the last four hand grenades from her waist, calmly pulling out the pins and dropping them one after the other close to the wall. The explosions that followed dismantled the ladder and claimed new casualties among those still clinging on, but when those survivors realized the gravity of the storm that was raging over their heads, they threw away their weapons and plummeted downwards toward more lenient climes.

And only at that sight did a satisfied smile spread across the Amazon's face, but it instantly vanished from her lips when she turned to her companions and noticed that one was missing: her pupil. "Where is Antatlochaa?" she asked with her heart in a vise.

"She was close to me when we came down into the tunnel," one of them replied, "but with all that dust…"

Atzcha blanched. "You stay here," she ordered in a trembling voice. "Never again will these sons of bitches want to come up here and bother us. Keep an eye on them, but don't lean out too far…and fire on anyone who dares to play the hero." With that said, she turned around and started on the way back alone.

The white powder in the tunnel, as fine as talc, was dispersing, depositing on the warrior's sweaty body; like a white angel of death who preferred not to allow for fake deaths and injury, she proceeded back up the tunnel while systematically stabbing left and right at every body she encountered along the way with a spear that she found on the ground. Her heart was caught in a vise but for a glimmer of hope, which was immediately shattered when she found no trace of her friend at the opposite mouth of the tunnel. And she did not even have time to mourn or wonder what might have happened because as soon as she cast her eyes on the meadow, she realized that the match was still far from over.

The surviving warriors, seeing that every way of escape was blocked and not hoping for the slightest mercy from their enemy, had closed ranks and were once again marching decidedly towards their opponents' stockade. Some of them had already reached it and were even able to climb the ladders were they entered into furious combat with the enemy; as decimated as they were in numbers, they were much more skilled in close combat and were still a serious threat, because Marco and Pueatl could not shoot into the fray without the risk of hitting one of their own.

Once again Atzcha was the one to change the course events and deliver the coup de grâce to the enemy. Blinded by hatred, she braced her crossbow and loaded it while aiming at the back of a warrior who had already reached the battlements. It would have been an impossible shot for anyone else, but not for her; she carefully calculated the elevation based off distance and hit the target on her first shot. More bull's-eyes followed and the warriors, pierced from behind, began to fall one after the other from the top of the wall, trouncing their companions until at a certain point they realized what was happening and jumped to the ground, finally giving up on their dreams of glory, giving in again to a stampede. At that point, though, the machine guns, rifles and crossbows came back into action to mow them down, and the fugitives were in total disarray. Indeed, many of them threw themselves deliberately into the booby traps in order to escape the carnage, quite heedless of the spikes or the dead and dying at the bottom. All others, who had not yet realized that they were in a death trap and could not in any way escape the crossfire that was decimating them, threw down their weapons and fell to their knees to kiss the ground in surrender.

Less than two hours had passed since the start of the battle. The incredulous women looked around in search of new enemies, and it was some time before they realized that the only sounds coming from the meadow were the moans of the wounded and the appeals of the defeated.

And then they finally realized that it was over, they were safe…they had won. Then pandemonium broke out. Cries of joy and shouts of victory arose from all sides. Soon after their avenging wrath exploded, because in the final stages of the battle the invaders had not bothered to capture live opponents. In addition to Atzcha's pupil who had fallen into the void, five other women had been killed among and seven were injured, one seriously so. It was nothing compared to the losses suffered by the inhabitants of the valley, but it was more than enough to unleash all the fury of the persecuted, and they began to swarm across the meadow to find survivors, hitting and stabbing mercilessly both living and dead. Even Atzcha, who had fallen back on the grass, continued to carry on with her relentless onslaught, systematically eliminating enemy survivors. Luckily for them she was delayed because the bridge had been destroyed, but she carried on her "work" and quickly recovered from her disadvantage.

Marco watched the scene from atop the fence for a long time. He seemed to be dreaming, it seemed impossible that everything had gone as planned, and he could almost not believe his eyes. Only after several minutes of enchantment did he realize what was happening below. He was shocked; he came back to himself rapidly, catapulted down from the battlements without even using the ladders and began to run across the meadow screaming like a banshee and even shooting his gun into the air to attract his companions' attention.

"No, stop, don't kill them!" he continued screaming to the bloodthirsty warriors. "Help me to get them to stop," he pleaded with Xeetha along the way. At that time she, too, was having a grand time giving her friends a hand, and remained nothing short of puzzled by the *tlatoani*'s absurd request. For a second she looked Marco in the eye as if to satisfy herself that he was not joking or out of his mind, wishing to deprive them of that legitimate and holy satisfaction. "I'll explain after. There's no time now," he assured her, reading the shock on her face. "But now help me stop them, please!"

Xeetha obeyed, albeit very reluctantly, and without another word Marco began to run at breakneck speed towards Atzcha, reaching her just in time to block the weapon that was about to cut right into the neck of some unfortunate survivor who had prostrated himself at her feet to beg for mercy. "Stop it Atzcha, do not fire, we need them alive!" The woman, interrupted in her course, turned on the man and glared at him. In a fit of rage, and with the snarl of an angry beast, she tried to yank her weapon from his hold and resume killing.

But suddenly something clicked in her mind, clouded by hatred as it was, and her arm loosed instantly: "Yes," she ruled, as though dazzled by a vision, "you're right, we need them alive…for the sacrifice!" Marco chose not to contradict her. If at that moment he had explained the real reason for his request, he would surely have triggered a murderous rampage and he could hardly hold the woman back a second time. "Get up, worm!" Atzcha ordered the prisoner who had just escaped a beheading, prodding him with the tip of her scimitar. The reprieved, little more than a boy, ashen-faced and with a dry throat, did not need to be told twice, and without any pleasantries she untied the cord of his loincloth and used it to tie his wrists and ankles together behind his back, leaving him unable to move. "Let's look after him well," she said, mocking her *tlatoani*, who had remained silent without interfering. Soon after she was racing across the meadow to give orders to capture all the prisoners alive.

Chapter 48

The nightmare was over. The conquest of the tunnel had not only robbed the enemy of their most insidious access to the World Above, but even more crucially it gave the victors the capacity to continuously oversee the last piece of land that until that day was hidden from view, and no further offensive action could be taken by the people of the valley without those living above being immediately aware of it.

A large quantity of weapons had been recovered from the battlefield and twenty-seven fleeing prisoners had miraculously escaped retribution. The five fallen women were buried with highest honors close to the graves of Karl and Chatì. Among the mounds there was also an empty grave dedicated to the memory of Antatlochaa, the girl lost during the attack on the tunnel, and Atzcha had shed all her tears above that unmarked tomb.

But in the World Above's cemetery there was no place for the enemy's victims. Marco was unable to curb the systematic looting because even a small piece of cloth could be useful to the community, nor had he objected when their bodies had been seized by the hands and feet and thrown into the lake without many pleasantries. But he had reacted alarmingly when, one morning, one of Atzcha's students had suggested feasting on the flesh of their prisoners; the mere memory of the violence inflicted on the body of his childhood friend and on so many sacrificed atop the pyramid made his blood boil and his stomach turn. The unfortunate girl was reprimanded so harshly that from that day on it was certain that no one else would dream of voicing such a proposal.

The prisoners were kept in a newly built shed, which initially had been intended for the storage of tools. Hands and feet tied constantly behind their backs, they were watched day and night by Atzcha's warriors who not only stood guard and hand fed them at meal times, but also had a bit of fun waking them in the middle of the night by ramming them with spear shafts and entertaining them with pleasant speeches relating to the sacrificial feast, drawing out in great detail the gruesome slaughter methods that awaited them.

Atzcha did nothing but feed her companions' aggressiveness, and never missed an opportunity to assume the role of pressuring her former lover with ideas of grandiose, choreographed ceremonies. Marco instantly diverted his route whenever he saw her nearby, and when he could not in any way avoid collision despite all his attempts at throwing her off, he stalled and invented some excuse or another to mollify her for a while. But he realized that his gimmicks would not be able to last forever; he saw that the woman was growing impatient with the constant delays and he felt in the air that the day would soon come when he would instigate her friends to take justice into their own hands. But the cannibalistic proposal made to him that morning which sent him into a rage had finally given him the right to deliver a speech to everyone. So after informing Xeetha of his intentions and receiving approval, he asked her to convene a general meeting.

"The gods have assisted us," the white *tlatoani* began after rising to his feet. So great in stature was he, with scimitar and dagger at his hips, flamboyant cloak over his shoulders and gnarled staff in hand, he towered over the entire semicircle, instilling respect and fear. Yet echoing in everyone's ears were the shouts directed at the unsuspecting warrior who had suggested the idea of feasting on human flesh. They had never seen him so angry before, nor had they ever heard him rage against one of their comrades with such vehemence. Such an impromptu, sudden gathering could not bode well. Even the children, who were usually free to roam the lawn during such meetings, were well-behaved on the sidelines, sensing a change in the atmosphere and palpable tension.

"But what gods came to our rescue? The gods of the valley people, perhaps?"

"Of course not!" It was Xeetha who spoke out into the silence, and everyone whirled towards her in silent reproach, fearful that the unauthorized interruption could exacerbate their ruler's anger. They were perplexed when, instead of flying into a rage, he graced the woman with a wide smile and began to speak calmly, as if no one had interrupted him.

"Perhaps it was these gods who enslaved you?"

"No!" some of them uttered, reassured by his previous reaction, joining their voices to Xeetha's.

"Perhaps it was these gods who drank the blood of your sisters and your children?

"No!"

"Or the gods who allowed the rulers of the valley to send their warriors to kill our companions?"

"No, no, no!" the entire assembly shouted back, increasingly excited and overcome by the *tlatoani*'s enthralling voice.

"Of course not," he replied when silence fell. "There have been many to assist us, to guide our hand, to be so benevolent towards us. Our gods are very different from theirs. Our gods—those worshiped by the fathers of our fathers even before the mothers of your mothers were enslaved—are not cruel and vindictive monsters like those worshiped in the valley. Our gods do not demand the blood of innocent, blameless children." The growing consensus was giving him confirmation up to that point that he had struck the right chord. He could even venture to spit it out while hoping that it was not too stodgy for some of his friends, one in particular. "In the great battle we took several prisoners. Men who came over here with the worst intentions: to enslave us, to go as far as to kill us, if they could not have done otherwise...and that is what happened to some of our unfortunate sisters, sadly. But, ask yourself: are they the real culprits of the evil we have been made to suffer? Were they really free to do anything else?"

He waited a few moments, letting the doubt creep into his audience: "Certainly not. If you think of the fate met by warriors who dare to disobey their orders, you'll understand that these men had no other possibility, that the young men were forced to fight us and to hurt us, they are poor people who are nothing by the victims of the lords who dominate the valley. Just like we were. That's why," and at this point the speaker scanned his eyes across the whole crowd before delivering the blow, "we will not sacrifice our prisoners to their gods, because we are not like them. We are a free people, a people who knows compassion, a people who knows how to distinguish the innocent from the guilty. We, therefore," he continued in a rush, so as not to give anyone time to respond, "do not kill innocent men, but will spare them, and with their livelihood, and we will grant them freedom. Freedom that they have never had, but which they too have dreamed of and desired."

These words shocked the listeners to the point that none of them even knew how to react, some thought they had misunderstood the meaning of the speech, and Marco took the opportunity to give the final jab: "Human sacrifice is not a custom of our people, and therefore they will be forever banished from our world, and woe to those who dare to feed on human flesh."

At these words, Atzcha jumped up angrily: "And you intend to free those bastards who killed our sisters and our children and wouldn't hesitate to do the same to each of us if they could?" she yelled, beside herself with rage. "Is that what you…you…You made a promise, and now…"

Marco had predicted that the affair would not end easily. The semicircle had again fallen silent and Atzcha's resentful reaction had the power to ruin it all, to create opposing factions, lead to open warfare. He had to act very tactfully if he wanted to quell the woman's combativeness without losing his hold on the crowd. "Try to understand," he interjected, trying to keep his voice calm and persuasive. "As I just said, the blame for what has happened cannot be attributed to these poor people waiting to be sacrificed, but to others, especially Chitoontecl and Mohotzuma, and all the *pipiltin*

285

who support those two evil dogs. They are the real culprits behind what is happening down there, they are godless, heartless men who deny an entire population their rights, and who consider the warriors of the lower orders to be animals for slaughter in the name of their own sordid interests…The people of the valley are slaves as much as you were before being released and they would ask nothing more than to live in peace and friendship with all of us one day if they were given that opportunity."

A murmur of approval made him realize that his declaration was gaining approval, but Atzcha was still on her feet, backed by the girls in her group and determined to fight to the end. But he certainly did not want to let the hard-won advantage slip through his fingers, so, being aware that he should give her something if he wanted to deter her from her criminal intentions, he then added: "I promise you that when we capture the real culprits they will be punished for their sins and they will be shown no mercy."

"Yes, and you're going to go get them down there?" the warrior growled at him mockingly.

Marco ignored her insolence and played the last card he had: "Listen, Atzcha. You were the first to say that yes, we have won a great battle, but we are still very, very far from total victory. Let us be under no illusions," he continued, taking his eyes off the woman to look over the semicircle for consensus, "those who rule in the valley live in hatred and the desire for revenge. They have already been defeated twice by a group of mere slaves, and this is a shame that they will never tolerate, and they will not find peace until they see us dead or reduced back to slavery. We can therefore be sure that sooner or later they will find a way to come and do us still more evil, and they will be much more cautious and dangerous than before. And on that day, what will be their best weapon?"

Marco then looked back to his rival before continuing. "You know it well, Atzcha, better than all of us: their numerical superiority. That's why we should grant freedom to our prisoners. So that they can become a part of our people, and live and work with us, so they may become…the fathers of your children. Only then can we too become more numerous and powerful, forever preserving our freedom. And then you'll see that there is no need to go and catch those greedy sons of bitches, because when the inhabitants of the valley rebel against their oppressors they themselves will deliver them to us."

The chorus of applause that followed this finale made it clear that he had hit his mark. The mention of the danger that still existed had rekindled old anxieties, but that which had perhaps worked its way into the ladies' hearts had been the reference to the non-strictly military potential of the young men, which caused them to see a new perspective that was certainly more attractive than simple human sacrifice.

Atzcha, looking around herself in search of support, saw that even her most faithful friends were beating their hands in applause, and at that point she realized that she had lost the game. With difficulty she managed to suppress her anger and, after casting a hateful look at the victor, she sat down stiffly without reply. "Now you'll have to work harder than ever to stay on her good side," Xeetha whispered into his ear with a barely concealed hint of satisfaction: "She's not one to forgive easily."

Chapter 49

Xeetha had known to warn him of Atzcha long in advance. The Amazon had actually not at all overcome her public humiliation and was far from accepting her former lover's decision to pardon the prisoners. There was something visceral in her that led her to wholly rejecting the idea of coexistence with former enemies and lately had taken to openly stirring the waters among her most faithful students and turning them against this new direction, and she never missed an opportunity to find new reasons to cause friction or quarrel with the newcomers.

As Marco had foreseen, the prisoners accepted their pardon as a divine gift, not so much for escaping retribution but for the fact that they became the absolute masters of their lives without the nightmare of ending up killed in the Flower War or at the top of the pyramid. And their enthusiasm for their new quality of life was such that they willingly shouldered the heaviest work, reclaiming it from the fairer sex so that after so much time the women were able to return to their timeless, preferred occupations. Almost all the males except for a few inveterate bachelors had long since found their soul mates and each girl had had her work cut out for her in the race for the best partner, showcasing merits and virtues that were more or less hidden.

Atzcha's attitude threatened to undermine the balance that had been so hard-won and Marco would not allow it. He had to find a way to mollify her and divert her once and for all from her malicious intent. He continued to mull it over during dinner, when everyone noticed he was unusually silent and deep in thought. But on the way to the shelter, there came a revelation; he would call for a new assembly and, in an unprecedented ceremony he would honor the warriors who had most distinguished themselves in the recent battles with accolades and honors. Obviously he would reserve the most prestigious award for Atzcha. I could even give her the watch, he considered, convinced of having at last found the perfect solution.

When everything between them was still milk and honey, on more than one occasion Atzcha had slipped the old Swatch off his wrist and clasped it onto her own to admire it from every angle with ecstatic eyes as though it were a jewel of inestimable value. And it was probably just this assumption that had kept her from asking for it as a gift.

Marco was whistling for the excellence of his plan when he reached the shelter. He was in high spirits and was just about to undress and go to bed when he heard the creak of his door hinges. His heart lifted when he turned and saw Atzcha's statuesque body on the threshold, just covered by a short tunic that left her legs and breasts almost completely bare. And he was struck breathless when he saw Peepty's radiant body appear behind her.

He had long since given up hope for that visit. He was almost unable to believe his eyes, and he stood stock-still for a time to contemplate in awe the two goddesses descended from Olympus, while his lively imagination ran over rapidly the forbidden summits that he would soon conquer. "What…what a surprise!" he stammered, rousing himself from his daze. "Now this is a surprise!" he repeated, tripping over a chair and bouncing up to meet them.

Spurring them gently by the hips, he accompanied them to the center of the room and sat them down on the bed, then in a very masculine manner straddled the chair that he had just righted. "Great!" he said, gracing his visitors with a beaming smile, as they continued staring at him without saying a word. He had never before felt so excited and awkward at the same time. "Would you like some cocoa? It's a real treat, I assure you. Xeetha brought it to me just last night," he added thoughtlessly, then immediately bit his tongue. The women's silence began to cause him some embarrassment.

"Well! I'm very glad to see you here," he continued in an attempt to break the ice by addressing Peepty directly. "I must confess that I have often wondered if it was shyness or too much pride that kept you from coming to see me without being invited. There were times when I almost thought that you were resentful towards me for having preferred the company of others to yours. But if that was your thought then you could not have been more mistaken, both because I've always desired a visit from you, and because I've never asked, nor forced anyone to see me. And although I have had some preference in the past," he added with a meaningful, complicit glance to his old lover, "I can assure you that I have never—"

"You never understood a damn thing," Peepty filled in for him scornfully, abruptly ending the soliloquy. "You never realized that men disgust me, they always have; ever since I was a child, I have been forced to satisfy their gross desires. And I hated you too. Yes, I hated you. Ever since the day I saw Atzcha leave your room with what had happened between you two written all over her face. If you hadn't been the one to release me and my sisters from slavery, I would have killed you with my own hands. You were about to take my beloved away from me," she continued, freewheeling, to an ever more astonished Marco, who was listening open-mouthed as his mind began to put together all the pieces of the messy mosaic. "Atzcha loved me too. But she is different from me, and I, knowing her, have always lived in terror that someone might take her away. So it was, but thanks to the gods, now she is back and I am finally a happy woman because she has sworn not to leave me ever again. And you see me here tonight because I can finally put aside all the hate that I have harbored against you and come in peace to your house to thank you for having freed me and my beloved from our life as slaves." That said, she threw herself tearfully into Atzcha's arms, who welcomed her warmly, pulled her to her chest and graced her with a long, passionate kiss.

"And two," the man remarked in his mother tongue, suddenly brought back to his former experience in Rome. Marco was stunned by the shocking revelation, he felt his masculine pride was wounded, an his disappointment reached its peak when he thought about the friends that Atzcha used to bring along with her during their nightly rendezvous: "So…it was not for me…"

He had to make a superhuman effort to swallow all the bitterness in his mouth and bring a less idiotic expression to his face. He tried to regain his voice, but when he started to speak his throat remained constricted, forcing him to clear his throat several times before he was able to make a sound. "Good," was all he managed to articulate, rubbing his hands almost as if wanting to revitalize them before resuming the topic of conversation, although at that time his only desire was to see them vanish from sight and be alone.

Luckily for him the two, given that the conversation was languishing, found it expedient to stand up and silently exit, leaving him sitting in front of his sadly empty bed, and meditate on his immense, blind stupidity. Atzcha had not opened her mouth once the whole time, but before exiting she had gazed at him intently, and her lips were just barely curved into a wicked smile. She had just gotten her revenge.

After some time, Marco stayed faithful to his commitment and called the general assembly. Dressed in full regalia and bearing his usual symbols of power, he conferred awards and accolades left and right. And when it was Atzcha's turn, he lauded her hyperbolically, emphasizing her key role both in training the army and acting in the course of the battle; as he revealed her heroism and many other merits in front of everyone, he renewed her role as supreme commander of the army of warriors of the World Above. "Because," he added, concluding emotionally, "as long as there are certain dogs making the laws down in the valley, we will be considered nothing but enemies to be eliminated. As a result, we can never afford to be complacent, we have to remain constantly vigilant, trained with weapons and always ready to face any attack…and no one can do the job better than Atzcha."

The ovation that followed his speech was successful in the near-impossible feat of inflating the chest of the fearless warrior even more; on this occasion she had enriched her vestments with a beautiful feathered coat given to her by Peepty, so bright as to compete with that of the *tlatoani*. During the long adulation Atzcha remained standing upright with a dazzling, proud smile on her lips, and she was determined to sit back down only after the prolonged applause subsided, when the ceremony seemed like it was coming to a close with her triumphant apotheosis. But it did not.

"And now," Marco continued, taking everyone by surprise, "I wish to draw your attention to another person. A person who, in silence and full humility, has worked and still works for the good of the community. You all know who I'm talking about," he added, raising his voice. "Xeetha needs no introduction, you all know her dedication to service and unparalleled talent. Out of nowhere and in no time, thanks to her practical sense, her shrewdness and deep knowledge of each of you, she has been able to set in place a perfect organization. Her work has been invisible, but we owe it to her that we were able to prepare for the confrontation without the worry of many everyday problems. For this and other reasons," Marco conspicuously glanced towards Atzcha out of the corner of his eye, "it is safe to act in the name of unanimous opinion when I give her a token of our infinite gratitude." He then invited Xeetha, who was sitting to his right, to stand up; he slipped the watch off his wrist and put it on hers.

"I've always said that you're a big son of a wall-rider!" she responded with tears in her eyes, throwing her arms around his neck while the whole assembly, at the peak of enthusiasm, stood up to applaud and scream their approval. Atzcha had a much harder time than others standing up and clapping her hands; the dazzling smile from before had disappeared from her face, and that delay and her drawn lips told Marco that he had hit the mark.

Maybe, he chided himself alone late that night after the usual solemn drinking, as he went up to the shelter on unsteady legs, he had not acted in a very lordly way towards his ex-lover; perhaps he should have let it go and proven himself superior instead of stooping to such a wretched level of revenge…because perhaps she had a valid reason for behaving like that towards him, maybe. But in spite of all these variables, he just could not feel any guilt or remorse for his less-than-chivalrous behavior. Indeed, though he struggled to admit it, he was immensely satisfied at having tied the score.

Two days later, Xeetha announced to him that she was expecting a child.

PART TWO

Chapter 1

There was already the scent of spring in the air. Yet another in the World Above for Marco. His hair had veered sharply from salt and pepper to pure salt. At first, he had not entirely appreciated the fact that he was the only one in the whole kingdom to go white so quickly, but with the passage of time he had not only resigned himself to the unwanted achievement, but even let them grow longer. Now the white ponytail which floated freely behind his back had transformed in everyone's minds into the inimitable symbol of his kingship.

The snow-white plumage, however, was the only sign imprinted on his person showing the passing of the years. His body, forged through all the hard work in the open air and the simple diet, still retained its former strength, and no one could compete with him in terms of athleticism. The former prisoners had become his instructors and from them he had learned all the secrets of the art of dueling, which had made him a true warrior. Of course, he would never come to match his masters' agility and plasticity of movement, who had dedicated their lives to a military career from early childhood, but he could make up for this deficiency with his height and the length of his arms: when he twirled the long scimitar around him, it became a heroic exploit approach him.

The idea to spare their lives had proven successful from all points of view. The men, apart from the inexplicable escape of two of them several years ago while they were on guard at the cabin, had embraced their new lifestyle with great enthusiasm, agreeing to the rules of the community with no chauvinist claim. In a short time they had almost all married their former enemies, who had started to give birth to one child after another, swelling the number of the *tlatoani*'s subjects. Marco had also entrusted to them the task of training young men to arms.

And warriors were surely needed in the World Above because, as they had expected, the danger had never ceased. It was actually getting more and more imminent and threatening every day. Though any possibility of a surprise attack by the losers was now unlikely, they were by no means willing to give up their primary intent and had decided to carry out their schemes openly, and years before had begun to dig a long tunnel on the opposite wall of the valley, which after bypassing the volcanic pole of the crater went straight up to the southern end of the terrace.

The great venture, which at first had aroused in the observer little more than simple curiosity—if not, indeed, some playful joke—was now close to its final goal. Along the entire route the workers had shaped some small slits on the outer wall of the tunnel, both to ventilate it and to work in daylight without exposing themselves to the fire of the machine guns, whose bullets they knew well now both in nature and consistency, although how they could be shot with such precision and such deadly violence at impossible distances remained a real mystery to them.

There were almost two hundred meters left before the completion of the project. For the third time the black specter of war was unfolding its wings on that land of freedom, and the fear and anxiety of its inhabitants grew day by day. But they had kept themselves busy all the while.

The community was enriched with fifty newborns, still too young to handle a weapon. On the other hand, those who were children the day of the escape had become great warriors. Too few, however, to face a large army.

Itzac, who was now almost a man by, was the oldest. Everybody still remembered with admiration his unforgettable boyhood venture, and his courage, his intelligence and his determination, which had gradually sharpened over the years.

Tall and strong, he had learned to deftly handle any weapon. But while his friends seemed to live on the basis of the conflict to come, devoting themselves completely to the martial arts, these aroused in him only a marginal interest. What distinguished him the most from the others was his inexhaustible thirst for knowledge. As an acute and careful observer, he had the rare gift of listening without interrupting and of speaking only after he had considered every little facet of the problem that was presented to him, but when he decided to intervene it was not easy to find faults in his arguments.

He had a passion for mechanics and in his free time, while his friends used to gather in groups for the usual pastimes, he preferred to spend much of that time planning out new and ambitious projects on his sheets of bark. One of his most important achievements had been to convey all the water of the numerous streams, which descended freely through the woods, in two large basins excavated on the two sides of the slit, to distribute it through an ingenious system of bulkheads and hydraulic lifting, at every point of the meadow and in every house, where it could be used both for irrigation and for domestic use.

The exclusive source of all his knowledge was the white *tlatoani*, whom he visited almost daily to ask for advice and new ideas.

Marco was quite glad to indulge his pupil's desire for knowledge; he was proud of his progress and felt an indescribable satisfaction in remarking how much interest and amazement any new notion was able to arouse in him. On occasion the teacher had a problem remembering precisely the operation of a device; it often happened, then, that it was the same Itzac, properly stimulated and guided, who found the right solution.

The young man also had the great quality of not showing off his superior intelligence to others, nor he did alienate himself from his friends, who continued to accept him in the group without envy or awe and followed all of his constructions with interest, though they felt for him a sort of admiring deference.

But there was one thing that was able to distract Itzac from his wonderful machines, and with increasing frequency he could be seen solitary and taciturn, almost indifferent to everything that happened around him.

Marco had noticed these changes and, thanks to Xeetha, he knew the reason behind them.

Itzac was not nine years old when he was taken from the house of slaves to be brought to the palace, where he had had to endure all kinds of abuse by the *tlatoani* and his entourage. A lot of time had passed since that tragic experience, but he still felt the stigma tattooed on his skin; he knew that all the atrocities to which he had been subjected could not be forgotten, he felt that everyone knew of his shame: the sudden silences, the rapid changes of topic when somebody talked in his presence of past incidents, certain looks and certain winks weighed on him more than if his secret had been shouted aloud for all to hear.

Marco had come to know, to love and to cherish Itzac as a son. He wanted to take him aside, talk to him, make him understand that what had happened was part of the past, that it did not matter at all, that he should not worry about it, but he feared that acting that way, letting him know that even he was aware of the secret that oppressed him, risked plunging the young man even more deeply in that state of grief and discouragement. On the other hand, he could not resign himself to the idea of watching him suffer. He wanted, he had to find a way, a method, a strategy to put an end to all that torment.

One morning, the teacher and his pupil were trying to finalize the design of a crane intended to lift and move large boulders. Itzac, however, was unusually distracted, he could not focus and he was struggling to keep up with what he was exposed to, until Marco could no longer restrain himself.

"Listen Itzac: you are old enough and mature enough to understand that you cannot continue to suffer shame and guilt for a sin you never committed and for something you were subjected to by use of force and against your will."

Sometimes at the end of winter an unstable and capricious wind sweeps away every cloud in its path, revealing in the fields and hills the first pastel colors of early spring, only to blot them out immediately with new cobalt blue clouds; Marco saw just this happen on the young man's face in its sudden changes of expression, as if it were a mirror of his inner turmoil: the initial look of anguish had been taken over by something akin to relief, full of hope, which had given way to despair, and had then resulted, finally, in tears of release.

"No one can ever erase my shame. I was hoping that you, at least…But I could not fool myself, I knew that sooner or later you would find out…"

"Enough!" Marco warned him, grabbing him by the shoulders and shaking him, as if he were to give life to an inanimate mannequin. "Stop creating a problem that does not exist! It's not the past that should trouble you. There are many other things that you need to worry about right now: the danger is lurking over our heads and if in the future we were to be defeated by the battle that lies ahead, I could never forgive you for having wasted the last days of your life. Do you understand?"

"Thanks," was all Itzac could utter, and finally Marco saw a serene and grateful expression appear on his face: the dawn of a new day.

Xeetha later complimented Marco for how he had acted. Then, feigning the sudden onset of a headache, she did not take part in the general meeting convened in the late morning. Itzac was called to sit in her stead, with an invitation from the white *tlatoani* himself. The fact did not go unnoticed in the eyes of the others, and especially in eyes of Atzcha, but no one had anything to say against this decision.

Chapter 2

"All this time, we have only ever sought peace with the people of the valley. We could have even forced them to peace. But we always let them live undisturbed, and we tried to make them understand in every way possible that there is space for all of us in the Curved Mountain, and that it is in everyone's interest to live in peace. Because we are all needed."

The words of the white *tlatoani* had immediately captured the audience's attention, and Marco could then continue undisturbed: "However, this was not enough to quench the hatred and the desire for revenge of the lords of the valley. They reject our friendship, and they will never be sated until they have defeated us, killed us, or even reduced us to slavery. The peace they have granted us is nothing but a fragile truce, a way to prepare themselves even better to move against us once again."

A murmur of approval ran through the assembly, but Marco was quick to resume his speech: "There is only one way for us to ward off such a powerful and large army, and that is to completely overturn the numeric law. You need to know that such a plan already exists. Xeetha and I are the only ones to know of its existence, but the time has come for all of you to finally know about it…that's the reason for this summoning."

There was no time for illusions anymore: the excavation was close to its completion, and while the tunnel proceeded towards the goal, their confidence in the now seemingly unattainable victory decreased, along with their trust in the future, making room for old fears. And if that was not enough, as had already happened a few years earlier, two men had vanished into thin air the night before, taking advantage of their guard duty. Marco had even fired some shots with his rifle, which had not only woken up his people, but also attracted attention in the valley.

"We," resumed Marco, when the buzz caused by the general astonishment ceased, "did not only save the prisoners, but we let them choose freely whether they wanted to stay with us or go back to the valley. They all eagerly accepted a place among us and with us they formed their families, they fathered children and built their homes. So the shock and the anger that came the day when Tlama-hatl and Actonuy disappeared into thin air was more than under-standable, and your desire for revenge against the men remained. And I can imagine that tonight's escape of Meyaui and Xaiput has rekindled exactly the same feelings; you would have never expected such a betrayal from them. Rest assured, then, because these men, in truth...they have not betrayed us. Xeetha and I are the only ones responsible for their escape."

The murmur which followed this revelation was suddenly cov-ered by the enraged voice of Atzcha: "And can you please tell us why you've been hiding something of this importance from us for all this time? You did not trust us, perhaps?"

Marco was not perturbed. "No," he answered quietly, speaking directly to her, "we had to be quiet to avoid compromising the plan. What would have happened to our friends and what would have happened to our people if one day, one of us, taken by despair, dis-trust or fear, had decided to run away and betray us for real?"

Atzcha, seeing that she was not even backed by her most faithful companions who were all carefully listening to the words of *tlatoani*, sat down rigid and stiffer than before. And the silence came back in the assembly.

"Our choice fell on Tlamahatl and Actonuy, not only because we were sure that they would agree with a great sense of duty and sacrifice to our proposal, but also because, knowing their very high rank among the jaguar warriors, we were sure that after the losses suffered in the great battle there would have been a great need for men with their qualities in the valley. And in fact, when Xeetha and I were almost beginning to despair about the success of our plan, we received their first message."

The audience was left speechless by the enormity of the revelation, they were completely unable to react or to interrupt Marco's story, who continued his exposition: "As many of you will remember, Tlamahatl was a great friend of the fisherman—he was the one to help Pahaleotalli to drop and pick up the nets in his free time—and it then seemed natural to everybody that, once free, he would go back to visit his old companion. It was then not difficult for him to sway his heart to our cause, and so the fisherman has been sending us the messages of our men along with the usual goods.

"And I can tell you," Marco continued, "that the news we are receiving is very encouraging. It seems that we can now count on the support of a fairly substantial number of jaguar warriors, but the work of persuasion carried out by our friends can only proceed in a very slow and careful way; Mohotzuma's spies are everywhere, and even the smallest mistake could turn fatal. Unfortunately, work on the tunnel is now coming to an end and the time left for finding new allies has almost run out. This is the reason Xeetha and I felt this was the right time to move to the second part of our plan, the riskiest and most difficult to carry out."

Marco paused for a moment, the time required for the final revelation: "Last night's escape was part of this plan, and if we have decided to reveal everything only now," Marco continued, intentionally staring in Atzcha's eyes, "we did it for a reason: we know very well the value of our friends and we are more than confident that they will tackle all the risks and the trials that await them with courage and determination. But we also know that none of us, though ready to die in battle, can know his own limits with torture…We could not take any chances; even Meyaui and Xaiput had to remain unaware of Actonuy and Tlamahatl's mission. And today Xeetha and I have decided to reveal to everybody our secret because now, betrayal is no longer possible. It is too late to back out."

Chapter 3

Chitoontecl, chief priest of the people of the Sacred Curved Mountain, looked down in silence at the two men kneeling at his feet, face and hands to the floor, kissing the ground. The arrow that had pierced the side of his cheek had cut his facial nerve. From that night on, Chitoontecl's left eyelid remained perpetually open, and a thick rheumy liquid dripped constantly from his congested eye, mixing with the drool dripping from the twisted corner of his mouth.

And on top of all that, the bullet that hit him with good accuracy some time later had truncated his thigh's inner tendons and the erector nerves, making him lame and impotent. The terrible impairments had kindled in him a blind, unquenchable hatred, and the pursuit of revenge had become his only reason for living.

He had been disturbed in the middle of the night by an excited clamor and he was already mentally listing the punishments to be meted out to the unwary souls who dared wake him when he heard the unsteady voice of his assistant from the vestibule, begging forgiveness and asking to inform him about particularly important news.

During the night, the sentinels stationed in every corner of the southern part of the valley had been alarmed by a succession of screams coming from above. They had also clearly heard the thunder-like sound of the cursed weapon and some distant splashes in the lake. Shortly thereafter, by the light of the torches that were immediately set aflame, the guards had seen two naked men appear at the shore, panting from the long swim. One of them, supported by his companion, was visibly bleeding from his calf.

The two had identified themselves and a sentry alongside whom they had fought before the battle had confirmed their declared identity. They were then hastily conducted into Aplaia; in the House of the Serpent, where Puqutec, who was *tlaccatecatl* after the *tlatoani* of all military orders and head of the Sacred Serpent, had questioned them a first time, after which he considered it worthwhile to inform the *tlamacazqui* as soon as possible without waiting for the morning. And once he had received the news, the *tlamacazqui* had ordered the fugitives be brought to him immediately, and they were now kneeling at his feet, kissing the ground while surrounded by a swarm of armed guards.

"So, after all this time, you were able to escape," said Chitoontecl after a long and heavy silence. Puqutec had already informed him of the outcome of the first interrogation, but he wanted to understand the whole thing in person.

"Yes, my lord," replied Meyaui, who had decided to speak for both, raising his head from the ground. "After the escape of two of our men, the surveillance up there had become unbelievable, but we—"

"But you've done it," continued the priest for him "and, coincidentally, just a step away from the big day…Well done, very good indeed."

"Thank you, my lord." Meyaui nodded, flying high on the priest's irony. "At night those bitches kept us locked up in a cage, with our hands and feet tied behind our backs…Look," he added, raising his arms to show the marks left by the laces on his wrists. "And during the day it was even worse: those damned women, after having sacrificed three of our men and satisfied their hunger with their flesh in front of our eyes, forced us to work from early morning till late evening as if we were two miserable *tlatacotin*."

"You wouldn't say that from your looks: you both look in great shape and very well fed for having been treated so poorly,"

Chitoontecl sarcastically remarked, far from being convinced by such a laughable account.

"Great *tlamacazqui*, you should not underestimate those wall-riders: it did not take them long to realize that only by satisfying our hunger they could get all they wanted from us. And if there is one thing they are not short of, that is food: they have as much as they want, and they surely don't need to deprive themselves of anything to feed their prisoners. What they have a great need of is arms to work. Without our help they would have never been able to raise the defensive walls and to dig the dozens and dozens of traps scattered all over the field. But we are the ones who dug those holes, we know very well where they are located and we know the paths to follow to avoid ending up trapped in them. And we know all the weak points in their defenses: when you want, my lord, we will point them all out to you, one by one…with the little time left before the big day, they surely won't have the time to change anything."

The latest news aroused some interest in the priest, but it took much more than that to dissolve his suspicions.

"Two moons ago," Meyaui continued, "I found a fragment of blade in the wood. I wrapped it in straw and hid it in my mouth, hoping they would not find it before they locked me up in the cage. The gods have stood by my side: I buried the blade in the place where I slept, and from that moment on, I just waited for the right moment. It was my cousin Antuacahatl who helped us. We got rid of the guards and he helped us climb down, but things did not go as planned. We had just grabbed the rope under the hut, when we felt something pulling us up very quickly. We had no choice, so we slackened off and we let ourselves go. Fortunately, the lake was not so far away and everything went well for us, but they continued to shoot from above with the thundering weapon and Xaiput was hit in the calf before he had the time to touch the water. Thank the gods, I was close to him when that happened, and I was able to grab him by the arm and drag him to the shore."

"That's a lot of luck!" the priest commented sarcastically.

"That's true, my lord," acquiesced Meyaui. "They probably found my cousin while he was making us climb down, and I would not want to be in his place right now…"

"I'm not interested in that," the priest interrupted him. "Tell me about the Son of the Mountain. Who is he? Where does he come from? And why did he come here?"

"If I have to be sincere, my lord, I did not have many chances to see him from up close. But I can assure you he is five heads taller than the tallest of our warriors, and it is also easy to recognize him from far away because of the long, white ponytail going down his back. Nobody knows who he is, where he comes from, or why he came to the Curved Mountain. They say he was conceived by the mountain, but I think the slaves know as much as me. He is also a man of few words, and you see him only rarely around. They say he hides weapons of incredible force in the cave where he lives, weapons which could destroy the entire mountain in a day, and—"

"Shut up!" commanded Chitoontecl, who realizing with no sense of timing that his grudge and his craving for information pertaining to his despicable nemesis had induced him to ask for information in the presence of too many curious listeners. But the damage was already done: the guards had heard, and even if he had threatened them with death, the news would have surely been quickly spread around the entire valley.

"As you like, great *tlamacazqui*," Meyaui promptly obeyed. "But you should know that you will be able to beat him in spite of all his weapons, if you will listen our advice. So then in one fell swoop, you will be able to undo the disgrace of old losses and we will be able to avenge all the suffering we have endured these long years…Act as you think it's best, my lord, but—we beg you—grant us the honor of taking part in the battle when the time comes."

"We will speak of that later. But…don't fear, you will soon have the opportunity to demonstrate your courage to everyone," the priest interrupted him with a wholly discouraging tone. "For the moment, you will remain guests of the Serpent House. But in separate rooms. And woe to you," he said, raising his sinister gaze to the guards, "if you allow them to communicate with one another or with others without my authorization: it will be a pleasure for me to tear your heart out if you dare disobey this order…and this goes for you two as well," he added, lowering his eyes to the runaways. "Understood?"

"You have our word, Enlightened One," replied Meyaui quickly. "We are intelligent men and we know that you cannot trust us yet. Nonetheless, we dare ask you to accommodate our plea."

"You are not in the position to make requests!"

"Of course, my lord, and we beg you forgiveness twelve times over for our audacity, but…knowing your generosity and your benevolence, we miserable servants still dare ask you this."

"Let's hear it, then," the priest acquiesced, not fooled by their flattery, but very curious to know what the man kneeling at his feet could ask him of such importance to dare challenge his anger.

"From the day we fell in the hands of those she-hounds, I have had no news of my parents. And he…" Meyaui continued pointing at his companion, "has had no news of his woman, who had just—"

"It's true, great *tlamacazqui*!" Xaiput interjected, raising his head from the ground.

"You are not allowed to speak!" screamed Chitoontecl.

"Forgive him, my lord," interfered Meyaui, quickly pushing the insolent man's head back to the ground, "but you need to know that he lives only in the memory of his woman and that it is only to see her again that he decided to face the risks of an escape…my lord, if you allowed us to see our loved ones again…we would be extremely grateful."

"We'll see," Chitoontecl cut short, without promising anything, signaling to the guards to take the two men away.

"What do you think about this?" asked the priest when the vestibule remained empty.

The grim-faced Mohotzuma, Chitoontecl's éminence grise, appeared from behind the curtain facing the bedroom. He lived in the shadow, but everyone knew him too well and everyone had learned to fear him—often at their own cost—even more than the high priest. Nothing escaped his eyes and his ears; the network of spies and informers he had at his service was wide, and his thugs were there to systematically hush up every protest with threats, intimidations and physical elimination in the more severe cases.

For this, several *pipiltin* had preferred having him as a friend rather than an enemy, and the few who still dared to challenge him and openly express their dissent could be counted on one hand. Year after year, he had conquered yet more freedom of action, to the point that no initiative of importance could be carried out in the Curved Mountain without his prior authorization.

He had always executed the dirty jobs commissioned by the high priest, and with time his power had exaggeratedly increased, and it could be compared to that of his protector. To whom he laid always more urging and costly claims.

"He doesn't convince me at all. I don't believe a word of what he has said…give them to me for a day, and I'll let you know how things really are."

"Forget it. I know your methods very well, and I already know how they'll come out of it. By now everybody knows of their escape, and you still can't get into that bald head of yours that not all of the *pipiltin* are our friends. If those who don't agree with us come to know we have tortured them or if we eliminate them without the council's approval, they will incite the people against us rapidly. And you can never tell: they could turn out to be useful. There could be some truth in what they have said. No, let's let them be for the moment, let's pretend we've taken for good the story they have told us. What damage can they do in the little time left before the big day, since they're locked up and closely guarded day and night?"

"As you wish, my lord," Mohotzuma agreed reluctantly.

"Good! Subject closed, then," Chitoontecl said, walking towards the bedroom.

The conversation was over, and Mohotzuma could only swallow his annoyance. He could not take any more of that powerless cripple who only impeded his plans. Chitoontecl had even advanced the possibility of having him elected as *tlamacazqui*, once the senior priest, who was old and in bad health, decided to take his leave.

A lot of time had gone by since that proposal, but Chitoontecl seemed to have had some second thoughts about that; he did not mention the possibility anymore, he beat around the bush and changed topic when his subordinate tried to bring him back to that. He had clearly realized the excessive power his henchman had accumulated, and he had started to fear the possibility of seeing his transformation from an obedient perpetrator of his orders into a dangerous rival. Needy of his services, though, he kept him on a string with false promises.

Mohotzuma had got the hang of that a while ago and, tired of the continuous delays, he had taken his own route, which in his plans should lead him soon to the power he craved. With or without the support of his protector.

Chapter 4

"One of my men was there when they were questioned by the *tlamacazqui,*" Peheptel said while she continued brushing Tlahaxtala's long hair. "What the fisherman learned was all true, but it was nothing compared to what those two have told."

"Come on, Peheptel, speak and don't keep me waiting."

"Uh, don't be so impatient, sweetheart," the woman reprimanded her with a motherly smile, happy of having found a topic that could awake the interest of her sad and afflicted mistress. "They reported that he lives in the heart of the mountain that conceived him, that he's as tall as a tree in the wood, and that he has a very long white ponytail behind his back. But he isn't old. It seems like his face doesn't know time, and that his extraordinary beauty has enchanted all the slaves of the *tlatoani.* They fear him and adore him as a god."

The light coming from the perpetually blooming garden lit up the room, reflecting on the gold of the storiated columns and exalting the vivid colors of the hunting, fishing and farming scenes depicted on the vault and on each wall. The dreaming eyes of Tlahaxtala reflected like two emeralds on each side of the great crystal mirror.

Her eyes were the only green eyes in the history of the Curved Mountain. At her birth, the news had spread like fire from mouth to mouth and all had rushed to the house of her parents, humble basket makers, to see the prodigious event in person. A then beardless *tlatoani* Cuzupuma—successor to his father, who had prematurely died in mysterious circumstances—informed of this, had ordered the baby to be brought to him in the palace, and was so enchanted by the light of those eyes that he did not want to leave them anymore: that marvelous toy had to be his own. And Chitoontecl, who at the time was only at the beginning of his climb to power, had made it so that the young, spoiled sovereign could be pleased once more, all in order to garner support for himself in the council.

The conclusion: the high priest had given her to the then eleven-year-old *tlatoani* as a wife, pontificating on the sacredness of those eyes, and then sent her mother to serve in the temple and her father to top of the pyramid. But the *tlatoani* was developing a peculiar erotic taste, and once he got tired of the initial excitement, he completely lost interest in the child, relegating her to a wing of the palace very distant from the one he lived in.

Tlahaxtala had grown up there in loneliness, far away from her family, flattered and envied by the courtesans for her extraordinary beauty, which had increased exponentially while that young flower blossomed into a woman. On her face, though, a sad and absent expression could often be observed, with a lost look, as she dreamed of different and faraway worlds. She had already turned twenty-three and her illustrious spouse had never touched her. But this was the least of her worries: that fat creature with his shrill voice, whose only concern was to surround himself with callow youths to satisfy his depraved inclinations engendered only disgust in her, and knowing he was far away was a relief.

Her only consolation was Peheptel, who was also of humble social origins, and who had been her wet nurse when she was taken away from her family. The woman had the joviality and the good spirits of simple, chubby people. Her belly always preceded her and her jokes were the only things that could comfort the young girl from the pain of isolation in her gilded cage. She was a mother to her, a friend, a confidant, and she was also her eyes and her ears for everything that happened in the palace and the valley. When she became an adult, the courtesans tried to take Peheptel away from her and substitute her companionship with that of their daughters and consorts. But Tlahaxtala, who was always moderate, docile and almost indifferent to what happened around her, had caused such pandemonium that to keep the peace the *tlatoani* had given in: they could continue staying together.

The almost complete isolation had led Tlahaxtala to abandon her prison by dreaming up different worlds inhabited by surreal characters, which changed face and role according to her mood and frame of mind. The lack of contact with other children had made her mature prematurely, but in a different way from her peers; it made her seek refuge and comfort for her loneliness in those fantastic worlds even as an adult.

For some time, though, her daydreams were permanently and obsessively monopolized by one single character. Not an imaginary one anymore, but a real and concrete one, although unfortunately unattainable: he came down from the top of the mountain and he freed her from her imprisonment to lead her with him in their enchanted world, where she would serve him, give him children and love him until the end of his days…

The wing of the palace in which Tlahaxtala and Peheptel lived was also frequented by many members of the court—wives and daughters of *pipiltin*, especially—who took turns in assisting the sovereign in her various activities: weaving, painting, music, gardening and all the rest. The two women, though, had learned to be wary of the gentleness and helpfulness of these unreliable characters, among which they were sure Mohotzuma's spies were hiding. For this, they dared to confide in one another only when they were sure that they were alone. Just as they were that very moment.

"They reported that he's a tireless lover, and that every woman who has laid with him lives in the memory of those moments and in the desire of living them once more. They also said that—"

Tlahaxtala's dreamy expression changed immediately. The mirror was reflecting the image of the grimy face of Mohotzuma, who had appeared from nowhere, and had silently entered the room without being announced.

"Who gave you permission you to come in!" she cried indignantly without tearing her gaze away from the mirror. The man was unfazed, and his face bore a grimace that intended to be a smile; he proceeded quietly forward, and when he reached the women, he directed a meaningful glance to the maid.

There was no need for words. Peheptel lowered her head, put down the comb, and as she held back her anger with difficulty, she silently left the room.

"Forgive me, my lady," Mohotzuma began, moving behind Tlahaxtala's shoulders to better admire the reflection of her wonderful curves in the mirror, "I wanted to announce my arrival, but nobody was there to watch your room…I think we should take some punitive action against whoever has failed in his duties."

Tlahaxtala did not comment; she knew perfectly well that all the women assigned to her service had been chosen by him with the express purpose of surveying her and reporting to him every move she made and word she said.

A bony, claw-like hand shot out from the sleeve of his gray tunic and grabbed the comb laid on the dressing table; he took up the task that he had interrupted Peheptel doing. But Tlahaxtala was ready to block his wrist with one hand.

"How dare you touch me," she hissed trembling with rage and repugnance. "If the *tlatoani* came to know that…"

Mohotzuma sneered amusedly. "Cuzupuma has his mind on other things right now. When I left his room a few minutes ago, he was trying to track down his last purchase, who knows where he's hiding…Poor man," he went on mockingly. "Since the slaves escaped, he has lost his personal breeding ground, and he's obliged to select them directly from the general populace. And from time to time…heh…another young boy disappears. He thinks that nobody knows who instigates these kidnappings. But it's so well known that only terror of the guards can stave off the fury of the people. The situation could get out of hand and turn into open revolt at any time, and if something unpleasant should happen to your divine

315

spouse…well, you know very well what destiny will be reserved for his beloved, virgin wife."

The reference to her chastity hit Tlahaxtala like a slap in the face. She loosened her grip and her hand fell lifelessly to her knees while a cramp twisted her stomach as she pictured her skin, bloody and freshly torn from her body, draped over the high priest's shoulders. Mohotzuma's skinny hand resumed combing her hair while the poor, speechless girl continued to stare at the mirror with a lost look.

"But there could be a way to avoid this sad destiny," the man continued, winking at her through the mirror. "It's been years since Chitoontecl started saying I could become *tlamacazqui*, but I have the feeling he has changed his mind recently…and guess what I found out. That son of a wall-rider has worked for many moons to have Claloch elected in my place."

Mohotzuma let out a brief laugh, then he went on. "But I want to tell you a secret: Chitoontecl doesn't know I was the one to let Claloch in the *tlamacazcalli* and to make sure he became the first pupil, outdoing every other aspirants to the position. That sweet boy knows he owes his quick ascent to me, and now his only wish is to somehow return the favors he has received…who knows, I could even aim to become *tlatoani*, and oblige you to surrender yourself…"

"Enough!" the woman screamed, jumping up and hitting the dressing table on which the mirror rested. The mere thought of having to lie down with that repugnant human being behind her gave her the creeps, to the point where the idea of being skinned on the altar seemed less painful. The noise caused by the crystal mirror as it smashed to the ground in a million fragments made the manipulator jump, cutting off his monologue and making the comb fall from his hands.

"As you wish, my lady," Mohotzuma said, collecting himself with ill-concealed disappointment. "As you can see, I have no fear of confiding in you my secrets. Because I trust you completely, because I'm your friend, and because my only desire is to help you and defend you from any danger. Think hard about my proposal, divine lady. As you know, I can be very, very patient. If it were up to me, I could wait on your decision forever, but time is running out…"

After this last threat, Mohotzuma bowed formally, turned around and slowly left the room while bitter and silent tears of despair streamed down the immaculate face of Tlahaxtala.

Chapter 5

Tlamahatl had just reached the top of the tunnel, walking at the head of his men, to relieve the workers on the latest shift. The tunnel was about to circumvent the southern pole of the crater and from its slits the entire valley could be glimpsed from above, including the faraway walls of Aplaia and the place where the river disappeared into the mountain. Even with the air-shaft windows, the rock was still affected by the heat of the underlying volcanic area, and the tunnel was a furnace. The workers, who were completely naked but for thick wooden clogs to be able to bear contact with the soil, drank from their rabbit-skin waterbags both to quench their thirst and refresh their bodies.

Even in the stifling heat, the work proceeded in the best possible way. Five men attacked the wall with heavy clubs and stone wedges while other workers arranged for the rubble to be removed and collected in conical wicker baskets, which were transported to the valley at the end of the shift. The shift was reduced to the minimum, and the constant turnover of relaxed and refreshed arms allowed the workers to maintain a very fast rhythm, day and night, without any interruption, and it also made working in such a hostile environment more tolerable.

It had been Tlamahatl who suggested that rapid cycling of men, and when they realized that such a well-structured organization went much faster than before he had received the recognition of his supervisors, who wound up appointing him director of the entire construction. Tlamahatl had then maneuvered in such a way as to make it seem like they were entrusting to Actonuy the task of forming the teams.

Since Tlamahatl and Actonuy had taken over direction of the labor, the digging had quickly accelerated and this had contributed to dispersing suspicions against them. Nonetheless, the old companions still continued to avoid meeting each other; if not in the presence of other people or in apparently occasional situations to the eyes of other people, and only in those circumstances did they dare to briefly exchange information and to take stock of the results achieved. At this point, considering the trust they had earned in the eyes of their superiors, these precautions could even appear to be excessive, but they had produced excellent results. By acting in secret and only after having carefully studied the ideas and reliability of each possible candidate, they had won over a large group of supporters to their cause—former brothers in arms, especially—who had also continued to deceive their comrades, acting with the same infinite caution.

"Those two were always locked in the House of the Serpent," Tlamahatl told Actonuy while his men took the tools from the workers who were finishing their shift, dripping in sweat and covered from head to toe by a poultice of white powder. "I know for sure that they haven't touched them at all, and that they are even treated as two *pipiltin*, but it's impossible to approach them or even exchange a single word with them…and what's more, those up there refuse any bartering and nobody can explain the reason for it."

"It certainly is quite strange," considered Actonuy, "just two moons are left before the end of the digging and it can't be that they were sent down on a similar mission to ours."

"If they didn't escape for real."

"No, I don't think so. Even though, just like you, I don't understand much of it yet…For the moment I'm afraid we can't do anything but wait and see, in the hopes of learning something more." After having said this, Actonuy took leave of his friend and quickly caught up to his men who were already walking on the way back.

Mohotzuma, with his hands perennially hidden in the sleeves of his gray tunic, was silently listening to the words of Cohocotl, a short, dull-looking man, who was always the first to be informed on everything that happened in the Curved Mountain.

"Meyaui's parents are still alive. Even though they're old, they're still well and they continue producing baskets near the cave. His brother Antapuoi, instead..."

"Antapuoi?"

"Yes, my lord, it's him, the first coil of the Order of the Serpent."

"Ah, I didn't know he had a brother. And what else can you tell me about them that I don't know?"

"Oh, nothing that hasn't already been around for a long time. I think it's no mystery that Antapuoi is a protégé of the *theoticatl*, even though we must acknowledge he has reached his position only thanks to his qualities: he captured twelve enemies alive in the previous Flower War, and this venture made history. His men adore him, also because he never took advantage of the insignia to obtain riches and favors."

Cohocotl snickered: "He's an honest man," he continued, "who doesn't accept bribes. You only need to know that he didn't even think of asking Puqutec for permission to visit his brother when he found out that Chitoontecl had prohibited anybody else from meeting him...because he probably knew what answer he would have gotten," he added with a giggle. "Puqutec can't stand him, he knows he is his first rival..."

"Okay, okay, but what can you tell me of the other man?"

"Oh, well, there isn't much to say on Xaiput. His parents died a long time ago, and his only brother went to meet them in the *Mictlan* in the last flower war. There's nobody waiting for him around here."

"But I heard it with my own ears that he only escaped to see his wife again!"

"He can forget his wife too!"

320

"What do you mean?"

"If you only knew, my lord, she's an amazing woman, a goddess," the short man informed him with dreamy eyes. "Xaiput was crazily in love with her, and he was so consumed by jealousy that he obliged his parents to lock her up in the house until the wedding...you should have seen the scenes he made with her father," Cohocotl sneered amusedly, "when his friends told him they had seen her around at night with another suitor."

"Get to the point!"

"I beg your forgiveness, my lord, but I can't help laughing when I think about it...well, to make it short, the wifey, some days after her beloved spouse went missing, thought it was time that Puqutec consoled her...the poor girl couldn't stand the pain anymore..."

"Puqutec?"

"Yes, still him, my lord, the *tlaccatecatl*, the head of the serpent."

Mmm, I'm really starting to get old, Mohotzuma thought to himself, amazed at being completely unaware of that as well.

"Just like that, my lord. And you can guess if that bitch is ready now to renounce all the *tlatlacotin* who serve and revere her from morning to night in her beautiful *tecalli*, to go back to cooking and weaving for that miserable *macehualtin* that her husband is...you understand why I said Xaiput can forget his wife too now, and that—?"

"Can you repeat that?" Mohotzuma interrupted him, suddenly interested.

"What?"

"Son of a bewitched chicken, I asked you to repeat and explain what you just said!"

"Yes, yes, my lord, but don't get mad, I beg you...well, as I was saying, Cuanpooca, that's her name, was waiting for just that, and she welcomed her husband's disappearance like a liberation. And, thanks to her...qualities, it didn't take her long before she was welcomed by Puqutec with all honors," the informer concluded, with a complicit, knowing smile.

321

"Enough with these useless details!"

"Forgive me, my lord. It was only to tell you that Puqutec, too, wound up losing his head for that woman, and that even though he knows that Chitoontecl has promised her as a prize to whoever can capture the Son of the Mountain alive, he already considers her his own."

"You finally gave me the important news!" Mohotzuma shouted out radiant, and then he added: "Unlike you, I'm convinced that our little widow will be very happy to see her beloved spouse after having been separated from him for so long."

"But…what about Puqutec?"

"Puqutec is the least of my problems," Mohotzuma concluded scornfully. "I don't think that he will have anything to say when I make my request…Go, find that woman, Cohocotl. And bring her to me immediately."

Chapter 6

"How I have missed you!" Xaiput cried out, sitting on the pillows, bewitched by the figure of that delightful being, who moved naked along the room sinuously, like a cat. In the valley he had left behind an absolutely beautiful, but still immature, unready woman. Now he had in front of him the body of a woman of unrivaled beauty; time had smoothed the rough edges of her adolescence to enrich her body with soft, sinuous curves. She was bursting with sensuality, and you could only be left enchanted by the face of such a desirable creature. "I never stopped thinking about you; this made my imprisonment unbearable, but the desire and hope of holding you in my arms again one day also kept me alive." While he talked, the man could still feel the woman's flavor in his mouth, and his nostrils were pervaded by the heady smell of recently consummated sex.

Puqutec had reacted vehemently to Mohotzuma's requests, the arguments he had laid out to persuade him to reason had been so convincing that even before he was done listing them, the eminent leader had kept himself from protesting too much. Cuanpooca, on the contrary, had promptly accepted the clever manipulator's offer.

In her excessive craving for wealth and social advancement, she had believed every promise made by the almighty character, and she had not hesitated for an instant before complying with each of his requests. And in that moment, she was with her former husband in Puqutec's wonderful *tecalli*—and Puqutec, mad with rage, had to endure this second affront without saying a word in order to avoid displeasing his persuasive protector. Mohotzuma, in his endless benevolence, had decided to give the runaway this gift "for the braveness shown in his escape and his revelations, which were to become a crucial contribution to future offensive strategizing."

In the past few days, Cuanpooca, who was determined to see out the task assigned to her, had put so much effort into the display of her skills that she was by now convinced that she had ensnared her former husband to the point that he would have killed his father and mother—were they still alive—to go on enjoying her services. She could now enjoy the fruits of her patient and hard-earned labor.

"You need to come to terms with this, my love: I'm not your woman anymore. I have been given to the *teocalli*, and you know you can't take back from the gods what has been given to them. Only the *tlamacazqui* has the power to decide if the servant has to remain in the temple, sacrificed to the gods or given as a gift to a hero. And Chitoontecl chose to give me as a gift to whoever succeeds in capturing the man who rendered him impotent and crippled...how I wish you were to be the lucky one!" Cuanpooca whispered to him, bringing her pelvis to the height of his face.

That smooth flower full of promise awoke in her lover that insatiable desire, which brought him to instinctively place his lips on it.

Xaiput had never stopped loving and desiring Cuanpooca during his long absence. Through the fisherman he had always been informed on the events of the valley, including his wife's betrayal, which had aroused in him rage and despair, and an uncontrollable desire for revenge, his grudge had melted away like snow in the sun as soon as he saw her in all her unrivaled, amplified beauty before him, and his desire to have that lovely woman all to himself was revived.

"My heart," Cuanpooca gasped, grabbing his head and pushing it onto her groin, "cries to think that all of this will have to end soon. Only two moons are left before the digging is done, and this time there will be no way out for those people. I will then be given to another man, I will become his, and we will be separated for the rest of our lives."

"Shut up!" Xaiput shouted, clawing at the woman's thighs. "You are mine, and mine only…and you will never belong to anyone else!"

"No, Xaiput, we need to resign ourselves to this, we are nothing but miserable *macehualtin*, we can't go beyond the law of the Book. Let's try savoring each moment the gods have conceded us in their infinite benevolence."

"No, Cuanpooca, I will never be satisfied with this only; you must be mine forever and not for a short time only."

"You need to come to terms with this, Xaiput, you know how things are. Only death could change them. And if you ask me, I won't hesitate to die with you."

"No, Cuanpooca, you will be mine again and alive, not dead."

At these words, the woman's heart skipped a beat, but she was too clever to reveal her emotions, and showed nothing.

"Stop dreaming, my love. Only the one who will capture the Son of the Mountain alive will have me forever. And you think Chitoontecl will allow you to take part in the battle when the time comes? And even if he did concede you this honor, what makes you think you'll be the one to capture him?"

Xaiput, tormented by opposing forces, stayed silent for a long time before he answered.

"You'll be mine again, but not through that path."

"And how, then?"

"I can't tell you, but…trust me. You only need to know that many things might soon change in the Curved Mountain, and that if everything goes the right way, nothing will impede our love anymore. Don't ask me more. I don't want to put you in danger as well."

Cuanpooca felt she was one step away from the aspired goal, and had no intention of letting up then, on the finish line. She decided to play all her cards.

"I understand. You don't trust me. And you're right," she added bursting to tears and wiggling out of the man's embrace.

"Why do you say that, Cuanpooca! Why should I not trust you?"

"Because…because I lied to you, Xaiput. I lied to you and I betrayed you. And I don't deserve your trust and your respect any-more…a few days after the battle I went to Puqutec's *tecalli*, this *tecalli*, and I gave myself to him…that's why you don't have to trust me: I know I don't deserve you, Xaiput, and I also know you'll never forgive my crime. But I didn't want to be sacrificed, I didn't want to die…I wanted to live! Do you understand me?"

Hearing the woman confess those secrets he knew about already, Xaiput flung himself at her and embraced her. "Don't cry, Cuanpooca, I…I already know the truth. Nothing of what happens here in the valley is a mystery for the people up there. The news that I received about you tore a piece of my heart away every time. I got the point of hating you for what you'd done to me. And I decided to…escape from up there, just to have my revenge; I wanted to make you suffer, to make you endure everything I had had to en-dure…but then I saw you again. And I understood. I understood that it's not right to dismiss the only true, worthwhile gift life has given us to satisfy a wounded pride, and that we can't be ashamed of our weakness when gods present us with trials larger than us. Cu-anpooca, I…I forgave you in the moment I saw you again. Because seeing you again I understood I couldn't live without you. And after your confession, I feel I love you even more than before."

"You have a great heart, Xaiput. I always knew that. And I wish so much that I could remain close to you to make you forgive me for all my faults," the woman whispered, pressing the length of her body against his, "but soon this possibility will be taken away, and we won't be able to fulfill our dream."

Xaiput let go of her embrace and started to nervously move around the room.

"The last word hasn't been said yet," he hazarded, almost talk-ing to himself. "The last word hasn't been said yet," he repeated, touching his chin as he used to do when he had to take a controver-sial decision. "But…"

"But what?" she urged him, knowing very well what that insecure gesture meant.

"It's not easy to explain."

"But what's so difficult about it?"

"When I escaped, I was sure things would go in a certain way. But now...I'm not so sure about it anymore: everything is getting more and more complicated..." The man turned around to stare with possessed eyes at his beloved's face, as though tormented by an invisible fire which burned inside him. And then he finally resolved himself: "It's a long story, Cuanpooca. It's very hard to believe. But after what you've confessed to me, I think it's time for you to know. And maybe...not only you..."

Chapter 7

"You're a spy, then."

While talking, Mohotzuma carefully observed the man kneeling at his feet, controlling each one of his reactions. He had reached the *tecalli* by the river during the evening, accompanied by a handful of armed guards. They had positioned themselves in the vestibule overlooking the garden to be ready for anything, after they had carefully inspected every corner of the building. Cuanpooca slept in Aplaia that night, at her parents' house.

"Yes, my lord, that's the truth," Xaiput replied. "Almost nothing of what I told you at the *tlamacazqui* is true. Shortly after the first moon following the day of battle, the Son of the Mountain untied our laces and let us free to go or stay with them. We all chose to stay, and many of us coupled with of the *tlatoani*'s slaves. My lord…our escape was part of a plan."

"And how do you explain Tlamahatl and Actonuy's escape then? Was it part of the same plan?"

"The reason behind their escape is still a mystery for everybody. But I don't think their escape was planned: those women almost killed us all like animals, for how angry they were…Tlamahatl and Actonuy were warriors, born and raised to fight. After the initial excitement, they must have grown tired of working in the fields as miserable *mayeque*, waiting for a war that would never come. So, at the first occasion, they took off and went back home. And without saying anything to anybody, of course, because nobody would have let them go, since they knew all of our secrets."

"Go on. And give me information that *your* woman hasn't given me already."

"Well, there isn't much more to add. I think what you're most interested in, is knowing how you can capture the Son of the Mountain. Alive. And in a very simple and safe way. But you need to promise me that—"

"I think I've already given you my word," Mohotzuma interrupted him, continuing to stare at Xaiput right in the eyes, looking for any sign of falsehood. His nature always led him to be wary of everything and everybody. Nothing—he was thinking to himself—could assure him that the man kneeling at his feet was not lying for a second time. But why would he? And what damage could he do, isolated as he was and watched day and night? And what if there was some truth in what he was reporting, what if he really knew how to capture the great enemy? What risk would he run in trying?

"And why did you choose to speak only now?"

"Cuanpooca...she is the one and only reason for my choice to speak. If it wasn't for her, I would have never even dreamed..."

"All right, all right...I'm still waiting for you to tell me what you came here to do."

"The son of the Mountain assigned us a task. A risky one, but with good chances of turning out good, nonetheless."

"You don't mean to say you thought we would have let you go freely around once you came down."

"We expected a much worse welcome, to say the truth. And I can guess the reason behind my dear wife's sudden display of affection. But that doesn't matter: I'm ready to do anything to have her back. But you need to know that it's not because of your slyness that I decided to collaborate, but rather because I couldn't believe I was offered this opportunity for which I hadn't dared to hope. I've always known she doesn't love me, but unfortunately she's the only reason that I live, and I have no intention of losing her again."

"So you're not as stupid as you pretended to be..." Mohotzuma complimented him. "But now come to the conclusion, if you please."

"No sooner said than done, my lord. Our task was to contact a person. And we were sure to meet this person, even if we were to be locked up in the depths of the mountain. But the impossible happened: the encounter never took place and by now I'm afraid it never will. And if our plan fails, the Son of the Mountain, even with all his weapons would have very few chances of winning against such a powerful and large army as yours...or he wouldn't have had to make up this whole mess, don't you think?"

"If you knew you wouldn't be allowed to communicate with anybody, how could you be so sure you would meet that person?"

"My lord, when you will know the name, you will easily understand how."

"Then tell me this name, for the gods' sake, if you don't want me to force it out of you my way!"

"Yes, but...you will keep your promise?"

"Again? How dare you question my word, you filthy dog, you traitor!"

"Forgive me," Xaiput excused himself, resolutely staring at the enraged look of the dreadful interlocutor. "But this is an irrevocable condition for me. You can even kill me with atrocious tortures if you want, but you won't get anything from me until the *tlamacazqui* gives Cuanpooca back to me in front of the whole Holy People..."

"All right, all right, you will have everything you've asked," Mohotzuma said, getting a grip of himself. "But you need to speak now once and for all, if you don't want me to change my mind."

"I'm getting there, my lord. Our only task was to contact Antapuoi, Meyaui's brother and the first coil, and propose something to him. We were more than convinced that he would have done anything to see his brother back, and we were also sure that, with his insignia, there wouldn't have been any problem in seeing him, but..."

"I can guess the proposal you would have made to Antapuoi: an alliance with him. Am I right?"

"Yes, my lord: if he accepted, with the weapons of the Son of the Mountain, and the support of all his faithful men, things wouldn't have looked well for you. Meyaui and I had to meet Antapuoi and combine a meeting between him and the Son of the Mountain, to let them discuss the entire operation."

"And when was the meeting planned?"

"My lord, if you don't mind, this I will tell you only when you have fulfilled your promise."

"Mmm, okay," Mohotzuma consented, holding back a temper tantrum. His mistrust was slowly vanishing, though. As suspicious as he had always been, he could not find any gaps or inconsistencies in the confession he had just received. "Now listen to me very well," he said, making a decision.

"I'm listening, my lord."

"I will fulfill your wish. But you will continue to behave as if this meeting never happened…if you speak one word about this, Cuanpooca included, you'll regret being born."

"You don't need to threaten me, my lord, I know what I have to lose behaving any other way."

"Right. Understood then: everything will have to proceed as planned…with a small variation," he added with an evil snigger.

Chapter 8

It was a moonless night when Marco was lead in chains inside the walls of Aplaia. The news of his capture had spread like lightning, and in spite of the hour the entire population had turned out, crowding the streets around the parade of armed warriors that escorted the prisoner to the House of the Serpent.

Nobody could believe that the great enemy, the almighty being who had twice defeated an entire army on his own, the demigod with horrible weapons, was right before their eyes, a helpless prisoner, a mere mortal. But the powerful figure of the Son of the Mountain, who was pushed through the crowd with his head high though bare and chained, still commanded respect and fear. Nobody dared to insult him or raise his voice, and only a low murmuring accompanied the parade.

Waiting for the prisoner, on the steps of the barracks floodlit by the torches of a band of warriors, stood the high priest and Mohotzuma.

Chitoontecl could still not come to terms with the event: the nightmare of many of his sleepless nights, the enemy who had robbed him of his lover, had made him impotent and crippled for life, was there, in front of him, and his prisoner. He was already savoring his merciless revenge.

Mohotzuma was already flying high as a dragonfly, at the height of exaltation. And he had many good reasons to feel so blissful. First of all, the credit for the whole operation had to be given to him alone. When he had gone to Chitoontecl to let him know that there was a concrete chance of capturing his despised enemy alive even before concluding the tunnel, the high priest had not hesitated in granting him carte blanche, as excited as he was for the long-desired eventuality. And he had gone rapidly along with the business of undoing Cuanpooca's relationship with the temple and giving her back to her husband.

The nuptials had been celebrated grandly on the esplanade of the *teocalli*, which for the occasion had been completely covered by a phantasmagorical flower carpet. Not even the *tlatoani*'s own wedding had been so pompous. Mohotzuma did not take part in the abundant celebrations during the sumptuous nuptial banquet, which took place in the heavenly park of the defrauded Puqutec's *tecalli*. He had stayed aside, limiting himself to observing the merrymaking and the two lovers' displays of affection while mentally reviewing all possible ways to make the bride a widow again and forever without attracting any attention. This would have let him satisfy his faithful and red-hot henchman, who had already shown he was not pleased at all by the recent impositions.

Once he had obtained all the crucial information from Xaiput, the éminence grise had moved to prepare the perfect trap, and he had informed Chitoontecl of his enemy's capture only once it was accomplished. The sly man made sure he let everybody know immediately that the origin of the master plan was his own, and this would surely pave his way to power.

Another great reason for his satisfaction was the simple and bloodless way he had captured the coveted prey. The dreaded enemy was attracted to the trap like a bee to the flower, and captured alive without the sacrifice of any man.

Mohotzuma's first move was to hunt down Antapuoi, and once he had explained everything he forced his hand: Antapuoi's collaboration in exchange for his traitor brother's life, and for the promise that nobody would attempt to take his position as first coil anymore, once the air had cleared. In return, he would go visit his brother and, pretending he was unaware of everything that was going on, enthusiastically accept his proposal, extorting all his useful knowledge to be put to use for the great enemy's capture.

During his confession Xaiput had revealed that for safety reasons he had been assigned a secondary role in the plan, and that Meyaui was the only one who knew how to send reliable messages above by the fisherman. As Antapuoi's brother, he would run less of a risk of being tortured than his escape companion, and it was also logical to think that Antapuoi would not have trusted anybody other than his brother.

After fifteen days of heated negotiations and secret contacts the Son of the Mountain had climbed down to the watercraft for his decisive meeting with Antapuoi, but suddenly a horde of warriors had emerged in ambush; they had taken advantage of darkness to follow the craft to the predetermined spot in perfect silence and without disturbing the waters.

Marco had tried to grab the rope hanging from the cabin, but it was useless: a sudden thrust had thrown the craft off balance, plunging him into the water. He had tried everything to wriggle out of his enemies' grasp, and he had even succeeded in clinging onto the outer parts of the boat to return aboard, but beaten down in a single strike to the head by a helmsman's oar; it was the fisherman, whose collaboration was granted by a few well-planned threats. He had been seized, lifted aboard and immobilized with fiber laces while he was still unconscious. Only ashore was he put in chains; the price to pay if he were to fall into the water and sink from the weight was too high. The order was peremptory: the Son of the Mountain had to be captured alive.

The boat had then proceeded towards the shore with its precious cargo. During the agitated capture and along the whole journey, no sign of life had come from above.

"Oh, there is the…what do they call you? Oh, yes, the Son of the Mountain. The almighty god has fallen into a trap like a dumb, blind rat…before long you will curse your stupid bitch of a mother for giving birth to you," Chitoontecl shouted as soon as he had Marco in front of him, unable to resist to the impulse of slapping him with a powerful back hander.

334

Marco, careless of the blood that was dripping from his nose and the stabbing fits he felt continuously behind his nape since he had come round, did not let a single moan slip out of his mouth and continued to stare at the despised enemy in the eyes. Chitoontecl, overcome by the force of his look—although he had placed himself two steps higher than Marco to avoid being in a state of inferiority—turned to the side to indicate the entrance of the barracks.

"Lock him down in the depths of the House and don't lose sight of him at any time," he ordered, opening even his good eye wide on the warriors around. "And treat our friend well," he continued on a softer note, "I want him fat and strong for the celebration day. I want him to be able to fully appreciate the service I'll do to him when I pull his heart out…and it will taste even better when we roast him," he concluded with an unrestrained laugh.

Chapter 9

"You told me the digging was almost done."

Tlahaxtala lived in anxiety; Mohotzuma's words kept whirling in her head. She felt helpless, she hated and despised the *tlatoani*, but just the thought of being touched by that the high priest's unctuous lackey made her blood boil…what had she done to deserve such a punishment? What misdeed was she guilty of that made the gods continue to torment her so cruelly? She felt she did not deserve such a horrible punishment, and her sense of rebellion and her determination to somehow change her destiny was ever more pressing. There must be an alternative, she repeated to herself. And if it did exist, she was resolved to find it.

"Yes, sweetheart," Peheptel replied. "The big day is approaching. Aplaia never saw so many warriors coming and going. This time it will be Puqutec in person who leads the army and all three orders will follow him. I'm afraid this time those poor women won't have any chance."

"And what about him?"

"My baby, he's always there, locked up in his cell and nobody can approach him or talk to him without Chitoontecl's permission. They don't ever let him out of their sight."

"I have to meet him."

Peheptel suddenly spun around thinking she had misunderstood her precious girl's words, but the firm expression she saw printed on her face made Peheptel realize she had understood them very well.

"But…" she tried to object.

"No buts. I have to meet him. At any cost," Tlahaxtala resolutely replied.

"But what is wrong with your head! You know I would do anything to make you happy, but what you ask is impossible. I just told you Chitoontecl denied everybody permission to approach him, even the *tlatoani*, and you think he would concede that to you, with all the love he has for you."

"I don't expect anything from him. But…but I think I know the right person to make him change his mind."

"But…"

"No buts. Go call Mohotzuma. And tell him…tell him I want to talk to him about something he cares about very much…you'll see, he won't make any trouble."

It was a peremptory request which did not allow any response. Peheptel had become distressed the second she had heard that dreaded name; she would have wanted to know her protégée's intentions better, to prevent her from making hasty moves, safeguard her from any danger, but she had never seen her so resolute and determined. Therefore, even though she was concerned and her maternal instincts urged her to make the girl desist, she left the room without replying.

Mohotzuma, as usual, snuck into the room unannounced. Tlahaxtala was hardly able to repress a temper tantrum and once again she swore to herself that she would have let those treacherous slaves feel her anger. She knew they were out there only to eavesdrop on her. As soon as Peheptel left, she rushed to change her dress, to don some much more suitable clothing for the next meeting, and then she waited for her illustrious guest; she was seated in front of an even larger and brighter mirror than the one that had shattered shortly before.

"Forgive my being so late, my wonderful la…" Mohotzuma began, stopping on the threshold and opening his eyes wide in front of that magnificent body, veiled only by a very thin dress, which exalted even more the wonderful curves of the woman for whom he longed.

With considerable effort, the sovereign succeeded in overcoming her repulsion and flashed her brightest smile. "I thought a lot about what you told me recently, Mohotzuma, and…"

"And?" he uttered with bated breath.

"And I realized Cuzupuma doesn't deserve me. He has been keeping me locked up in these walls for too long, without even knowing if I'm dead or alive. During all these years, the thought of coming to look for me, to conceive an heir, has never even crossed his mind. The *pipiltin*'s wives only laugh behind my back at how I am treated and they rejoice for the future that awaits me…I can't stand this prison anymore, and this continuous fear of ending up on the stone. But those molting chickens will regret their insolence; it's time they learn to understand who has the power."

"This is what I like to hear, my lady."

"Yes. But I certainly can't hope for the help of that half-man I married, if I want to fulfill my goal."

"Well, I don't mean to insult you, but I need to agree with you on this as well, light of my eyes. And what would you do, then?"

Tlahaxtala, in that moment, slowly stood up, turned around towards her admirer, and looking straight into his eyes she replied, "I have decided to accept your proposal."

Mohotzuma swayed. After years and years of infinite passion he was about to fulfill his greatest dream. He had never loved anybody in his life, apart from that divine being, the unattainable woman who now stood before him. Once he was elected *tlatoani* he could force her to be with him, but it would be completely different if she willingly decided to concede herself to him. And now, when he least expected it, his dream had suddenly become reality. The woman's words were music, he still could hardly believe his luck, such an unforeseen grace, and for the first time in his life he felt almighty and gratified in every desire.

"But I have several conditions," Tlahaxtala continued.

Mohotzuma's eyes snapped back to reality, although the euphoria of the moment overcame his suspicious nature.

"You only have to ask, my magnificent flower. I will be very happy to grant your every wish," the chosen one ended up promising, unable to resist the impulse of grabbing the woman's hand and of placing his lifeless lips on them. The scent of her silky skin, loaded with promise, stunned him and intoxicated him to the point that in that moment he would have even walked on hot coals if she asked him to.

"First of all, I will have to be free to leave this room and roam every corner of this palace, without asking for anybody's permission anymore…"

"Of course, my lady."

"…And to choose my own friends, and not those envious women who can't wait to see me skinned atop the pyramid."

"This is also your undeniable right."

"Then…I will have to be free to organize parties with whom I want and when I want. And the dear *pipiltin*'s wives will have to kiss the ground I walk on if they want to be invited."

"A very legitimate aspiration."

While he was listening to her, Mohotzuma silently laughed hearing that long list of very feminine requests. To be sincere, to hear such a shy and discreet woman claim all that disconcerted him a little, since she always seemed to be so resigned to her condition, without desiring anything more. Maybe, he considered, in his blind and infinite passion, he had idealized the beloved woman so much that he had judged her superior to those frivolities. All in all, however, he was pleased to discover so much grit and determination in her. *That is better,* he thought: the two of them, together, would rule over the entire Curved Mountain in perfect harmony.

"And I will also have to be able to go out of the palace when I like, to walk around the streets of Aplaia, to go to the river, to bathe in the lake, to…to do everything that comes to my mind…I can't stand this closed prison anymore!" the woman blurted out, not having to simulate enthusiasm in listing all these desires she really felt.

"I understand, you, my lady; it's the minimum a person with your insignia can aspire to."

"And then…" and here Tlahaxtala had a deliberate pause. "But I don't know if I'm daring to ask too much."

"Nothing is too much for you, my love."

"I would like to be elected a member of the council of the wise."

Mohotzuma was floored by this last obscure request. But it did not take him long to gather his thoughts. After all, he thought, there had been several cases in the past of *pipiltin* women that had become part of the council, so it would not be impossible for him to overcome the doubts of some members, and the hostility of a few others to grant her this request as well. But he had to make her believe that this would have implied a significant effort from his part.

"What you ask is not easy, my lady…but I will do my best to satisfy even this wish of yours," he conceded magnanimously.

"I'm extremely grateful to you for this," Tlahaxtala said, delighting him with another bright, though forced, smile, offering him her hand to seal their pact and to make him understand at the same time that their conversation was over.

Mohotzuma was euphoric, radiant, he could not believe he had obtained such a complete and absolute capitulation at such a derisory price, and he felt like he was twirling in the air, while he walked on stilts the few meters that separated him from the exit. But while he was about to disappear from the room he was blocked on the threshold by the woman's voice.

"Ah, Mohotzuma."

"Yes?"

"Sorry if I'm holding you back for another moment, but…I forgot something."

"I'm listening, Emerald Eyes," the promised lover chirped, happy to turn back.

"I have another small favor to ask you for. A small thing, a woman's whim, if you will, but…I would really love to see it carried out."

340

"Your every wish is my command."

"I thank you infinitely for your willingness. And I will be sure to appropriately express my gratitude to you," Tlahaxtala promised, visibly swaying her hips as she approached him. "Knowing your power, I think this will be terribly easy for you to grant this last stupid wish of mine," she continued, grabbing his hands and bringing her half-naked breasts under his nose.

"You…anything you want, my lady," Mohotzuma stammered in a choked voice, unable to tear his gaze away from all that beauty.

"Well, I found out that the Son of the Mountain is locked up in a cell of the House of the Serpent and that Chitoontecl has prevented anybody from seeing him or even approaching him without his authorization."

"That's true, my lady."

"I'm sure all the wives and all the lovers of the *pipiltin* would turn the whole Curved Mountain upside down to meet him…"

"Just like you say, my lady," the man admitted with an unsteady voice, feeling he was about to be drawn into a trap.

"I have to see him!" she said with vehemence, strongly holding his hands as if she did not want to give him a chance to escape. "And I also want everybody to know that I was the only one to be given the opportunity of meeting him and of talking to him before the sacrifice…like that, everybody will start to understand where the power lies, and that many things are about to change, here in the palace and in the whole Curved Mountain. I will make them all die of envy, those chickens. Instead of laughing at me, they will learn to fear me and to understand that it's much better to have me as a friend than to pity me."

She had spoken with nonchalance, as if it was the most stupid request.

Mohotzuma swallowed his breath. He had given his word. He could not back out, he could not make a fool of himself to the eyes of the woman, not when she had finally made him the promise he had so long waited for. He could not show he was unable to grant this wish, which to her seemed so simple. He had to please her.

Absolutely. He would have to clash with Chitoontecl much sooner than he originally thought. That was not a problem. The showdown had to come sooner or later anyway. So, better to deal with it immediately and resolutely. He would claim both of his greatest aspirations in life on the same day.

"You will be satisfied in this as well, my lady," he then promised straightaway, speeding up towards the exit, though, to prevent his beloved from making any other "trivial" requests.

Chapter 10

"How could you promise her something like that without asking my permission?!"

Chitoontecl was raging mad because of Mohotzuma's request. His paralyzed eye was blood-soaked and the contraction of his facial muscles seemed to bring his mouth to bite the ear on the healthy side of his face.

"But she's the *tlatoani*'s wife, my lord. How could I reject her request?"

"Make up another excuse! Say rather that you were fooled by those beautiful eyes of hers," Chitoontecl commented scornfully. His impairments had brought out in him a sort of visceral grudge against all the flowers he could no longer pick.

"That wall-rider will wind up fooling everyone around her, though. I can't wait for the day when I'll have her skin on my shoulders and the heart of that damned fool in my hands. This is the only way my revenge will be full and complete."

"I'm afraid...my lord...I'm afraid you will have to be content with the Son of the Mountain."

The priest thought he had misunderstood him on the spur of the moment, so he stared at him in the eyes to ask for explanation, but the firm expression of challenge he saw sculpted on his face made him understand he had perfectly grasped his words.

"How do you dare talk to me like that, you filthy dog!" he shouted, his face turning red. "Have you already drunk too much pulque this morning, by any chance?"

"You know I'm a teetotaler, my lord," remembered Mohotzuma absolutely unimpressed by his outburst of rage. "But I think you haven't realized there have been a few changes in the Curved Mountain recently."

"What's this nonsense?"

"I know, my lord, about your decision to have Claloch elected as *tlamacazqui*, and I know the council willingly accepted. Even though, if you remember well, you had promised me that position."

"So?"

"You couldn't have chosen better: maybe you don't know that Claloch is…how do I put this…like a son to me. I was actually the one who sent him to the *tlamacazcalli* and to convince his teachers to assign him increasingly important tasks, in order to make strides along the whole holy road. And Claloch knows he owes to me his entire rapid and decorated career, and when he found out about your choice he quickly came to kiss the ground at his benefactor's feet…at my feet, to be precise."

"And what is that supposed to mean?" Chitoontecl asked with disdain, but he was visibly alarmed by his treacherous assistant's revelation, although he still did not understand where he was going with the information.

"The other day," Mohotzuma continued quietly, "I went for a walk with the elder member of the council. As you know, Nahualcatl is very highly regarded inside the council: many owe their insignia to him, and many are by his side in every decision." Mohotzuma felt a sadistic pleasure in continuing to keep his hateful master on a string. "Guess what he proposed to me? He sees me gifted enough to wear other insignia, those of…*tlatoani*, my lord."

Chitoontecl was shocked, but Mohotzuma did not give him the time to respond: "According to him," he continued in one breath, "the time has come to free ourselves of that half-man of Cuzupuma, who is only able to fill his belly and steal children. That mound of lard is only a danger to us, and Nahualcatl is convinced that there's no more time to lose, and that we should anticipate our enemies' moves. And the only way would be to elect a new *tlatoani*, a real sovereign who is able to govern with resolve."

The high priest finally understood the where the man he had always considered his watchdog was leading with his words.

"I'm convinced," Mohotzuma relentlessly continued, "that as a *tlatoani* I would be in the condition to express my unrivaled qualities at their best, and to demonstrate my remarkable ability to lead the Holy People…"

"And…and what did you reply?" In spite of himself, the sentence slipped out of Chitoontecl's mouth in a whisper.

"It's simple: I promptly accepted his proposal. And this morning, to avoid losing any time, I went to chat with the *tlatoani* Cuzupuma…When I informed him of Nahuacatl's idea, it didn't take him long to understand how serious the situation was, nor to accept all of my suggestions. He also told me in confidence that the insignia were becoming too heavy for him, and that he was already thinking about giving them to somebody else, to dedicate himself more freely, as he has always done, to other interests."

It was done. Mohotzuma had waited an entire lifetime for that moment, pleasing his master in every stupid request and enduring all his insults and humiliations without saying a word, but with infinite patience and always acting in the shadows he had continued to weave his intricate net, waiting for his pray to entangle itself. And the great day had finally come.

In that moment, the servant was at the height of his exaltation; he felt almighty as he savored an unspeakable satisfaction in observing the astonished and flabbergasted expression of the other man. His face, ready to react with vehemence until a moment before, had suddenly blanched and sagged, wan and inexpressive as the face of a dead man; Nahualcatl had most of the members of the council behind him, and Claloch, the infamous Claloch, was nothing but a sharp claw on the hand of the bastard in front of him.

He had to admit it: his arrogance had completely blinded him to what was happening behind his back: he had been led into the maze of one of the many evil nets set by his perfidious servant and, knowing him, he knew perfectly well that if he had tried to disentangle himself, he would have only ensnared himself further, and he would see his already precarious situation take a turn for the worse. He had been fooled, he had been duped, he had been…defeated.

Chitoontecl had to make a herculean effort to hold back the ocean of insults and threats that was mounting in his throat. He had to buy some time. Yes, he only needed time. After all, he thought in his inner tumult, he still had a lot of "friends" who owed him, and who knows, maybe he could have turned the whole situation in his favor and he could take his revenge, but at that moment he did not see any way out. He had to suffer.

Swallowing his bitterness, the high priest stayed silent and, for the first time in his life, he did not reply as he wanted to do. "But…the Son of the Mountain is still mine," was all he was able to pronounce with a shaking voice in a last, desperate attempt at reaffirming his authority.

"I certainly don't want to deprive you of this sacred right," Mohotzuma magnanimously conceded. Now he was the one to concede, and Chitoontecl could not help noticing that his servant had not called him with the appellative "my lord" for the first time since he had started to work for him.

"I also want to thank you for having authorized Tlahaxtala to visit the prisoner," Mohotzuma added, well aware of not having received any promise in that direction, but feeling a sadistic pleasure in pouring salt into his deep, smarting wound. Then, without the usual formal bow, he turned his back to the priest and silently walked towards the exit, leaving his despicable former master in the middle of the room, motionless, with his eyes staring wide into nothingness.

Chapter 11

She was the first one to be amazed. Sneaking into the cell, Tlahaxtala thought she was about to meet a worn-out man, exhausted by his prolonged confinement in the gloomy cellar of the House of the Serpent. Instead, before her stood a strong, awe-inspiring man, in perfect shape, looking like a statue, and although he was in chains and half-naked he still had the power to intimidate. During his long days of imprisonment and almost complete isolation, Marco had not let himself go. He trained continuously, and his body was even re-invigorated, and preserved from the dangerous disorientation his mind could have gone through in the complete absence of stimulation.

Before letting the sovereign in, the jailers had chained his hands and his feet to the wall, but even in that position he still preserved a certain austere and dominant look. The perpetual darkness had not whitened his bronze skin. His muscles were toned and vigorous, and his long ponytail that went down his left shoulder seemed to emanate luminescent reflections in the dim torchlight provided by the visitor. She was convinced that she stood before a supernatural being and was enchanted by that magic vision; she contemplated at length the titanic figure without uttering a word, while her womb was suddenly crossed by an indescribable, almost painful, feeling she had never felt before.

The eyes of the prisoner, dazzled by the light after so much darkness, could hardly perceive the outline of the stranger: "Who are you?" Marco asked.

The unforeseen and peremptory request startled the woman, interrupting her state of ecstatic contemplation. With uncertain and timorous steps, Tlahaxtala approached the prisoner and when he was close, she lowered the hood covering her head and her face. And this time he was the one to be amazed, breathless, cut through by the light of two huge eyes, green as emeralds, set in a face of extraordinary beauty.

As soon as the door had opened, Marco had prepared to stand his ground against another persecutor, but the sudden apparition had cut off his breath. "Who are you?" he repeated, recovering from his dismay. But his voice had lost its challenging tone, and had reduced to a murmur, almost a prayer.

"My name is Tlahaxtala," she replied, mustering her courage.

A window opened in the man's mind: Tlahaxtala Emerald Eyes, the prisoner queen pitied even by her slaves. An air of mystery lingered around that solitary, unreachable woman. Marco had heard people praise her unrivaled beauty an infinite number of times, but he had long learned to be wary of the information that was spread by word of mouth and always emphasized along the way, magnified and distorted. But this time he could not avoid seeing the truth in front of him.

He felt an absurd sense of shame and embarrassment for the sight of his dirty, stinking body, and he also felt a ridiculous and narcissistic regret at not being able to show himself to the visitor in the full splendor of his regalia. But a terrible suspicion immediately seized him: what was the *tlatoani*'s spouse doing there? What had brought her to enter his cell if not the morbid desire of seeing the dreaded man in person before his sacrifice?

As much as he wanted to believe otherwise, Marco could not find any other possible explanation and the thought of being the object of mere curiosity, and of being observed by those beautiful eyes as a freak-show, broke the spell and sent him into a rage. He was about to fire a series of enraged imprecations at the woman when, once again, he was floored by her words.

"You must help me!"

Marco was speechless. He thought he had heard an invocation for help, and he grasped a desperate note in the woman's voice, but it made no sense, he had probably misunderstood her words.

"You must help me!" Tlahaxtala repeated with an anguished tone.

The disconcertment was followed by irony. "Of course, *my lady*. As you can see, I'm in perfect condition to help you out. If I make a good effort, I can even get at least an arm's length away from the wall, and…"

"Please, don't mock me," she begged. "I haven't been given much time to speak to you, and it's important that you listen carefully to what I have to tell you."

Marco was even more confused; the queen of the valley was asking his help, although he was a perfect stranger, a man she had never seen or met before. And then, putting aside the absurdity of such a request, how could she request or hope for any help from a man whose hands and feet were chained, and who was one step away from being sacrificed? No, none of that made sense, he wasn't convinced yet. It was probably a setup, a tragic farce, or even worse, a deceitful attempt to draw some secret from him…However, something in the desperate tone of her voice still brought him to consider that the plea for help was sincere.

"I'm listening," he acknowledged, becoming serious again.

Tlahaxtala did not wait much longer: "My husband is *tlatoani* Cuzupuma. But that half-man only wears the insignia of the great orator; in truth, he is a fearful chicken, a puppet of the priests."

"I knew that already."

"But you don't know he's very close to losing the little power he has left. Only me and a few others know this secret. His insignia will soon go to Mohotzuma, a ruthless man, hungry for power and even more wicked than the *tlamacazqui*…"

"I am intimately familiar with those two as well," Marco said in a voice laced with hatred.

"Mohotzuma, unfortunately, is madly in love with me. He wants me at all costs and he has already informed me that when he rises to power I will have two opportunities only: become his woman, or be sacrificed to Huitzilopochtli...But I hate that man, and I would do anything to avoid ending up in his hands, dirtied with the blood of many innocent men..."

"So what?"

"I heard that you are the Son of the Mountain and that inside the mountain that formed you, you hide very powerful weapons."

"I admit that there is some truth to what you said," he conceded without denying nor confirming, but curious to understand where she was heading. "There is still this problem," he added, clinking the chains that clamped his wrists.

"I will do anything to help you...I can guess what you're thinking right now. I know you can't trust somebody you don't know and who could be here to steal your secrets and report them to your enemies...but I beg you, I implore you with all my heart, believe me: I'm not hear to cheat you! I know there's no way I can prove that to you, but you could ask me to burn myself alive in front of you and I would do, if that's what it takes to convince you," the woman begged fervently, bursting into tears and bringing the torch dangerously close to her dress.

No, it could not be a trap, the tears pouring out of those wonderful eyes were sincere, and there was a real determination in that desperate gesture, a part like that could not be played in such a way, she could not pretend so much, with that rapture, with that voice. Marco would have loved to comfort that suffering soul, to free her from so much affliction. The pain kept him silent, to avoid any risk, to avoid trusting anybody, but those tears had torn his heart apart and moved him to pity; they had...convinced him. And his rational self had stopped warring with him a long time ago.

"You can't do anything for me," he then said to her tenderly. "But...I will save you. I promise." He could not, would not add anything else. He had even said too much. But he was happy with having said it.

An enchanting smile appeared on the woman's face, with an expression of infinite gratitude. She did not want to hear anything else, what she had just heard was enough for her, because she believed in him, because he had never deceived her in her dreams, and she knew that dreams were messages from the gods. She was not supposed to know how and when the man in front of her would act, but she was more than sure that he would keep his promise.

In a rush of gratitude, Tlahaxtala stood on her toes, surrounded the man's neck with her arms and kissed him on the lips, then she leaned her face on his chest and she embraced him passionately. Had she been caught by the guards like that she would have been in serious trouble, but Peheptel was watching outside the door and presently she could not even think of releasing that embrace: she was happy in those arms, she would have let herself go in them, she would have gladly died in those arms.

"Chatì," Marco whispered, suddenly brought back in time: the same hair on his chest, the same gestures, the same scent…he tried to draw that fragile and vulnerable being to him instinctively, but his arms stayed chained to the wall. "Chatì," he repeated with a whisper.

Tlahaxtala did not hear him, or she pretended not to hear, and stayed silent for a long time, gripping the man's body, as if she were afraid to lose him. She had had faith in him even before she met him, and she had placed in him all her hope. In the moments of greater discomfort she had come to doubt her crazy plan, she had come to consider her intention to entrust her fate to the hands of a stranger as absurd and meaningless, but now that she had met him, she was more than convinced she had chosen the right thing to do.

And there was more to that: the contact with that vigorous body was provoking that strange, new, uncontrollable feeling that had pervaded her from the first moment she stepped into that cell. A feeling that stunned her, made her body grow weak and her legs unstable.

Love, what she was feeling in that moment could not be anything but love. The love she had so long aspired to and never known, the love that existed in the many stories she was told, but whose existence in reality she had started to doubt. Yes, she was

351

convinced of it, it could not go any other way; after so much struggle the gods had finally acknowledged her, her pain, her torment, and moved to pity they had fulfilled her greatest wish, giving her knowledge of that sublime feeling in all its overflowing plenitude.

But Marco had also been deeply upset by that meeting. As if by magic, something ancient but never forgotten had awoken in him, something he never thought he could feel again, if not in memory. From the day Chatì had abandoned him, he had been with many women, he had felt excitement for them, physical attraction, esteem, tenderness, but nothing even close to what he had felt for his beloved one. Somehow, he was almost proud of the fact that nobody after her had succeeded in undermining the memory of his one true love, and with time he had convinced himself he could never again feel the same heartbreaking passion for a woman.

Now, though, something ungraspable was mining that conviction, while a vague sense of guilt tried to impede that feeling to come out, to filter through in its entirety, to possess him. But how could something like that happen? How could somebody he did not know, a perfect stranger, arouse in him so suddenly, the same feelings he…? No, it was absurd, impossible, it was probably only because of his forced isolation. And yet…

A noise of voices from the corridor broke the spell and turned them away from their thoughts. Three short knocks were heard at the door. The arranged signal. Tlahaxtala reluctantly detached herself from that embrace. "I will wait for you," she said with a sad but hopeful smile, before she lowered her hood on her head. Then, without adding anything else, she left the cell.

Chapter 12

"I see you're a little sad this morning, Son of the Mountain. Tell me the truth, you miss your darlings, right? You shouldn't have let them down like that!" Not a day went by without Chitoontecl coming for a visit to torment him. He came at any moment during the day or night and talked to him through the peephole in the door, maybe because he feared his powers, but more likely to avoid showing his hateful nemesis the injuries inflicted upon him.

"I'm afraid they felt a bit hurt when you got caught. Since the day we locked you up, they haven't made a peep; not a chant, not a sound, not a single movement…it seems they just disappeared," the priest added with a sneer. "They even pulled up the revenge hut. They are probably so frightened that they don't know what to do to try and defend themselves. How I wish they could see you right now, so they could understand once and for all what a chicken-god they adore! But your beauties won't have long to wait. They will soon come to keep you company and then we will all go for a nice walk together up to the top of the pyramid. And there we will have a huge celebration…a fantastic one, incomparable to any other!"

The peephole suddenly closed with a rap and the unmistakable dragged steps of the priest resounded in the silent cell, while he moved along the corridor to leave the room, and his gloomy laugh faded in the distance.

As usual, the prisoner had not given his persecutor the satisfaction of the slightest reaction to his words, remaining motionless and absolutely silent the whole time.

The day so feared by the inhabitants of the World Above and so craved by Chitoontecl, the day of the final battle, the day which would decide the fate of the two opposing peoples once and for all, had finally come.

Even the weather seemed to have realized the exceptionality of the event, as had happened on the occasion of the last battle: up at the mouth of the crater the wind blew anxiously, as it had had not done for many years; the sun, climbing ever higher, was probably obscured by nimbus and cumulus clouds because the valley was illuminated by an icy, crepuscular light.

The entire army was moving up the length of the tunnel and the warriors, as they sweated and milled about, eagerly awaited the moment when their sledgehammer strikes would bring down the last bastion that separated them from glory, their dull rumble reverberating on the stone walls.

This time Puqutec, *tlaccatecatl* of all the military orders and head of the sacred serpent, did not want to run any risks: he would personally lead his army to victory. The stakes were too high to leave the command to someone else and take credit for the victory; what's more, the outlook for him would have been too bad in case of defeat. In the last months he had not given his officials any breaks in the fear of making mistakes; he summoned them continuously in the bleakest hours of the day and night to ask their advice or to propose new war strategies until they developed a plan that seemed surely victorious, then ran through their infinite doubts only to change both tactics and opinions.

In the first rank he had marshaled a squad of muscular soldiers with the singular task of carrying big, rectangular shields with supporting posts at their edges. Dense troops of archers followed them, and behind them, the head of the guard. The eagle and jaguar contingents closed the ranks, naked and armed only with spears and crystal swords. Four hundred and twenty warriors, a third of which flaunted the bright uniforms of the guard.

About a hundred men were left to safeguard the walls and the palaces of the city, all members of the Order of the Serpent. For the occasion, the main gate remained shut even during the day and in the streets of Aplaia there were only chickens and stray dogs: as Puqutec had commanded, until more orders came all the inhabitants had to stay closed in their homes.

The surveys done through the slit opened in the stonewall before breaking in had confirmed every detail the information offered by Xaiput. As he had reported during his long and detailed confession, the inhabitants of the World Above had not rested on their laurels during the long wait, and had made up for the scarcity of the labor force with a rudimentary but efficient revolving crane projected by the white *tlatoani* and his irreplaceable apprentice. A few steps away from the point in which the tunnel would end, according to their calculations, they had erected wall a few meters thick which could not be spotted from any angle by the inhabitants of the valley because it was hidden by a palisade of about the same height, built much earlier on the border of the terrace.

The defensive wall ran parallel to the crater's internal wall just a few steps away from it, starting from the beginning of the palisade. After about seventy meters, it turned at right angles, to meet the mountain. Between the wall and the mountain there was a long, narrow corridor dominated by the steep vitrified channel that closed the southern pole of the crater.

Puqutec sneered when he saw the wall: even if he had not been informed of its existence, that meager rampart would surely not represent an insurmountable obstacle for his men, who were equipped with ropes, grappling hooks and long ladders divided into several segments. Everything went as it was supposed to go. He could proceed.

The last barrier fell, and the first rank of men started out of the tunnel's opening protected by the heavy shields, to go and place themselves on a long row at the wall's feet. A second contingent of men followed and paired up with the first to create a testudo formation sustained by the supporting posts and designed to protect the other warriors as they left the tunnel.

To tell the truth, the warriors expected a much warmer welcome, as they had had in the previous, tragic experiences. What they found instead was deadly silence, and even when they tried to look up, protracting their necks several times out of the canopy, it seemed like nobody was up there with the intention of spoiling their day. All that quietness certainly was not enough to reassure them. However, staying on their guard, they moved forward out of the tunnel undisturbed, and placed themselves in three rows until they filled the whole corridor, obliging most of their comrades to remain inside the tunnel.

The quietness did not last long. After a blow of horns, the heralds raised their banners and the invading army let thunderous cries of war out into the air. The archers shot up arrows equipped with ropes and grappling hooks and the assembled ladders were leaned on the wall. Shortly after, a throng of shouting warriors started rapidly climbing up the wall.

But the besieged responded immediately: the first assault was staved off with a rain of rocks, pushed down with wooden levers from the top of the wall, where they had been placed a long time before. And the boulders kept falling on the attacking army when the crossbowmen appeared on the bastions. They came out with perfect timing, aimed, and let their arrows fly before they retreated to load their weapons, leaving space for the following wave of shooters.

Swarms of arrows flew in both directions, and those coming from above almost always hit their mark. But Puqutec had been well-informed by Xaiput and he had already taken those casualties into account; he was more than certain that the top of the wall would be conquered by his valorous men anyway. And nothing, from that moment on, could impede his advance.

But then something showed up to foil all his plans.

The right wing of the army was crowding the narrow corridor bordered in front and on the side by the defensive wall and at its shoulders by the mountain's wall. At a certain moment, at the bottom of that blind alley, an intangible fog started to rise from the ground, and it quickly turned into a blanket of smoke so thick and acrid that it blinded them and took their breath away. And shortly after, burning wells started to open under their feet and swallowed them in groups of three or four at a time.

During his long, circumstantial confession, Xaiput had revealed to Puqutec every detail of the defensive strategy adopted by his former compatriots to counter the invasion, describing in the smallest detail the configuration of the ground, the length and height of the wall, and its distance from the tunnel's opening, to allow him to precisely calculate the length of the segments of ladder to be assembled. He had also warned him about the boulders that would be thrown down, and he had even given him a map of the many traps scattered along the field. But for some reason he had completely forgotten that fire trap. Even if he had grown calluses all over his hands, just like his comrades, excavating the final section of the alley to obtain a large, deep hole in the ground. A hole which was later to be covered by wooden platforms masked with a thick layer of topsoil on which grass had continued to grow high and luxuriant.

The platform, supported by a colonnade of pillars, was nothing but an ensemble of hatches that could be manipulated from the other side of the wall, erected in that section on solid underground barrel vaults, that would open wide when the ropes of the closing devices were destroyed by the fire or cut deliberately. The cell under the platform had been filled to the ceiling with dry, resinous bundles of sticks.

The fire was lit as soon as the invaders had filled the space available to them. Once the flames touched the resin they burned up and rapidly spread under the entire platform attacking the tie-rods of the levers. And soon they started to clash against each other.

When the hatches started to open with sudden and frightening bursts of fire and swallow dozens upon dozens of men, their comrades, choked by the smoke and sure of being one step away from death, retreated together to the left flank creating a dreadful crowding at the base of the wall. The boulders kept falling on the shields covering with their dull rumble the fearful cries of the escaping warriors, the groans of the wounded and the shouts of the commanders, who ordered their men to withdraw composedly. And the confusion reached its peak when these men found their way blocked at the opening of the tunnel.

Tlamahatl and Actonuy had sent the others forwards and stayed back with their men inside the tunnel, and when those who had come out tried to retreat back in, they had stumbled upon a human barrier that shouted and kept pushing forward to go out.

Some time went by before the boldest men could win over their fear and decide to attempt the wall again. But they had just taken the ladders and the grappling hooks in their hands when the rain of arrows and boulders stopped as suddenly as it had begun. The attackers then conquered the top, ready to even the score in a more equal and direct confrontation, but quickly found with amazement that there was not a soul up there waiting for them: the defenders had all left and in that moment they were crazily running through the field towards three narrow boardwalks bridging the crevice. At the opening of two of these, there was a long row of runaways, but the third one, the closest one to the defensive wall, was already deserted, and those who had just gone through it were cutting off the supporting ropes with furious ax strikes.

Puqutec had been one of the last to reach the top of the wall and to realize the danger he was facing: if all the bridges had been taken down he would have had to stop dreaming about glory once more, and he was not ready to experience the humiliation of another postponement.

"Faster, filthy dogs, faster!" he started shouting to the troops, enraged out of his mind. "Reach the bridges!"

A chaotic race against time started. While the runaways impatiently waited at the end of the queues to take their axes in hand, the invaders soon realized at their own expense that Xaiput's map of booby trap locations was not so precise, so they proceeded in a breathless run interrupted now and then by continual stops and starts, as if they were trying a new dance step. The boldest men, trying their luck, ran without any precaution, often ending up in the insidious traps, but the luckiest ones reached the crevice before the last bridge was taken down, and the invaders were obliged to run away to reach their comrades under a hail of ever thicker and increasingly precise shots; many had already taken shelter behind the old palisade on which the order of the bastions had been inverted.

The attackers did not wait any longer to jump on the only bridge left intact and to launch their chase, but close by the palisade they were wiped out by the crossbowmen barricaded on the terraces; this convinced them to maintain a safe distance. And only when the backup arrived and they found themselves protected by their big shields and with their ladders and hooks did they dare attempt the bridge again and resume their advance in three ordered and solid rows, about a hundred meters away from the fortification.

Despite the heavy losses, the invading army still stood out in its overwhelming power, and the warriors, by then sure of the outcome, were only waiting for the order to attack, but the rain of arrows suddenly stopped; this had already happened shortly before at the wall. From behind the palisade, thick columns of smoke started to rise. A huge amount of resinous bundles had been piled there, and the fire lit at the same time in several points had not taken long to burn and create an insurmountable barrier of flames and smoke, which went from the threshold of the wood up to the external border of the terrace. At that sight the commanders instantly reconsidered the idea of a frontal assault and they ordered their men to go around the obstacle, cutting on the right, through the wood. But even there, on the path the warriors were forced to pass by, a thick web of traps had been arranged and many experienced that on their own before their comrades could pass them with care, and before they could reach the palisade limiting the wood in the northern part of the field. As soon as they tried to climb it, though, they were greeted by the shots of the machine guns positioned at the tunnel's opening above the waterfall and they were forced to retreat again into the woods in a hurry.

While the invaders were looking for a safe passage through the woods, the inhabitants of the World Above had taken refuge in the old tunnel above the waterfall only after lighting the fire, and once they had pulled back the boardwalk, they had placed themselves on it, sheltered by a solid protective barrier.

Puqutec, who was ever more enraged and on edge, saw that immediate victory was once again slipping between his fingers, so he ordered a rapid council of war to review the situation and to carefully study the following steps to avoid new unpleasant surprises and to end the affair once and for all with their insidious enemy.

His officials were a little more optimistic than himself, perhaps because they knew they were not facing the same risks, and did not consider those unforeseen difficulties to be as grave as their commander did; they even seemed euphoric in their certainties.

"With a boardwalk made of logs and protected by the shields it shouldn't be too difficult to get up there," one suggested.

"No," affirmed another. "I think we should take it easier: they have trapped themselves up there, and they will sooner or later starve, no matter how many supplies they have."

"True!" Puqutec interjected, jumping at what seemed to be the last possibility to avoid the looming threat of being sacrificed. "Even though we won't get our victory today, we will still obtain it, and without sacrificing any of our men. Time will work for us: they can bring water up with buckets, but you can't live with water only, and in a short time their bellies will be empty. And they will have to decide then: starve, jump into the lake, or give battle...whatever their choice, and in spite of all their damned weapons, those wall-riders and infamous traitors won't stand a chance."

"To speed up the process," answered the best of them, earning the plaudits and blessing of the commander-in-chief, "we could lead them to believe that they will be safe if they surrender without resisting. That way the *tlatoani* could have his slaves back—the slaves' sons, I meant," he corrected himself causing a general laughter. "The *tlamacazqui* will be able to take all the prisoners he wants for his sacrifices, and we—"

Then something horrible happened right in the middle of that animated discussion.

Tlamahatl and Actonuy were the last ones to come out of the tunnel with their men and follow behind the others, but at a certain point they took advantage of the fact that most of the army had retired in the woods to wait for new orders and they had doubled back. Without attracting attention, they had crossed the bridge again, demolished it using the axes abandoned there by the runaways, then they had quickly dispersed on the other side of the wall.

Their absence had been noticed only when a few warriors, going back to retrieve the dead soldiers' weapons, had found their path interrupted at the crevice. Puzzled and understanding only in part what had happened, they had come to warn the commanders, but in the meantime the deserters had already entered the tunnel that went down to the valley. Only Actonuy had stayed behind outside of the tunnel longer than the others. As instructed, he had gone to look for the end of a rope hidden in the grass, very close to the opening. He had pulled it back to him. Then, not intending to remain out to enjoy the expected show, he had rushed inside the gallery as well. And he hardly had the time to cross the threshold when the silence was broken by a sudden explosion.

Then, it was the apocalypse.

The southern end of the field was surmounted by a steep and bent canal dug into the rock by an ancient current. The rope pulled by Actonuy had pulled out the pins of three hand grenades that it held. The grenades fell and exploded in unison in the same place, dismantling the supporting post of a wooden bulkhead, and as soon as this had been overturned a huge rock that had been leaning on it, started to roll in the canal underneath. It had demolished several supporting posts in quick succession along its way, and just as many bulkheads blocking stones and small rocks.

An avalanche poured into the canal, carried by the steep and polished walls, and it collapsed like a flooded river overfilling the entire space between the defensive wall and the mountain. When the dust cloud was dispersed, the opening of the tunnel was covered by a gigantic amount of stones and debris.

As soon as he was informed of the inexplicable defection of a large group of jaguar warriors and by the demolition of the last bridge, Puqutec had rushed with his officials to hunt the traitors down, prompted by a dark misgiving, but he had to interrupt his run at the border of the crevice, from where he could only watch the tragic situation unfold, confused and powerless. Even if they had succeeded in crossing the crevice in a short time, it would take them a lifetime to remove the mountain of stones they saw erected beyond the wall.

The unimaginable had happened: they had been fooled once more by a scant minority of enemies, once more they would have to renounce to their dreams of glory. Once more…they had been defeated.

And soon, they would have to face an even worse and more disconcerting problem: in the whole World Above, there was nothing to feed them, apart from the water flowing from streams. Each plant had been deprived of its fruits and all the grass of the field mown. Not a single chicken, not a single rabbit had been forgotten in the hen coops in front of the houses, and not a single stray dog walked around that damned lifeless place. Even the easily accessible nests above the gravel had been removed. Some of them had been placed in long aviaries hung on the walls of the tunnel, others had been collected and moved during the night, along with their inhabitants, to unreachable heights with the use of very long ladders. Many more had been sacrificed, and this surely was the saddest and most painful decision the inhabitants of the World Above had made before the final confrontation. A terrible heart-breaking decision, that proved itself successful.

During the battle, about a hundred invaders had died, and there were many severely wounded soldiers, but there still were many mouths to feed. Too many. The roles had been reversed, the besiegers had become the besieged and their rage had soon turned into discomfort and dark desperation, after a rapid and heavy reconnaissance mission; they would soon be starving, and only the flesh of their comrades could feed them. But that would also run out. And then…

The warriors started to look at each other with circumspection and in their eyes a dark light of diffidence suddenly appeared.

Chapter 13

"Let's get a move on," Antapuoi ordered.

The avalanche's rumble was the agreed upon signal. When he arrived at the House of the Serpent with a squad of five men, the soldiers on duty were caught up in frenzied discussion. They had heard the enormous uproar and they were wondering what had caused it, unsure if they had to send somebody to the gate to ask for news or stay, as ordered, to guard the barracks.

"I have Chitoontecl's official order to lead the prisoner to the *teocalli*," Antapuoi communicated to the official on duty.

"But…my lord, Puqutec has prohibited anybody from…"

"Don't waste my time, Xahyotl," Antapuoi interrupted him. "There's no need for you to remind me what Puqutec ordered; he has his mind on other things right now, and if you truly earned the insignia you have now, you should know that when he's absent, the first coil is in command. And the first coil is right in front of you right now. If you want, I can go back to Chitoontecl empty-handed, but I suggest you consider the consequences of that very well…"

The official felt a shiver running down his back. He had never had to face a situation like this before, but nothing of what was happening that day had ever happened before. The rule was indeed exactly as Antapuoi had just explained, and if Puqutec had some objection, he would use that rule to justify himself. And since everyone was well aware of the friction between the two commanders, what reason should he have to doubt the upright Antapuoi, renowned for his incorruptibility and his superior sense of duty?

"As you wish, my lord," Xayhotl pronounced with a dry throat, only partly reassured by these considerations. He ordered his men to bring the prisoner to the high official, but not before they slid a big chain in the rings that locked his wrists and his ankles.

Under Xahyotl's and the other soldiers' anxious gaze, the group led by Antapuoi, with his men beside the prisoner, descended the stairs and rushed through the small square in front of the barracks to follow the route that led to the temple.

The street was deserted, doors and windows were all barred, and the only noise to be heard was the clanking of the chains which slowed the prisoner's steps considerably, even though he did his best to increase his speed. The squad did not meet a single soul along the entire route. Just before they reached the main square where the *teocalli* was located, they suddenly deviated into a narrow, lateral street to stop after a few steps in front of a simple house with no windows.

Antapuoi knocked three times on the door. Inside he heard footsteps and the noise of a sliding bolt, then the door was half opened to admit the seven men.

When the prisoner's eyes adjusted to the dim light, they focused on a man that was about forty years old, short, podgy, with sparse hair and a worn-out fiber skirt which was almost completely hidden underneath his overflowing belly. He held big pincers in his hands, which he used to cut the chains and the rings at Marco's wrists and ankles with rapid and experienced movements. Marco recognized only afterwards the tool the blacksmith held: the first utensil that had come out of the mouth of his furnace. And there were other objects he knew lying on the worktable, which almost entirely filled the small room: the cowboy belt, with its holster and Colt on one side, a scimitar on the other side, a crossbow with a full quiver and a little further on, the amazing *tilmatl* that Chatì had given him as a gift.

It was all thanks to Pahaleotalli, who was faithful to the cause of the World Above, and who had taken the items and hidden them in a safe place in preparation for the fateful day. The fisherman had only pretended to follow Mohotzuma's orders when Marco had been captured, but the old man knew he was part of a brave plan organized by the white *tlatoani* himself.

Just after the Son of the Mountain was caught, Itzac had dismantled the winch and had brought it from the crevice to the opposite opening of the tunnel above the waterfall. The old cabin had been replaced with a booth made with bamboo-like stalks, light but able to bear the weight of about ten people with no problem. The pulley had instead been affixed to the end of a pine trunk hanging from the tunnel's ceiling by transversal beams on which it was free to rock back and forth, to remain hidden until the very last moment. The echo of the landslide had just faded when Atzcha had ordered the trunk to be pushed out and slid down with the first contingent of Amazons.

On the battlements of Aplaia's walls all eyes were turned upwards, in the direction of the opposite side of the crater. Judging from the level of noise and from the cloud of dust that rose into the air after the explosion, something quite worrisome must have happened up there. The discussion was extremely animated among the guards, who were interpreting the event in many different ways, when the attention of one of them was attracted by something moving near to the rocky spur. It was the booth going up for the first time, and the warrior opened his eyes wide when, lowering his gaze, he noticed the people along the gravel bed of the creek.

His cry of alarm distracted everybody from their own hypotheses. Excited screams, and horns blowing were heard from one side of the wall to the other, and on the battlements armed and startled warriors were running along the communication passages, shouting and calling to their brothers in arms.

When the main gate of Aplaia was locked, the city of the golden rooftops was unassailable. Even a small garrison could oversee it and stave off siege by a whole army. As planned, Tlamahatl and Actonuy's men would have to be inside the walls when the first contingents, led by Atzcha and Itzac, slid down, and once inside they would not face many difficulties surprising and overwhelming the guards while keeping the gate open until the backup arrived.

But a well-studied plan had also to foresee some possible variations, in case for some reason they would not get there in time, and the gate would still be closed. In that case, Antapuoi as an authority figure could potentially order it opened, but such an attempt, with the enemy already lined up outside the walls, would seem quite suspicious in the eyes of Puzutlan, second coil of the serpent and commander of the garrison at the walls, brother of Cuanpooca, protégé of Puqutec and arch-enemy of Antapuoi.

Puzutlan would surely override the order and it was very unlikely that he would comply with his superior's request. At that point, only an intervention from the inside could offer the strategists further possibilities of success. And this was the task Marco had assigned to himself, when he decided to let them capture him.

Among the many solutions he had considered, nothing seemed better. In the World Above, they had realized a long time before that Antapuoi would not be allowed to take part in the invasion, but with all probability—and this was an accurate conjecture—almost all of his men would be sent to follow the rest of the army.

Puqutec in fact did not want to allow his greatest rival the opportunity of earning honor and glory on the battlefield, but since he did not trust him, he only let Antapuoi stay behind with a few of his men. They would clearly be outnumbered and have very few possibilities of damaging the much larger contingent of the *tlacuatecatl*'s faithful soldiers who had been charged with guarding Aplaia. But with the help of the Son of the Mountain and his weapons, they would surely have many more possibilities of success.

It was a dangerous move, filled with uncertainties, almost solely based on the hypothesis that Chitoontecl, in proximity of the battle and more than sure of impending success, would postpone the sacrifice of his despicable nemesis for the final celebrations. If he decided to anticipate it, a nighttime invasion had been planned, supported from the inside by Antapuoi's men and by Tlamahatl and Actonuy's jaguar warriors. With the whole army still in Aplaia, though, this would have surely been a very difficult and much bloodier path to take.

The alarm sounding on the walls had also been heard inside the city, and the men guarding the *teocalli*, the House of the Serpent and the palace of the *tlatoani* had finally decided to proceed towards the gate, leaving almost all of the buildings in their custody undefended.

Some inhabitants, alarmed by the rumble and the repeated blowing of horns, had dared to come out into the street, but the discouraging passage of that multitude of armed, breathless soldiers convinced them to retreat.

Tlamahatl and Actonuy's men were also running in then. When the alarm had sounded, they were just coming out of the lower opening of the tunnel, more than two kilometers away from Aplaia's gates. There were just a few of them and they were running considerably behind schedule; they were slowed down by the weight of a man carried on their shoulders. Their operation, which had begun with perfect timing, had undergone an unforeseen and catastrophic event.

Tragically, the huge stone sphere that had started the landslide had gotten into the tunnel and as it rolled down the smooth, inclined path it had gained speed and begun to heavily bounce from wall to wall in the tunnel. In its blind and uncontrolled descent, it had soon reached the last unaware runaways, who had not heard it coming over the echo of their clogs, and were mown down underneath its weight. Only the men in the first ranks who were alerted by their comrades' screams had succeeded in avoiding it by a hair and the few survivors, grief-stricken and dismayed, had stopped there to provide first aid to their comrades and to count the losses, which were disastrous.

Actonuy had been the first to be hit by the rock, which had almost crushed his leg. He had implored his men to continue their run and leave him there, but to no avail; they had refused to listen to his reiterated objections and had carried him along the whole route. In the end, only a small number of survivors had come out of the lower entrance of the tunnel. And severely behind schedule.

Tlamahatl had miraculously escaped the tragedy, though he was stricken by the gravity of the losses and tried to make up for lost time by anticipating his men in a breathless run. But in spite of all his efforts, he had got to the gates of Aplaia only after everyone on the walls had been alerted by the sight of the invaders.

"Open!" he shouted breathlessly to the men on the battlements once he reached his destination. If he had gotten there just a few minutes before he would have faced no objection, but the presence of the enemy had alarmed the entire garrison and Puzutlan, even though he welcomed gladly the arrival of backup, took great care in granting this request.

"And what are you doing down there?" he shouted back.

"A disaster. It's unbelievable, my lord. There was a landslide. The whole mountain up there came down and the tunnel was blocked, the serpent warriors and the eagle warriors had already come out when it happened, but we were trapped inside. We even tried to open up a passage, but with these blades..." he continued, brandishing his short crystal sword. "So we decided to come down to pick up better tools, but when we were just out of the wood we saw those people there," he continued, gasping for breath and indicating the invaders, "and we left the tunnel and ran here straightaway to your aid...but you will have to let us in, before..."

"You can forget that!" Puzutlan blocked him, intending to take advantage of the providential help in a completely different way. "Since you're there, if you really want to help us, go to meet those sons of bitches and try to keep them far away from the walls until we get backup from the center...you're much more useful out there than inside right now."

Puzutlan's scorn did not garner any reply: if he insisted, he would only lose time and engender suspicion. If he wanted to make the best out of the situation, he had to immediately look for some other expedient.

"As you wish, my lord," he replied quickly, as his other comrades were catching up. "But we have a severely wounded man, it is commander Actonuy, and he needs urgent care, or else..."

"We'll treat him with all available care at the right time. Now execute my order. Understood?"

Tlamahatl promptly changed his strategy. "Right away, my lord," he replied respectfully. "Achteuatl," he continued, talking to one of the two carriers. "Assemble the men and marshal them in two ranks. But you, Cuathinicque," he ordered to his strong, faithful assistant who had just reached him, "you will stay here with Actonuy...he could need some help while we're gone." Then, lowering his head to Actonuy to comfort him and lowering his voice to ensure that only Actonuy and Cuathinicque heard him, he added: "Try to get them to open the gate for you. And inform me with the usual signal if you succeed. I will try not to go too far in the meantime."

"I'll do my best," Cuathinicque answered, tightening his grip on his club.

"You, follow me," Tlamahatl immediately commanded the marshaled men, raising his voice and after turning his back to the walls, he led them at a trot to face down the "enemy."

"Something must have gone amiss," Atzcha said to Itzac.

The booth was already going up for the third time and both commanders were following the evolution of events from far away, trying to make sense of what had happened.

"Those men should be Tlamahatl and Actonuy's warriors...but there should be more of them, and they should be inside the walls already, according to the plans," the warrior added.

"I don't know what to tell you," Itzac commented worriedly. "I think it's them. Maybe the others were already out of the tunnel when the landslide came. But this doesn't explain why they took so long to get there and why they're coming towards us, instead of going in."

"Maybe they were ordered to."

"That could be, but if the gate remains locked, it will be trouble for us."

"And what if it isn't them?"

"I don't think so. But it won't take us long to find out," Itzac replied. Turning around towards his men, he said: "Those who are coming towards us should be our men. But we're not completely sure about it. So, we'll proceed as planned, but without lowering our guard…and don't shoot without my order, for any reason."

On the opposite side, Tlamahatl was struggling with an even tougher problem. He had to be recognized by his enemies without raising the suspicions of those who observed the scene from the top of the walls, but he also could not get too far from the gate, to avoid the risk of being too far away if Cuathinicque succeeded in having it opened. He had to improvise, he had to quickly make up something credible if he wanted to satisfy both these opposing needs.

The two densely packed squadrons advanced, studying each other. When the formations were within firing range, Tlamahatl ordered his men to stop and the adversary commanders did the same. A quick secret meeting followed and shortly after a team of five men detached from Tlamahatl's ranks. Screaming and raising their swords and shields in the air as a sign of defiance, they advanced against their enemies, inviting them to combat. Such a move, considering they were obviously outnumbered, would seem objectively hazardous to say the least, or even suicidal, but the outcome seemed quite predictable in the eyes of the observers. Only cowards would have backed out of such a challenge. It was an unwritten rule, but it was rigorously observed by any true warrior since the dawn of time, and who dared to infringe it, would only attract contempt and a bring great dishonor upon himself.

Itzac did not wait long, and he left his ranks with four men, and resolutely advanced to meet their rivals.

A cry of war broke the silence and the two groups launched their assaults together. The clash of shields on shields was heard at a long distance. A clinking of swords followed, to end a few seconds later: at first contact with the tempered steel swords, the frail crystal swords of Tlamahatl's men fell to pieces. Three men had immediately run away, one had fallen to the ground accidentally wounded at the hip, and the other, disarmed and with a sword placed at his throat, had kneeled to kiss the ground at the winner's feet. And when the victor prepared to immobilize his arms behind his back for live capture, he spoke quickly.

"We are on your side. It was a disaster in the tunnel, we couldn't get there in time and that bastard Puzutlan wouldn't let us in, he ordered us to keep you away from the walls until backup from the center arrived. Maybe we can still find a way to get that damned gate open, but we will have to try being in its proximity when and if that happens...pretend to attack us, now. Tlamahatl will retreat...being so outnumbered by you, this should seem normal to the men watching. Keep behind him, but don't get too close to the gate, or that son of a *tepuli*-sucker will get suspicious and he won't open it."

"Alright," Itzac said, pulling him up and pricking him with the tip of his sword to push him towards his formation, to make the scene seem more realistic.

Immediately after, Tlamahatl's men started to retreat towards the city with their face turned to the enemy and slowly going towards the northern corner of the walls, away from the main gate. During their retreat, they continued to taunt and throw insults in the enemy's direction and to beat their swords against their shields as a sign of defiance, while the two enemy's contingents pursued them, although keeping their distance.

At a certain point, one of Tlamahatl's men broke off from the group and started running towards the walls.

"Go tell Puzutlan to send us some backup immediately!" he shouted, gasping to the guards on the battlements when he reached his destination. "We will never be able to hold them back alone with these useless blades, but if you come down to help us we can take them on both flanks. It will be a walkover to eliminate them all...but tell him to hurry!"

A sentry immediately left his lookout to run through the battlements and report to the commander, who had gone up to some kind of vantage watchtower shortly before to better follow the development of the events. Since Antapuoi was in the center of the city, he was the highest in charge to oversee the walls and it was the first time he had had to make a decision of that importance. He had never been known for his intelligence or initiative, and if he had come to that position of command he owed everything to the fact that he was Cuanpooca's brother and that he had always blindly obeyed the orders he received without question. He was shaking when he thought about the consequences he might face if he were to make a wrong decision, but at the same time he felt the intoxication of command and he burned with the desire to show the entire world his abilities.

What had just been reported to him was a simple objective truth: Tlamahatl's men could never hold back the overwhelming enemy force with the few weapons they had, but with that flank move that had just been suggested to him. On the other side, he was continuing to consider, the enemies were far enough from the gate in that moment: what risks could they run, in opening it and closing it immediately after the men were out?

He was still hesitating when his rumination was brusquely interrupted by Actonuy's heartrending moans; the man had recommenced his moaning without even having to fake too much to make the scene more realistic.

It was the last straw. And Puzutlan finally took his decision.

"Prepare to exit with a squad of three dozen men!" he shouted to the assistant in the field. "But only with arrows and spears...our blades are good for nothing against theirs...and close that man's mouth immediately," he added, raising his voice even higher to cover the wounded man's screams of pain, "or I'll shut him up for good myself!"

Chapter 14

The huge gate of Aplaia started to open, groaning on its ancient hinges. When there was enough space to let a single person through, a disarmed man ran out through the narrow passage to help Cuathinicque transport the wounded man inside, but as soon as they were about to lift him up he began to struggle in pain and emit such a heartrending noise that the two were forced to lay him on the ground again, right at the entrance.

"Listen, my friend," the rescuer told him wrathfully, since he had been ordered to do as quickly as possible, "if you don't want us to leave you here to the dogs, calm down and keep quiet, or else—"

The unfortunate soldier never had the time to finish; his speech was brusquely interrupted by a tremendous blow that smashed his skull in, killing him on the spot, and after a pleased grunt to commemorate the deed, Cuathinicque brought two fingers to his mouth to emit three powerful and prolonged whistles interrupted at brief intervals.

"The signal!" Tlamahatl shouted to his men, changing his direction immediately and starting to sprint breathlessly towards the gate, chased at a distance by his fake pursuers.

Puzutlan, who was ready to enjoy the spectacle of this ingenious operation from his magisterial vantage point and planned to take all the credit for it, was surprised by the sudden about face of Tlamahatl's men and he was forced to wonder what kind of tactic he had decided to adopt to hold the enemies back.

"Treason!" he suddenly screamed to the amazed sentinels the second it dawned on him. "Close the gate! Now!" he kept on shouting, hurling himself down from the lookout post to sprint down the elevated battlement that led to the top of the gate.

Those in charge of the gate, who were not seeing what was happening outside the walls, were baffled by their commander's unexpected change of mind and were a little late in executing the order, but as soon as they changed the direction of their pushing, the shutters were unexpectedly blocked by the corpse that Cuathinicque had thrown in there after dragging Actonuy away. With some soldiers pushing to close the gate and some trying to drag the dead man out, the gate ended up being blocked for a long time; but as soon as they were about to remove the body they also had to face Cuathinicque's club. Protected by the big architrave above him, he had in fact resumed doling out death blows with his club, continuously crushing shoulders' arms and heads.

The victims fell on each other, forming an ever more imposing pile of dead and wounded men, and it took their comrades a long time to start shooting towards the entrance after they recovered from the amazement; this allowed Cuathinicque to several retreats behind the door while other soldiers, protected by shields, tried their best to clear out the passage.

After several useless attempts and another copious dose of blows, the last body was removed and the two freed panels of the gate started to close slowly and relentlessly. In a last and desperate attempt to keep them open, Cuathinicque snuck between them; he was being crushed by the gate, and obstructed in his movements. Before too long a spear pierced his thigh and an arrow dug halfway into his left shoulder. But he did not give up.

Grabbing the arrow with his free hand, he pulled it out with a furious scream while blocking the blows with his other hand as best as he could. He felt his forces fade from blood loss, as a deep red poured out from his yawning wounds, and from the gate's pressure, which in spite of his vigor was just about to crush him. He held firm nonetheless, and kept fighting like an animal until another arrow ran through his wrist, and his club fell from his hands. He was then left disarmed and defenseless, standing only because of the gate's strong grip.

"It's over," he said staring defiantly straight into the eyes of the warrior stood before him with an evil smile on his lips and his sword raised in the air, both arms tensed to deliver the death blow.

But it never came.

Cuathinicque thought he was hallucinating and maybe already in the realm of the dead, when he saw the man in front of him open his eyes wide, let go of the sword and slowly collapse to his knees with an astounded expression, while his hands numbly grabbed at the tip of an arrow that had magically appeared in his chest.

His comrades were as amazed as he was and believed it to be a tragic mistake; they turned around in fury towards the improvident shooter, but as soon as they discovered who he was, they were breathless: at the opposite end of the square, the titanic figure of the Son of the Mountain had suddenly materialized.

They had only seen him once, and briefly, the night he was captured, but that had been enough to permanently engrave the giant figure in their memories, who appeared to them now in a very different guise than that of the defenseless, barefoot and half-naked prisoner that had been led in chains through the streets of Aplaia. The long silver ponytail now trailed down a splendid, plumed cloak under which shone a menacing blade. He held an object with an unusual shape and he was protected on the sides by six fully equipped warriors. And their bewilderment reached its maximum when they realized that those warriors were wearing their same uniforms, and it turned into complete dismay when they noticed that one of them bore the insignia of the first coil. The insignia of Antapuoi.

Time seemed to stop infinitely, and then Puzutlan's hysterical scream sounded again. He was still commanding his men to bar the gate, but his screams turned into a choked gurgle when Marco's second arrow run through his throat.

The high official, impaled, fell forward from above, and the precision of an arrow shot from such a formidable distance made his men shiver much more than the dull thud of the body on the cobblestones of the square. But their morale was raised instantly when the backup from the garrisons at the center started to come in waves out of the main and side streets.

"How many of these damned men are there?" Marco swore through his teeth. He had taken into account the possibility that Antapuoi would be left in Aplaia with a few faithful soldiers, and even the more disadvantageous possibility that Actonuy and Tlamahatl's men would not reach their destination in time, but he had not at all expected that multitude of people pouring from the garrisons in the city center.

In the meantime, Cuathinicque's body was released by the gate's pressure and he collapsed to the ground unconscious between the narrow opening and the sentries. The latter, growing bold thanks to the arrival of their backup and protected on their flanks by a barrier of shields, resumed the initiative: they barricaded in front of the gate and once the obstacle was removed, they recommenced their attempt to force the gate until they were able to pull it shut with a dull rumble. And they had almost succeeded in making Aplaia unassailable by locking the heavy blocking post in place when a powerful push coming from outside hampered their efforts: Tlamahatl's men had just reached their destination.

Pushed by opposing forces, the gate was forced back and forth repeatedly. In some moments it even closed completely, but on the outside more and more support was turning up and at a certain point, under the growing pressure, the doors started to give way until they finally opened wide.

Tlamahatl's warriors flew into the square, engaging in furious hand-to-hand combat with the sentries. They screamed and fought like furies at the height of exaltation, proud of finally being able to face the disdainful serpent warriors and unloading all the rage and bitterness they had accumulated throughout the course of their entire existence.

A few moments later Itzac's men arrived, followed closely by Atzcha's Amazons. The two machine guns with the last magazines had been left in Xeetha's and Puehatl's hands, who had stayed behind to control the tunnel above the waterfall, but to make up for it the invaders were equipped with a new and smaller kind of crossbow, no less lethal than its predecessor. The small and lightweight weapon could be used with one hand only like a gun and the shooters, with their shields braced on their left arms, could shoot their arrows without having to expose themselves, at the same time keeping both hands free to reload it.

The men guarding the gate were overpowered in minutes, but new backup was arriving, while the warriors on the battlements, taking advantage of their elevated position, continued to bombard the raiders from above and behind them. They ended up being in the midst of an extremely dangerous crossfire, and they would have had a very hard time if Marco hadn't decided to give the word to an old friend of his, immediately grasping the extent of the danger.

After finding it in the helicopter, he had painstakingly freed it from any trace of rust, paying a lot of attention to avoid streaking the interior of the barrel. He had then greased it, disassembled and reassembled it an infinite number of times to make it shine like new. And in the moment of truth, the Colt, like a perfectly tuned violin, responded obediently and faithfully to all its commands without ever getting jammed: aiming in the direction of the central terrace, he fired six shots in quick succession.

Four of the six bullets hit their mark, and the targets had just dropped from the terraces when the hastily reloaded gun spit out its second round of bullets.

The unluckily men who happened to be in the lethal trajectory of the firing saw their comrades falling one after the other and were deafened by the rumble of the shots in the closed square; they stopped shooting on the crowd and raised their eyes to scout ahead and try to determine the source of the carnage. When they realized they had been aimed at by the white giant that was pointing the hellish weapon towards them, they ran for an escape, scared to death. Some went down the stairs two by two, others ran towards the side terraces and some even jumped over the wall, risking their lives.

The terrace above the gate was cleared in a few seconds, but from the side arrows and javelins continued to rain down. To shoot in those directions, Marco was forced to abandon his defiladed position and expose himself to the fire of the soldiers on the walls and by those at the opening of the other streets. At that moment, though, Antapuoi's men came to his aid. They ran to protect him on the front and on the sides with their shields, during the lightning-fast forays.

At the same time, the jaguar warriors led by Tlamahatl were rapidly running up the stairs onto the now deserted central terrace, while Itzac's and Atzcha's warriors had closed ranks and spread in two concentric rows in the center of the square. And while one was standing up, shooting arrows every which way, the other one was kneeling down, rapidly reloaded their weapons while protected by the shields.

The sentries were not that naïve either, and they succeeded in hitting their enemies with well-aimed shots. But their tactics had always been based on individual combat and direct confrontation, nothing like the disciplined group action and organization based off closed ranks for which the warriors of the World Above were trained. Marco was intransigent on this subject, and he had to curse a good deal to convince Atzcha and even Itzac that this would be the best way to fight and to reduce the number of losses as much as possible.

In confirmation of his predictions, the warriors who had positioned themselves at the opening of the streets suddenly launched their attack. If they succeeded in closing the distance between them and the enemy huddled in the center of the square, their uncontested superiority in direct confrontation would create many problems.

It was time to put everything they had into it.

Marco, with his gun firmly in his hands, definitively abandoned his position and under the continuous protection of the shields he began to resolutely advance towards the attackers, relentlessly shooting at the vanguards. At the same time, the consolidated ranks of Atzcha and Itzac were able to focus their fire in a unified front; in

379

perfect harmony with the Colt's bullets they did not have to cover their flanks or rear anymore, since the shooters on the terraces had been by then decimated by Tlamahatl's men, and their arrows devastated the enemies.

Many froze in dismay as they watched their comrades collapse to the ground in front of them, and they were unable to decide if they should persist with their suicidal mission or run away as quickly as they could. Most of them, realizing in a second that they would never fulfill their objective and that they were by then too far away from the square in which they could seek shelter, let go of their weapons and of their shields, and began to kiss the ground as a sign of surrender. Their comrades lost all hope after seeing that, and turning their shoulders, they took flight.

Marco pointed the weapon on the last lingerers, and he pulled the trigger when the man was about to disappear behind the corner of the main street. But the shot did not come out: his faithful companion had just shot its last cartridge.

All the eyes were now staring at the openings of the streets fearing new arrivals. But there were none.

The attackers, barricaded in the square, slowly stood up, looking around with a bewildered expression, as if they were oppressed by the sudden quietness after the thunderous chaos of the battle. Just then Tlamahatl's men had finished clearing the terrace of any remaining resistance and were cautiously walking down the stairs to join them. And time seemed to stop in the anguishing wait before anyone could understand the true meaning of that unreal calm.

Nobody had yet come to terms with the fact that the nightmare was over, and that an impossible dream had turned into reality. They had all wanted to believe in that dream, even though they were very often overcome by the awareness of the enormous difficulty precluding their aspiration. They had lavished all their energy and sacrificed everything to see it fulfilled. And their sacrifice, in the end, had been rewarded beyond measure. It was an absolute victory, unconditional and definitive.

Dozens and dozens of enemies were strewn across the ground, in the square and on the terraces, and even among the ranks of the people of the World Above there were losses and wounded to count, but the euphoria of the moment prevailed over the pain.

And time started flowing again.

Isolated exclamations were heard here and there, and they quickly turned into a rumble of shouts of joy and of victory. Laughing and crying, each one embraced the friend beside him, many kneeled to the ground and thanked the gods, while those who were more pragmatic jumped at the surrendered men to immobilize them in the appropriate way to avoid any unpleasant surprises. But they were not without mercy: the white *tlatoani* had been peremptory about this and all of them were extremely careful to avoid getting carried away by their desire for revenge, ever mindful of his distant but unforgotten outburst of rage.

Atzcha was still examining every corner of the square when her eyes accidentally locked with Marco's.

They had not been on such good terms since that infamous night many years before. After that night, they had seldom met, and only when they had to make operative decisions, but even on those occasions they had continued to treat each other in a very formal and detached way. They had both practically decided to ignore each other, to go their own way, and neither of the two had made any effort to repair their former bond.

They stared at each other from far away as if studying each other. Then, as if pushed by a single force, they started to move towards each other with slow and uncertain steps, which became increasingly rapid and resolute, until they embraced each other. And their cry of victory joined the general din.

Their joy was indescribable. Apart from the catastrophic carnage that had occurred inside the tunnel and the dangerous, unforeseen difficulty at the gate that had been remedied by Cuathinicque's heroism—he was still alive, although quite battered—the whole plan had been executed perfectly. They had completely and definitively swept away the terrible weight that oppressed the souls of the people of the World Above.

But the nightmare was only beginning for some.

Once the euphoria of the moment passed, Atzcha let go of Marco's embrace and stared him in the eyes. "Will you keep your promise now?" she asked.

There was a moment of awkward silence, during which Atzcha feared a new change of mind.

"Yes," the man conceded resignedly, not convinced at all that his reconciled friend would scrupulously obey the orders. He then turned away from her and began to take control of the situation, loudly ordering those close to him to gather everybody in the center of the square.

It took them a while to calm the more passionate spirits and to placate the last cries of joy. Then, in the general silence, the white *tlatoani* gave the directives.

"Atzcha, you and your comrades will take care of the *teocalli*. And…please…" he added, leaving the sentence hanging, but staring at her eyes once again in a meaningful way.

She did not linger. After gratifying him with an enigmatic smile, she turned her back to him and made a sign to her faithful companions. She marshaled them into a wedge formation, with herself leading and the impenetrable shields on the sides, and resolutely advanced.

Marco kept staring at the departing handful of warriors with some apprehension, until they disappeared from his sight onto the main street. Then he moved again and resumed: "Antapuoi, you take Tlamahatl's and Actonuy's men, and you lock all the prisoners up in the House of the Serpent. Along the street, try to reassure the people, tell everybody they have nothing to fear, but they should stay in their houses, it will be better for everybody if we keep the place calm. And don't even think about going into their houses, even if you're sure of finding more enemies in there…as few and isolated as they are, they can't hurt anybody. But if you were to find some resistance, break it off without ceremony…it will serve as an example for the hot-headed ones. And you," he added, turning to Itzac, "you will come with me to the palace, but before you assemble the men, send somebody to the tunnel to reassure Xeetha: she is surely concerned about us, and anxious to know what has happened. Any questions?"

Nobody uttered a word.

"Good. Let's not waste any more time then. There is still a lot to do."

Chapter 15

Chitoontecl was struggling to reach the upper steps of the House of the Serpent. He was in a good mood. He had also heard the rumble and the horns, but he gave that no importance, since he took an imminent victory for granted. He was dying to enjoy the reaction of his hateful nemesis when he communicated to him that only seven days remained before the score was settled.

"Lead me to the prisoner," he ordered the official on duty that had thoughtfully come down to meet him.

"But…but he was already brought to you at the *teocalli* shortly after sunrise," Xahyotl stuttered, blanching at the scent of impending trouble.

"What prisoner are you talking about?" the priest addressed him indignantly and irritably.

"Well…the Son of the Mountain, my lord," the poor man stammered, ever paler and more frightened by the expression on the priest's face. "Antapuoi came…came to pick him up with his men…on your orders, he said."

A dreadful presentiment ran through Chitoontecl's mind in a flash. He pushed the official aside, and climbed up the last steps to reach the cell.

The door was wide open. Inside it: nobody.

"No!" he screamed with all the breath in his body, mad with rage. "I'll tear Antapuoi's heart out, and I'll do the same to all those behind that dog! And as for you…" he continued, looking the official up and down with bloodshot eyes, "gather your men. And follow me."

Leading the armed squad, the priest descended the steps of the barracks and headed straight towards the main square.

Along the route, Chitoontecl was trying to make sense of what had happened. The less he could work it out, the more his fervid imagination exaggerated the punishments he would inflict upon the traitors and the official on duty, who had dared disobey his orders.

When he entered the main square, he found it deserted. He had never seen it so lifeless. Considering the orders Puqutec had issued, this should not have surprised him much. Nonetheless, that immense emptiness and that unnatural silence still gave him an unsettling feeling.

Approaching the temple, he noticed a strange object at the foot of the steps. It was dark in color, and it clearly stood against in the whiteness of the esplanade. Looking at its shape and its size, you would probably say it was…yes, it definitely was the sacred turkey skin ball with which the eagle warriors and the jaguar warriors competed after the sacrificial ceremonies, and the thought that somebody had taken advantage of the peculiar circumstances to remove it from the *teocalli* without being authorized to do so only augmented the priest's ire. He widened his good eye when, a few meters away from the thing, he was finally able to identify it: it was the shaven head of one of his young novices.

A sudden cramp tightened his stomach, twisting it like a rag, but his blind hatred and desire for retribution overcame his fear.

"Go…go before me!" he ordered to the guards, continuing to cautiously walk up the stairs behind them.

At top of the stairs, on the temple's parvis, lay the beheaded bodies of the guards. Of their heads, there was no trace, but a long trail of fresh blood went beyond the main entrance.

"Hunt down and kill those sacrilegious dogs who dared profane our sacred *teocalli* and spill the blood of its servants! Show no mercy!" Chitoontecl screamed. But his voice had lost its usual firmness and arrogance, and it had turned into a choked sigh when a sudden hissing of arrows broke the silence and he saw all the warriors preceding him crumple to the ground.

Immediately after, at the opening of the temple from whose dark depths had sprung the lethal arrows, a majestic, dreadful figure appeared.

A black helmet with an unbelievable plumed crest atop it hid her head and most of her face. The right hand held a long blade of an unusual shape and the left arm bore a small shield adorned with shining plates. Underneath that, three severed heads hung at her belt by the hair, streaking her bare legs and her shoes with blood as they swung grimly. Behind her, many other characters as tragic as her were stepping onto the scene, armed to the teeth.

Chitoontecl was petrified.

"Do you recognize me, filthy bastard?" Atzcha questioned him cold-heartedly, pulling her helmet up from her head and throwing the shield to the ground. During her long absence, she had kept her unmistakable haircut and Chitoontecl immediately realized there would be a very slim chance of escape for him. He had in fact been the first to rape her, when she was little more than a child, and he was the one who fed her to his pupils when he was tired of her.

The priest stepped backwards, instinctively bringing his hand to the sacrificial dagger perpetually hidden inside his left sleeve, but while he extracted it and raised it menacingly he did not consider the limit of the parvis. His good foot stumbled into emptiness and his body tipped back. An inhuman scream accompanied his fall down the entire flight of stairs.

Chitoontecl gave no sign of life when the warriors reached him at the bottom of the last step. At that sight, Atzcha, who used to face danger with disdain and a smile on her lips, felt her blood freeze, and she only collected herself when she verified the man was merely unconscious. The orders of the white *tlatoani* had been very clear on this issue: the high priest had to be captured alive.

"Tie him up and lock him up in the House of the Serpent," the warlord ordered the first two warriors that reached her, heaving a sigh of relief. "And if you allow him to hurt himself, even just a scratch, I'll gut you with my own hands."

Her subalterns, not at all convinced that the commander in chief was only talking figuratively, rushed to pack up the prisoner like a salami, and after picking him up off the ground they heaved him onto their shoulders before he had regained consciousness.

"Well done," Atzcha said, observing with satisfaction the departing trio. "Now we're free to go pay a visit to our old friends. Let's hurry up, though…they will feel insulted if we make them wait for us." And a chorus of laughs rose from the group of Amazons, while they resumed their march towards unforgettable places.

Chapter 16

"Today, my dear, marks the close of a sad and dark era, and the beginning of a new one, bright and full of great promise. We lived in shadow until yesterday, obliged to satisfy the desires of that half-man Cuzupuma, and to follow the orders of an impotent and ever more arrogant *tlamacazqui*, but from now on we will be the true rulers of the Curved Mountain and we will forever live in splendor and glory," Mohotzuma recited inspiringly, resting his hands on the woman's shoulders while she sat beside the door leading out to the garden.

A shiver ran through Tlahaxtala's body and she could hardly subdue the instinct to flinch away from that repulsive touch. She had just woken up when the unwelcome guest snuck into her room. After her "promise," he actually felt more justified than before in visiting her at the most unreasonable times to overwhelm her with his never-ending monologues.

"I just finished talking with Cuzupuma," the intruder continued. "I must say that weakling is behaving quite well; he accepted my advice in a flash when I informed him of the gravity of the situation, and he also immediately and fully accepted my proposal. He even suggested I leave the task of announcing to the people the passage of the sacred insignia to him, to avoid rumors about his sudden retirement."

I had no doubts, Tlahaxtala thought, guessing at the arguments Mohotzuma had used to induce the coward to take his leave.

"He also promised me that tomorrow morning he himself will communicate to the people and to the council his decision to retire and nominate me as his successor, and he will announce his decision to give you as wife to the new *tlatoani* as a sign of high esteem towards me and of continuity in my enlightened path."

And the people will jump for joy when they find out that on the throne of the kid-kidnapper, they will have the most hated and feared man of the Curved Mountain, the woman thought, continuing her sarcastic commentary with bitterness.

"He confided in me once more that he couldn't stand his responsibilities, the rituals and the ceremonies anymore and that his only great wish now is to retire in his *teocalli* by the river, where he intends to open a school for young men to teach them his precious lessons."

Yes, until they find him one morning on his bed with his throat cut, Tlahaxtala concluded with certainty.

"By now, my dear, we can consider ourselves one being, and nothing remains to inhibit us from enjoying the fruits of our feelings," Mohotzuma continued, at the peak of his excitement, letting his fingers slide down almost to her breast.

Tlahaxtala, frozen on her stool, hardly listened to him. *But*, she was considering, *he seemed very confident when he made his promise. But how can he keep it, locked up and chained inside that cell? I could try to convince Mohotzuma that he's much more useful alive than dead, for all he knows. And then he could even make the high priest change his mind*, she continued dreaming, although she allowed herself no illusions. The promised spouse, who was no naïve man, had in fact surely considered that in spite of recent changes in power Chitoontecl could still count on the support of several potentates, and that it could turn out to be counter-productive—if not dangerous—to prevent him from taking his long-sought revenge.

Unfortunately, with how things were going, the possibility of altering the course of events was minimal. Nonetheless, she could not surrender, but she had to proceed with a good deal of circumspection if she did not want to arouse suspicion, showing she was too interested in the prisoner's fate. With the intention of advancing her requests in a more opportune moment, and trying at the same time to avoid affecting her admirer's susceptibility, she placed her hands on those repulsive claws, blocking his advance a step away from its goal.

"A little more patience, noble Mohotzuma," she said, "I couldn't bear the shame of conceding myself to one man when I belonged to another. There's not too much time left before the day in which we will be forever united."

Annoyed, but pleased at the same time for that noble display of feminine virtue, Mohotzuma resigned himself to retract his bony fingers and he took his leave, happy and delighted by his lover's behavior. As soon as she was left alone, she burst into tears, and even her faithful maid was not able to comfort her when she rushed in the room.

"I cannot allow that disgusting creature to touch me anymore!" she shouted, sobbing. "I'd rather kill myself!"

"That won't be necessary."

Tlahaxtala jumped and she turned immediately towards the entrance.

He was on the threshold. Wearing the magnificent regal *tilmatl* that reached the ground and brandishing the scimitar in his hands, still red with the blood of the sentries. The sight of him could have inspired terror, but she was out of her mind with joy, and still unable to believe her eyes. She stood up, and hardly freeing herself from the arms of a frightened Peheptel, who tried her best to hold her back and to protect her from that menacing presence, she rushed towards him. And she continued crying for a long time, as if she was whispering, when she found herself in the embrace of his arms.

Marco let her unburden herself, remaining silent the whole time. He felt on his chest the heaves of her sobbing, and when this finally came to an end, he delicately raised her face with one hand.

"You see? I kept my promise," he said to her simply, staring in her eyes. The woman's lips then opened in a wonderful smile of gratitude, and they instinctively moved up to join those of her liberator.

Peheptel, who had feared for her child's fate until a few seconds before, was observing the scene in ecstasy, alternating between incoherent sentences and sighs of relief. Which turned into enraged imprecations when she saw the ghostly figure of Mohotzuma appear behind the couple's shoulders, tightly held by two muscled warriors. The man, looking even paler than usual, had lost all his boldness and he appeared confused, bewildered and completely incapable of explaining what had occurred. Peheptel was the first one to regain her thoughts and to take the initiative. Shouting unrepeatable words and interpreting the wish of her protégé very well, she approached the prisoner and after spitting on his face, she delivered a very powerful and unrefined kick to his groin. The hit made the unfortunate man bend over on himself, but this did not elicit much sympathy from the men, although it did send a shiver down their backs.

"Don't rough him up too much," Marco entreated with a smile. "Try to leave something for Atzcha and Peepty as well, if you can."

"No, not those two!" Mohotzuma screamed, hearing the dreaded names.

"I'm sorry for you," Marco told him insincerely, "but I made a promise, and I," he continued staring at Tlahaxtala with a knowing gaze, "I keep my promises."

At his sign, the prisoner was taken away by force while he continued to alternate curses and requests for mercy between intervals of kicking and screaming.

The echo of the screams dissolved in the distance and Peheptel, who had realized she was in the way, rapidly left the room, continuing to mumble incomprehensibly.

An embarrassing silence fell in the room, during which Tlahaxtala was suddenly struck by an inexplicable feeling of anxiousness. Her dreams had magically been fulfilled beyond all expectation and everything in her life had changed in a moment. She should have felt like the luckiest woman on Earth, she should have cried aloud for the miracle…but, against all logic, she felt oppressed by an unjustified feeling of dissatisfaction, as if everything she had always desired and everything she had just obtained were nothing to her anymore. This was her second meeting with the Son of the Mountain, and just like the first time, she felt a strange listlessness that made her legs shake and almost fold. She felt irresistibly attracted to the man before her, she wished she could continue clinging to him forever, she wished she could melt in his arms. But the harsh reality hit her like a slap in the face: she was now just a normal woman like any other...indebted. She had never cared about her rank and even less about power, but at that moment, though she realized how absurd it was, she wished to be the envied spouse of the *tlatoani* again, the most powerful woman in the Curved Mountain, the sovereign who could claim whatever she wanted...

"I'm your slave, my lord," she stammered reluctantly, melting from his embrace, and she was about to kneel, to excuse herself for the liberty she had taken in throwing her arms around the new sovereign. But he swiftly pulled her to his feet.

"What are you doing?" he laughed, raising her face with one hand once more. "You are a free woman, now; from today on, there will be no more slaves in this land." He was extremely attracted to her, to her wonderful eyes, that charming face, the angelic sound of her voice...he knew almost nothing about that woman, but he felt like he had known her forever, and he embraced her again, urged by an uncontrollable instinct. His lips found her lips and they united in the kiss they both craved and longed for.

Chapter 17

Cuzupuma reclined on a thick layer of soft, colorful pillows and admired the curves of the young boy he had received as a gift from Mohotzuma as a sign of gratitude for his "generous collaboration." A charming boy, mild and even accommodating, as he had never succeeded in finding during those last years of great shortage. The boy had just undressed and he was already mentally running through the wonderful plans he had for the night when the boy was startled by something and immediately covered his naked body with his hands, staring at the entrance with wide eyes.

The astonished *tlatoani* whipped around to look in the same direction.

A stranger was standing on the threshold in absolute silence. Maybe he had been enjoying the show for a long time already.

"Who…who are you! Who…who authorized you to enter my chambers without my permission!" he shouted in a squeaky voice, made even more strident by his fear.

"What, you don't recognize me?" Itzac accused him, while slowly stepping into the room with a long banner shaft in his hand, which he had taken from the palace's entrance. "I'm almost offended: it's been a while since we saw each other last, but after so many beautiful moments we spent together, you should remember me!"

"Guards!" Cuzupuma screamed, with his face growing paler, as he clumsily attempted to stand up.

"It's a shame, but I think they'll have a hard time hearing you with their heads chopped off of their necks."

"Help!" the god incarnate shouted with all the breath he had in his body, starting to foresee the worst.

After several vain attempts, Cuzupuma finally succeeded in standing up again. He breathlessly dashed towards the exit of the vestibule, but he was immediately blocked by Itzac's men, who were already lying in wait at that exit.

"I've been waiting for this moment all my life!" Itzac continued, stepping inside the room and approaching him. "I feared it had to remain a dream…but, here I am. All for you. Ready to give back some of what you gave me so long ago."

Cuzupuma, with his tongue tied by fear, kept on staring at the stranger with a dazed look. And the stranger, while walking towards him, continued to rapidly work the shaft of the banner with his sword, knocking the edges of its extremity to form a long, barbed point. And he jumped when the man said: "Undress him and hold him in his favorite position."

The poor man was still alive when the shaft was planted back at the palace entrance with its macabre trophy. Shortly later, atop another shaft, his aspiring successor appeared to keep him company, and the revenge the Amazons had enacted on him had probably been less merciful. At the feet of the two impaled men were exhibited the severed heads of many counselors, aspiring priests, and several people of high rank, along with those of some of their lovers and consorts.

Marco had reluctantly released Tlahaxtala's embrace. He was the happiest man ever when he left the room to join his men, but his mood changed immediately when he was presented with the fait accompli, as soon as he was outside the palace.

He had been no saint, and his hatred towards those who had obliged him to fear and silence for an infinite time, and towards those who had taken away from him not only freedom, but also the being he had most dearly loved in his life, was equal to, if not beyond the hatred of those who had committed that horrible massacre. He also knew the story well, though, and he was well aware of the revenge and hatred that would inevitably bring cleansing and retributive justice; that was the worst mistake they could make in such a critical, delicate moment. With much reluctance, he had kept faithful to the promise he had made to Atzcha, foreseeing her moves, but at the sight of her people dancing around the murdered enemies, he could not hold himself back anymore.

"Take those two men down," he shouted to the people who were there, "and remove these as well," he added with his face reddening, indicating the heads spread on the ground. "Take them as far away as possible from the square and burn them, before the people leave their houses and realize what you have done!"

Shortly after, Atzcha and Itzac, who had rushed to protest against the removal of the two bodies, earned their share of Marco's anger.

"You have had your revenge. Enough!" the white *tlatoani* screamed. "Do you want to make the people believe we're just like those who oppressed them for their entire life? Do you want them to learn to fear and hate us just like they feared and hated them? Remember that almost all the inhabitants of the valley have been persecuted like us and more severely than us by our same oppressors, and that many of them have paid with their lives for being our friends. We'll celebrate together with them the liberation that has finally come, because only this way will we be able to say we really won and we really brought an end to the days of hatred and fear."

He was staring with inflamed eyes at the people who were assembling at the foot of the stairs: "Anyone dares to kill, persecute or even offend the inhabitants of the valley, taking advantage of the victory, will be in deep trouble. And anyone caught stealing a single grain of *mahis* from its legitimate owner will be judged by a council of wise men formed by members of both peoples. Let the absent know what I just told you and go call Antapuoi. Now!"

His words required no reply. The last time they had seen him so enraged was when they had suggested eating human flesh. Everybody started to immediately execute the orders they had received, without even hinting at a protest.

Shortly thereafter, Marco rethought the situation and he regretted having treated with so much vehemence those who had always loved him and respected him like a god, and who would not hesitate one second to sacrifice their lives for him. Maybe, he said to himself, he should have been less harsh, more understanding towards them, but he soon absolved himself: he could not compromise on that matter. For no reason. Everybody had to get a clear idea of the importance of a peaceful coexistence of the two peoples, and if he had not acted the way he had, if he had not shown he was more than firm and inflexible on that matter, he would have risked seeing the final fruit of all his efforts go to waste.

Chapter 18

In the World Above, the old refuge of the persecuted, the warriors of the glorious army of the Curved Mountain were now wandering around in isolated and opposed groups. Almost three moons had passed since the day of the disastrous venture.

At first, those belonging to the Order of the Eagle and the Jaguar had continued to obey their high chief, but as soon as they had started to starve they realized that their only possibility for survival was cannibalizing their comrades, and that even with the division of the little food that was left, they were still being treated as inferiors, and the first grumbles started to rise. When they were then repeatedly ordered to attack the tunnel above the waterfall and had been decimated by the hails of machine gun fire, the first insubordinations had arisen. And these turned into open revolt when Puqutec, to reaffirm his authority, had committed the fatal error of putting five of them to death because they were guilty of refusing to return to that massacre once more.

Two opposing groups had then formed, with those faithful to Puqutec on one side, and the Eagle and Jaguar warriors on the other. The latter had sought shelter in the higher ground of the wood, where they had discovered an unexpected source of food in the few nests that had been forgotten there, but the news had spread and from that moment on that area had become a theater of daily battles among those who defended tooth and nail the little they had at their disposal and those who, blinded by hunger, tried to steal it from them. There had been enormous losses on both sides, and after every attack, there had been a rush to snatch up the bodies.

When the nests were exhausted too, hunger ended up dividing the opposed factions even more, and in a short time a total anarchy was reigning, where the strong killed the weak and united to the others only to procure more food.

Marco had followed the progressive barbarization of those people with his binoculars. Only half of the many warriors that had gone to the World Above, so self-assured and questing after honors and glory, were still alive, and they were wandering around the wood like wild beasts consumed by hunger. They were the mere shadows of what they had been, and they were resigned to starve to death or to be brutally killed. There was no danger anymore. Marco considered this the perfect time to play his last card.

Antapuoi, preceded by a herald and protected by the fire of the machine guns, went down to the field with no weapons, and after having identified himself promised that those who would have give up their weapons and swear obedience to the white *tlatoani* would be spared.

The Eagle and Jaguar warriors accepted the unexpected proposal with elation, followed closely by several representatives of the Order of the Serpent, reassured by the presence of their old commander. Only Puqutec and a few of his most faithful men, realizing that their bloody crimes and their infinite oppressions would grant them no forgiveness, tried to impede the capitulation in every possible way, but they had by then been completely stripped of all authority. Within a few hours they were surrounded, overwhelmed and massacred by the blind fury of all the other survivors, who reunited for the occasion.

Now the nightmare was finally over.

Chapter 19

At the foot of the great pyramid there was a united people: The Free People of the Curved Mountain. Only a whispered murmur ran through the whole square, from one end to the other. All eyes were staring at the *tlatoani* in that moment; he was slowly ascending the high steps of the central stairway, followed by a small group of comrades. He kept his scimitar at his hip, and the silver flashes of the weapon fused with the golden glow of the stairs and those of the iridescent royal *tímatl* that wrapped his body, while the long, knotted and carved staff preceded all of his movements on the highest step.

Once on top, the man turned around to look down. And he felt a sense of wonder and dizziness.

It was not the height that caused him the vertigo: a multitude of adoring people was down there, and he was the object of their adoration. Those people were his people, and he was their Liberator.

That new appellative had been conferred to him by a council with representatives of both communities, and Marco had accepted with real pride the title of *tlatoani* conferred to him by acclamation in an unforgettable ceremony during which he had offered his blood to the gods, as his predecessors, piercing his earlobes, calves and tongue with agave thorns.

The gods. He had never believed in the gods of the Curved Mountain people, nor had he ever been a zealous or practicing Christian in the past, but he had been raised in a religion which had grown into him, bringing him to believe and hope in his God. But he had not lived that religion with ease, since it had given him no certainties, but had just succeeded in imbuing him with guilty feelings and the fear of eternal damnation.

He had always been convinced that all religions had been dictated by a single God but, by the very fact that they had all been touched by the hand of the imperfect being that is man, none could claim to be superior. Trying to convert other people to your own belief therefore made no sense. Nonetheless, he had never succeeded in completely freeing himself from the old fears, but for that very reason he would have never allowed his sons and his beloved people to be possessed by those fears. In truth, he felt at times a vague guilt feeling for this very un-Christian determination to deny his neighbor a possible way of salvation. However, bringing back to mind the crimes, the vileness, the oppressions and the sea of innocent blood that was shed in the last millenniums in the name of the infinite religions that were all born and destined to sooner or later sink into oblivion, he was reassured: if there was a God—and he was deeply convinced of that, like Karl—then that God would weigh the actions of men, not their knowledge of the sacred texts or their frills.

"Chitoontecl's merciless gods have never been your gods," he had reaffirmed in his inauguration speech. "Those were the gods of the Lake People, the people that for many cycles has oppressed the fathers of your fathers, disseminating hatred and death among your people. Therefore, you will never again worship the gods of death, but those of life, of tolerance, and of love. None of these gods will ask of you human sacrifice anymore, and he who dares to raise his hand to harm his fellow man in their name once again, will be punished by the justice of men."

His arguments had been very convincing, and they had found their way into his subjects' hearts and they had contributed to making the transition from the old to the new regime almost painless. When the inhabitants of the valley had seen with their own eyes that the white *tlatoani* did not make empty promises and that, in fact, "not even a grain of *mahis*" had been stolen from their houses, they had abandoned any suspicion towards the victorious army and their fears had soon turned into loyal and open collaboration.

The priests would continue to officiate the ancient propitiatory rites, offering the products of their lands or some yard animal to the gods, but they would be excluded forever from politics and from the possession of goods; their main task would be to assist the sick and to support the needy and those who could not look after themselves, along with the women of the temple.

While the Liberator had now been elected *tlatoani* by acclamation, things would go a completely different way for his successors. Every new sovereign would be nominated—and controlled—by the council, and the council, in turn, would be elected by the entire population.

Military orders had been abolished. A unit of urban police had been established in its place—and its officers, not too numerous—to which the task of monitoring the deeds of the citizens and the well-being of the environment was assigned. As head of this new institution Antapuoi was nominated, and Marco had to sweat his own blood to overcome Atzcha's resistance, since she was demanding that desired title for herself.

"Fortunately times have changed, Atzcha," the former lover had tried to explain as tactfully as possible. "Once we were at war, we had to defend ourselves from an enemy. Now that enemy doesn't exist anymore, it's part of a united people and we can't occupy all the high offices with our representatives. If we don't want the people of the valley to feel oppressed, and to really trust us, we have to give prestigious insignia to both the defeated and the defeaters, in equal measure."

But he had not succeeded in making the warrior give up her obstinate claim, and in the end Marco had got his own way only after granting her and her partner the beautiful *tecalli* by the river, which had belonged to the deceased Puqutec and the unfaithful Cuanpooca.

The latter had certainly not dared to fight against the eviction. She was still young and beautiful and, considering her resources, she would surely soon find an accommodation that suited her aspirations. She had to thank all of her gods that she had managed to avoid the worst, though she had contributed to the Cause—although involuntarily—by offering her former husband, commended for his success in duping the despised Mohotzuma, the unexpected opportunity of making his own "revelations" without passing through crueler methods.

Xaiput was still madly in love with Cuanpooca, and when the woman was brought to the special tribunal to be judged, he had exposed her and covered her with insults and scurrilities at first, confronting her with her double betrayal, but immediately after he had intervened in her favor, saving her from certain, harsh punishment. But he had rudely and theatrically chased her away when she had gone to him to offer her "services" again, to ask for his forgiveness, or perhaps to find a new "place in the sun," according to the most malicious gossip. A rumor spread, though, that shortly after that unforgettable scene, Xaiput had had some afterthoughts on his firm decision to forever remove her from his life, and that, during the night, he quite often paid her a visit.

The eyes of the white *tlatoani* lowered on the altar, still encrusted with the blood of so many human sacrifices, when they met Chitoontecl's terrified eyes. His face was wan and he was waiting for just this fatal moment. The former uncontested master and lord of the Curved Mountain had screamed and railed so much when he had been dragged by force to the top of the pyramid he had no breath left to breathe. He was wearing rough fiber underwear, and he had his wrists and ankles firmly tied to the convex sacrificial stone, which arched his back to better offer his chest to the executioner's hand. The Liberator was now occupying the position that was formerly his.

"The New Book prohibits human sacrifice," Marco commenced, standing tall, and staring at the condemned man in the eyes. "But you were judged *before* the new law was written. And the verdict was unanimous: death."

402

The sound of that word succeeded in the impossible accomplishment of making the tortured man's face even paler.

"But when the people called upon me to wear the insignia of *tlatoani*, they also meant to attribute some powers to me, powers that will never be given to anyone else in the future. Well, I decided to take advantage of this privilege, and I have therefore made my decision: you will not die on this stone."

Incredulity, relief, amazement and diffidence appeared in the same moment on the priest's face, restoring some semblance of life.

"Also, because I'm convinced that death for you would be too moderate a punishment," the accuser continued implacably, instantaneously obscuring the feeble glimmer of hope that had ignited in the priest's eyes. "Therefore, I…condemn you to live."

That said, the Liberator extracted his long scimitar from its sheath and raised it up with both arms.

"This is for all the crimes you have committed towards the people you should have served and that you only mercilessly oppressed instead," he sentenced, swinging his blade a first time. "And this," he added with rage, swinging it again, "is from Chatì."

Both blows hit right where they were supposed to, and an inhuman scream came out of Chitoontecl's mouth. Not held by his arms anymore, he crumpled down to watch with horror the blood squirting out in streams from the stumps of his wrists that had just been amputated, while the two truncated hands still clawed at the hard sacrificial stone with worm like movements.

The *tlatoani*'s assistants, who were already prepared, immediately blocked the hemorrhage with some tourniquets and they cauterized the wounds with red-hot iron, ripping fresh, atrocious screams of pain from the tortured man's throat.

"From now on," the Liberator continued, not moved to pity in the slightest, "you will be fed by the people you have persecuted. And each time they will remind you of the crimes you have committed during your wicked life. Maybe one day you will come to repent for your misdeeds, and who knows, maybe even to long for forgiveness."

Chapter 20

Kneeling on the field, Xeetha was adjusting the finishing touches of Chati's tomb. After the invaders' surrender, the reinstatement of the small cemetery—appropriately disguised in anticipation of the coming confrontation—was one of the first preoccupations of the inhabitants of the World Above, who almost all preferred to continue living in their houses.

"Good morning," the woman said without turning around, recognizing the footsteps.

"Good morning to you, Xeetha," the man answered, stopping behind her.

"I already relocated the orchids. There will be an amazing bloom."

"Thank you, Xeetha. As always, you beat me to it."

"She was also my sister."

"Of course, I'm sorry."

Contrary to his usual ease during their interactions, Marco felt awkward. He felt a vague feeling of guilt and embarrassment towards the woman. In the last weeks he had only thought about the best moment to speak to her, to expose his problem, and he had racked his brain to find the appropriate words to avoid hurting her, to make her understand he would never abandon her, that…tormented by these thoughts, he had not slept all night, and that morning he had woken up quite early, firm and resolute, but once he stood before her, so frail and defenseless, kneeling in front of the graves of her loved ones, he lost his courage. *I can't give her this sorrow as well. She doesn't deserve it. It would be too much for her.*

He had decided to give up and was almost going to make up a subject of discussion when the woman's voice distracted him from his thoughts.

"I know what you're trying to tell me."

"Xeetha, I..."

"No, don't speak. You don't need to," she interrupted him, continuing to work on the grave. After a brief pause, she continued: "Eyes have an unmistakable light when they're filled with love and passion...and I've seen that light in your eyes only when we talked about Chatì and when, on the day of your investiture, I saw you looking at the woman with emerald eyes."

"Xeetha, I don't..."

"No, you don't need to justify for something that's not your fault. The fire you have inside you cannot be put out by your own will. It's the gods that light it up, and once it's lit, you can't do anything to put it out...that light never appeared in your eyes when you looked at me. But I can't blame you, because I know for sure that you hold me dear, and that you always will. And that you will respect me. You have all my understanding...and also my blessing."

"Thank you," was everything Marco could say with a sigh of relief, as if Xeetha had removed a heavy weight from his shoulders.

"You don't need to thank me, not you," the woman continued. She had turned towards him and in the morning light. Marco could glimpse the reflections of the tears that until a few seconds before had streamed down her face. But now she was smiling at him "I always looked for a way to repay you for everything you've done for me, and now that I finally have this opportunity I'm the happiest woman of all, because my only wish is to see you happy. I only ask one thing of you: allow me to build my new house in this part of the field. I could not live in the valley, and even if the two peoples are now on good terms, I feel that only up here has the air the true scent of freedom."

"No, Xeetha, I will never be able to fulfill this wish of yours."

The woman looked at him with incredulous eyes, but her amazement did not last long.

"I can't satisfy your request, because I need you. And I also need your children. Our children. We will build a house together, up there, in front of our shelter. From its terrace we will rule the entire World Above. And inside it, there will be space for everybody. For our children, for their wives, and for the children of our children. Because you're part of me, and I can't do without you, without your voice, without your advice."

The woman stood up and approached him, awkwardly rubbing her hands dirty with earth on her immaculate tunic, then she threw her arms around his neck and cried with gratitude, while Marco, assailed by new guilty feelings, tenderly caressed her hair.

Chapter 21

The palace was no place for him. The vaulted rooms, whose walls were frescoed with scenes of hunting and war, were wonderful, the plumed curtains of iridescent colors were amazing, the garden charming; but all that magnificence, instead of gratifying him and pleasing him, made him feel out of place. During the day, the continuous coming and going of officials and people in charge of taking care of the palace bothered him; in spite of his reiterated remonstrations, they kept kneeling and kissing the ground each time he passed by, and he felt even more uneasy when, in the night, he remained alone in his huge and unfamiliar bedroom.

Almost four moons had passed since the day of the battle and things were settling down in the best way, thanks to the contribution of his valid collaborators. The new setup worked at full speed, as if it had always been like that, and everybody in the fields and in the city had resumed their usual occupations. Work had resumed even in the stone cave and in the mines, but there were no more slaves and the workers were happy to do it, because they received a fair and regular salary.

There was no more distinction between the elite school of the *calmécac*, which only the children of the noble potentates could attend, while the *telpochalli* were destined to the poorer ones. Now there was a single school for everybody, where every student could follow the most appropriate path for his own abilities and inclinations. The tribunal and the city hall, with its unit of urban police, had become perfectly efficient organisms, and nothing was lacking in the markets and in the shops of Aplaia.

Marco had had the far-sightedness of leaving the old functionaries in their places, or at least those who were more prepared and who had been less complicit with the past regime, assigning equal charges to representatives of both the old communities, and he was still amazed by the ease and enthusiasm with which everybody had welcomed the new system, adjusting rapidly to schemes of life so innovative and vastly different from before.

The new organization was working so well, that he could have left before, delegating to others all that was left to do. Only one torment had kept him there, in those cold and unknown walls, but after he had clarified things with Xeetha, he had finally decided to put aside his last reservation once and for all.

Tlahaxtala was about to lie down. "Don't be sad, my lady," Peheptel implored her once more with a maternal demeanor. "You'll see, he'll show up sooner or later."

Tlahaxtala seemed not to hear her. Lately her mind was dominated by a single and discomforting consideration: the gods had fulfilled all of her greatest desires, but in contrast with all logic, she continued to harbor an inexplicable feeling of dissatisfaction mixed with sadness. From the day of the liberation, *he* had not shown up again. Nonetheless, she had felt passion, rapture and desire in the kiss they had exchanged. She still felt it on her lips, that kiss, and each time she thought of that moment, she was pervaded by the same languid and heart-breaking feeling of their first encounter.

On more than one occasion, while she was freely wandering around the corridors of the palace, she had glimpsed him in the distance, caught up in intense discussions with his functionaries. Each time her heart had started, and had opened to a new hope, but he had maybe not even noticed her in those moments, or even worse, not even recognized her.

He already has his woman, his sons, Emerald Eyes had considered, broken-hearted and melancholy, *and I already had much more than I could ever wish for. I can't claim anything more.*

She was absorbed in these sad and not reassuring considerations, when two knocks on the door suddenly distracted her from her thoughts.

The woman had just the energy to stare at her faithful maid with supplicating eyes: "Excuse me for the time, Tlahaxtala," Marco awkwardly began while Peheptel passed by him in a rush out of the room with a bright smile of complicity.

"My lord," Tlahaxtala whispered quietly while kneeling down, ashamed for the shabby clothes she was wearing in front of her sovereign. "If I had known…"

"What are you doing?" he reprimanded her, rushing to keep her upright.

"My lord, I…I didn't think that—"

"I can't blame you, Tlahaxtala," he interrupted her, misinterpreting the woman's embarrassment. "I realize I have chosen a quite inappropriate time to visit you…I could have warned you at least. I ask twelve times your forgiveness for this intrusion, but it was absolutely necessary that I speak to you and I couldn't postpone this further."

"No, forgive me my lord, I…I didn't mean that. I…I meant to say that…I thought that you, by now…Oh, gods of heaven, help me!"

That chain of disjointed and mumbled words succeeded in making Marco smile, and in loosening the tension that had almost made him get off track. He had received Xeetha's blessing, but he still felt guilty about her, and also towards Chatì. What mysterious force had brought him to that room at that time of night? More than once, reason had advised him to desist, but, for once, his rational self had only increased in him the desire of seeing that woman who had charmed him once more.

"I desire you, Tlahaxtala. I felt I wanted you from the first moment you showed your face to me. Don't ask me why…I will never be able to explain. I wanted to make you understand something about me, before I came here to confess my feelings to you, but I feel the time is running out, and I have no intention of wasting more time on pleasantries and small talk. Therefore, please forgive my curt and abrupt ways, I...I ask for your hand in marriage."

The woman was listening to him as if spellbound; she did not believe her own ears. She could not tell if she might cry from joy, kneel and thank the gods, throw her arms around the beloved man, or do all of this at once.

"Soon, though, I'll be back up there, where there's a house to be built and fields to be cultivated, and this is the life I came to propose to you. You're free to accept or refuse, and if you decided to stay here, I will ensure that you may continue to live in this *tecalli*, as you always did, until the end of your days. Don't be afraid to hurt my pride if you decide to refuse my offer...I prefer to know you're happy here, rather than living a life of obligations. And also—"

"What are you saying, my lord?" she interrupted him, placing her hands on his arms. "These walls are my prison, the prison I've been locked in from the day I was taken away from my parents...poor basket makers, as somebody has probably told you already. I always dreamt of going back to my people one day, and find a man to love and a house in which to raise his children. And now that you're here, fulfilling all the desires of an entire lifetime, you think I would be crazy enough to refuse this? You were in my dreams even before our *tonalli* brought us together. I'm ready to follow you wherever you want to go. For me it will be a privilege to serve in your house...I'm your slave, my lord."

After saying this, to seal the promise, Tlahaxtala brought her hands on her shoulders and pulled aside the strings supporting her dress. It slid down with the lightness of a whisper, revealing a perfect body with alabaster skin.

Such a call could not remain unanswered.

Marco silently approached her, pulled her into his arms and whispered to her, "You will never be anybody's slave. You will be my queen. And I won't let anyone take you away from me."

Epilogue

He had lain down shortly before, when they came to notify him that the last barrier was about to be removed. Almost twenty years had passed since he had come back to live in the World Above, and Marco had fulfilled his dream.

Now his house was as he had always dreamed it would be. Constructed entirely of wood, it rose in front of the old shelter, which was still part of the home. It rested on eight strong pine columns, and during the spring the climbing plants which surrounded it from end to end, brought the whole balcony to bloom, and the intoxicating scent of jasmine reigned uncontested.

He had spent wonderful years in that house, peaceful and in perfect harmony, with Xeetha, with Tlahaxtala—who had given him two more children—and with all the other members of the family, alternating between work in the field, household chores and the ever rarer administrative tasks.

But he had not succeeded in keeping his word. Last year Tlahaxtala had been seized by a sudden and mysterious fever which had killed her in three days and his desperate attempts to save her from death were in vain. Now she was resting beside Chatì and his friend Karl, and not a day went by without Marco paying a visit to their graves, and chatting with them about the day's events.

He needed all of Xeetha's love to overcome that new, tremendous detachment. A month after Tlahaxtala's passing, Marco resigned from his appointment as *tlatoani*. Itzac had been elected to succeed him by acclamation. The young man had increasingly been admired for his talents over the years by all the inhabitants of the valley. They had gone as far as adoring him when he taught them the use of the wheel, which had by then become an irreplaceable instrument.

But the real sovereign of the Free People of the Curved Mountain was always him, the Liberator. On the very rare occasions in which he came down to the valley to attend some public ceremony, his high stature and the aura of mystery that continued to surround him instilled great apprehension, especially among the new generation, for whom he represented a true living legend.

Xeetha was already up. Her eyes were red. While Marco consumed his frugal breakfast, she had stood there the whole time, off to the side, reviewing the content of his sack several times to make sure she had not forgotten anything. There was no space for more words; they had already discussed the matter to the point of exhaustion in the last months.

Marco could not deny it: he had lived an incredible adventure in that crater, finding what he had sought after in all the remote corners of the Earth. He had accomplished unimaginable ventures, ones that could satiate the most egocentric expectations, but since Tlahaxtala had left him, an ancient and untamed desire had reemerged forcefully in him, growing each day into an always more pressing need to cross the boundaries of those reassuring walls, to move towards the rediscovery of a world that was now far away, not his own anymore, but which he felt he had to face again.

He actually did not miss that frenzied, chaotic world very much, but he could not go on pretending there was nothing outside of that crater, and before anything else, he had to understand if his intention of keeping away from it, was indeed a surrender, denial in the face of a harsh reality, or if it was dictated rather by the deep awareness that he had finally attained that which he had longed for. And only out there he could have found an answer to that.

Before leaving the shelter, Marco held Xeetha in his arms, almost hurting her, and while he was embracing her, he covered every corner of the room, as if he wanted to impress in his mind every possible detail of the walls that had protected him for so many long years.

He had to force himself to let go of that embrace. Then, he started to descend the steps in front of the balcony without turning around. At the threshold of the wood, he had an afterthought, and before he went towards the wooden bridge, over the waterfall, he took a sudden detour towards the small cemetery. He had already been there the night before, but the desire to go back for a last salute had uncontrollably reemerged in him.

Over the years, the pulley had been turned into a much quicker and safer instrument of communication with the valley, although it could only be accessed through the tunnel at the other end of the terrace, that had been made passable again a few months after the final confrontation. The person in charge of the pulley permanently lived close to the cabin, which ended its journey on the old pile of detritus leaning against the rock. From there, through convenient zigzagging stairs, one could easily descend to the right bank of the stream, where a wooden bridge united the two banks to give access to the valley.

Waiting for him on the opposite shore were Itzac, Antapuoi and four of his men, equipped with torches, who placed themselves ahead of the group and led everyone along the left bank, until the point where the river disappeared inside the mountain. The tunnel under the ancient sacrificial altar had been reopened and huge piles of detritus were obstructing the gravel bed of the river for a long section on both sides.

When the small procession stopped at the opening of the tunnel, Marco turned around to look at those accompanying him. Even though he had already said his goodbyes to them one by one over the previous days, and he had requested that they behave with dignity, none of them could hold back their tears. He stood still, silent, for a long time. Then he moved, turned his back to the valley and, preceded by two men, he resolutely entered the narrow opening.

Spring had just begun, but the stream was already swollen with water from the thaw. From time to time the rumble of small rapids

413

filled the tunnel, drowning out the voices of the torch-bearers and any other noise. Marco proceeded quickly, but he had given his sack to the man preceding him, and on more than one occasion he had to ask his comrades to help him to overcome the most dangerous and challenging spots. Inside the tunic had been sewn some emeralds of unrivaled purity, which would grant him ten lives as a nabob, though his skinny figure would have never lead anybody to imagine that he carried such a fortune.

After more than an hour of an exhausting hike, the group reached its destination. The end of the walkway had been obstructed by a pile of stones and earth, but close to the ceiling they had opened a small hole, and the airstream that rushed in lifted long strips of fire from the torches, which lit up the gallery, and Marco could not hold back a choked exclamation when he saw the image of the Sun God sculpted on the wall beside him.

His comrades, after securing the torches on the walls, immediately got started and it did not take them long to widen the hole as much as was needed for a person to crawl through it.

"That's enough," Marco said, starting to clamber onto the pile of gravel, heedless of the mud that was dirtying his tunic, and once he reached the top of the detritus, he pushed himself without hesitation into the narrow opening. He had to struggle to get his sack and his shoulders through but then, leaning on his elbows and knees, he came out easily on the other side. The sediment that had accumulated there over the centuries had created a sort of slope and Marco, who was not supported by the narrow opening anymore, ended up sliding down it; when he reached the bottom, his nostrils were suddenly pervaded by a strong and ancient smell of moss and wet ground, emanated by the soil in which he had face planted. Once he regained his breath on his elbows and knees, he crawled forward until he reached a horizontal position, then, pressing with both his arms, he kneeled up, and finally stood with difficulty.

The low ceiling of the tunnel obliged him to walk those last meters bending forward, almost doubled over, but as soon as he was out he stood up completely and—maybe because he feared he might

414

miss what he was looking for—he immediately lifted his gaze towards the sky.

Fate was benevolent to him. It was a wonderful September night and not a single cloud obscured the sky, where millions and millions of stars were shining for only him. Many years had passed since the day in which he had last greeted them, but in that moment he felt he had only left them a few moments before. Probably because they had always burned bright in his heart.

He felt a small pang in his chest. He had already noticed this a few times recently, but he was at peace with himself, and he had learned to accept those premonitory signs with a serene and ready soul.

When his eyes adjusted to the obscurity of the night, by the light of the feeble gleam of the stars he glimpsed a huge stone with the weird form of a camel's back in front of him. He climbed onto it quite easily, sat down on the cavity between the two humps, laid his head on the bare rock and from that moment on, he never took his eyes off of the sky.

The view was not the same as it was before, and he could not make out any of the known constellations; but suddenly in that sea of stars, he recognized the smiling face of Chatì. "I'll wait for you among the stars," she had promised him before leaving him. And she had kept her promise.

"You won't have to wait long, my love," he said aloud to her. "Soon we'll be together again. And this time, forever."

He continued chatting with her for a long time, until the last star was eclipsed by the light of the dawn.

The sun had risen already on the other side of the mountain. If he had had the patience to wait a little longer, he would have seen it rise above his head. But he could not wait. He had already made his decision.

With some difficulty he stood back up, stretched his legs numbed by the stillness and humidity of the night, and turning his back to the world outside, he went straight towards the opening of the tunnel.

415

"Start closing the passage," he ordered to the amazed sentinels, by then resigned to infinite shifts, when they saw him reappear after just one night. They were frozen stiff, and could not wait to go back to their homes. "I can go back by myself," he added, "stay here until the next shift comes...they won't be late." That said, he took an extra torch from the ground, lit it using the one that burned secured to the wall and left alone down the almost inaccessible tunnel.

His commotion was great when he got to the valley, and he saw the crowd.

The news of his departure, which had remained hidden until the last moment according to his wishes, had spread from house to house during the night, and before the morning, in dribs and drabs first, then all together, all the inhabitants of the valley and of the World Above had begun to gather beneath the ancient altar. On that altar they had laid down flowers, left offerings, and prayed their gods. And they had also paid the God of the Liberator, who more than any other god could have interceded for them. The gods had listened to their supplications and the Liberator, once he had won his last battle, had gone back to his people.

The first to catch sight of him was Itzac. Not resigned at all to the departure of the man he considered a father, and a teacher, he had continued to stare at the entrance of the tunnel, and his cry of exultation in seeing him appear again instantly turned the crowd's sad lament into a roar of joy. They all ran towards him to embrace him, shake his hands, kneel at his feet, or just touch his tunic. Each and every one of them, with gestures or words, wanted to transmit to him their happiness and their gratitude for not being abandoned. They offered him the few things to drink and eat that they had brought with them.

That day there was a great celebration in the Curved Mountain and the crowd only started to diminish in the late evening, once the Liberator had had the opportunity to exchange some friendly words, a gesture of affection or encouragement, with each one of them.

Only Itzac had waited for him until the very last moment. Xeetha had not shown up, but she surely knew. And she was waiting for him.

"Well, what are we doing here below?" Marco said. "It's almost night, and I haven't even watered the garden yet."

He wanted that to be a grouchy reprimand, but a knot in his throat distorted his voice, and he was dying to see Xeetha again. Now he knew which was his world, the place in which his bones could rest forever. He was sure that nothing out there could have added anything to what the sky had gifted him that night. And he was finally at peace with himself.

"Show me the way, Itzac," he said, placing a hand on his shoulder. "Now I want to confess a secret," he continued along the way, "my only regret since I ceded my insignia to you is that along with the title I had to give you my cane as well. I've tried an infinite number of times to make another one like that, but as comfortable and handy as that…never mind. You're all here to support me anyway."

While they were walking at a quite fast pace towards the bridge that would lead them to the cableway, Itzac asked him out of the blue: "What did you see, out there?"

"Oh…" Marco began, going back in his mind to the night that had just passed. Lost in thought, he was about to speak of the stars, but when he grasped the look in his pupil's eyes, turning towards him, he stopped immediately. In those clear, honest and knowledge-thirsty eyes, he recognized all the expectations of his far away past and he suddenly remembered what he had really left beyond the tunnel. The pain and hate, the stupid obligations, the dishonest interests that infected the outer world: all of this, and much more, came clearly back to his mind in the blink of an eye. He chose, therefore, to answer: "Nothing that could be compared to the scent of the soup that Xeetha has surely cooked."